THE
FISHER OF DEVILS

(A LOVE STORY)

BY
STEVE REDWOOD

Published by
Dog Horn Publishing
45 Monk Ings, Birstall, Batley WF17 9HU
United Kingdom
doghornpublishing.com

ISBN 978-1-907133-42-8

Cover design by
Sandra Sue

Typesetting by
Jonathan Penton

UK Distribution: Central Books
99 Wallis Road, London, E9 5LN, United Kingdom
orders@centralbooks.com
Phone:+44 (0) 845 458 9911
Fax: +44 (0) 845 458 9912

Overseas Distribution: Printondemand-worldwide.com
9 Culley Court
Orton Southgate
Peterborough
PE2 6XD
Telephone: 01733 237867
Fax: 01733 234309
Email: info@printondemand-worldwide.com

First Edition published by Prime Books, 2003
Second Edition published by Dog Horn Publishing, 2013

THE
FISHER OF DEVILS

(A LOVE STORY)

TABLE OF CONTENTS

PART ONE

THE TREATY OF EDEN

1.	Eve (and Adam)	p.9
2.	The Devil Drops In	p.27
3.	Death of a Sardine	p.37
4.	The Devil Meets His Match	p.42
5.	God Has a Rather Good Idea	p.50
6.	The Archangel's Arent Happy	p.54
7.	Surrender!	p.59
8.	The Treaty of Eden	p.63
9.	An Apple is Eaten	p.81
10.	God Plays Dirty	p.90

PART TWO

A VISIT TO HELL

11.	Journey to a Very Warm Place	p.99
12.	The Kings of Hell	p.113
13.	First Encounter	p.122
14.	Belail is Suspicious	p.136
15.	A Stroll Through Hell	p.144
16.	The Immaculate Infant	p.163
17.	Bugrot	p.173
18.	Fisher of Devils	p.184
19.	Belial isn't Fooled	p.191
20.	Mephistopheles	p.203

PART THREE

BLOOD OVER HEAVEN

21.	Atrocity in Limbo	p.219
22.	An Old Acquaintance	p.222
23.	The Message of the Serpents	p.244
24.	The Devil Hears Confession	p.256
25.	Blood Over Heaven	p.267
26.	Judgment	p.277
27.	Beginnings	p.285

PART ONE

THE TREATY OF EDEN

Chapter One
EVE (AND ADAM)

Finally, the Lord God formed man of the Clay of Zindor, and breathed into his nostrils the breath of life: and man became a living soul. And he planted a garden eastward in Eden; and he took the man, and put him into the Garden of Eden to dress it and to keep it.

And regretted it almost at once.

For this man proved to be a troublesome creature, always moaning: the flowers were too fragrant, the honey too sweet, the air too balmy, God too bright...

And what on earth, he demanded the first evening, was he supposed to do with that thing dangling between his legs?

"It's for you to play with," said God, a little crossly.

"To play with?"

"Yes, it's quite easy: you just grab it with your hand, like this, and..."

"But that's ridiculous," said Adam – for that was the name of the man – as God, in human form, of course, demonstrated how to activate the toy. "You look so silly! If that's all you've given me to play with, then, quite frankly, I don't think much of it."

God stopped, hurt. "It's an organ of exquisite pleasure, it's..."

"What's the thing called, anyway?"

"It's a dangly."

"And these?"

"Wobblies."

"Hmm, pretty useless things, if you ask me! Dropping off, were you, when you made them, having a doze?"

And to God's amazement, he marched off, muttering something about gross ineptitude, and tripping on a serpent lying on the ground meditating. He prodded it angrily to one side.

"Hey, God!" shouted the serpent indignantly, "did you see that?"

"Oh, shut up, you elongated maggot!" snorted Adam, and plodded on.

"Oh dear," said God, "what have I done?"

****

On the second day, however, the man busied himself with his gardening, and made no more allusions to his dangly. Indeed, he would frequently disappear behind a bush, to emerge slightly out of breath and with a satisfied smile on his face.

But another problem immediately arose. God had asked the Archangel Gabriel to organise a small band of angels to keep a protective eye on the Garden, and late in the afternoon Adam met him. After less than five minutes' conversation with the Archangel, he came storming up to God, who was having a quiet chat with the trilobite, and demanded brusquely:

"Is it true you made Gabriel?"

"Why, yes."

"Just like you made me?"

"Well, yes." No need to mention that man had been an afterthought.

"Then why," said Adam, in an ominous tone, "is Gabriel bigger and brighter than me?"

A small silence. God licked his lips. "Well, he's an angel, and you're a man..."

Another silence thinly coated with the grinding of Adam's teeth.

"And angels are, I mean, they happen to be...er...well, bigger and brighter than a man."

"And just *why* do angels happen to be bigger and brighter?"

God pondered this while Adam's teeth continued to engage in civil war. He was, being a god, rapidly able to establish a powerful synthesis of the latest findings of anthropology and angelology, to subject this to rigorous teleological and cosmogonical principles, and to arrive at the following irrefutable conclusion:

"That's the way it is."

"That," stated Adam severely, "won't do. There are too many things that just *happen* to be the way they are. That awful serpent, for instance, insolent worm! Whatever possessed you to make such an execrable excrescence?"

"The serpent is a fine philosopher, an excellent..."

"Jumped-up spaghetti, that's all he is! And all those other ridiculous creatures I have to put up with here! The frog, the ostrich, the poodle – and that silly sea urchin and hedgehog you're so fond of!"

"And just what," inquired God in a dangerously quiet tone, "do you consider silly about the sea urchin and the hedgehog?"

"Just look at them! A bunch of spines, that's all. What earthly good are they?"

"Could you," retorted God, stung, "ever have conceived of making living creatures from spines?"

"Certainly not, that's just my point! The whole Garden is a biological shambles, and I'm expected to look after it. And on top of it all, you go and make the angels bigger than me."

"And brighter!" chortled a voice from the undergrowth.

"It's that dressed-up worm again!" shouted Adam furiously. "Creeping and sneaking around all the time..."

"I wasn't creeping or sneaking: I just happen to locomote this way. You might try doing the same, so we wouldn't have to put up with the sight of you all the time. This place was a paradise until you came."

"You hear that? Not a leg to stand on, and this overgrown slug dares to argue with me! And it's high time you did something about all those other animals wandering around here. This morning I found a giant – a *giant* – elephant dropping right next to my bower! Have *you* ever tried picking up a giant elephant dropping?"

"Gods," replied God with dignity, "do not go around picking up elephant droppings, giant or otherwise."

"Exactly! Yet you expect *me* to! There's going to have to be some changes around here, let me tell you! And soon, too!"

And again he stormed off, nearly slipping on a fallen apple as he did so.

"And that's another thing," he yelled, "when are we going to get some decent food? Fruit, fruit, fruit, and nothing but fruit! I'm sick of it!" His voice trailed off as he receded into the distance. Then, "I wonder what serpent tandoori would taste like!"

God stroked the trembling serpent. "Oh dear," he said again, "what have I done?"

****

On the third day, God was tempted to forego his evening stroll round the Garden, but decided this would be akin to cowardice. Sure enough, though, no sooner had he Manifested himself than he heard the clomp of very determined feet, and a voice announced without any preamble:

"I want a new dangly."

God decided to count to ten, but before he reached three, Adam continued:

"How many angels did you say you'd made?"

"A hundred thousand."

"And they all have danglies?"

"Certainly."

"So it's fair to say you've had some experience in making danglies?"

"I", said God proudly, "am the greatest dangly-maker in the universe." Perhaps not completely accurate, but Adam wasn't to know about the Saragashim in Hell.

"So how come mine's breaking down already?"

"Breaking down!"

"Yes, breaking down, broken down, kaput, dead! Most of yesterday it was OK. But last night it just didn't feel the same, the third time it took ages, the next time it actually hurt, before breakfast this morning it was hardly a trickle, and after breakfast," Adam's voice rose, "not so much as a shudder!"

"Oh well, of course, in that case," God felt immensely relieved, "what can you expect? You're not supposed to activate it that often."

"Is that so? And just how long am I supposed to wait before I can activate it again?"

"It should be fine by tomorrow morning," God assured him.

"Tomorrow morning! And what about tonight?"

"I'm afraid you'll have to wait."

"So what you're saying is, you've fobbed me off with a dangly that won't work more than three times a day! Can't you do anything right?"

And yet again he stomped off, stepping on the serpent who had come to enjoy the altercation.

"Hey, God, did you see that?"

When God didn't answer, the serpent looked at him closely.

12

To the serpent, of course, he appeared to be a serpent.
"Why, God, what's the matter?"

****

Back, back in a time before time, he has almost finished making his first angel, a magnificent combination of head, torso, and limbs, and nothing else. Realising that getting rid of waste matter through the mouth might well affect the sweetness of the angel's breath, he makes a hole between the legs, and slaps on a bit of Zindor Clay to cover it, a kind of small hemisphere with a valve that can be moved aside when necessary.

His Clay is still a bit too wet. His neat hemisphere loses its shape and drips downwards into three unequal blobs. He mutters a Nebulan imprecation, and is about to tear them off and start again, when he stops, stands back, and begins to smile. He can't help it: the blobs are so odd, so incongruous. Almost a pity to remove them, but of course he can't expect anyone to walk around with such quaint appendages as these...

Or can he?

The universe is a violent, wild, ultimately deadly place. Novas, supernovas, exploding galaxies – why must everything be conflagration, cataclysm, and catastrophe? Destruction, doom, and disaster? Why is there no humour in it? Nothing to smile at?

He gazes at his angel: by the Cosmic Crab, he'll do it! Other gods will wander past, and see one of these angels, and chuckle, and go and tell others, and they too will come to look and chuckle, and the universe will be altogether a chucklier place.. He can just imagine his old friend Xonophix hearing about it...

What to call them? Well, the longer bit in the middle dangles, so let it be a dangly; and those kiwi-shaped blobs, they wobble, so let them be wobblies.

But at this point he quails before his own audacity. Whatever will these new creatures think if they find themselves saddled with these odd lumps? Compassion floods him, and he again stretches out his hand to remove them, but then the answer comes to him!

Build in a pleasure principle! If these angels could derive pleasure from their blobs, surely they would soon get over their whimsical appearance. If intense pleasure were within reach at all times...

He teaches himself the rudiments of hydraulics, applies these principles in his own idiosyncratic fashion, and within a few hours has produced the first working prototype.

"God," he says to himself, as he shapes a dainty waterproof cap for the dangly, "though I say it myself, there's a touch of genius in you."

Well, there's the first angel completed, and very nice it is, too. Raphael. God gives the heart an almighty thump to get it going – his methods aren't too refined as yet – and steps back, feeling not a little nervous. This, after all, is his first independent act of Shaping. Raphael blinks, says hello in a friendly yet respectful manner, flexes a couple of muscles, and nods approvingly at God, who smiles shyly and feels it's all been worth it. But then he notices his appendages, frowns, mutters "What's this?", and tries to pull them off.

"Wait," says God, "you mustn't do that! Just hold the thing in the middle, and you should get a feeling of intense pleasure."

The angel looks a bit dubious, but dutifully does as God suggests. A minute passes, nothing happens, and he looks even more dubious.

"That's odd," says God, "I don't underst... ah, maybe it needs winding up. Try rubbing it a bit to get the blood flowing. Here, let me help you. There, you see! Now you do it yourself."

And he watches proudly as his angel expresses his satisfaction.

"Hey, that was great!" exclaims Raphael when he gets his breath back. "Allow me to say I'm more than pleased to have had you as my creator."

It is moments like these that make it worthwhile being a god.

So he goes ahead and incorporates danglies into all the other angels. And then what joy it is to witness them gratefully and vigorously disporting themselves, panting loud hosannas in his praise. Of course, the Saragashim Affair in Hell will later be a great shock, but for the moment God feels serenely proud.

****

On the fourth day, God did some yoga relaxation exercises, calming his mind for the inevitable evening encounter. And sure enough, he had been in the Garden for only a few minutes, chatting with the duck-billed platypus, when his Mistake approached.

"Ah, Adam, perhaps you could help me. My friend here isn't sure which species he belongs to. If you could..."

"No, I couldn't! I've got all my time cut out doing the

gardening, let alone bother with all this naming of the species."

"Yes, yes, but if you could just tell him which..."

"How should I know? Looks like a bungled attempt at a duck to me, but I won't know until I can examine him properly, and I can't do that until I've finished with the insects."

"What, you haven't finished them yet?"

"No, I have not! Do you realise how many you made?"

"Maybe a million." Pause. "Or two," he added.

"Or three! Perhaps if you'd spent more time on my dangly instead of piddling around with all those bugs...anyway, since you've brought the subject up, I need help."

"I'll ask Gabriel to..."

"Bugger Gabriel! Ruins my eyes just looking at him! No, I want you to make another man."

"Another man!"

"Yes. To help me get through all this work."

"I'm sorry, but I used up my last bit of Clay making the anteater."

"The anteater?"

"The anteater."

"Is it supposed by any chance to eat ants?"

"It may be," snapped God, "that sometimes in a mysterious way I move my wonders to perform, but in this case, yes, I made an anteater to eat ants."

"Better make some ants then, hadn't you?"

"I made some, you bad-mannered biped!" So much for yoga! Adam glared at him. "Well, *I* haven't seen any."

"What do you think those are? Those, near that stone over there."

"Those scarab beetles?"

"Scarab beetles? They're ants!"

"Excuse me, I should know! I named them. They're scarab beetles: order *Coleoptera*, genus *Geptrupes Typhoeus*."

"Excuse ME, I should know! I MADE them! They're ants."

"You mean order *hymenoptera*?"

"Er, well, erm..."

"There, you see, you've no idea! You may have made some creatures – right little horrors they are, too! – that you thought were

15

ants, but since you gave me the job of naming everything here, and since I named those things scarab beetles, then scarab beetles they are. I don't take it on myself to go around making things, which is your job, and I'd thank you not to go around naming things I've already named, which happens to be my job. I certainly hope this kind of thing won't happen again."

For a weak moment, God imagined an Adam-eater. His mouth watered.

"However," his Mistake went on, "I'm a reasonable man. You say you've made an anteater, and so I suppose you've designed it – though one can never be sure with you – to eat those beetles over there, so, just this once, I'll rename them ants. And don't you look at me like that," he added to the platypus, who had been listening to all this with open-billed indignation, "or I'll rename the lion a platypus-eater! And the next unnamed insect I see I'll call a scarab beetle. Can't be fairer than that. However," and he gave God a no-nonsense look, "there is a *quid pro quo*."

"Which is...?"

"Another man to help me here. An odd job man."

"I've already told you, I..."

"...used up all the Clay! Bit careless, wasn't it? Rather cocksure? Well, you'll just have to undo something. You could start with the serpent. Or the elephant, who, when he isn't leaving giant droppings everywhere, is always playing with that utterly silly sardine, when he could be helping me shift logs. Make him smaller. Or send away for more Clay. Do *something*! You're the god, not me. But just don't take too long about it."

Yet again Adam marched off, not stepping on the serpent this time only because the latter had taken the precaution of hanging from a tree.

Undo something! The words rolled round God's mind like a particularly delicious peach. He knew temptation.

The platypus said quietly: "The whole Garden would understand. Adam is not good for the Garden. He will destroy it one day. He does not love the Garden."

God nodded slowly. Yet he had made Adam what he was. Did not the fault lie rather with the creator than the created? And could he destroy what he himself had created, destroy therefore a part of himself, and remain a god? Why, after all, had he not destroyed

16

Lucifer?

"No," he said, "Adam has committed no crime. I'll get Gabriel to ask the other animals if they would be willing to give up some of their flesh. But", he added lightly, "that's a job for tomorrow. The hedgehog has, I believe, prepared a surprise supper for me, so I must get ready to be surprised."

****

The fifth day God arrived early to confer with Gabriel, but the news was bad. Nobody wanted another man, so nobody would give up any flesh. God took a deep breath, and went to find Adam.

"Right, that settles it!" shouted that personage. "I've already put up with too much, from now on I'm working to rule – if I work at all!"

And, furious, he slung his shovel away. By chance it landed right on the serpent's forehead, scoring a nasty V-shaped scar.

"Hey God!" spluttered the serpent, "did you see that? I'm telling you, I'll swing for him one day, so help me, I'll swing for him!"

"Oh shut up, you herpetological horror!"

"Adam," God reprimanded severely, "you ought to show more goodwill and care towards the other creatures here. They have rights too, you know."

"Acting as if I *meant* to drop the shovel on his silly head! 'God, oh look, Adam's done this, God, oh look, Adam's done that!' all the time! If he did a bit of work instead of always getting under my feet, it wouldn't happen. *I'm* the one who does all the work. Look at my hands! Bet *you* don't have calluses like that! Come on, feel them! Feel them!"

"Gods," replied God with dignity (and just a twinge of guilt?) "do not go around feeling calluses!"

"...any more than they go around picking up elephant droppings, of course! 'Adam, do this, Adam, do that'! Well, that's it, until I get an assistant, I'm going on strike."

And go on strike he did. For seven days he just reclined in his bower and, like Achilles in his tent, disdained to venture forth when God paid his daily visits. The Garden itself profited from this inaction, the vegetation and foliage swiftly recovering from the scars

17

inflicted by the man in his attempts to impose an alien geometric order upon it. Once again, impossible colours gambolled through the bushes, skitted over the ponds and rivers, leapt recklessly from tree to tree, while a myriad fragrances intertwined in dizzying airborne dances, gyrating to the sensuous pulse of bud and blossom. True it was that the as yet unnamed creatures queued up glumly day after day, clutching their blank name tags, but the other denizens walked with a lighter step, freed from the disturbing presence of man.

God, however, was troubled. For now he knew the answer to the riddle of Adam's behaviour. Before Adam, every animal, every bird, every fish, every insect, had burned pure and fresh from his mind into the glowing Clay of Zindor. Tremendous forces had fused and exploded, and something of that power, of that sheer *exhilaration* of Shaping, had entered every creature.

But Adam hadn't been a new MindShape, merely a reduced copy of the angels who had gone before him. *Why am I not as big and bright as the angels?* Because he'd been created with practised, effortless ease, almost as an afterthought: it had seemed natural to create an angeliform animal to be titular head of the Garden.

Adam had, God realised sadly, been born without love and wonder.

So he resolved that he would, after all – somehow – make a helpmeet for Adam, a man to share his work and, more important, give him companionship and understanding. On the evening of the seventh day of Adam's protest, therefore, he glided towards his bower. His thoughts on the task ahead, he stumbled over the serpent who was as usual stretched out in meditation – this time upon a thesis he planned to write proving beyond all reasonable - and unreasonable – doubt that horizontal forms of life were innately superior to vertical ones.

"Hey, God, did you see that?" shouted the serpent before he realised who it was.

Adam was prodding his dangly tentatively, as if wondering whether it was ready for another outing, when the Lord God caused a deep sleep to fall upon him.

Then he eviscerated him.

"Oh lovely, lovely, lovely!" chanted the serpent, before God's frown silenced him.

God removed most of the three-foot-long appendix, four of

the six kidneys, and half a dozen ribs, sure that Adam would have been unaware of the existence of the kidneys, or the appendix – he couldn't even remember himself what it had been for – and hoping that he hadn't got round to counting his ribs. Nowhere near enough. Better have half the liver, too: what remained should just about be enough, if treated with care.

He contemplated the Clay thus released, while the serpent drooled in ecstasy. Still not enough. He'd have to make Adam – and the new man – smaller than before. And that would mean trouble!

The rest of Adam snored blissfully as God surveyed his innards.

Just then the dog came by and urinated. The puddle was quite large. Not for the first time, God found himself wondering whether his system of ingestion, digestion, and elimination was not perhaps unnecessarily complicated. But there was something so satisfying and almost mathematical about the various circulatory and lubricating systems. About a quarter of the body weight of his mammals, for instance, consisted of water.

Water! Of course!

One quarter. Two quarters. Three quarters. Did it matter?

All he had to do was top Adam up with water to replace the purloined innards, and then do the same after forming the second man!

Whistling an ancient Nebulan starsong, he rearranged the depleted contents of Adam's body, added water, and then, to the serpent's great disappointment, carefully replaced the skin so that, externally, Adam was exactly the same as before.

"He'll sleep now for a few hours," he told the serpent, "and when he wakes up, you're to say nothing about all this. You understand? Nothing."

"Does he *have* to wake up so soon? Oh well. But won't he guess what you've done? He knows you had no more...what do you call that stuff?"

"Zindor Clay? You're going to tell him I found some, after all."

"*I'm* going to tell him?"

"Yes."

"And why not you?"

"Gods," said God with dignity, "do not go around telling

lies."

"Oh, of course. Silly me!"

God carried the purloined innards to the spot where the Cloud of Unknowing narrowed down into four dimensions: he might need to draw on some of that power. There, he first cast a rough mould of the new man, watched by the serpent, who looked a bit unhappy, but said nothing. Remembering Adam's complaints, he wondered whether he should perhaps dispense with the dangly and wobblies. But in that case the new man would be without a pleasure principle...

And then he remembered the Saragashim.

****

After the creation of the angels, a few centuries years passed before some early explorers, led by the Archangel Michael, returned from an expedition with halo-raising stories of a hideous cauldron of a planet called Sheol, and of a savage cannibalistic race, the Saragashim, who peopled the smouldering shores of a huge brimstone lake.

Some of the Saragashim had danglies!

Not exactly the same as the angels', it is true: there were three wobblies instead of two, and the dangly itself, which was apparently used in combat as a last resort, had a sharp serrated edge on the underside; but danglies and wobblies they undoubtedly were.

God felt quite miffed by the discovery. Surely only he was capable of MindShaping a system at once so intricate and idiosyncratic. Unless... could it possibly have been Xonophix? His old Nebulan classmate rarely billowed outside his own galaxy, but who else could it be? The similarity of their artistic temperament had frequently been noted. Well, that question would soon be settled at the next Godmeet, scheduled only a few aeons hence.

But just as remarkable as the existence of another dangly was the simultaneous discovery of what could only be termed an anti-dangly. Where the dangly came out, the anti-dangly went in. As simple as that. A blank. An emptiness. The natives had even given it a name: snuggery.

And what really shocked the explorers was that the danglied natives, instead of deriving pleasure in the proper angelic manner, enthusiastically directed their danglies into any available snuggeries, and then wriggled and squiggled in a most unbecoming and undignified way which made a mockery of the whole noble concept of the dangly. Worse, the snuggery owners seemed to take a perverse delight in contributing to this abomination, wriggling and squiggling, and even giggling, in their turn, before finally ejecting the dangly-owners yards into the air to the accompaniment of wild abandoned screams. This heinous desecration of the dangly, moreover, was performed half a score or more times a day.

The reaction of the angels to this barbaric ritual was extremely restrained. They said "Yuk!", and vomited all over the participants, a fact the latter didn't notice until they had finished their frenzied grappling.

A day later, an even blacker abomination came to light.

Once again, the whole expedition yukked uncontrollably, clutching their stomachs or writhing on the ground in sheer horror. The Saragashim gathered round in some consternation, seeking to help the stricken angels to their feet. But they were pushed away with loathing and disgust, the angels preferring to bury their heads in their own steaming yukhills rather than have to look at the baffled natives. When they recovered, they determined to return to Heaven, and seek permission from God to come back and exterminate these creatures.

It had at least been possible to understand, if not condone, the insertion of danglies into snuggeries for purposes of pleasure, utterly perverted though that pleasure might be. The dangly had been designed as an instrument of joy, and what was at fault here was not the end in itself, but the means chosen to achieve that end: for a quiet, personal, contemplative rapture, the Saragashim had substituted a noisy, violent, wanton public demonstration; still, the principle of recreation remained.

Recreation. Not **procreation.**

For the second mass yuk had been brought on by the horrendous discovery that these Sheolites had the effrontery to reproduce themselves, committing this ultimate sacrilege through the selfsame abuse of the dangly! There existed, therefore, sentient monstrosities WHO HAD NOT BEEN CREATED BY A GOD!

Anathema! Uncreated beings, begotten of savages, twice-removed from the Wellheads of Zindor! UnShaped, unBlessed by the hand of any god!

The Archangel Michael trembled as he reported these depravities to God, half expecting to be incinerated in a flash of almighty wrath.

"Fascinating," said God – was there a touch of envy in his voice? – "really most remarkable. Now calm down, and tell me again..."

A hundred thousand angels. It had been gruelling work. By the time he'd finished, he'd been on the point of collapse. A hundred thousand angels – when he could have made a couple of hundred, and left them to reproduce themselves!

If only he'd thought of it!

****

He had not, of course, allowed the destruction of the Saragashim, but neither had he allowed any more angels to visit their planet; the trauma would clearly be too great for them. And it became doubly off bounds when Lucifer and his followers happened to fall to the same place, which they renamed Hell, to reflect their opinion of its less desirable properties. As time passed, God gradually forgot the whole Saragashim affair, and the unique symbiosis of dangly and snuggery. When he came to make Adam, he simply made him, on a smaller scale, the same way he had made the angels.

But now, about to create his second man, he remembered the Saragashim. And he realised he might be able to solve the problem of man.

He had brought into being an extremely flawed creature, and since the fault lay with himself, not with Adam, uncreation was not a solution to be seriously considered, even if occasionally drooled over. Was the purity of the Garden, therefore, to be forever vitiated by the presence of this imperfect man? Must he face the mute reproach of the sea urchin and hedgehog day after day?

But if he could adopt the Saragash system, and if Adam and the new man could together reproduce a third, maybe that third man would have only half of Adam's faults; and if that third man also reproduced, might not the fourth have even fewer?

"Quick," he shouted, "bring me some peas!"

Why he chose peas will never be known, but he planted them in a patch of earth touched by the Cloud of Unknowing, and with the aid of that power, grew and crossbred them, and worked out the Mendelian laws of inheritance, all within half an hour.

It worked! By number twenty, man could become very different from the first man. And, with twenty men to help him, even Adam would have little cause for complaint.

Almost trembling with excitement, God rapidly gauged out

22

an anti-dangly in his new man, made a few internal alterations to produce a reproductive system, and stepped back to observe the effect. Yes, it was OK. Slap hair on all over the place, breathe life into him, and the job would be done.

Before he could finish, the serpent spoke.

"Now don't misunderstand me, God, as usual you've done a fine job, an excellent job, but...isn't he just a little bit too much like Adam?"

"Well, of course," answered God, surprised. "I'm making another man, so what do you expect?"

"Well," said the serpent, with some degree of embarrassment, "this may appear presumptuous, but...well, does this man have to look exactly the same as the first one? I mean, he's already a dangly short. Does he need to have hair all over him, for example? I think I may say in all modesty that my own person shows how attractive a smooth skin can be. And perhaps if you altered the face – just a little – so he wouldn't remind everyone so much of Adam..."

"Serpent," exclaimed God, ripping off the beard he'd just stuck on his new man, "you're absolutely right! Sometimes I overlook the most elementary things, I don't know why. By the Great Crab, I'll show you whether I can make a worthwhile man or not!"

Later, much later, when he stood shyly in the Amphitheatre of the Universe to receive the Grand Prix for Creation, the greatest moment came, not with the presentation of a beautiful gift-wrapped galaxy for his own personal use, but when Xonophix (who had indeed been responsible for the creation of the Saragashim) approached and bowed smiling before him, saying simply, *"Il miglior fabbro'"*. And this despite the fact that the two main innovations, the antidangly and the breasts – a portmanteau combination of 'brace of chests' – had both been based on the Saragash prototype.

He worked with Cloudlight throughout the whole night, softening, curving, rounding, refining. The breasts he reShaped a thousand times until they seemed less like additions to the basic Adam-body than the very essence of the new being. They swelled in a warm-cool pledge of joy and peace and excitement all at once; offering so much, the unknown with the known, assured yet strangely vulnerable, the mischievous triumphant thrust of the nipple suggesting, too, the hesitant bud of the unborn flower. They promised a world of dreams while pleading to be clasped lest they fade

23

into dreams themselves. They swept forward with sensual defiance, yet swayed to the gentlest touch like unopened Andromedan wraith-bells bobbing in their silver pools.

The snuggery, too, became so much more than the mere absence of a dangly. God MindShaped the Clay with such intensity that the flesh itself became subtly different, moist and resilient, strange potencies wound within, deceptively cloaked with delicate folds of skin that beckoned and siren-smiled, and urgently whispered of fire and sanctuary, puissance and surrender. If the dangly lay poised to flare in a quick, impetuous conflagration, this new wonder simmered and smouldered and hinted at a peace that passeth all understanding.

But these were just the more superficial differences. There were a myriad other minute changes, a perceptible softening of the whole body – softening, not weakening, for the brash physical strength of Adam's muscles had been squeezed out and distilled into the poignant power of beauty: the slope of the neck; slender arms with just a trace of fine down and an undercurrent of timid veins; the sweeping andante of waist and hips, curling arpeggios of hair stroking the belly, cool languid cadences of thigh and calf. A new kind of beauty. A new kind of harmony. A new kind of power.

Power. For as dawn broke, other animals came to join the serpent, who had curled himself round a branch overhanging the crucible of creation and gazed, transfixed by the great thaumaturge, throughout the hours of darkness. Even though they could not yet see the face, hidden by a gleaming mass of dark hair, they already felt the power, and croaked and quacked, squeaked and clucked, and barked and bleated, bayed, brayed, and buzzed, their awed delight.

And finally God looked up, seeming to shimmer and waver before them, for the effort had drained him, and only with difficulty could he retain the thousands of shapes whereby he appeared to each in his own image.

"Behold," he said, "Woman!"

And he breathed gently into the mouth, and for a second an eerie blue glow hung over the body – was the Zindor Clay itself paying final homage to him? – and then the breasts rose in the first breath of life.

"'Wo'", remarked the hedgehog, whose eyesight was rather poor, and who was therefore less spellbound than the others, "is an ancient Nebulan word meaning 'that which goes beyond' or, more precisely, 'that which contains within itself the potential to go beyond', and is often, as in this case, used to denote a new development, generally of a self-sustaining nature, from which further, but not entirely predictable, developments might be expected to arise, provided that the original development does not retrogress into what might be called the larval stage which preceded the application of the 'Wo' principle."

God had lent him a small booklet containing the basic billion trillion words necessary to accomplish phatic communion within the Nebula Cluster, and he was delighted to be able to display his knowledge so soon, even though he felt his definition was a bit rough and ready.

But no one was listening to him.

For when the Woman sat up and swept back her hair from her face, all the animals fell quiet; and the breeze, though the tree-tops still swayed and the leaves still fluttered, seemed to hover in silence; and the serpent's eyes glazed over and, murmuring "My Queen!", he slipped from his bough and thudded to the ground.

And even God gazed at her wonderingly, before he said, "At last."

It was not just the beauty of the Woman that brought this sudden hush over Eden. There was something else...

****

A long, long time later, as Eve sat by her pool in Heaven, staring unmoving into the depths, Raphael murmured to St. Peter, who was gazing at her, troubled and fascinated:

"Yes, Peter, it's as if God trapped himself, a part of himself, in his creation, and it is weeping to escape."

And St. Paul once called her, enigmatically, 'the unfinished one', and it wasn't until much, much later, as she leaned sobbing over a broken Archangel, that Peter realised he meant she was greater than them, not lesser.

****

No such thoughts as these occurred to the animals as they clustered round the new creation. They were conscious only of the beauty, and did not ask themselves why, or how, the Woman could appear so beautiful, when each had such differing conceptions of what beauty was. Yes, her hair was rich and midnight-gleaming and rainbowed out slivers of light and sparkled and crackled, and her cheeks were smooth and petal-clear, and her nose nestled delicately above lips of dawn promise and sunset fulfilment. But what was the tenderness of her skin to the crocodile, the roundness of her lip to the pelican, the suppleness and grace of her body to the barnacle? Would moonlight-smooth skin impress the eel, would the wasp wonder at the narrowness of her waist?

Only the serpent had understood what the other animals had seen and responded to without understanding why, for he had *felt* the blazing power and love of God. It had been the eyes, the eyes, ocean-green with purple-blue depths, deep, deep, some other reality rocking behind them...

And then they were just the puzzled but calm eyes of a being facing life for the first time.

"Hello," said Eve, "who are you?"

God smiled, for Adam, as Lucifer so long before him, had said, "Who am I?"

Chapter Two
THE DEVIL DROPS IN

Satan arrived in Eden a week later: by then, a small problem had arisen with God's plan to generate twenty human beings.

Adam refused point-blank to go through the requisite actions.

It was partly to do with Eve's birth. At first, he had loved and admired her as much as anyone else. He had touched her hair wonderingly, felt dizzy looking into her eyes, run his fingers over neck and shoulder and breast. The love that was within her swept over him like warmth from a sun just freed from a cloud, and he felt at one with the others, and put a beetle back on its feet, and even told the dinosaur his dancing was coming on nicely.

It was therefore quite by accident that he once again stepped on the serpent. Both of them were so busy thinking about Eve that neither was really looking where he was going. But the serpent thought it was deliberate as usual.

"God, did you see that? I'll do him one day, the ribless cretin!"

Unfortunately, God wasn't there, and Adam enquired, while banging the serpent's head against a tree to a steady woodpecker rhythm, why he had chosen to use the word 'ribless'.

The spluttered answer quite destroyed his good mood, and that evening he accosted God and complained with great vehemence about the unauthorised intrusion into his internal structure and the purloining of parts.

"Adam," said God quietly, too quietly, "I made Eve for your sake, to help you and to give you pleasure. Your ingratitude doesn't please me. In fact, it displeases me greatly. Indeed, I'll even go so far as to say you're beginning to get up my nose: and if you travel any further up my nose, I may be left with no choice but to sneeze you back into Clay, and let Eve alone represent the human race."

Now this was pretty tough talk from God, but he was very proud of Eve; it wasn't every day that four kidneys, six ribs, a couple of feet of appendix, and a slice of liver underwent such a wonderful metamorphosis. Moreover, he was angry about the further damage inflicted on the serpent, whose head, from once being a perfect oval, was now looking both flat and splintered.

He wasn't aware of it at the time, but he was suffering his first attack of Righteous Indignation, later bouts of which were to prove so costly to the human race in general, and the Sodomites, Egyptians, and Philistines in particular. He reflected afterwards that he might have been more understanding towards Adam's sense of outrage.

But the damage was already done. Until now, Adam had shared in the general admiration of Eve, but now that God had not only shamelessly ransacked his body, but had even threatened to supplant him with the new creation, he saw in her only his stolen organs, and a threat to his own continued existence.

And the love that Eve inspired in all the other creatures only fuelled his resentment. They much preferred her to him, and the smaller and slower ones made no secret of it when he wasn't around, while the larger and fleeter ones made no secret of it even when he was around. The giraffe would pick the most succulent fruit for her, the termite would build mounds for her to sit on and the weaver bird matting for her to lie on, the crocodile would raft her along the streams, the hedgehog would scratch her back. And the serpent worshipped not only the very ground she walked on, but even the ground she *might* walk on.

They all found her beautiful because she found *them* beautiful, they loved her because the love she gave them filled their beings and left a surplus. Every creature had felt the love of God, but just because he *was* God, because he was their creator, the love they returned was filtered through respect and gratitude. When they loved Eve, they were responding to the aura of himself that her creator had left in her, but now it was love between equals. She gave every creature significance and dignity. It was, for instance, generally agreed that the hedgehog was horrendously erudite and the slug regrettably unintellectual; and when she spoke to the hedgehog, he still felt erudite; but when she spoke to the slug, he also felt, if not exactly erudite, at least *interesting*, and soon discovered that he really did have ideas hidden under his sloth.

Eve loved Adam, too. But she was still young, and didn't understand that the human male is a weak, insecure creature who needs to be loved more than others. Instead of being healed by her love, he only became more resentful; resentful that she loved others, resentful that others loved her.

Under these circumstances, it was not surprising that his dangly continued to visibly sulk in her company, and when once or twice, it did show an inclination to defy both its master and gravity in her honour, Adam marched away and put down the rising as he had done before.

And it wasn't long before he became aware that Eve's admirers weren't limited to the animals in the Garden.

****

The Archangel Gabriel – Seraph of the First Circle, Deputy Vice-President of the Council of Seven, Protector of the Garden of Eden – was not, despite the titles, overmuch concerned with rank or hierarchy. If he'd thought about it – which he rarely did – he would have made a simple distinction: God – and Everything Else. God was God and that was that. So when God had announced his intention of performing a second Creation, Gabriel had been mildly surprised but otherwise quite unruffled. God was God, and if he chose to create more beings, that was his privilege.

Nevertheless, when it was done, and the Whiteguard took their first walk around the Garden, Gabriel did wonder why God had bothered to make all that effort. There was clearly only one reasonable shape – angeliform – and an optimum size – his own: was it not just a little bit ludicrous to be a spider or a starfish, just a little bit pointless to be a tick or a bacterium?

So he was polite and courteous towards each creature, but a little distant because he couldn't really see the point of their existence. Perhaps the nearest he came to friendship was with the dinosaur, with whom he had good-natured wrestling matches. There was, of course, the man, Adam, who had the right shape and a size not to be ashamed of, with whom he was quite prepared to be friendly; but the man spent all his time complaining, an attitude which Gabriel found both offensive and shocking.

He was therefore only mildly interested when word came to him on the thirteenth day that God had created a second human, and Eve was already half a day old before he finally flew across to meet her. The creatures surrounding her parted for him as he approached, and he saw Woman for the first time.

And stared straight into his own worst nightmares!

For beneath the calm pragmatic Gabriel of the daytime lurked the furtive sweating angel of the night, tormented by the images brought back millennia before by the explorers who had discovered the Saragashim. He had listened in horror to the lurid descriptions of the Saragash rituals. But that night, his own dangly had glowed in the darkness as he recalled with terrified fascination the stories he had heard.

From then onwards he had lived a double existence, deeply ashamed of the dreams that ravaged the dark hours, until with the passage of time they came less and less frequently, and he began to feel that he was at last cured.

But now a creature far more desirable than any he had ever imagined was standing naked in front of him with an open smile and, worse, a hint, just a hint, of the first anti-dangly he had ever seen, and he knew at once, from the throbbing in his head and veins, that his disease had never been truly vanquished, but had simply lain dormant. He noticed his treacherous dangly begin to glow, and tried to bring his wings round to cover it, but they would not reach, and all he could do was stammer a quick greeting and stutter that he was needed elsewhere, then stumble away terrified of his sudden desire, knocking over the elephant in his flight.

"Oh dear, doesn't he like me?" asked Eve anxiously.

Not until the terrible business of the Virgin Mary was Gabriel to suffer such torment as he did that afternoon. He had been able to live with his fantasies for a few thousand years, since they had been totally removed from his daily existence, but how was he going to live with himself now that there was a real snuggery in the Garden?

That very evening, however, God explained his plan to dilute Adam, as it were, by letting the humans produce eighteen more of themselves. He also explained how it would be done. For most of the angels, it was a severe shock: the underlying assumption of all angelic thought, the foundation of their morality, was that danglies were for self-gratification only, in no way designed to probe and pry in other bodies.

But Gabriel was delighted. God obviously felt it was OK for human danglies to venture into realms unknown, and though it was true he hadn't had the same intentions for angel danglies, that was, as he had just openly admitted, simply because he hadn't thought of it. The idea was not, after all, as unnatural as he had thought.

And so, freed from guilt, Gabriel allowed himself to fall in love with Eve. Not in the innocent, asexual way of the other creatures: if the serpent always chose to lie curled round her breast, it was simply because he found the nipple so handy for resting his head on; if the spider liked to snuggle up in her pubic hair, it was because it saved him the effort of weaving a web. It was only Gabriel who felt *excited* by these things.

But was it fair that the one and only snuggery in Heaven and Earth had been reserved for a rude surly fellow like Adam?

****

For the unfortunate Adam, Gabriel's open admiration for Eve was yet another reason for turning against her. He felt inferior to Gabriel. He *was* inferior, the fact was self-evident. Not through his own fault, but through the injustice of God, who had made them both. And now even this superior being seemed to lose no opportunity to be near Eve. All right, so everyone loved her! Well, he, Adam, would show her she couldn't have it all her own way! Let her play for admiration and worship! *He* would not be so easily added to her list of adulators! And he certainly wouldn't give her the pleasure of taking advantage of his dangly! So there!

So when, seven days after Eve's birth, Satan arrived in Paradise, the two humans were far from being the happy couple Adam, in his memoirs, later claimed them to have been.

****

Satan, who had heard of this new world from two Saragash Fliers, had fully intended - or so he had convinced himself - to sweep into Eden with the fury of a thousand tornadoes, dealing death and destruction to all. But the damage inflicted on his wings in the Great Rebellion and during his submersion in the Brimstone Lake, and the further ravages of centuries of hell-fire, poor nutrition and extremely bad habits, had so weakened him that he was hardly able to withstand the four days' buffeting by the nightmare storms of Chaos. When he finally reached the new world, the first thing he saw was the dinosaur

31

trying out some new ballet steps, and he just had time to wonder whether he had pushed himself past the point of sanity before his wings gave one last despairing flutter, and he plummeted like some monstrous wounded bird into the Garden itself.

It was lucky for him that the Whiteguard, and most of the inhabitants, were on the far side of the Garden, where they had been summoned by Gabriel to witness Adam stand trial on a charge of nothing less than attempted murder. Only the serpent was on this side of the Garden for, just before Gabriel's summons, he had been trodden on yet again by Adam – deliberately this time – and had come here knowing it to be one of Eve's favourite haunts, and hoping to bump into her and get some sympathy.

He was smearing some ointment on his latest bruise and limning, in his imagination, a new treatise he intended to bring out, arguing that homicide in certain circumstances – i. e. the gratuitous abuse of serpents – was morally defensible, and perhaps even imperative, when Satan's clumsy landing jerked him out of these pleasant ruminations. He slithered painfully towards the source of the noise.

"Blimey!" he said. He could see that the creature was an angel, although he had never come across a pitch black one before.

Satan's first instinct was to destroy this odd-looking creature before it could raise the alarm, but he could hardly move and, besides, it immediately began to rub some of his worst abrasions with some ointment.

"I don't remember seeing you before," the serpent said, "is this your first visit here?"

Satan cautiously answered that this was so, asked the serpent to tell him about the place, and had soon learnt, among other things, that one of the humans, Adam, was a detestable creature who ought to be done away with, and – more important – that there were twenty angels protecting the Garden, including Gabriel himself.

Gabriel! Solid, blunt, blindly loyal to God, never a close friend like Raphael or Beelzebub, but nevertheless a link to the past, a pillar of the edifice that he had brought crashing down to his own destruction.

Satan fought down the feelings, the memories. Hope had given him the strength to get here, the hope of striking back at

God by destroying his new creation. But the Saragashim had not mentioned the Whiteguard. Even in his wildest self-deceptions, he knew he could never defeat twenty angels. It was no longer a case of easy revenge, but a question of his own liberty.

"You look like an angel," the serpent was saying, "but why are you so dirty, the wrong colour...?"

Satan switched on Automatic Lie while he pondered his next move.

"The *right* colour! In my line of work, it wouldn't do to reveal how bright I really am."

"You mean, God made you as bright as the others?"

"*Made* me? Do you think your God would be capable of making someone like *me*?"

"Why not?" asked the serpent, unaware that in other circumstances this reply would have meant the end of him.

Satan forced a smile. "I can see your experience of the Universe is rather limited. Indeed, this world here, from what you've told me, is quite primitive. The man, Adam, head of the Garden? Ridiculous! In the worlds I protect, serpents are the dominant life form, not humans."

The serpent nodded. He wasn't really surprised.

"In fact," Satan went on, realising the value of having an ally here, "if you want, I could take this Adam away with me, if he really treats you as badly as you say."

The slight doubts the serpent had felt about this new angel were immediately dispelled. He was prepared to like anyone willing to remove the owner of the heel which constantly bruised him.

"But that's a wonderful idea! I'll take you to him now, if you like. Or shall I ask Gabriel to help carry you?"

"No, no, it's better if we keep this to ourselves. I'm really here to defend you from the Foe, and if..."

At that moment, he heard a sound he had not heard since his Fall. Singing. He had, reluctantly, on the insistence of Belial, his *éminence grise*, had singing banned in Hell, for it was an action too closely interwoven with praising God, too symbolic of all that they had fought against. But this singing was different. Not a massed, exultant, reverberating paean of praise, but a little, plaintive melody, unsure of itself, sad, lost.

As thin as a blade of grass, it lanced into Satan's being.

"Don't worry," said the serpent, mistaking the reason for the spasm that crossed the visitor's face, "it's only Eve, she won't hurt you."

Then she appeared, the melody stopped, she gasped.

One of the oldest beings in the Universe and the newest gazed at each other: he, blackened, scarred, feverish, huge but huddled into himself, shock and disbelief in his eyes, and something like fear; she, slight, delicately strong, the afternoon sun behind her silvering even her midnight hair, and projecting her forward as if she had stepped from its very heart. Light and dark, heat and cold, promise and despair. The serpent gazed from one to the other wonderingly. Then the tableau cracked, and she who was to be the Mother of Mankind uttered her first words to he who was to be the Adversary.

"Oh dear, you've been cooked!"

Satan had long ago left the straight and narrow path of the angels and most of the devils, and was therefore no stranger to the female form – the *Saragash* female form. This being was different. Beautiful, at first glance, she was not. On the contrary, she was quite odd: no claws, no fur on her chest, and her teeth just didn't seem long or sharp enough to tear living flesh; neither was she as supple, as gracefully deadly, as the Saragash Fliers. And yet everything that Satan once was, and might have been, ached towards her and, without knowing why, he felt the same pain he had felt when he had first pushed his way to the shore of the Great Lake and turned round and seen his followers still writhing and screaming in the brimstone. A repetition of that pain was too much, a shutter snapped down in his mind and screened him from her influence and even from his own real existence. The puppet that Belial had helped to create and sustain took over.

"He's an angel," explained the serpent, rather proudly, "who protects worlds full of serpents, and he only looks black and ugly because he's in disguise."

"But you're hurt!" cried Eve, darting forward. She had spotted a jagged cut running out from under his chin. She laid her hand on his cheek and tilted his head gently to see the extent of the wound.

"I've used up all my anti-Adam ointment on him," the serpent informed her, as Satan quivered beneath her touch.

"But you're cut and wounded all over!" Eve's eyes were full of pity. "And your wings are ... all twisted and misshapen..."

With his inner self hiding in terror, shrinking from the grief her presence carried, Satan wondered what to do. These two could help him until he recovered his strength, but one word to a single angel, and he was doomed. He needed a story which would explain his presence and his condition, but also persuade them to reveal nothing to the others. Mistaking their innocence for lack of intelligence, he continued with the story he had already begun to invent for the serpent.

"These wounds are the inevitable but honourable price for defending the Universe. You've been warned about Lucifer, of course?"

"Who?"

"Perhaps you'd know him by the name of Satan."

"Who?"

Satan was hurt. He had fondly imagined that God would have warned all his new creatures about him.

"Lucifer is a mighty, indomitable, fearsome enemy who could destroy you all."

"Whatever for?" They both stared at him, puzzled.

"Because a great injustice was once done to him and he swore everlasting vengeance. Since then," and he rolled his eyes, "the Universe has quaked, the Great Miasma itself has heaved with the force of his passing, and palpitations have shredded the threads of infinity!"

"Oh," said Eve. Then, "You must be hungry; would you like a pear?"

"The very Axis of Time is unbalanced when this Fell Foe passes, the Music of the Spheres screams in disharmony."

"Or a peach?" added the serpent helpfully.

"The very Nerves of Existence shriek in terror and ... oh, all right, a pear then." He would have preferred a peach, but it was Eve who had offered the pear.

"So who are you?" asked Eve.

"He says he'll take Ad..." began the serpent.

"I cannot reveal too much," interrupted Satan, "except to say we seek to guard the Universe at every point against this Foe."

"But why are you so black?"

35

"Camouflage," replied Satan promptly. "If I didn't hide my natural brightness, the Foe would spot me hundreds of miles away."

Eve nodded. "Yes, I think God does the same thing. Sometimes, when he's in a hurry, or," she smiled sadly, "angry with Adam, a bit of his brightness escapes."

"Are the wounds camouflage, too?" asked the serpent.

"Oh no, they're real. When you've spent as long as I have defending the Universe, you're bound to get a few scratches."

"Well, I think you're very brave," said Eve, "but I must go now. Adam's in some kind of trouble again. I'll ask one of the angels to come and help you."

"No, no angels!" said Satan sharply. "You mustn't tell anybody I'm here yet. My mission is top secret. That's why God didn't tell anyone I was coming."

"All right," answered Eve, without any hesitation. No one, not even Adam, had ever lied in the Garden – the very concept was unknown – so she, like the serpent, believed everything she was told. "I'll come back later, and see if I can clean some of those wounds. But I have to go now. Would you like Squiggly to stay?"

"Well, we do have a small matter to discuss."

"Goodbye, then," and she was gone before he fully realised it.

As he fed the serpent more lies about himself and the serpent-worlds, while learning as much as possible about Eden, the same question swirled round and round his mind: one word from Eve to anyone, and he would, at best, be thrown out of this Garden even quicker than he had fallen into it.

So why hadn't he even tried to stop her?

He would have been unable to accept the answer.

"About Adam…" repeated the serpent for the third time.

Chapter Three
Death of a Sardine

Earlier that same day, the sardine had lodged such a serious complaint against Adam that Gabriel had called a meeting of all the inhabitants of the Garden to discuss it. Except Eve. He'd been tempted to summon her, too, but in the end his better nature had prevailed.

Although the details of the charge hadn't been revealed, the meeting place was still packed. Gabriel and five of the Whiteguard sat on tree trunks, forming a semi-circle, in front of which Adam and the sardine (the latter in a banana leaf filled with water) faced each other across a table roughly fashioned from bamboo.

Gabriel rustled a few papers (they were blank, but he sensed this gave the requisite air of gravity to the proceedings) and asked the archangel Uriel to give a brief summary of the facts of the case, about which there was apparently no dispute, only the interpretation thereof. The sardine claimed that Adam had been about to eat him, and Adam claimed that he had only *pretended* to be about to eat him.

The incident had arisen, said Uriel, following a heated exchange between Adam and the sardine, during which the latter (perhaps made over-confident by his friendship with the elephant) had forcefully suggested the possibility that there might well be twice as much intelligence inside Eve's bowels as inside Adam's brain, but that he wouldn't stake his reputation on this calculation since the existence of the latter organ was as yet purely conjectural; to which Adam had replied that, since the sardine clearly felt the presence of brains in bowels to be somehow advantageous, and since, by happy chance, the sardine was indisputably a creature of impressive intelligence himself, it was obviously incumbent upon him, Adam, to arrange the immediate transportation of this impressive intelligence to his own deprived bowels.

Neither Adam nor the sardine disputed this summary of their quarrel, nor indeed the fact that Adam had then proceeded to wrap the fish in some vine leaves with a dollop of parsley sauce, and, after saying grace, to raise the wriggling sandwich to his open mouth.

"There you are – he was going to eat me!" screamed the sardine, almost falling out of his makeshift bowl.

"Nonsense!" retorted Adam, "I merely intended to frighten him. I wanted him to *think* I was going to eat him..."

"He *was* going to eat me! He opened his mouth wide..."

"You see?" interrupted Adam. "That proves I'm telling the truth. I've just told you I intended to make him believe I was going to eat him, and now he's admitted that he *did* believe I was going to eat him..."

"... wider and wider, with his stinking horrible hot breath..." The sardine's eyes were even glassier than usual, and he thrashed about so much that his bowl wobbled precariously on the table.

"... and since he's clearly here uneaten," continued Adam calmly, "I really can't see what all the fuss is about – his accusations are obviously as empty as his head, and as that bowl is going to be if he doesn't simmer down a bit. And if I were an Archangel supposedly conducting an impartial enquiry, I wouldn't allow irrelevant – and quite exaggerated – comments about my breath."

"... and then he pushed my head inside and I saw ... I saw ... I ..."

No-one ever did discover just what the sardine had seen, for at that moment he did a quite unexpected and impolite thing.

He declined to finish his testimony.

In fact, he declined to do anything at all; he just lay there floating in the banana leaf.

It was some time before someone muttered "He's gone to sleep!" because his eyes had become so wide from remembered horror that his body had practically disappeared behind them. Nonetheless, despite the wide-open eyes, it soon became clear that he really had gone to sleep, because he completely ignored all Gabriel's impatient promptings and just continued to float there on his back.

The Edenians muttered among themselves: it was very rude to just drop off during a trial. But mixed with the astonishment and indignation was a growing sense of unease. This was a very strange sleep, with the eyes staring, no movement of the gills, and ... wasn't his skin slowly changing colour?

Gabriel's brightness had perceptibly dimmed, and the animals nearest him distinctly heard him whisper to Uriel: "Kahraman – in the War – that's what happened to Kahraman and the others! Call God at once! Now we're in trouble!"

And even as Uriel flew towards the Cloud of Unknowing, Eve ran forward out of the crowd.

Despite Gabriel's well-meant precautions, she had heard about the meeting some time before, and had in fact been on her way to it when she had come across the serpent and his strange new friend. She had arrived in time to hear the last altercation between Adam and the sardine, and been as baffled as the others when the latter ceased to move. But then she felt a pinpoint stab of that foreknowledge that God hid from himself, but a wisp, a sliver, of which had unintentionally lanced into her at her creation, and she rushed towards the source of her uncomprehended grief. She lifted the sardine and clutched him to her breast, keening in an alien voice that made the animals start with fear. Adam, too, after a moment of shocked immobility, touched Eve's arm as if to take the sardine himself, but something in her expression made him flinch and draw back.

Then the sun burst!

That at least was how it seemed to the watchers. An unbelievably bright flash, a light that seemed to fill the sky and beyond ... and then God was standing there, the terrible light gone, but the after-image still visible.

"Give me the sardine," he said to Eve quietly.

She obeyed without speaking.

"Thank you. I'm sorry if I came ... rather carelessly. I will return soon, and if any of you have been hurt, I will ease it. But I cannot stay now."

Everyone expected another burst of light. But God just walked away into the trees, carrying the sardine.

****

The Zulf had escaped!

God held the sardine in his hands. Gone, all gone. It should have been impossible, but the Zulf had escaped, and his whole creation was doomed.

The Zindor Universal Life Force, the ultimate mystery of the

Universe, found in one place, and one place only, and that a place known only to the Nebulan gods – the terrifying Wells of Zindor! Pits so deep they pierced the fabric of the Universe itself, and at the bottom, heaving, roiling, pulsating with potency, the Clay itself.

The source of all life.

God recalled his descent into the Wells, and he remembered the ascent, but everything in between was struggle and wrenching and disintegration – until suddenly the Zulf had yielded to his mastery, accepting his control, willing to allow the destructive anarchy of its concentrated life force to be channelled and limited. And he had learned to Shape the Clay, and set Trammels to lock it into its new form, with a hundred thousand angels testifying to his success. Yes, during the War in Heaven, a few of the angels had been destroyed, the Trammels torn down by extreme shock and violence, the Zulf streaming out into the cosmos. But otherwise, no angel had ever lost its Zulf, or shown any sign of mortality.

So why should the sardine be any different? He realised the answer even as he formulated the question.

Zindor, Heaven, and Hell existed in the Fifth Dimension, but most of the rest of the Universe, including the planet on which he had constructed Eden, had only four Dimensions. He had known this, of course, but at the time it hadn't seemed important. But now...

He entered the Cloud of Unknowing to reach the Fifth, and sure enough, quickly came across something huddled against one of his Trammels. A small blob of Fifth Dimensional matter, very much like a large rabbit dropping.

"Oh, God, I'm so glad to see you! I've just had a terrible nightmare!"

It *was* the sardine! It was even the sardine's voice, though there was no tongue or even mouth to contain it.

The Zulf had seeped back into its own Dimension!

God sat quietly stroking the trembling blob, while grief threatened to overwhelm him.

The sardine was saved – and not saved. The body it had had in Eden was now, simply, rubbish, like the husk of some fruit. Yet the *essence* of the Zulf remained, here in the Fifth, and, moreover, still retained the consciousness of the sardine, which had, as it were, almost a second life.

But what kind of life? Trapped in this amorphous blob, unable to move, to glide delicately through the waters?

And it was very probable that his reckless attempt to bind the Zulf into a four-dimensional world had condemned the rest of this second Creation to extinction, too. The sardine might not even be the first; possibly there were already other creatures in the Garden without Zulf, without life. And, if so, he must find them quickly, because he had no way of knowing how long the Zulf retained the personality and memory of the creature it had suffused.

In Eden, only a few minutes had elapsed before God reappeared, and quietly ordered Gabriel to have the Garden searched at once, and any bodies kept safe until his return.

He was on his way to Zindor as the Whiteguard began to fan out through the garden.

Chapter Four
The Devil Meets His Match

Midnight in Eden. A full moon streaming down on the Garden, gliding over the lush vegetation, tiptoeing through silent glades, creeping along the banks of rivers, stroking the water. Midnight in Eden, Paradise in repose, a million creatures slumbering in tranquillity, wing and foot, tail and horn, fin and paw touching air and earth and water without fear. Midnight in Eden, and the sounds and scents of night stolen and borne away by a breeze that flowed like the hair of the Woman as she sat hunched over a stream, her attenuate shadow fragmented into slivers of darkness drowning in the ceaseless current.

Lying in the grass, the serpent watched, troubled, wishing to speak to her, but wary of intruding on her sadness.

A million creatures, and now one of them was gone for ever. Eve knew it, had known it at once, and the other animals had sensed something of her grief. Whether Adam had really intended to eat the sardine remained unsettled, though most of the animals were inclined to judge him guilty of nothing more than ungentlemanly conduct, and possibly advanced halitosis. Only the elephant, who had frequently sucked up the sardine into his trunk in fun, and sent him sprawling, giggling helplessly, down his huge back, spoke directly to him. "I will not forget, Adam," was all he said. Gabriel had immediately brought the meeting to an end. What mattered was that something had gone wrong in Eden, and Adam, as always, was somehow implicated.

The evening had been spent mostly in tense silence, with Adam sprawled restlessly on the ground outside his bower. Eve sat quietly, lost in her own thoughts. Once she knelt beside him as he lay supine, staring up at the tree tops surrendering to the dusk, and laid her hand gently on his forehead. His own hand came to rest on hers for a second, then he pushed it away brusquely, turning his head stubbornly away. She regarded his averted face with compassion, then rose and walked slowly away. The serpent followed, wanting to help, not knowing how.

The animals were still discussing the afternoon's dramatic events. The hedgehog, as the self-appointed expert on Nebulan affairs, had been speaking continuously for two hours, but both his diction and his theories were so complex that he had long before lost his audience, except for the frog, who was unaccountably in love with him.

As Eve passed near them, the creatures had fallen silent. For the first time ever, they felt uncomfortable in her presence. It was, after all, her appointed mate they were discussing. So they shuffled and scuffled and avoided looking into her eyes. When she spotted the hedgehog, it was with something like eagerness that she asked him how he was.

"Oh, fine," said he, and looked at his feet.

He had never before been known to make an utterance of less than five minutes' duration, but Eve saw the affection and sympathy in his delicate face, and nodded with understanding. Nonetheless, as she walked on, her eyes were glistening.

And now she sat by the river near where the visitor had been, although he himself was no longer there. She sat by the river, as she was later to sit by her Pool in Heaven, her arms clasped round her knees, her head resting on them, her hair trailing over her feet. From where the serpent watched, only her back was visible, slender and vulnerable in the moonlight, as she stared into the water that tried in vain to carry away her shadow

The serpent had followed her with no clearer purpose than to be near her. Should he approach her now? Perhaps if he said nothing, just curled quietly round her breast as usual, she would understand that he shared, without fully comprehending, her sorrow. Soon everything would be all right, for wasn't Adam the cause of her sadness, and hadn't their new friend promised to take him away? Where was he now, he wondered. At some vantage point scanning the skies for signs of the terrible Foe? Perhaps already doing battle in the heavens?

Just then, Satan hobbled into sight, and softly called Eve's name.

****

43

"Come and sit by me," she said, without looking up. Then, as if there had been no break in their previous conversation: "Why does the Foe want to destroy our world? You said there was some injustice, but we have done him no injustice."

"That is true. The injustice was in Heaven. Lucifer – the Foe – should have been King. That's why there was a terrible war in Heaven."

"But God is King in Heaven. Gabriel told me."

"I know, but Lucifer *should* have been King."

When you are just seven days old, and have spent all your life living in Paradise, the concept of imperfection, that things may not be as they ought to be, is not easy to grasp.

"But if Lucifer should have been King, then why wasn't he?"

"That's what Lucifer asked."

"But why should Lucifer have been King? Gabriel told us God made everything in Heaven, including the angels."

She had just made a statement that, in Hell, carried the Triple Death Penalty.

"A pack of lies! Nobody could have *made* Lucifer! He was the brightest, the strongest, the cleverest! If your Gabriel stood beside him, he was so dull by comparison he couldn't even be seen! Lucifer was to those puny angels as a sun to a moon, to the *shadow* of a moon! Everyone worshipped him..."

"But you said there was a war in Heaven."

"Yes, such a war as shook the very foundations, toppled mountains, caused..."

"But if everyone worshipped Lucifer, how could there have been a war? Who was there to fight him?"

The fact that Satan's mouth stayed open at least three seconds was an enormous tribute to Eve's logic.

"There were perhaps a few," he mumbled, "who didn't ... who couldn't recognise his greatness."

"How could a few cause a whole war?"

"And a few more who were jealous of him, so they banded together against him, and..."

"If Lucifer was so mighty and invincible, how did he lose the war?"

There was no disbelief in her voice: she was simply seeking an explanation for something she couldn't understand. Her body remained hunched over the stream, but she had now placed one elbow on her knee, and was supporting her face on her hand, looking across and up at Satan calmly and evenly. The moon carved her in silver.

The same innocent curiosity had resulted, in the early days in Hell, in many thoughtful Saragashim meeting untimely and messy ends. Later, the definitive *History of the Great Rebellion* had pre-empted such questions by proving that the rebels had been utterly victorious, but had then chosen to turn their backs on the effeminate luxury of Heaven. Even many of the Companions, as the Fallen Angels now called themselves, had almost come to believe this version of events: it lessened the pain. It had thus been a long time since Satan had admitted even to himself that the war had been lost.

He now gave Eve a potted version of the *History*. In the process, as usual – he tried to stop himself, afraid of Eve's clear-sighted innocence, but the habit was too deeply ingrained – Lucifer grew mightier and mightier, ever more terrible, ever more magnificent. By the time he had finished, he himself felt awe for the peerless being he had portrayed. This Woman – bright and intelligent, yes, but so limited in her experience – must be vainly trying to imagine such a supreme being. He waited for her to express her awe and wonder.

"It seems to me," she remarked, "that Lucifer was a very silly angel."

"SILLY!"

"Why did he need to revolt? Why did he need to be King, if everyone already knew he was greater than God? What was the point in causing all that trouble, hurting all those angels?"

If Eve had simply disbelieved him, it wouldn't have been so bad. But she *did* believe him – and still seemed not at all impressed.

Before Satan could react to this astonishing evaluation of his semi-fictitious self, she went on: "Where were you?"

"Me? When?"

"In the war."

Satan was about to reveal that he had saved Heaven from the Foe when Automatic Lie sent an *'Error: Retry or Cancel'* message, as he remembered he had just claimed that the Foe had been completely victorious. It was becoming difficult to do justice to himself both as the invincible Foe and as the invincible enemy of that invincible

Foe. It was also becoming increasingly pointless, since Eve remained unawed by either of these *dramatis personae.*

Worse than this, her dismissal of Lucifer as 'silly' had struck an invidious blow to his self-esteem. Even as one part of him was outraged, another, long-suppressed, momentarily saw with her eyes, and all his boasting, even had it been true, appeared hollow and meaningless. As Automatic Lie Back-Up explained how he had been occupied saving another part of the Universe from creatures deadlier still than the Foe, he suddenly saw himself as if from outside: an old, defeated, cast-out devil, with only the memory of true glory tossed away in vain, sitting beside, and aching for, a creature that did not even know the meaning of age, or defeat, or exile.

"It seems to me," said Eve, "that Lucifer must have revolted because he was unhappy. Perhaps because he didn't have many friends."

This was too much! "Everyone loved him, I told you!"

"You said they worshipped him."

"It's the same thing."

"Oh no, it isn't," retorted Eve decisively. "If they'd really loved him, they wouldn't have minded him being greater than them. They'd have been glad, just as I am when God appears, or when I see the angels skim over the trees. No, I think nobody really loved him, and that's why he became unhappy."

Satan wasn't to know that Eve was partly thinking about Adam and his resentments, seeking to interpret the war in Heaven in the only terms she knew. She had stripped away his layers of illusion with every word she uttered, then casually stamped on the real being lurking behind them. A long-submerged pain inside him screamed "It isn't true, it isn't true!", as the embers of the real Lucifer stirred. He hit back at the pain.

He spoke of those early days in Heaven, when he and Raphael and Beelzebub had been of one heart, if not of one mind. He yanked memories from the bowels of his being, reckless of the grief that came with them, memories of days of light and joy, the three of them almost never apart, plucking life, drawing the juice from it, letting it dribble wantonly over their lips. Beelzebub, dark eyes, and arms of steel touching the dulcimer like a whisper; Raphael, sturdy as the ground he trod but airy as the currents he flew, compassion and preternatural knowledge compacted within him; and Lucifer, truly the brightest of the three, Lucifer the restless one, the daring one, the proud one, the questioner and the quester...

Like barnacles wrenched loose from the rocks of his delusion and despair, their undersides vulnerable and soft, the memories came; and as he recalled what he had been, he forgot what he had become, sheltered from his own bitter reality by the warmth and wonder now at last shining in the Woman's eyes. The young Lucifer crept back into his scarred and blackened body, his scarred and blackened mind, given tenuous existence by the magic of moonlight in Eden and the Woman's gaze. Still he boasted, but now it was of comradeship and trust, and the thirst to test their powers.

When at last he stopped, Eve waited quietly for a minute, and then asked:

"And so, after the war, when Lucifer left Heaven, Beelzebub and Raphael, they left with him, of course?"

With this innocent question, the ghost of Lucifer fled with a cry of desolation, and Satan crawled back into his own hideous corpse.

"They ... they weren't ... great enough to share his vision..."

And as if the ghost of Lucifer had struck her in its passing, Eve winced in sudden comprehension.

"They didn't fight with him in the war!"

"They weren't great enough to share his vision," Satan repeated tonelessly, as if he were but an echo in his own skull.

Eve turned her gaze away from him and stared into the water that lapped delicately against the bank. "Thousands of angels, you said, fought with Lucifer, and thousands travelled with him to find a better life. It seems to me that *they* were his real friends, not Raphael and Beelze..."

"They were!" Denial, defence, anguish. "Beelzebub came to Hell afterwards, he gave up everything to join ... Lucifer."

"Hell?"

"Where Lucifer went. A place of pain and unspeakable hardship..."

"Why did Lucifer choose to go there if it was so bad?"

Automatic Lie was no longer working. Satan ignored the question. Instead, he said:

"Even though Beelzebub didn't ... see everything the way Lucifer did, he still followed him to Hell."

47

"So they *are* still together!" Eve touched his arm impulsively. The final thrust. The Woman was destroying him.

"Beelzebub ... left. But he said he would always love the Dark Lord." *Well, he had said it once, hadn't he? Maybe not right at the end; at the end, it had been fury and scorn and ...* Satan snapped off the memory before it could choke him. Beelzebub *had* loved him, he had!

"And Raphael?" Eve prompted softly, as he had known, and feared, she would.

He didn't answer. He couldn't.

The old image welled up, *the silent horde implacably barring his path, and as he came near he prayed that his scouts had reported falsely, that they had mistaken the leader of that army, surely it was Michael, or Gabriel, or ...*

Sacrificed, all sacrificed, and for what? The innocence of this Woman had scraped away the patina of lies and illusions, and then raked cruel nails over the quivering creature within. Belial for Beelzebub, Mammon for Raphael, adulation of inferiors for respect of his peers. And not even that, for the Saragash chieftain Mephistopheles had never bowed the head and never would – *but what peers? Fair outsides without the courage to defy God, false friends, false memories, chimeras projected by the proximity of the Woman ... no, not false friends, that never, only perhaps the memory was false, perhaps it really had been Gabriel leading that golden army that shimmered like a million stars ... and Beelzebub* had *come to Hell, he really had...*

He looked up at the Woman wildly, seeking he knew not what, but without it he must explode, be rent apart by his own grief. She nodded in that strange way she had, tracing a deep scar down his cheek with her fingertips, and gave him the release he craved.

"You're Lucifer, aren't you?"

"No, I'm not Lucifer!" Sudden knowledge. "I am ... the ruins of Lucifer."

Later, when the Woman was not there to give the hurt meaning, he saw this only as a moment of utter humiliation, a weakness brought on by exhaustion and pain. Later, he did not understand, because he did not dare to understand, that the unique purity of the Woman, the love that spun out almost palpable threads over all who came near, had plucked out his own heart and thrust it before his eyes, forcing him to behold the agony and the glory of it.

He swayed towards her, and she cradled his head against her breast, and gently rocked him, while the serpent, too far away to hear, waited and watched and wrestled with the doubts that were creeping in.

Moonlight in Eden.

Chapter Five
GOD HAS A RATHER GOOD IDEA

It worked! God made a rough-and-ready sardine shape from the Clay at the top of the Wells of Zindor – Clay which no longer contained Zulf – and, murmuring 'Brace yourself, little chappie!' to the rabbit-dropping lookalike, he eased it into the new body.

"Are you there?" he whispered.

"You should know, you shoved me in here!" Being the first creature to die on Earth was a trifle upsetting.

"Are you comfortable?"

"Comfortable! You must be joking! I'm pinched all over, bits sticking into me everywhere! It's like being in an inside-out hedgehog!" The sardine wasn't given to fanciful language; this simile, God mused, must result from the abrupt change of dimensions.

Clearly, the old Zulf and the new Clay hadn't completely fused. The Zulf was no longer as malleable, as free, as it had been, indeed it was now something slightly different, a Stability-Oriented Unbound Life-force: S.O.U.L. But he was sure this soul would adapt to the new body with time. And the Zindor Wastes, unlike the Wells themselves, were almost endless: he would, if necessary, be able to rehouse the souls of all the Edenians and save the whole creation.

"When we get to Heaven, I'll work on your new body a bit more," he promised, "make it more user-friendly."

The sardine was still groaning, so he took the soul from the body, and massaged it.

"Can't I stay in Eden?" enquired the sardine-soul rather nervously. "I don't know anyone in Heaven."

"I'm sorry, that's not possible. But don't worry, you'll soon be joined by all your friends."

"The elephant?"

"Yes, everybody, the elephant too."

Silence for a moment. Then, shyly: "And you?"

"And me what? I don't quite understand..."

"You'll be in Heaven, too, won't you? You won't spend all your time in Eden? Please?"

God was touched. "No, in the end everyone's going to leave

Eden, and then I'll be in Heaven all the time."

The sardine sighed contentedly, and murmured drowsily: "So everything's going to be all right, then; we'll all be together again in Heaven – you, Ellie, Eve ... **ADAM!**"

He jerked so spasmodically that God nearly dropped him.

"Will Adam be in Heaven, too? You don't know what it was like! He opened his mouth, and I saw inside, and..."

"There, there," soothed God, rocking him gently. "It's over, don't worry. I won't let him do it again."

"Then Adam *will* be in Heaven!"

The sardine felt the protective grip on him tighten ever so slightly.

"You know," said God, "I hadn't thought of that."

****

He is just about to take a quiet evening stroll round Heaven. He looks forward to these walks. Since the departure of Lucifer and the rebels, the remaining angels, with notable exceptions, are on the whole a rather humdrum lot, but he feels an abiding affection for them. This evening, who will he meet first? Uriel, bright-eyed and ebullient? Amiel, still trying to write a treatise on the mystery of the Cloud of Unknowing? Michael, immaculate as usual?

He steps out of the Cloud, and allows the rays of the setting sun to flood his being. He gives a contented sigh, turns around – and there, petulance and complaint wrapping him about...

Adam!

"Since it appears you made yet another almighty cock-up and we're stuck here for eternity," announces that figure, "we'd better get a few things sorted out. Those angels, for a start. Haven't they got anything better to do than flutter round all day singing those ridiculous hymns and disturbing my siestas? I hope you don't expect me to put up with that all the time! And another thing..."

God turns to flee into the Cloud, but Adam has got hold of his foot.

"That's right! Typical! Abrogating all responsibility as usual! Well, I'm not putting up with it any more! You've been hiding behind the feeble excuse of being a god far too long! I have no choice but to give

you a good spanking!"

Five huge slippers appear in Adam's five huge hands. God shrieks, and falls back into the Cloud, panting: and there, stretching out into the illimitable Universe, looms a monstrous Adam-face with a monstrous Adam-scowl, and a monstrous Adam-voice pounding at his ear: "And another thing and another thing and another thing..."

God came out of his sudden nightmare, shaking. "Come on," he said to the sardine, "let's get you to Heaven."

****

A few hours later, just before dawn, as Eve was returning quietly to Adam's bower, God was preparing himself to face the inhabitants with the news of their imminent demise. He'd spoken to the Whiteguard, who, informing him that half the Garden still remained to be searched, had given him three other creatures found in the same inert state as the sardine. Well, he'd expected it, and had already instructed the Archangel Michael to come to Eden to co-ordinate the work.

Now, as he sat in the Cloud looking out over Eden, pale and spectral and so very very vulnerable in the pre-dawn, his earlier mood of optimism was gone.

One by one, every one of these perfect bodies would fall lifeless, a million fascinating forms laying a carpet of detritus over the new world. The living canvas shrivelling to dried parchment, flaking into undifferentiated dust. And unheard, unfelt winds would whip together the trusting eyes of the dog and the bunched muscles of the cheetah and the curving breast of Eve and the wispy wing of the bat, and scatter them contemptuously over the dead Garden. Disintegration. Desolation. Death. A foul, meaningless illogicality.

Yes, they would exist again in Heaven, but they would exist as the angels existed, without change, without flux. Eden was to have been different: he had built in the Principle of Mutability, hoping to watch this cauldron of life heave and seethe with its astonishing richness, spawning new patterns, new independencies, new mysteries. Now all that would be left of this magnificent undertaking would be a kind of celestial museum, the whole wonderful creation transposed to heaven, transfixed forever in its infancy.

God looked down on the doomed Garden, and sorrow and

52

rage welled in him.

"NO!" he said, "I am a god. I will not let this be!"

And even as he spoke, the answer came to him, an answer that he had possessed all along, and had even employed as the solution to another problem.

God smiled. And the waves of his joy rippled through the Garden. The elephant hadn't slept all night, but suddenly the grief for his departed friend was lightened by the memory of a picnic they had had together, during which the sardine had grown angry over something, and had threatened to give him a good beating. "Oh heck, why not!" chortled the salmon, and in sheer exuberance, instead of swimming round a rock, he triumphantly launched himself over it, nearly colliding with a fish coming the other way who had had a sudden urge to glide. And so it was all over Eden.

He had created Eve, and her reproductive system, simply in order to 'dilute' Adam, and the whole process would have come to an end once there were twenty humans. But now that these humans were no longer to be immortal, he could simply allow the process to continue. And just as he had created a mate for Adam, *so he could create a mate for all the other creatures, and give them the means of reproducing themselves in the same way.* Each new creature, moreover, provided he again built in the Principle of Mutability, could become different from its progenitors. There would be more change than he had ever imagined possible.

An endless experiment. A creation that could even become independent of its creator, as dynamic as Heaven was static.

The ultimate work of art.

And not only the conquest of death; not only an Eden more varied and fascinating than would otherwise have been possible; but Heaven itself would be rejuvenated, revitalised, as a constant influx of new souls arrived. The angels would remain to give continuity, stability, guidance; their own lives, perhaps till now rather meaningless and stagnating, would take on new purpose and vigour.

At that very moment, at seven o'clock in the morning of Day Twenty-one, he spied Gabriel in the distance. Almost tingling with excitement, he left the Cloud to tell the Protector the good news.

Chapter Six
THE ARCHANGELS AREN'T HAPPY

The Archangel Gabriel, however, didn't consider the news good at all, and was indeed so upset at God's Afterlife plans that he quite forgot to mention that two of the Whiteguard had failed to report in at dawn.

Yes, he was glad that all these inhabitants would be saved from annihilation, and neither did he object to God's plans to create mates for all these creatures, thereby allowing them to produce their own young, although he knew many of the other angels would find the idea repulsive.

Of course, he was acutely disappointed when he realised that Eve wasn't going to be in the Garden for ever. Now her eternity would be spent in Heaven, under the watchful eyes of God, and, worse, the other angels. On the other hand, he quickly realised, there would soon be, not just one, but thousands of Eves, tens of thousands...

"Your dangly," God had remarked, "is glowing. It makes me happy to see how enthusiastic you are about the New Order."

No, what made him unhappy was something quite different.

After God had gone, Gabriel had a word with Uriel, and together they intercepted the Archangel Michael high above Eden, and flew south to an area of dense foliage where they were unlikely to be seen.

Given the choice of living forever, in an enclosed space, with excruciating toothache but no Michael, or with Michael but no toothache, Gabriel would unhesitatingly have stocked up large supplies of aspirin. But this was a time when the angels, and especially the Seraphim, must stand together: if the whole Council united to protest that God's plans for the Second Creation were unjust to the First, he might be persuaded to modify them.

First he told Michael and Uriel about God's discovery of the mortality of the Edenians, and his plan to cheat death by taking their souls to Heaven and giving them new bodies there. It was for him a novel situation to be explaining an *idea* to someone else. His satisfaction was vitiated, however, by the fact the Michael had guessed a lot of this from God's visit to Heaven, and, in between yawning, began to paint his nails.

There was one strange incident, though, that stopped Michael mid-yawn. Uriel had just asked if Eve too would suffer the same metamorphosis as the sardine – she had, after all, been created later – and received an answer in the affirmative, when a most unusual noise came from the surrounding undergrowth. It was not speech, yet near enough to it to make all three angels mentally visualise an anguished 'grrrkkk'. They looked in the bushes, but saw nothing: it must have been some passing creature. Gabriel raised the pitch of his voice, just in case, to a level inaudible to any but angel ears. It was time to enlist Michael's support while simultaneously puncturing his ostentatious pretence of insouciance.

"I like to think," he began, "that I have an open mind. I have nothing against any of these creatures whatsoever. But, really, angels sitting down to breakfast with the skunk? The slug asking you to pass him the salt? The dung beetle sharing your cutlery?" His examples were chosen to make the fastidious Michael wince.

The fastidious Michael winced.

"But we won't *have* to mix with them," protested Uriel nervously. "They'll probably be in another part of Heaven – in the Flatlands, maybe."

Gabriel snorted. "God's so smitten with them, I hardly think that's likely. Now, we all inherited some of the Abominator's land. I took over a small part of his garden, you, Michael, had the lawn with the gazebo..."

"And the rest was converted into the golf course," added Uriel.

"Quite. And the lands of all his followers are also now in our possession. But what do you think will happen when all these souls start to arrive? They'll have to live somewhere."

"You may be right," conceded Uriel, "but they still won't take up that much space. Why, the whole lot would almost fit into Michael's garden."

"I trust," remarked Michael languidly, "you are not indirectly objecting to the fact that the Vice President of the Council of Seven has a garden befitting his rank and status?"

Uriel coloured slightly. He had only been elected to the Council after the departure of Lucifer and Beelzebub had left vacancies. It was, Michael felt, occasionally necessary to keep him in his place.

"Of course not. What use would I have for such an enormous garden?"

He realised he had chosen his words badly, and stammered: "What I meant was, this Eden is quite a small place, and so the inhabitants would take up very little room."

"I would not consider a hippopotamus, a whale, and an elephant splashing around in my pool as taking up little space," retorted Michael acidly. "Apart from which, Heaven was meant for angels, not these new-fangled creatures."

"Exactly," agreed Gabriel. It was time to drop his bombshell. "But we're not talking about *one* hippopotamus or *one* elephant." And he proceeded to tell them about God's plan for the Edenians to be fruitful and multiply and all go to Heaven.

Although he himself was quite dismayed by God's Afterlife project, it was almost worth it to see the effect on Michael.

The relationship between the two Archangels had always been strained, especially since the discovery of the Saragashim. Of all the angels in that expedition, Michael had been the most disgusted by the Saragash desecration of the dangly. Not just because it led to the ultimate blasphemy of reproduction. For him, the dangly was too precious, too delicate, too *personal,* to be allowed out of one's own hands: and to actually hazard it inside another creature's body, where all kinds of unpleasant things might lurk...! And how revolting had been those other bodies! Shapeless, sticky folds of flesh where the exquisite dangly ought to be! Useless lumps of fat wobbling about on their chests, with warts stuck on the ends! This female shape was a horrendous caricature of the beautiful male body.

Because God had shown only interest, and even admiration, when learning of all this, the exploring angels had made a gallant attempt to conquer their early disgust, freely confessing to themselves how narrow-minded they had been. Of course, there would always be the *angelic* way of doing things, but there clearly were also other ways (for other creatures) of doing things (if they really *had* to).

Michael tried. But failed. He had almost the same nightmares as Gabriel, but whereas Gabriel's dangly responded by glowing, Michael's cringed and whimpered in outrage. He had once been so proud of it, almost never being absent from the communal dangly celebrations, but now, it realised, the Universe was not a safe place, and it steadfastly laid low. This public humiliation only fortified his initial prejudices. The female form was grotesque, intercourse abominable, and reproduction anathema.

All during those years, then, as Michael's denunciations of any deviation from the norm grew ever stronger, Gabriel felt ever more vulnerable, ever more guilty, whenever they met.

And now how beautifully the tables had been turned! Gabriel well and truly had God on his side! Not just Eve: the Creator was about to legitimise, in every single species, the moral crimes that Michael loathed most!

Michael's reaction was everything Gabriel could have hoped for. His face passed from a dull cabbage butterfly white through stagnant pond green and hence to German measles red. His wings fluttered feebly as if trying to fly away from this information. His whole body seemed about to undergo spontaneous combustion.

By now, Gabriel was engaged in a battle of his own with a smirk which refused to be suppressed. First it tried for a foothold in one corner of his mouth, sneaked round to the other, then captured the whole of his face for a full two seconds when he was distracted by an agile snigger which made a sudden break for freedom.

The wonderful thing was, Michael could say nothing! Condemning the Saragash acts as perverted and repugnant was one thing: saying the same about God's creations and intentions was quite another.

When Michael had returned to something resembling his former silvery self, Gabriel continued; but not so joyfully this time, because now he was touching on his own objections.

"Now maybe some of us find the manner of multiplication unusual, but God is free to do what he wants," (he paused, daring Michael to contradict him) "but you both seem to have missed the implications of all this. Each pair of creatures will produce one or more young creatures, who will then themselves produce one or more young creatures, who will then produce ... You see? One and one is two. Two and two is four. Four and four is eight. Eight and ..." He stopped himself: why risk spoiling his advantage with a mathematical error?

Michael tottered. "They'll ALL go to Heaven in the end!"

"Not just one hippopotamus, but eventually a thousand, a million hippopotamuses! A million vultures, a million skunks, a million dung beetles! If these creatures reproduce for ever, then they'll be coming to Heaven for ever!" He looked at Michael's lower lip trembling, and couldn't resist it. "If one hippopotamus makes two piles of dung a day, then how many piles of dung will an infinite number of hippopotamuses make in an infinite number of days?"

In a small, secluded spot of Paradise, three Archangels stared at each other, and tried to imagine the odour of an infinite number of hippopotamus pats.

Chapter Seven
SURRENDER!

He was sitting side by side with Eve on a magnificent double throne while God, bowing obsequiously, served them with fruit cocktails, and Michael and Gabriel vied with each other for the honour of serving as footstools. Beelzebub lounged comfortably on a couch nearby, chatting with Mephistopheles: no need for ceremony with them, *the loyal friends who had helped him retake Heaven! He took the drinks, and gave God a gracious smile: let bygones be bygones, he wasn't such a bad old chap after all. He knew his place now, and in the evenings he was quite superb in his other role as court jester. Ah, but life was good! Eve nuzzled him, and mischievously slipped a hand under his cloak, secretly caressing his member: she loved to do that on state occasions, while some boring old Council of Doom minister rambled on about something or other. He smiled at her, and ran a hand through her hair. Life was good, yes, but today was going to be even better. Raphael was coming! The stubborn old warrior had defended Heaven with all his cunning, and when the inevitable defeat came, had taken to the hills, vowing never to surrender. Surrender? Lucifer did not want surrender! It would have broken his heart to see his old friend bow the head. Raphael had done what he had to do, just as he himself had done. No, Raphael would enter this palace as his equal, and they would laugh at the memory of the tremendous battles they had fought, and Raphael and Eve would embrace, and she would cry, her tears would splash the throne itself, she would weep with happiness and pride that her beloved Lucifer had such wonderful friends. Ah! A noise, a commotion, at the door of the chamber, voices, Raphael was coming...* But that wasn't him coming through the trees, and why was the throne so hard and damp, and what was that pain in his shoulder, and the throbbing in his head, and semi-darkness all around him...

"...no point going any further; nobody would be this far away."

"But Gabriel said to check the whole Garden: some terrible danger, this whole creation threatened..."

"Yes, but this far out? Shareel, there's someone here!"

Jolted into instant wakefulness, one thought had burned into Satan's brain like a firebrand: if these angels reported their discovery, he would be cast out of Eden and never see Eve again.

Never see Eve again!

It was over in seconds, his tiredness and weakness conquered by a fear stronger than any he had ever experienced before.

The fear of losing the hope she had kindled in him.

The two unprepared cherubim unconscious at his feet, blood pounding in his head, panic churning his stomach. 'Some terrible danger'! They were searching for him already! *Only one chance of happiness, only one chance!*

Panting, he bound the cherubim securely with vines, and sat back to think.

He had flown here, far from the middle of Eden, while it was still dark, hoping to spend the next few days resting and building up his strength for the even more difficult journey ahead of him. *For he had already made up his mind to take Eve back to Hell with him.*

It was hardly a decision, for decision implied conscious thought. It was something he had *known* since the first notes of her song had trickled over the desiccated corpse within him. The possibility that Eve might not wish to join him, that the love she had shown him might not be very different from the love she would have offered any desperate broken creature, never entered his head, any more than a creature drinking water questions whether the water wishes to be drunk.

All thought of the destruction of this new Creation was gone. Indeed, though he would never have admitted it to himself, he could not have destroyed them, even without the unexpected presence of Gabriel's Whiteguard. The pitiless Destroyer was a part of his fantasy, the warm cloak of self-deceit he clutched around him against the biting cold of the loss of Heaven. The fantasy had served to power his twisted wings on the journey here, but if faced with creatures who truly were helpless and at his mercy, the dream would have faltered.

But how had they known he was in Eden? The serpent? But it was the serpent, hoping to be rid of Adam, who had brought him food...

Suddenly, the beating of wings, angel wings. He looked up, and there they were, three angels, and not just any angels, but

Gabriel and Michael themselves, and a third he did not recognise. Swooping down towards him! So soon, was it all to end so soon?

But they landed the other side of the bushes. Incredibly, they hadn't seen him! He still had a chance, if he crept away quietly...

But then they began to speak. He listened.

And heard Eve's death sentence.

God had botched it! Eve was going to die! Like the Saragashim died. The breath that had so recently intermingled with his would rasp through her lips one last time, the eyes would film over, the cheeks become cold. What if he did escape to Hell, and hold her close for ten, twenty, fifty years? One day, inevitably, her body would stiffen and decay and crumble in his arms.

A hundred thousand angels living for ever, and she was to die!

He didn't realise he had cried out in despair until there was a sudden silence from the three Archangels. But again his luck held, no one came through the bushes to the other side.

Half of him continued to listen, while the other half writhed in the hopelessness of it all.

Gabriel was still talking. So they were worried about these Edenians taking up their precious space in Heaven, were they? What was this compared with *his* loss? Whatever he did -- even if he destroyed God himself -- he had lost Eve. God alone had the means to make her immortal: to take her from him by force would be to eventually destroy her.

Ah, so *that* was what Gabriel was worried about! God was planning to let these creatures reproduce like the Saragashim, and they were *all* going to go to Heaven! Good! The more the better! Let the hippopotamus shit a million times in his old gazebo, and fill the holes in the cowards' golf course!

He felt another grrrkkk coming on. The injustice of it all! The one and only way he could have Eve would be if God *gave* her to him, voluntarily and without compulsion, which he would never do.

Unless...

The force of the thought that burst into his mind nearly gave him an embolism.

Gabriel and Michael didn't like God's plans at all. Not one little bit. They didn't like the idea of hippopotamus shit squelching between their delicate toes. For the first time ever in their miserable lives, these goody-goodies sounded a mite miffed! A touch rebellious! And two of them – maybe the third, also – were members of the High Council of Seven. God would listen to them.

He would have preferred to speak to the serpent first. But with the Whiteguard (as he thought) hunting for him, they might capture him before to could do that. In which case, he would probably never get the chance to speak. No, he would have to gamble on seeing the serpent afterwards. He had to make his move now, while the Archangels were still under the effects of shock.

He stepped out of the bushes.

Chapter Eight
THE TREATY OF EDEN

What do you say to one of your own creations who five thousand years before had attempted the greatest *coup d'état* in the history of the Universe? You can't just say hello...

"Hello," said God.

"Hello," said Satan.

"Lovely weather today," said God.

"Beautiful," said Satan.

Silence.

God: "You had a good journey here?"

Satan: "So-so; bit on the stormy side."

Silence.

"You haven't changed much," remarked Satan.

"Thank you. And you..." God didn't want to lie, so he coughed, ordered tea, and looked in turn at Satan on one side, and Gabriel, Michael, and Uriel on the other. "Well, here we all are. Erm... was there anything in particular you... um.... wanted?"

Satan: "Well, actually... You've got a nice place here."

"Yes, it *is* rather nice, isn't it?"

"Though I hear from my good friends here there *is* one small problem,"

God looked enquiringly at Satan's 'good friends', all three of them covered with bruises, lumps, and other sundry swellings.

"We...er... had a slight misunderstanding," muttered Gabriel.

"Lucifer ... um... forgot to let us know he was coming," added Michael.

Satan's bruises, lumps, and other sundry swellings being considerably bruisier, lumpier, and sundrier than the others', God said nothing. Still, given the situation, and the personages involved, one could hardly have expected fairness.

Satan coughed, and seemed to grind the few teeth he had left.

"Anyway, we had a little chat – old times, you know – and we agreed that maybe I was to blame for ...well ... that little spot of bother in Heaven."

"Yes, we definitely agreed on that," said Gabriel, rubbing his bruised knuckles lovingly.

"Unanimous decision," nodded Michael, removing a slice of black flesh from his nails.

Uriel blushed.

"I was, you might say," went on Satan, grimly bland, "a bit of a rotten apple."

"Quite rotten," added Michael supportively.

"To the core," agreed Gabriel, backing Satan up loyally.

"I see you've ... erm... grown claws," remarked God conversationally.

"Sorry," said Satan, battling to retract them. "What was I saying?"

"That you're a rotten apple," prompted Gabriel helpfully. "To the core."

"I was a rotten apple. I see now I caused a lot of trouble in Heaven."

"Nothing that couldn't be handled, though," said Gabriel reassuringly.

"Don't be too hard on yourself," chided Michael. "You didn't really cause that much bother, you know."

Satan twitched and said: "Well, my good friends here told me that all the inhabitants of this Garden will eventually be going to live in Heaven..."

"...and all the future inhabitants..." added Gabriel.

"...including the females..." pointed out Michael.

"...and clearly you don't want any more rotten apples in Heaven..." went on Satan.

"...but with so many creatures going to Heaven that would be difficult to avoid..." remarked Gabriel.

"...what with half of them females..." added Michael.

"...terrible crowded..." Uriel, making his first contribution.

64

"...standards, shared cutlery..." said Michael, not awaiting his turn.

"...overpopulation..." muttered Gabriel.

"...the dinosaur is awfully big..." ventured Uriel.

"...not to mention the hippopotamus..." Michael.

"...and all the future hippopotamuses..." Gabriel.

"...we'd need an awful lot of toilet paper..." Michael.

"...it's true, ambrosia *does* need a very pure soil..." Uriel, gaining confidence.

"...and so I thought..." continued Satan.

"...the golf course would be ruined if all the hippopotamuses played together..." interrupted Uriel, now getting carried away.

"...I mean, *we* thought..."

"...do you realise how much the dinosaur *eats?*..." Uriel, face flushed.

"...there are the other angels to think about..." Gabriel.

"...Heaven for the Heaven-born!" shouted Uriel, his wings flapping.

"SHUT," said God, "UP!"

A sudden hush fell over the group. There was an audible hiss as Uriel deflated.

"Are you saying," said God, "that you disapprove of my idea of taking all the souls to Heaven?" His voice was stern.

"Oh no," stammered Uriel, "it's a wonderful idea."

"Marvellous," enthused Gabriel and Michael together.

Satan glared at them pityingly.

"So," said God, "what's the problem?"

Uriel looked at Michael, who looked at Gabriel, who looked at Satan.

"It's none of my business," Satan said, after glaring pityingly at the others a moment longer, "and it makes no difference to me, since I live elsewhere. But we were having a chat, catching up on the news, and these lily-liv... these gentlemen, while welcoming your plan with great enthusiasm, did mention a few reservations..."

"...not exactly reservations, just a tiny doubt or two..." Michael corrected him

65

"...not even exactly doubts, just the odd thought or two..." added Gabriel.

"...did mention a few reservations," went on Satan doggedly, "as you've just heard, because they are naturally very concerned that Heaven should remain a happy place. As I am."

God said nothing, but the corners of his mouth twitched a bit.

Satan gazed fixedly into space as he continued: "In five thousand years I've had time to reflect a little, and I'd like to make amends. These gentleangels have mentioned their ... thoughts on sanitary arrangements, possible food shortages, and so on, but I suspect they were trying to avoid hurting my feelings. I believe I'm right when I say that what they're really concerned about is that Heaven shouldn't have to put up with any more rotten apples like me."

"That's it," said Michael. "I hope I didn't give the impression I was against females being in Heaven."

"Personally, I greatly admire many of the creatures here," added Gabriel.

"Who cares about golf, anyway?" said Uriel, starting to recover.

"Anyone's welcome to share my garden," said Gabriel generously.

"Or mine," added Michael. "And if some animals don't use toilet paper, well, it's just a matter of custom."

"Why shouldn't everyone have the right to enjoy Heaven?" asked Uriel belligerently.

"Rotten apples, that's the problem," decided Gabriel.

"Exactly," assented Michael. "the rest is practically irrelevant."

Amazing, thought God, the effect of a single 'SHUT UP!'

"You were saying?" he prompted Satan.

"I fully admit my responsibility. And that of my companions, too. For I wasn't, of course, the only rotten apple."

"The rottenest, maybe," said Michael, "but not the only one."

"That's true," said Gabriel. "There were plenty of others, perhaps not quite so rotten, but rotten enough."

Uriel opened his mouth, saw Satan's expression, and closed his mouth.

A pause, while Satan again subdued claws and teeth. He then went on: "So you were quite right to send us all to Hell."

"I didn't send you," said God, almost smiling. "You went."

This sophism induced the faintest suggestion of skulls dancing in Satan's eyes, but his self-control was remarkable. *He must want something very badly.*

"So you see, what is really worrying my candid friends is that they don't want any repetition of the trouble I caused. At the moment, of course, there's no likelihood of that. The creatures here, they tell me, are very well-behaved."

"No trouble at all," said Gabriel.

"Exemplary," said Michael.

"But what about the future? Who can guarantee there'll be no more troublemakers?"

"Especially since they'll be procreating themselves," added Michael, with a grimace.

"...in quite significant numbers," said Gabriel.

"...lots and lots and lots of them!" said Uriel.

"Now Hell, as you may know, is much, much bigger than Heaven, and there's no problem with sanitary facilities or golf courses, since we don't have them anyway."

"Because the place is full of rotten apples," explained Gabriel helpfully.

"Not full," emended Satan, "that's just what I was coming to. Most of the planet is completely uninhabited. Now I'll be quite honest with you..."

"He will, really," said Uriel, as God fought to keep a straight face.

"We could do with more inhabitants. There just aren't enough Companions to manage the whole planet. Whereas Heaven is in danger of being overpopulated, we are seriously underpopulated. So, you see, I have a little self-interest in what I'm about to propose."

"But he really does want to make amends, too," said Uriel anxiously.

67

"Since Hell already contains a lot of people who weren't really suitable for Heaven, we wouldn't mind accepting a few more, if that would help you."

God still said nothing. Satan hesitated, and turned to Gabriel for support.

"He really is only thinking of himself," said Gabriel earnestly, as if Satan's despicable character were being questioned. "All he's got to rule now are a few renegade apples, and those - what are they called? - Soggywash creatures..."

"Saragashim."

"Saragashim. And a few other monsters. Not much for an arrogant bast... for someone who actually wanted to rule us!"

"Thank you," said Satan, "for clarifying my position. You may, or may not, believe me, when I say my first consideration is Heaven's well-being, but you see it would be to my advantage, too."

There's something wrong here, thought God. *It's clear what the others want, and they may have a point. And it* seems *clear what Lucifer wants, too. Which means there must be something else. But what?*

"So what you're all suggesting," he said finally, "is that if any of the inhabitants here, or future inhabitants, turn out to be rot... difficult, their souls could go to Hell instead of Heaven."

"We don't ever expect it to happen, of course," said Gabriel, "but..."

"You think it's as well to be prepared? And you, Lucifer, would be willing to look after them?"

"It's the least I can do."

"Your idea certainly has some merit, and I thank you for your kind offer. But don't you foresee considerable difficulties in deciding who should go to Heaven, and who to Hell? There is, I believe, a significant difference between the ... erm... amenities of the two places. One couldn't decide lightly that any of my creatures should be sent there."

"*I* was," muttered Satan, almost inaudibly.

"You *arrived* there," God corrected him, "but you weren't sent there."

Satan's mouth formed a strange shape that God supposed

68

was meant to be a smile. "Yes, that's true. However, might I suggest that Hell isn't as bad as you may think? Have you ever actually been there?"

"No. Michael and Uriel have, though, and they didn't think much of it."

"It was terri... ," began Uriel, before noticing Michael glowering at him.

"Maybe it wasn't quite as bad as I first thought." Michael shuffled his feet.

"No, be honest, Michael!" chided Satan gleefully, "it used to be pretty grim. But since then, we've introduced civilisation to the place. Why, in some ways, it could even be considered better than Heaven: it's warmer, for a start, the terrain is quite exciting, and the indigenous population are really, when you get to know them, quite interesting."

God gave a slight smile. "But if Hell is no worse than Heaven, there would be no disadvantage in being sent there, would there?"

"Though, for people less hardy than ourselves, it might perhaps be considered *too* warm, the terrain *too* exciting, and the natives possibly *too* interesting. And, most important of course, anyone sent there wouldn't have the company of yourself. Or the archangels."

The archangels glared, and God twitched perceptibly.

"I will be there, of course," said Satan, "but these creatures are used to you."

"Yes, you have a point there." *This is turning out to be a memorable day. I never thought I'd ever have to act the straight man.* "However, I really don't think I'll need to take up your kind offer. The creatures here will, I'm sure, be a credit to Heaven, and we'll worry about overpopulation nearer the time." *Right, your turn; let's see what you're really up to!*

Once again Satan and the Archangels exchanged glances. Gabriel licked his lips.

"What about Adam?" he said.

"Pardon?"

"Adam," said Michael.

"Have you met him?"

"Not yet," said Michael, "but I've heard about him. It appears he's insolent..."

"...disliked by everybody..." Gabriel.

"...refuses to procreate with Eve..." Uriel.

"...tried to eat that poor sardine..." Michael.

God recalled his recent waking nightmare about Adam, and suddenly found himself sweating. He could almost taste the balm in Satan's following words.

"It seems this Adam might fit in very well in my place."

Get thee behind me, Satan!

"Of course, it's entirely up to you."

No, no, no! "Adam does have a lot to learn. But there will soon be other humans, children of Eve, and they'll be different, and Adam will no doubt change under their influence."

"But if he doesn't?" asked Gabriel sharply.

"Eve?" asked Satan innocently. "Ah yes, Adam's mate. Gabriel told me about her. She seems quite nice. I'm sure her children, too, will be very nice. Except..."

Despite the Nebulan ban on Foreseeing, in moments of stress it was impossible for a god to completely shut off the faculty. *NO, NO, NO!*

"...her children will also be Adam's children. What if half of them take after the father and not the mother? Say there are a hundred million humans in the future; fifty million would be like Adam, wouldn't they?"

"Even if only a quarter of them turned out like Adam," added Michael, "that's twenty-five million."

"And if *three*-quarters turned out like him, that's ...er..." Gabriel trailed off into silence.

An eternity, not just of one Adam, but hundreds, thousands, millions of them. Why had he been blithely assuming they would all turn out like Eve? *An eternity of Adams!*

And what if Adam *had* eaten the sardine? *How would the sardine feel spending eternity with someone who had eaten him?* Perhaps the idea of some kind of Afterlife separation wasn't such a bad one

70

after all. Would it be fair to inflict an eternity of unpleasant creatures on pleasant ones?

And he had always intended sometime to do something about the Fallen Angels. It had never been his intention to leave them in Hell for ever. Might this not be a first step towards bringing them back into the fold?

Besides, if he hadn't been so soft with Lucifer and the others in the first place, the Rebellion might never have happened. Perhaps a god ought to be just, as well as loving. Heaven should be a reward, a privilege to be earned, not just an automatic right.

And look how upset poor old faithful Gabriel and Michael were! In that rebellion, they were the ones who'd done his fighting, they were the ones who'd had mountains hurled at them. How could he allow the possibility of another rebellion by allowing in more troublemakers?

Bad apples, Lucifer had said. Should he ignore the advice of the greatest expert on bad apples in the Universe?

It was NOT – absolutely NOT – just a case of Adam personally. Nothing at all to do with his nightmares. Or the hurtful criticism of his dangly-making prowess. Or the suggestion that a god should go around picking up elephant droppings. Or the ridiculing of his most original biological concepts. These considerations, he was pleased to say, did not influence him in the slightest. Why, Adam would almost certainly reform, and live a contented eternity in Heaven. Nobody would ever actually be going to Hell – and even if they did, it didn't have to be for ever. And the place probably *had* been done up a bit.

All in all, the idea of a choice of Afterlives, based on good conduct and merit, was so apposite as to be almost inevitable. In time, he would almost certainly have come up with a similar idea himself.

So it really did have nothing to do at all, in the slightest, whatever, in the least, with his own personal feelings towards his first man.

Having thus discovered the balm and joy of rationalisation, God gave his answer. He expressed his gratitude to the Archangels for reminding him that he had responsibilities to Heaven as well as

71

to Eden, and to Satan for his perceptive enunciation of the Rotten Apple Theory. He reiterated that he really couldn't envisage any of the present Edenians not going to Heaven – one should not attach undue importance to the minor peccadillos of Adam, who was, after all, only twenty-one days old – but that it would indeed be a wise precaution to allow for the possibility that at some far future date alternative accommodation might be needed. And now, what about another cup of tea?

The angels looked at each other uncertainly, then they looked at Satan uncertainly, who was biting his lip uncertainly. *Ah ha, so there's more to come!*

"By the way," said God, "you still haven't told me what brings you here."

"Oh, just curiosity," answered Satan, his mind clearly elsewhere.

"Why did you come alone?"

"My friends can ... no longer fly."

God felt a pang of conscience. Ah well, contact had been made. "Give it time," Xonophix had said, "these things can't be hurried." He was about to ask about the other Fallen Angels, but Satan had already returned to the previous topic.

"I'm glad that I'll be able to help you, should the need ever arise. But as you so wisely pointed out yourself, one couldn't decide lightly whether a soul deserved your place or mine."

The three Archangels had an air of expectancy about them, as if they knew what was coming. A most unusual alliance. A most disturbing alliance. Of course, it *could* all be explained by the reasons already given...

"I assure you, I wouldn't decide lightly."

"Perhaps," offered Gabriel, "we, I mean you, could establish some criterion."

"Yes, some guidelines, some ground rules, for conduct in Eden," suggested Michael.

"Now that's an interesting idea!" exclaimed Satan, looking at him with an admiration only slightly spoiled by a twitching claw. "Yes, indeed, that would only be fair. Then everyone would know where they stood. Take that Adam, for instance. I hear he tried to eat the... what was it called? Sardine! Now that is really terrible! Positively nasty!"

"Revolting," agreed Uriel.

"But did you ever tell Adam he *couldn't* eat the sardine?" inquired Satan.

"Well, no," said God, irritated. "It was self-evident."

"Ah, but was it? He's only a few weeks old. Moral probity is something that can only be learned from experience!" Satan said sententiously.

How does he keep such a straight face?

"Were there any no-strike clauses in his work contract?" asked Michael.

"Was he ever actually forbidden to stamp on the serpent?" added Gabriel.

"Did you *command* him to procreate with Eve?" Uriel, emboldened by the others.

"Well, no, but..."

"So he's never actually broken any law, committed any crime?" Satan interjected.

"Eating another creature is clearly a crime," protested God.
How had they managed to get him on the defensive like this?

"Of course it is," said Satan soothingly. "*We* all know that, but we're considerably older. Perhaps Adam might not have done all these things if he'd been told beforehand that they were wrong."

"He's only a human," Gabriel pointed out.

"If," said Satan with righteous solemnity, "you were to request me to take Adam home with me right now, I would, of course, do it, but with a heavy heart. Poor unknowing sinner!"

"I have no intention," pronounced God, waxing more than a trifle wroth, "of requesting, or even *letting*, you take anybody home with you!"

Why do I keep growing angry so quickly? Guilt feelings? But I never said I was going to send Adam to Hell, did I?

Satan bit his tongue. Although his recovery was swift, his

73

articulation suffered.

"Exactly what I expected you to say. To commit an injustice would be impossible for you. When the Saragashim ask why we never complain, we always have the same answer: God is just, and we fully deserved everything we got."

"I'll say!" said the three Archangels simultaneously.

"It would only be justice, therefore," Satan went on, "for the inhabitants here to know exactly where they stand." Then, nonchalantly, "Why not give them some rules?"

"Yes," said Gabriel, "like, if you do this, or that, you won't go to Heaven."

"That's fair," said Michael. "Then it's up to them whether they go to Heaven or not."

"What a marvellous idea!" enthused Uriel.

"We don't really mind at all how many creatures come to Heaven," said Gabriel, "if they deserve to be there."

"Even the females..." Michael said magnanimously.

"If Adam changes his ways, he'll come, too." Uriel seemed relieved.

"Yes, yes! " shouted God exultantly. "It would be entirely his own fault if he didn't come!"

The others looked at him, amazed. He added rather sheepishly:

"But of course, that would never happen."

Satan had a look of intense excitement. "Of course not. That's the whole point. Once they have some rules, they wouldn't be silly enough to break them, would they?"

"*You* did!" Michael interposed.

"Of course," said Satan, "you'd have to think about what rules to impose very, very carefully. The creatures here are all so different, aren't they? You'd have to take into account all their diverse characteristics before deciding on any general rules. It could take years to make commands that would be fair to everybody."

"I'm glad you see the complexity of the problem," God said guardedly.

"The first prerequisite, as I see it, is that the creatures should learn obedience."

"To what?"

"To you, of course. I was foolish enough not to obey you, and look where I ended up!"

"Right where you belonged!" growled Gabriel.

"And none too soon, either!" snarled Michael.

Not the most solid of alliances! thought God.

"Why not give them," said Satan, "a few general rules, just to test their obedience, while you work out more complex commandments, suitable to each species?"

"I hardly think that's necessary. They all obey me as it is, and anyway, I certainly wouldn't want obedience to me to be the criterion of whether they go to Heaven or not."

Satan was taken aback, but quickly recovered his composure. "That's precisely what makes you such an admirable god – and lets people like Adam take advantage of you!"

Help!

"Just a simple test of loyalty, something ridiculously simple, so simple that only an irredeemable miscreant would even *think* of disobeying."

If Adam brought it on himself...

"In fact," pursued Satan, "the more ridiculous, the better. Some rule that nobody would even *want* to disobey... unless they did it deliberately to offend you."

"And what would you suggest?" asked God. "Mind you, I'm not saying I've accepted your proposal..."

Satan gave an ingenuous smile. "Oh, *I* don't know. Anything at all..."

Uriel looked inspired. "What about forbidding...?"

Satan swiftly cut him off. "*Apples!* Of course! Rotten apples! How appropriate!"

"...forbidding anyone to...?" Uriel was showing unusual determination.

"Perfectly ridiculous, and so ridiculously perfect!" went on Satan. "Just tell the inhabitants they mustn't eat the apples from a particular tree! Any tree, it doesn't matter which. If they do, it's a clear case of wilful disobedience, and off they come to me!"

"... forbidding anyone to make faces at angels?" concluded Uriel lamely.

"It would be a start," said Gabriel, obviously referring to Satan's suggestion, not Uriel's.

"Indeed yes," said Michael. "Simple obedience, discipline – that's what maintains standards! After that, you could ban the indecorous use of danglies..."

"...having excessive offspring..." Gabriel.

"...the public flaunting of breasts..." Michael, of course.

"Stop, stop!" exclaimed Satan. "Shame on you! God doesn't need us to tell him what's good or bad! I merely suggested a ban on an apple tree because eating apples in itself is patently neither good nor bad. The real commandments I wouldn't presume to suggest! I'm surprised at you!"

Gabriel and Michael gave him a look which suggested that if God hadn't been there, they would have added greatly to Satan's surprise in very unpleasant ways.

"It would, as you say," said God slowly, "be a start..."

"Though I wouldn't make a very good salesman," said Satan ruefully. "Why, even this Adam isn't remotely likely to do such a stupid thing. I don't mind telling you, I'm relying on your real commandments, when you make them, to swell the population of my Kingdom."

Which was only stating the obvious, God thought. Of course Satan didn't expect to get any of the present inhabitants of Eden. He knew very well that God would never consider such a thing. Which was why he had jokingly suggested a 'rule' which would never be broken. No, he was just building bridges with an eye to the distant future when the Edenians would have multiplied, and he might realistically look forward to the arrival of new subjects.

"I've decided," he said, "to accept your idea in principle. We'll begin with the tree, as you suggest, as a symbol, so that my new creatures can get used to the idea of right and wrong. We'll draw up a treaty so that we know exactly where we stand, though you appreciate, of course, that we'll have to leave blanks for my future commandments, about which I will immediately notify you. Is this acceptable to you?"

"Absolutely," said Satan. "For myself, I wouldn't even require it in writing, but it might please my Companions to see and feel a document indicating the possibility, however far in the future, that new arrivals might come to Hell to break the awful monotony there."

"Well then," said God, "that's that. Now I suggest we all have something to eat while you tell us something about your planet."

"Does he really need to stay here any longer?" asked Michael.

"Come, come," God rebuked him, "you must admit that Lucifer's suggestions have put some of your fears at rest. The least we can do is let him rest a bit before he makes what is clearly a difficult return journey."

"Thank you," said Satan. "Though I really would love to take a stroll around the Garden before I go back. There are so many fascinating creatures here. I'm sure I saw some huge creature actually dancing when I arrived! I'd love to meet a few of them."

Though he would have loved to show off his new creatures, God reminded himself that Lucifer was still Lucifer. So he said, tactfully, he hoped:

"The creatures here are, you will understand, still very young and impressionable, and have just suffered a terrible shock with the death of the sardine, so I really do feel it is better that you don't meet them just now. No, I think a good meal, deal with the paperwork, and then Michael and Gabriel here can escort you safely out of Eden. This is a very busy time for all of us, you understand."

"Of course," replied Satan with the appearance of meekness, though the muscles of his jaw had tightened. "Maybe some other time. Though," he added, after some hesitation, "there is just one thing. When I arrived, I fell and hurt myself, as you can see. In fact, I blacked out. When I came to, quite dizzy and disoriented, I saw two beings approaching me, and, as I said, I was still confused, and in Hell hesitation can be fatal, so I ... overpowered them, and only then realised they were angels. I really am sorry. Then I saw Michael and Gabriel and went to say hello to them, and there was ...

another misunderstanding, and I forgot all about the two angels. I really would like the chance to apologise to them personally. Maybe I could just go back quickly..."

"So that's what happened to Romael and Shareel!" roared Gabriel.

God frowned. Yes, Lucifer was still Lucifer all right! But maybe it was understandable in the circumstances, and at least he had been decent enough to tell them about it now.

"I'll send someone at once, there's no need for you to go. What's done is done. You'll get the chance to apologise before you go."

Satan seemed about to speak, but then nodded. God's euphoria was wearing off. The sooner this was over, the better. No telling what damage Lucifer might do – or might have done, if he hadn't met the Archangels first. No, he must not be allowed to meet any of the Edenians: they were, indeed, as he had said, too impressionable. *What if he met Eve, for example?* God shuddered mentally: she was so loving and innocent... Well, it wasn't going to happen.

****

Five hours later, Satan left Eden in the most undignified way.

"We're all terribly sorry you have to go," Gabriel said gaily, "and even more sorry that if we ever catch you here again, we'll turn you into a delicacy for the vultures. Give my regards to Belial, and urinate on him for me, won't you? And tell Moloch we often utter a prayer for his piles. And don't get into trouble with those Sogawash women" – a sly glance at Michael – "standards, you know. Now, I know goodbyes can be painful, and yours will be particularly so if you haven't taken off before my foot, which is now raised and will swing forward in exactly five seconds, reaches you ... five...four..."

"You wouldn't!"

"...three...two..."

And thus the Adversary of God and Man departed Eden, the

swish from Gabriel's foot whisking air currents over his posterior.

But under the feelings of indignity surged a boundless exultation.

Eve would be his!

But what a price he had paid! First, beaten almost senseless by the alarmed Archangels when he had stepped out of the bushes to offer the temporary truce based on mutual self-interest. Then the agony of being humble before God, because he, and he alone, controlled the destiny of Eve. She was inevitably going to die, and only God could resurrect her; but once in Heaven, she would be lost for ever. For him, the Treaty of Eden had but one object – the banishment of Eve to Hell after her death.

But the worst of all had been the knowledge that everything would be in vain unless he managed to see either Eve or the serpent before he left. Eve would only go to Hell if she ate the apple: and she would have no reason to eat the apple unless he gave her one.

Until the last moment, he thought his gamble hadn't paid off. God hadn't left him alone for a minute. It had been luck – but does not fortune favour the bold? – which had enabled him to spot the serpent as he was being escorted to an out-of-the-way spot in Eden from whence, God hoped, his departing flight would not be seen by any of the inhabitants. (They could have waited till night, but God was feeling unaccountably nervous, and wanted his 'guest' safely out of the way.) An immediate pretence that his bowels threatened dire things, feigned modesty while he went behind the bush where he had spotted the serpent, a few whispered words of deceit to enlist that creature's aid, and it was done. Or soon would be. God could not break his word. Eve would eat, she would be sent to Hell – and at last his life would have meaning again.

High in the atmosphere, he wheeled round, and looked down at Eden, and for a moment his exultancy died away. Ah, but this Eden was beautiful, mantled and cradled now by the tree tops, and among them the streams glinting like sudden smiles gladdening the face of the land, flowing away to a sea far to the west, over plains that sloped imperceptibly like the thigh of Eve. To the north, rolling mountains, their peaks now caught by the setting sun, glowing like the breast of Eve in the moonlight when they had been together by the water. Eastwards, huge tracts of forest, dense and intertwined to recall the hair that had nestled on her belly after they had bathed. And to the south one solitary river flowing lonely and sad like that single stray hair that had stuck to their lips as if to hold them together after that parting kiss. Eden *was* Eve, and, momentarily, the thought of her in Hell was too dislocating, obscene even.

But then his pride and his need rose up. Here, she was doomed to die, anyway. No, she belonged with him.

He turned and headed into the abyss.

Chapter Nine
AN APPLE IS EATEN

Day Thirty in the Garden of Eden, and God had completed the creation of mates for the inhabitants, give or take a few fastidious creatures, like the amoeba or the sea anemone, who said they'd rather reproduce by themselves, if he didn't mind. The ground, the rivers, the trees, were positively shaking, swishing, and swaying to the rhythms of joyous copulation. The Whiteguard, now increased to fifty strong, looked on aghast at the frantic goings-on. Most of them winced and closed their eyes and blocked up their ears, but none broke off so frequently to dash, retching, behind the nearest bush as the Vice-President of the Council of Seven.

The creatures were quite oblivious to the torment of their overseers. The very air hummed with their wanton rapture. And of them all, the serpent thought, he should have been the happiest. If anything, his Lamia was even more beautiful than Eve, sensuous, sinuous, sinewy – the exact replica of himself. And what a whirlwind courtship theirs had been! Three seconds after her birth, he had proposed marriage, and been accepted. Now, a whole day into their wedded life, he still felt not the slightest inclination to even look at another serpent – not that there were any, of course. A perfect marriage in a perfect setting.

And he *was* happy, ecstatically so. Only ... he had a small problem

He slithered and dithered in all kinds of geometrical aberrations which reflected his confusion of purpose, though, determined to be an ideal husband, he did stop every now and then to give his wife a quick peck on the cheek just in time to avert an open protest, thus pioneering a technique that was to be hallowed and refined throughout the ages. In the end, however, unable to bear his burden alone any longer, he told her what was bothering him.

He'd promised the Hammer of the Fell Foe that he would

persuade Eve to eat an apple from the Tree of Knowledge! He didn't add that the Hammer had told him that this was a kind of Test, and that when it was done, he would return to take Adam away.

"But, Squiggly, you know what God said at the big meeting! Any tree but that tree!"

"But do you know *why* it's called the Tree of Knowledge?"

"God didn't say."

"Exactly. Because the knowledge is about Hell."

"Hell?"

"It's a place like Heaven, but much, much nicer. Heaven's a slum compared to it!"

"How do you know that?"

"Because my friend, the Scourge of the Alien Hordes, told me."

Lamia sniffed. "But the angels say Heaven is even better than here. How could this Hell be better still?"

"Well, for one thing, serpents are the dominant life form."

"What do you mean, 'dominant'? All creatures are equal."

"They should be, yes. But when you're as old and wise as me, you'll learn things aren't always what they should be. Where do you think we got this 'V' from?"

"What a funny question! From God, of course."

"There you are! Jumping to conclusions! Typical woman! I got this 'V', my sweet – and God copied it when he made you – when Adam hurled a shovel at me."

"You let him do that?"

"Adam, my dear, has got hands, in case you hadn't noticed. I haven't. If I had, *his* head would have a 'V', or even a 'W', in it! But in Hell, as I said, the serpents are dominant."

"You mean, they've got hands?"

"I didn't ask him that. I suppose so, though."

"You'd look ridiculous with hands!"

"Yes, I suppose you're right there," admitted the serpent.

"Anyway," said Lamia, "if Hell is better, why should Eve go there, and not us?"

"Oh, we *can* go, if we want. I have a special invitation –

82

which would now include you, too, of course."

"I don't want to go to Hell, however nice it is. I like it here, so I know I'll like Heaven. And if all our other friends are going to Heaven..."

"Oh, it's not us I'm worried about. I'm sure I'd be happy in Heaven too, whether serpents are dominant or not."

"So your problem is Eve. But I don't see why you have anything to do with it. Why didn't this Hammer, Scourge, or whatever, simply invite her himself?"

"He had to leave suddenly – some danger in the Universe. He's so important that Gabriel and lots of the other angels saw him off personally."

"So why not just tell Eve she's invited to Hell, and leave it up to her?"

"Because my Friend is sure God will lie to her about Hell, because he'll want her in Heaven, naturally. She won't be able to see they're lies unless she eats the apple. That's why God doesn't want anyone to eat from it."

"But didn't you all use to eat from that tree before?"

The serpent looked crestfallen. ""Er... yes."

Lamia patted him on the head. "Don't fret, love. We all have to form hypotheses, before rejecting them in the light of new empirical discoveries."

The serpent gazed at her admiringly. *One day old!*

"So what are you going to do?"

The serpent came to a sudden decision. "I know! I'll talk to Uriel! I've heard he used to be a great traveller. Maybe he's heard something about Hell."

"Do you mean you don't trust your very important friend?" Lamia asked slyly.

The serpent looked uncomfortable. "I can't really believe God would ever lie. And if not, then my 'friend' maybe has been deceiving me."

"Squiggly, I said to myself when you proposed to me, 'This serpent is perfect except for one thing – he must be awfully vain to ask me to marry him before he's even said hello!' I'm sorry I thought you were vain."

"So I *am* perfect, then?"

"Of course you are, silly! Now, go and speak to Uriel."

****

Lies, lies, lies! The world where serpents ruled indeed! They *ate* serpents in Hell, and made condoms and footwear out of the skins! They even ate each other, and quite possibly made condoms and footwear out of their own skins too! And that Hammer of the Fell Foe, Arbiter of Destinies! Nothing but a rebel angel who'd been kicked out of Heaven thousands of years before – and a year, apparently, was quite a lot of days.

He thought nothing could be worse than his own gullibility. But as he wended his way back to Lamia, he had yet another unfortunate encounter with Adam. What happened next was partly his own fault, he admitted it, but that didn't alter his determination to finally exact vengeance.

Adam, after the big meeting, had been intercepted by the elephant, who, after a week of tearful and sleepless nights, demanded to know what had *really* happened with his friend the sardine. The discussion had grown heated, until Adam – who had only the evening before found another huge elephant dropping right at the entrance to his bower – lost his temper, and declared the sardine would probably have tasted foul, anyway, judging by the company he kept. Luckily, the elephant only hit him once, with the result that Adam had a worse headache than he had ever conceived possible.

The serpent couldn't hide a smirk when he saw the huge lump on Adam's head. And Adam, in turn, couldn't resist picking him up, rubbing him briskly across some stinging nettles, and then tying him in a sheepshank knot. Very tightly.

By the time the serpent had managed to undo himself, he had come to an irrevocable decision. Uriel had told him about the punishment for eating from the Tree of Knowledge, and since he could no longer rely on the Hammer's promise to take Adam away, he would make sure he finally received him in Hell, anyway! Instead

84

of Eve!

"It is nothing," he said fiercely to himself, as he gingerly stretched out his aching body, "to do with the indignities this man has heaped upon me. I am not influenced by the look in my wife's eyes when I told her how I came by my 'V', or the look that *would* have been in her eyes if she had seen me half an hour ago. I am above seeking revenge for the number of times I have been trodden on. I am a philosopher, beyond such petty, personal considerations. No, it is for Eve's sake, neglected and spurned by one so unworthy of her; it is for the sardine's sake, so cruelly terrified out of this mortal coil; and it is, above all, for Eden's sake, corrupted and soiled by the presence of this unlovely, unloving, disrespectful creature."

He, like God, had now discovered the joyful balm of rationalisation.

That night he made his plans.

****

"Hey you!" shouted the serpent. "Have you been scrumping my fruit?" It was the afternoon of the following day. Oddly, no one else seemed to be around.

Adam looked up. "What are you talking about?"

"That tree over there. It's mine."

"The Tree of Knowledge?"

"Yes, mine. Someone's been at it! Three apples gone since yesterday!"

"That's not your tree! No one's allowed to touch that fruit."

"That's right. Because it's been reserved for me."

"It has not!"

"Why do you think it's called the Tree of Knowledge?"

"Don't ask me! God never was very good at naming things!"

"Because it's my reward. Because I'm the cleverest creature here, that's why. The hedgehog nearly got it, I admit, but that's beside the point. Just keep your greedy hands off it!"

"Are you," demanded Adam in amazement, "telling me what

85

to do?"

"I most certainly am! Those apples are being saved for me! If you dare to touch... "

He wriggled away into the undergrowth as he saw Adam's foot, the underside of which he knew intimately, raised menacingly.

"You lumbering bully! By the Great Worm in the Sky, I'll teach you a lesson one day, when my apples begin to work! You'll see!"

Adam went back to bathing his head in the river.

Just then, the owl, a close friend of the serpent's, flew by.

"What on earth are you doing up this time of day?" the serpent asked loudly.

"I just wanted to congratulate you," answered the owl, equally loudly. "The hedgehog's very upset, though."

"I know. I think he deserved to win as much as I did. I'm thinking of sharing the apples with him."

"That would be a nice gesture. But tell me, I still don't see why God had to call a meeting just to tell everyone not to eat your fruit."

"I asked him to." If anything, his voice was now even louder.

"What!"

"I don't mind a few of my friends having one of those apples from time to time, but if word got out about their incredible effect... As you know, I had a modest part to play in the design of Eve, when we took that stupid Adam to pieces, so God was just returning a favour."

"Ah, that was clever of you! Well, I must be off. See you later."

The owl flew off, and the serpent wriggled over to the Tree of Knowledge, reached up, and took down an apple (from another tree) which he had carefully balanced on a branch earlier, leaned back against the trunk, and began to munch away.

Next moment, Adam was looming over him, a mixture of amazement and fury on his face. His nerve almost failed him, but with victory so near, he forced himself to look up and say, "I thought

I told you to keep away from my tree, you great lout!"

With an ominous calmness, Adam reached down, picked him up with one hand, with the other reached up, plucked an apple, held it in front of the serpent's eyes, polished it on the serpent's head, waved it in front of his eyes again, slowly and deliberately devoured it in front of him, wiped his lips, smiled evilly, and finally stuffed the core in the serpent's mouth, before tying him into another knot, hanging him from a branch, and marching off, whistling.

The twenty witnesses who had been hiding in the trees and bushes stepped out.

****

Poor Adam, unlike the apple, had been only too ripe for the plucking.

Since the serpent was the first Edenian ever to tell a lie, it hardly occurred to Adam to disbelieve that the Tree really had been given to him as a prize. God had said nothing to the contrary, merely that it was forbidden to eat from it. This was, for Adam, yet another example of the favouritism God showed to certain creatures. Moreover, he was still smarting under God's threat to replace him with Eve.

Then, to make matters worse, *he suspected Eve was having an affair with one of the angels!* The week before, after his trial, she had disappeared most of the night, and refused to give any explanation on her return. But the following day, there had been a glow in her cheeks – and mud in her hair - that hadn't been there before. It was Gabriel, he was sure of it! Although he told himself he didn't care, all that week God had been creating mates for everybody else, and all night long (and all day too) he could hear the cries of rapture, while he lay lonely and unloved.

It only needed, therefore, the splitting headache donated by the elephant to push Adam's nerves to breaking point. That, and the reminder that the serpent *had* seen all his innards laid out on the grass, and the subtle suggestion that these particular apples might make him somehow more than he was.

That was *Adam's* contribution to the growth of rationalisation in the Garden.

True, he had also broken a direct order from God: but that order had been arbitrary, and in any case no penalties had been specified.

What he didn't admit was that he was also just plain disobedient by nature!

****

"Eve?"

She turned at the sound of the serpent's voice. It was the following evening, and once again she was sitting by the river, her feet in the water.

"Why, you're crying!" He slithered on to her shoulders and tried to brush the tears away. But she turned her face away, and restrained him gently with one hand.

Minutes passed, until her weeping subsided, and she looked down at him with a strange expression, stroking his face with something akin to compassion.

A slightly petulant voice said: "Aren't you going to introduce me?"

"Oh my gosh!" and the serpent slithered to the ground and into the grass. When he returned, he was not alone.

Eve rubbed her eyes: was she seeing double?

"This," announced the serpent, both proud and shy, "is Lamia. My wife."

Eve stared at the two of them, identical even down to the 'V', though one 'V' looked somehow more *painful* than the other. Then she began to smile, and then, to their double astonishment, burst into tears again.

"Eve, Eve, what's the matter?" the serpent asked tenderly.

"Oh, I'm sorry, I'm sorry!" she said, wiping her eyes. "Squiggly, Lamia, forgive me, please forgive me!" and she held out both her arms to the newcomer, who looked a bit nervous, and turned to her husband for guidance. He nudged her towards Eve, who picked her up, and then him too, holding them both in front of her, seeming to take nourishment from what she saw.

The serpent couldn't resist boasting about his new mate. "Isn't she lovely?" he asked.

It took him a moment or two to comprehend Eve's sudden gust of laughter before he chuckled himself. It took Lamia a few seconds more before her frown of dismay dissolved into an identical chuckle.

Eve gasped, "Oh yes, you're lovely, lovely, lovely! Oh, if only this could last, Paradise for ever! All of you, every big, small, funny, finny, fat, thin, clumsy, graceful... and Adam too, he's not really bad, you know." *Why did she say that?* "Just a bit silly and immature. All of us here, for ever, sitting by the water like this..."

He's not really bad, you know. The serpent fought down a sudden feeling of guilt. "But it's all still alright, "he replied, "I know we'll have to leave here one day, but we'll be together again in Heaven." *But not Adam. What had happened to that glorious elation he had felt such a short time before?*

She didn't answer, but after a moment rose to her feet, and said lightly: "Let's go and see some of the other wives: I haven't met half of them yet."

They moved along, Lamia on one side of Eve, himself on the other, loving and loved.

And loved. That was the miracle. Later that evening, when he learned that she had taken another apple, taken and eaten it *before* she had met Lamia, in between the agony and the despair, his bruised mind lurched back time and time again to that miracle. She had eaten, she said – and would add not one other word of explanation – because Adam had been deceived into eating. She had *known*.

And still she had held him and loved him.

Chapter Ten
GOD PLAYS DIRTY

Day Thirty-three in Eden, and God, fully rested from his labours of rearrangement and re-creation, finally got round to giving more thought to the Treaty with Satan. He felt just a bit uneasy. He reminded himself that the bizarre idea of a forbidden tree had come from Lucifer, not from the others. And that called for caution! Perhaps, before he devoted himself to drawing up a set of *real* commandments, he ought to take a small precaution.

"Let's look at it this way," he said to the Archangels. "You realise, of course, that 'the quality of mercy is not strain'd, it droppeth as the gentle rain from Heaven upon the place beneath: it is twice bless'd; it blesseth him that gives and him that takes'. In fact, when you really think about it, it is 'an attribute to God himself', isn't it?"

The angels were most impressed with his way of putting things. However:

"What do you mean?" they asked.

"Mercy! Grace!" he answered promptly. "'The Grace of God', that's what I'll call it. I'll have it added to the Treaty right away!"

When again asked for clarification, he explained that 'Grace' meant that he reserved to himself the right to forgive sinners in exceptional circumstances.

"Isn't that cheating a bit?" asked Michael, not looking very pleased.

"Of course it is!" said God cheerfully.

He felt extraordinarily good-humoured and optimistic. The Afterlife was neatly sorted out: if any of the progeny of these creatures *should* turn out bad, they wouldn't be allowed to infect Heaven as Lucifer and Belial had done. From what had seemed like utter disaster with the death of the sardine had come glorious victory.

So when Adam and Eve appeared a little later, and she said quietly, "We've eaten the forbidden apples", he had a heart attack.

****

It took a week to get over the heart attack, and another hundred years to find an answer – a kind of answer – to the consequences of his own edict. The 'Grace' clause had come too late: Adam and Eve had eaten the apples while the original Treaty of Eden was in force, and there was no way to avoid sending them to Hell. Or, in all justice, the serpent, either.

The serpent, like the two humans, confessed his role voluntarily. He was never to fully recover from his grief. He frantically studied psychology, in a vain effort to understand how it was possible that Eve had not withdrawn one jot of her affection for him. She had said nothing to God about his part in the affair, nor, strangely enough, had Adam, which led the other animals to look at him with a new respect.

The serpent's action was explicable, as was Adam's: they had goaded each other to damnation. But Eve?

She never gave any other reason than that Adam had eaten, and so she had eaten, too. Of the three, she was the one who had most deliberately defied God. *No,* said God to himself, his heart filled with wonder, *she didn't defy me, she defied* my edict, *she defied what* wasn't *me. And she offered Adam something I never offered him.*

Even those creatures who could not look into her heart prayed that God would forgive her, not knowing that a Nebulan BondWord could never be Broken. The angels, too, felt drawn to her defence, and Gabriel even offered to go to Hell to plead with Satan for her release. Only the Archangel Michael remained obdurate, seeing in Eve's perfidy the unanswerable justification for his beliefs.

A hundred years, during which Cain was born, five months after the signing of the Treaty, and Abel, six months after that. Eve's first children, setting the scene for the crooked path that the human race was to follow, capable of becoming the greatest and the basest of all animals. Three candidates for Hell now, and only one for Heaven: not a good start for the human race. As if the grief of the first fratricide had unwomaned her, Eve's next pregnancy, twenty years later, resulting in the birth of Seth, took nine months instead of five, setting what was to be the pattern for all future gestations. Odd, thought God, wondering whether he'd made an error. He was still very innocent.

Adam changed. Only a few days after he and Eve had eaten the apples, he finally performed his matrimonial duties, spurred on, for some reason best known to himself, by the serpent, and he and Eve grew closer, though they were never to share a bond as close as that between Squiggly and Lamia. The murder of Abel shocked him deeply, but he somehow emerged with greater spiritual strength, and over the years the mantle of patriarch settled comfortably over his shoulders. As he neared old age, his memories became confused, and he told Seth, and his grandchildren, that Eve had eaten the apple first, led on by a visiting devil in the form of a toad. Eve just smiled, sure that no one would ever be likely to believe such a patently implausible story.

Eve remained Eve. As loving and as wise and as courageous as she had always been – and yet, paradoxically, as ultimately inaccessible and unknowable. It was not only Adam who gazed at her, uncannily beautiful even as her youth passed her by, in puzzlement and awe. In her eyes were mysteries unexplored, hints of a past and a future – a destiny – stretching well beyond the confines of Eden. The creatures continued to feel, as they had that first morning of her birth, when the very tree tops had stopped moving to welcome her, that they were in the presence of something they would never fully understand, a being at once simple and profound, ingenuous and subtle, close and remote, delicate and potent.

And gradually, pitilessly, the time drew nigh. God had already sent the first souls to Hell: Cain, the Venus Flytrap, a piranha fish. The hair of the first humans turned grey, their steps lost their resilience, the strength faded from their bodies. And as they aged, so did the serpent. It was as though Eden's first sinners had resolved to die together, so as to comfort and succour each other on that journey that loomed ever nearer and nearer, a journey not so much towards Hell, but away from Heaven, away from everyone they had loved, away from God.

I am a god, forged in the Nebulan Furnaces, all things are possible, all things must be possible for a god. But he had himself created the impossibility: no Nebulan could Break his BondWord without risking damage to the Universe itself. His first man, his first woman, his first serpent, were going to Hell. And why? Because he himself had ordained it would be so, he himself had given Satan the power he now possessed. And again why? Because his first man had been tetchy and bad-tempered, and hadn't treated him as he felt a god ought to be treated.

All things are possible for a god, all things must *be possible...*

And then he had it! He checked the wording of the Treaty,

and what could only be described as a devilish smile spread over his countenance.

Of course, he would have to get permission from Xonophix, but, considering their eternal friendship, that wouldn't be a problem.

****

A Saragash Flier came to Satan with some strange news. Far to the east of Hell, a region desolate and harsh even by Infernal standards, there had been an enormous earthquake – "almost like an invisible hand slicing through the ground", said the witness – and *a great chunk of the planet had broken off, and gone flying out into space, like a giant asteroid.* Satan didn't give the matter any importance, and returned to his facial exercises: he wanted to look good for Eve.

A few weeks later, however, he received a letter from God.

C/O The Cloud
Dy. 231, Yr. 98 (Edentime)

Dear Lucifer,
I trust you are pleased with the enclosed consignment of souls: five more humans, a lot more piranha fish, one kestrel, and one Black Widow spider..
You will undoubtedly be glad also to know that the piece of land that recently broke off from Hell is now in stable orbit round Zindor. While remaining, of course, still part of Hell, I felt it convenient to rename it locally Limbo. You, of course, still remain titular King, and your picture will be put on any stamps, should they ever be issued, and your health drunk on festive occasions, should there ever be any.
Adam has been in Limbo for some days now with his wife, and has asked me to thank you on his behalf. He is fully satisfied with the facilities in Limbo, to wit, one Vault, one Vat for the containment of souls, one Lid thereof, and one Keeper therefore. Since Limbo is really a part of Hell and hence under your jurisdiction (at least for the time being), Adam assures you of his fealty, and expresses a sincere hope that you will soon visit this far outpost of your Kingdom. As his stay there is unlikely to exceed fifty years (as per the 'Grace' codicil to the Treaty), he trusts that you will not delay your visit too long. He does not seem to realise that this is a complete impossibility because of the enormous distances involved.

Although I am absolutely confident that this situation will meet with your approval, I am aware of the unfortunate tendency of Belial, your Prime Sinister, to carp and cavil, so I suggest that you remind him that the Treaty states quite clearly that anyone who eats from the Tree shall be sent to Hell: it does not specify which part thereof. And nowhere, of course, does it say that they shall be delivered to the King of the said world.

Thanking you once again for your invaluable assistance, I remain, as always,

Unquestionably God.

Part Two

A Visit to Hell

Chapter Eleven
JOURNEY TO A VERY WARM PLACE

December 25, 1999. St. Peter quietly closed the Wooden Gates behind him, and set out on a journey from which he never really expected to return.

The first part of this journey – to the Way Station – he had made countless times before. As usual, all he could see through the Shuttle viewport as they approached Limbo were the Nets stretching into the depths of space like monstrous spiders' webs, ready to receive and trap the souls before they drifted inexorably back to the Wells on the dark side of Zindor. Even as he watched, a series of sudden blue flashes indicated where souls had fallen into the Nets. As the Shuttle came nearer, Limbo was a nightmare of swirling black mists and a bleak blank landscape broken only by the huge circular structure of the Station itself, and, on either side, the launching pads of the two Shuttle Terminals.

As soon as the Shuttle docked, Peter left his enormous trunk with three guards he knew he could trust, with instructions that it be unobtrusively taken to the Hell Terminal. He himself took the conveyer belt to the Earth Reception Centre, and thence marched rapidly, his beard stuffed furtively inside his cloak, down a long corridor towards the living quarters of the Station personnel. After knocking quietly on the door marked 'Judge Tobias' and receiving no reply, he let himself in with a master key.

He entered one of the most opulent rooms he had ever seen. None of the items – the plush furniture, the tapestries, statuettes, mirrors – were new to him, since it was he who had arranged for Tobias to receive them. But this was the first time he had witnessed a family gathering, as it were, of his bribes. Nearly six hundred years of corruption were here brought together in a magnificent display, a grandiloquent testimony to the strength of their partnership. He felt quite emotional, like a person rereading love letters sent over the years.

He paced feverishly around the room, waiting for its owner. A word scrawled on the cover of a video tape caught his attention. He felt his hackles rise and his beard curl. *Darren!* Was this the video that had been used against them? Had Tobias been punishing himself by watching it again, even though more than six months had passed since that fatal mistake?

Although he knew only too well what had happened, he had never seen the video itself. Since he had to wait for Tobias... He slotted the tape into the machine with the same sick feeling with which a man might examine the handle of a knife sticking out of his own chest.

The Courtroom appeared, and squelching on a small grimy table in the middle of it something resembling a tadpole, a greenish, musty, pond-idiot version of a tadpole. In front of it was the Bench of the Five Judges, although all that could be seen were the soles of four pairs of feet flanking a huge, jovial, white-haired old gentleman, with whiskers and hair running riot, a bulbous nose with obvious territorial designs on the cheeks, and champagne-bubble eyes promising warm shelter and safety, topped by a luxuriant foliage of eyebrows. With kindness lying round him like a fur cloak, this old gentleman gave the tadpole a welcoming smile.

"Welcome to the Afterworld, my lad! I'm Judge Tobias. It's probably been a bit hectic for you up to now, but you'll soon be able to settle down to your new life. Now, we'll make this as quick as possible, because this must be a trying time for you... a *trying* time! Ha, ha, ha!"

And he burst into peals of laughter, slapping his hands down compulsively on his generous belly.

"Oh, ho, ho, you must forgive me!" spluttered the merry Judge. "I've got such a wicked sense of humour... *wicked* sense of humour? *Wicked?* Of, dearie dearie me, you've gone and done it again, Toby, you old ram! God's Judge with a wicked sense of humour?"

It took some time before he regained control of himself, while the tadpole seemed to squelch more desperately than before. Peter could understand why.

"Right!" Tobias gasped, suppressing a final bubble of merriment. "Let's get on with the case. Now, as far as I can judge... oh no, not again, you old tiger, if *I* can't judge... Hector!"

A giant of a man, who clearly had robots among his ancestors, strode into view, looked at the tadpole as if it were an

100

escaped haemorrhoid and an aching tooth combined, then clanked round to face the Judge.

"I demand the Hell penalty for this soul!" he boomed.

"Well," beamed Tobias, "I know you to be a man of the highest integrity, who wouldn't demand such a sentence unless you had more than ample reason for it."

He turned to the soul with an apologetic smile.

"Well, that's it, I'm afraid. I do so hope you'll bear no ill feelings. But you'll only be there for an eternity, after all. I'm sure the time will soon pass."

He began to make an entry in a huge, leather-bound book in front of him.

A little, wizened old man appeared, and was just about to pick up the soul when it seemed to grasp what was happening.

"Wait a minute!" it screamed. "You can't do this to me! You haven't even heard any evidence!"

Tobias looked up sternly. "Are you acquainted with Hector, our Chief Prosecutor?"

"Of course not!"

"Precisely! If you were, you'd know what an honest chap he is. I for one am not going to insult him, to cast doubt upon his probity, by demanding to hear his evidence. I must say I'm a bit surprised you should even think of doing so yourself! You seemed such a nice lad."

"I want a lawyer!"

"Hector's a lawyer!"

"I want my own lawyer! It's my right!"

"Oh dear, what a fuss you're making just because things haven't gone all your own way! Still, just to show you the lengths I'm willing to go to give you every opportunity... Wilberforce! We have a guilty client here for you to defend."

A nervous-looking young man, with a thrush-egg complexion, and so many freckles they seemed to be playing leapfrog over each other, shuffled forward, biting his nails and staring at the ground.

"This," announced Tobias, "is Defending Counsel. I trust you realise you've vastly increased the work of this Court by insisting on this ridiculous formality. Right. We'll hear what Hector has to say again, then Wilberforce can answer in vain on your behalf. Hector?"

"I demand the Hell penalty!" boomed Hector again.

Tobias gazed at him admiringly, then turned to the trembling Wilberforce. "Well, Prosecuting Counsel has put forward, I think you have to agree, a cogent, compelling, indeed irrefutable case against the defendant. Perhaps, Wilberforce, you'd like to try to deal with the points he has raised one by one, bearing in mind that the lease on the apartment you're renting from me will shortly be up for renewal."

At this point, St. Peter winced even more than he had at Tobias' atrocious puns. *Of course, we never expected anyone to be secretly filming, and neither did we expect Darren to escape to tell the tale. But all the same...*

Wilberforce coughed obsequiously, showering the floor with bits of undigested nails, and continued to gaze fearfully at his feet, as if seeking inspiration from these extremities, which shuffled and wriggled like two giant insects caught in a sticky cowpat. His voice, when he eventually spoke, had all the force of a strand of overcooked spaghetti.

"I cannot argue with the evidence my learned colleague has put forward..."

"I should think not!" muttered Tobias.

"...or even with the evidence he has *not* put forward..."

"I assume you're referring to..."

"I am indeed, my lord."

"Yes, that on top of everything else."

"But I would respectfully suggest, my lord, that my client's very tender age might..."

At this point, a cluster of freckles broke free and floated to the ground like confetti, inducing a sneeze which caused a few of them to lodge like spring blossom in Tobias' wild hair.

"...very tender age might, though only if it pleased you, my lord, so to regard it, be considered an extenuating factor."

His own boldness at this stage so shocked him that he gulped into silence, glared accusingly at the soul as if holding it responsible for his discomfiture, and then fled the room, leaving a cloud of freckles homeless behind him.

There was a small silence while Tobias ascertained that Defending Counsel was not in fact lurking behind or within the freckles.

"Well," he breathed, turning to the tadpole, "you're a lucky lad, a very lucky lad indeed! I've never known Wilberforce make such a moving plea for mercy in all my life. A *tour de force*, if ever I've heard one! It's true he wasn't able to refute a single one of the points Hector made so tellingly, but what is justice if not tempered by mercy? You are indeed, as Wilberforce reminded us, very young – sixteen days, wasn't it? – and many of your crimes may perhaps be ascribed to the folly and hot-headedness of youth. It therefore gives me pleasure to commute your sentence to Purgatory. Now off you go, my lad, and reflect on your good fortune."

Once again he commenced writing in the book.

This soul, though, was a fighter. "I demand the right to appeal!"

"What!" Tobias' whiskers sprang to shocked attention. Their owner hesitated, then:

"On what grounds do you wish to lodge an appeal?"

"On the grounds that I'm innocent."

"Innocent of what?"

"How do I know? There hasn't been any charge yet!"

"How," expostulated Tobias, "can you claim to be innocent when, on your own admission, you don't even know what you're innocent of?"

"Everything!"

"Everything? Look here, my lad, this is a Court of law, you must be more specific."

"I'm innocent of whatever you're charging me with."

"Do I have your word of honour on that?"

"My word of honour."

Tobias pondered, then seemed to come to a decision.

"After due deliberation, the Court is prepared - just this once, mind you - to accept your word of honour alone, without placing on you the onus of proof."

"Thank you, my lord." Suddenly, the tadpole seemed less greenish and musty.

"Hector," said Tobias, restraining some whiskers which were trying to explore his ear, "you have heard the Court's decision. It is magnanimously accepting this gentlesoul's word of honour. Have you anything to say?"

"Yes, my lord."

"Well?"

"The Prosecution withdraws the charge to which the defendant has just pleaded innocent. However, we have no option but to demand the Hell penalty on the second charge."

Tobias swung round on the astonished soul, his bulbous nose now tumescent with indignation, his eyebrows contracting together into a bristling palisade of irate hairs.

"Ah ha, what do you say to that, you grubby little urchin! Right nasty piece of work *you* turned out to be! Show a bit of kindness to you, and you can't wait to abuse it! No sooner do we free you on one very serious charge than you're back here before us on another even *more* serious charge! I take it this charge *is* more serious, Hector?"

"It certainly is, my lord."

"Well, in all my years as a judge I've never come across such gross ingratitude, such lack of all common decency, such turpitude! I shudder when I think I was about to quash your previous ridiculously mild sentence."

He caught sight of Wilberforce, who had slipped back into the courtroom.

"Well, I hope you're proud of yourself and your liberal nonsense! I allowed myself to be influenced by your rhetoric, your spurious appeals to leniency, and what has been the result? A hardened criminal, deaf to everything that is good. Or would you try to excuse his latest crimes, would you try, once again, to pervert the course of justice with fine words and honeyed phrases?"

Wilberforce gazed at the soul with tears in his eyes.

"After all I did for you, the risks I took..." he said brokenly.

Tobias donned the black cap.

"The prisoner, having been found guilty on all charges made, and even more guilty on all charges not made, is hereby sentenced to eternity in Hell on the first group of charges, and to a second eternity in Hell on the second group, the two sentences, for technical reasons, to run concurrently. In short, to put a long sentence in a short one, you're damned! Oh my gosh, did you hear that? 'A long sentence in a short one'? Oh Tobias, oh dearie me, how *do* you do it! Well, off you go, ha, ha, to eternal torment! Next prisoner, please!"

"But I'm innocent!" yelled the soul again.

Tobias, the ripples of his rich Christmas-pudding chuckles

gradually receding towards the back of his neck, admonished him with a plump forefinger.

"Don't you go trying to court favour with me, my lad... oh no, not again, 'court fav...', oh Tobias, you absolute tiger, did you hear that?" And once again he went into paroxysms of laughter, bouncing around behind the Judges' Bench like a buoy in a storm.

Which was his undoing.

For Hector suddenly shouted, "Look!" and pointed to the far end of the Bench. Tobias looked, and his laughter died an abrupt – and, it seemed from his expression, a painful – death.

Two of the eight feet were beginning to move.

"Get that blasted soul out of here!" hissed Tobias.

But Hector had already violently seized, not the soul, but the little, wizened old man.

"You fool!" he snarled, "how many tablets did you put in the wine?"

"T...t...two." stammered the little wizened old man who, under this harsh treatment, was becoming littler, wizeneder, and noticeably older by the second.

"We told you four!" And Hector shook him so hard that the sound of his testicles clanking together was distinctly audible.

"I said get that soul out!" repeated Tobias urgently.

Too late. The feet disappeared below the bench, the torso appeared above it, and the head above that. Thus was revealed a stern-faced man, a tiny bristly moustache clinging precariously to his upper lip, and what looked like another tiny bristly moustache clinging even more precariously to the top of his otherwise bald head.

"Good heavens, Tobias, whatever on Limbo's happening? Do my eyes deceive me? Are my senses playing me false? Has Hector got his hands round the usher's throat? And our colleagues – are they *sleeping*? How dare they? Tobias, I repeat, what on Limbo's going on?"

The foliage smothering Tobias' head had suddenly withered, but his tongue battled on.

"Hector's just trying to calm the usher down. We just had a particularly nasty piece of work come before us, and when we sentenced him, he became quite insulting. Now, Hector, just take that soul out, so we can continue."

Hector grabbed the soul, and began to stomp out. But from his huge fist a voice yelled:

"You can't do this to me! No one's looked at my c.v. or listened to my evidence! My parents are Jehovah's Witnesses, my uncle's a Jesuit, another uncle's a cleaner in the Vatican, my aunt's a member of Opus Dei, my grandfather was a missionary, my grandmother..."

"Take him away!" shouted Tobias.

"Wait!" commanded the stern-faced Judge. "If all that's true..."

"Nonsense, Cuthbert. Some of these lost creatures will say anything to escape justice."

"But I must admit I don't remember seeing this soul's c.v."

"You were sleeping."

"Pardon?"

"You were sleeping."

"Tobias, am I, or am I not, Chief Judge?"

"Well, yes, of course you are."

"And are we, or are we not, in the Courtroom?"

"Where else?"

"Is it therefore likely, I ask you, that I, the *Chief Judge*, would sleep in this place, a *Courtroom*? Is this a proposition worthy of the most remote consideration by those aware of the duties of a Judge, and the functions of a Courtroom?"

"They're *still* sleeping."

"I fail to see what *their* sleeping has got to do with me." And he frowned challengingly, both moustaches bristling, so that he seemed like a tentative sketch of a hedgehog.

"Well," said Tobias placatingly, "perhaps you were just lost in thought."

"*Deep* in thought maybe, not lost," retorted the other.

"Exactly, that's what I meant," sighed Tobias, glancing towards Hector, who had been edging towards the door.

But although Hector's knuckles were white, a voice still squeezed through his fingers.

"I was only sixteen days old, and my parents refused to let me have a blood transfusion, but they *promised* me I'd go to heaven, but this horrible fat man..."

A look of doubt filled the space between Cuthbert's two

moustaches.

"Is it conceivable that...? Hector, bring that soul back here!"

Hector unwillingly returned to the centre of the Courtroom, squeezing the soul so tightly it now had the shape of an hourglass.

Cuthbert frowned him. "Put it down," he ordered.

Hector obeyed, but his huge hand hovered over the soul like an incensed crab.

"What is your name, soul?" asked Cuthbert sternly.

"Darren, sir, and I was martyred by my own parents, so I *must* go to Heaven."

"Pass me the record book, Tobias."

Tobias hesitated, then picked up the huge Book, made as if to pass it, seemed to notice something in it, looked more closely, shouted "Oh my God!" scrambled over the Bench, picked the soul up, examined it minutely from all directions – a somewhat unnecessary procedure, since it presented the same featureless form from all angles – dashed back to the Bench, fumbled through some papers, extracted one, stared at it, and finally flopped back into his seat.

"Hector," he gasped, his voice trembling.

Hector tanked across, gazed at the paper and then at the soul, then clapped his hands to his head so hard he knocked himself backwards. Wilberforce followed on this pilgrimage and, after one look, took a sizeable chunk out of one of his fingers. Then all three turned and stared ominously at the little wizened old man.

By now, the process of wizenization had progressed so far it was difficult to see him. His fading remains backed away from Hector, who advanced on him with murderous intent.

"Fiend from Hell!" thundered Hector. With one mighty blow, he ensured that the little wizened old man would wizen no more. He then threw himself down, ignoring the remnants of his victim showering down on him, and proceeded to beat his head against the ground.

"Ah, I tried to stop myself, I tried! But because of his mistake, a pure, spotless soul..."

His voice broke off, and vast shudders peristalticked through his body. Tobias, himself almost weeping, put his arm around his shoulders.

"Are my senses deceiving me?" inquired Cuthbert, "have my

colleagues all gone mad?"

Tobias approached the soul, ripped off a piece of his ermine gown, folded it into a tiny cushion, and settled the bemused soul gently upon it. Brushing his hands through his wild white hair that broke like surf over his head, he spoke thus:

""Oh, how narrowly has tragedy been avoided here this afternoon! That devil's minion, that treacherous snake that Hector struck down in his righteous wrath, almost deceived us – nay, did deceive us, I confess, to our everlasting shame! He swore this was soul number six six six, who was a damned soul long before he came here. But, of course, that is no excuse: we should have seen immediately that this was a superior soul before us. Indeed, at first, as he himself will confirm, even though I believed him guilty of the most heinous crimes, I felt compelled to absolve him. But that traitor," indicating one of the bits of the little wizened old man that had fallen on his sleeve, "must have done something to our lunchtime wine. Why, our colleagues are still asleep! It beclouded our judgement and our vision. Oh, kind sir," wringing his hands, and looking imploringly at the soul, "will you ever be able to forgive us?"

****

St. Peter switched off the video: he knew the answer to *that* question only too well.

At that very moment, the door opened, and in came Tobias, whose plump arms descended on Peter's scrawny shoulders and subjected him to a hug that left him breathless.

"Peter! I didn't expect you so soon! Ah, but it's good to see you again!"

Peter stood back and gazed at the jovial old man with affection and the stirrings of pity: better not to tell him the worst yet.

Tobias' smile faded. He looked questioningly into his friend's eyes.

"This time it's something really big, isn't it? Not just the usual nonsense with Michael or the Virgin. I could hardly believe it when I got your message, but I hoped..."

"Yes, it's big. That's why I need the safe-conduct."

"But, Peter, are you sure it can't wait? In a few days everyone will be so busy with the Apocalypse... To risk going to that place now of all times..."

"But that's just it. Toby, I *can't* tell you everything now. Later, you'll understand. But did you get that safe-conduct or not?"

Tobias opened his mouth to protest, saw Peter's expression, and desisted. Moving slowly and dejectedly, he reached into a drawer, and pulled out a pink parchment charred all round the edges and spattered with what looked like tear stains.

Peter took it. The words *'I hereby agree to sell my soul for the sum of ------'*, in beautifully embossed calligraphy, had been scored out and replaced with the following rough scrawl: *'The Bearer is to be allowed to enter Infernal territory without let or hindrance. No claw may be raised against the Bearer, on pain of extreme torment.'* Two signatures were appended, the first brash and buccaneering, proclaiming *'Satan, Master of the Universe'*, the other wispy and cramped, saying simply *'Belial'*.

"It doesn't look very official," Peter muttered.

"You can hardly expect them to have official safe-conduct passes when you're the first person ever to want to visit there! The whole point about Hell is precisely that it *isn't* safe to go there! It's hellishly *un*safe!"

Tobias sounded upset. Peter gave him a wan smile.

"Anyway," said Tobias, "I've checked the signatures, of course, and they're absolutely genuine. But I still wish you wouldn't go, even with this. Satan isn't exactly renowned for his integrity. I've made photocopies, naturally, so we'll have evidence if he breaks his word, but that won't help much if he's already broken you!" He paused and hesitated. "I know it's something to do with Darren. And it was all my fault..." A bead of sweat appeared on his brow, his pink cheeks began to tremble, his plump hands clenched and unclenched like an accordion. "If you *must* speak to Satan, let me... let me go instead!" The bead of sweat bounced off his cheek.

Peter was touched. "Thank you, Toby, old friend, thank you. But Darren was as much my fault as yours – I should have dealt with him as soon as he arrived, before Michael got to him. No, I have to go myself, I'm the only one who..."

He stopped as a look of horror invaded his friend's countenance.

"Duck!" hissed that portly personage.

For a moment, Peter was a bit hurt: here he was about to go to Hell itself, and Toby was thinking about his stomach! Then he saw what had occasioned the exclamation. The window of Tobias' office opened on to a quadrangle, across which was now approaching the stern Judge of the video. *Cuthbert!* Chosen by the Archangel Michael, when the Way Station was first set up on Limbo, to be Chief Judge. Probably responsible for the presence of the secret video camera in the Courtroom. And certainly responsible for the unending stream of complaints reaching Heaven about the workings of the Court of the First Judgement. He would undoubtedly inform Michael if he saw Peter here. So Peter ducked.

"He's headed right this way!" whispered Tobias. "We must hurry. Quick, follow me! I'll get you safely into the Hell Terminal. I've already arranged with the Captain, a good friend, to get you on the Shuttle."

"No, you get to the Courtroom, and behave yourself like a good boy. I know the way to the Terminal. But tell me quickly, did you manage to find the Serpents?"

"I tried! I have friends who can communicate with the Lost Souls, who have a legend of two Serpents who are completely Unbound. But that's all I could find out. But why...?"

"Eve has a message for them."

"*Eve!* You haven't told *her*...!"

"Toby, I'm only half crazy, not completely! But Eve *senses* things...all I know is, if Eve has a message, then somehow I'll be meeting them."

Tobias noticed the tension in his voice.

"Peter, if I thought you could ever be afraid of anything, then that Eve..."

" 'Afraid', no, it's something almost...worse. Toby, I must go! Cuthbert's nearly here."

Tobias looked at him. Protest in his eyes. Protest in the stiffness of his body.

"Toby, I've got the safe-conduct. In Hell, they can't possibly know what's been going on in Heaven. For them, I'm God's representative. And anyway, I still *am* the Keeper of the Keys, even if they *have* gone a little rusty. They wouldn't *dare* harm me." Tobias still looked decidedly unconvinced. "And since you're still looking decidedly unconvinced, let me tell you what I've got in my trunk."

No sooner had he done so than a curious mixture of fear and relief came over his friend's face.

"So you see," said Peter, with what he hoped was a light laugh, as he moved towards the door, "there's really nothing to worry about."

Tobias followed him out, locked the door, and tried to return the smile.

"Have a good holiday. Don't get into bad company." Were his eyes moist?

"Toby, if by any chance I don't..."

"No, I won't hear it, I *won't*!" He touched Peter's cheek, then turned abruptly and strode along the corridor, puffing, without looking back.

****

Three hours later, Peter was in Hell. Well, the Terminal, he reminded himself. The distinction was more than academic: in Hell itself (as in Heaven) there was no technology; indeed, the only technology he knew of, apart from Earth, was in the Way Station, and the Shuttles and Shuttleports dependent on it. Maybe the Vaults too, if they really existed. Something to do with Dimensions, he had heard.

The journey from Limbo to Hell had not been greatly different from the journey to Limbo. The Shuttles were identical, following a fixed trajectory from which it was impossible to deviate – Satan's early optimistic attempts to hi-jack the Shuttle were now part of the folklore of the Station. There were, of course, differences *inside* the Shuttle: the viewports, for instance, had all been blocked out (the first group of souls had mutinied upon seeing what Hell was like from the air), and most of the seating had been ripped out in order to be able to pack in more damned souls, now, of course, in their replacement bodies. But the Captain, as Toby had said, was a friend, so Peter spent the journey comfortably seated beside him in his cabin.

He had expected trouble with his trunk in Hellport, and indeed the two Customs officials, minor devils but still towering over Peter, started off arrogantly enough – would he mind opening his luggage before they opened *him*? – but were both reduced to trembling obedience when they saw the second signature, that of Belial, on the safe-conduct, and not only allowed the trunk to pass unopened, but even helped drag it into the Hellport Lounge.

So here he was, in front of a phalanx of giant air-conditioners, and not fooled by the fact that he was only sweating moderately. He tried to take his mind off the forthcoming danger, but this became difficult with the antics of a guard who, when he was not ostentatiously sharpening a vicious-looking trident, and pointing it experimentally at him, as if calculating the exact force necessary to impale him, was equally ostentatiously reading, with many a throaty chuckle, Foxe's *Book of Martyrs*.

He therefore found it impossible to suppress a slight tremor when a loud trumpet blast reverberated through the Immigration Hall, the great portals swept open, a wave of heat hurtled towards him, and there at the entrance loomed the Lord of Darkness.

Chapter Twelve
THE KINGS OF HELL

Less than an hour before, Satan had been presiding over the traditional Christmas Feast in the Great Hall, along almost the whole length of which ran a vast table tastefully fashioned from the bones of earlier menus, and inlaid with teeth and gallstones. Even the vegetarians among the devils – and they were the majority – forced themselves to eat a few slices of damned soul (or at least the bodies containing them) on this special day. Christmas, after all, was Christmas.

The great Heresiarch watched with a falsely avuncular smile as his Companions tucked into their food, he himself waiting patiently for his own second dish, which was obviously far from done, since it still twitched and shrieked on the spit in front of him. While he waited, he nibbled abstractedly at some marinated virgins' nipples, occasionally wiping his lips delicately with a gaily-coloured foreskin.

He bore little resemblance to the being who had left Eden so precipitately so many thousands of years before. Then he had been wounded, bruised, humiliated, but informed with the rekindled energy and fire of the original Lucifer. Now the fire had long since gone out. The scars and gashes which had then borne witness to his strength and courage were now mocked by the ointments and perfumes and powders with which he tried to hide them. It was the same powerful body, the same imposing stature, but the *impression* it gave was of something shrunken, stooped, diminished. The shell remained intact, but a vacuum had been forming over the centuries. A vitiated splendour, with more than a hint of the ridiculous. Belial's creation.

And yet today there *was* something different, a new alertness, an expectancy, a stirring. The more perceptive devils who noticed unconsciously touched their weapons, for, they thought, it could mean only one thing. At last.

"A few jellied testicles, sir?" an attendant inquired respectfully.

"No thank you, my bad fellow. Though if there should happen to be any pickled breasts... ah, delicious! That Way Station Fitter really is a master of verisimilitude. An actress, I presume."

"A transsexual, sir."

"Really? Whoever would have guessed? What do you say to that, Moloch?"

The person thus addressed, a huge devil beside whom Falstaff would have seemed dangerously under-nourished, had nothing to say to that, since he was too engrossed in the thankless task of trying to find some meat to scrape off the loin of yogi he had deliberately ordered in order not to spoil the diet he had recently begun. Satan was very concerned about his friend's weight – he had no aesthetic objection to a devil weighing three hundred kilos, but now, with Bugrot and the Nefilim in almost open revolt, was not the time for Hell's leading warrior to go to flab.

He thrust aside this depressing thought, and turned his attention to the conversation around him.

"...absolute nonsense! While it's clearly inferior to buggery, bestiality, masturbation, and so on, there's not a jot of proof that it causes a health hazard. On ethical grounds, of course, it's greatly to be deplored – it's unnatural in the extreme. But let's not confuse medical with ethical questions. This rumour that it can cause blindness is arrant nonsense!"

"But surely, even so, it's a useful rumour, and one we ought to encourage. If you, as Health Minister, were to declare it true, people would get frightened, and the filthy practice would soon be stamped out. Let the Saragashim stick to their own perversions!"

The Health Minister – a twisted, whorled creature garnished with suppurating sores that hissed and erupted so violently that the topography of his skin was constantly changing – snorted, dislodging part of his nasal membrane in the process.

"And if it's proved our evidence is faked? No, the whole issue should be fought on moral grounds, where our arguments are unassailable."

114

Satan nodded with seeming approval. *Prudish old farts! You're still angels at heart, the lot of you! Still, it's a relief to know I won't go blind.*

At this point, Moloch gave up on the loin of yogi, squeaked forth such a weak belch that the others glanced at him with compassion, and then began doggedly squeezing the marrow from the metacarpals of a former pianist.

"When's this rationing going to stop?" asked another devil, perhaps unaware that Moloch was dieting by his own choice. "Today's the first decent meal we've had for ages."

"As soon as we invade, you know that," a companion answered testily.

"That's what everyone keeps saying. Meanwhile, the Beast is eating half our food, and if we wait much longer, it will eat *us*!"

At this point, the others became immersed in a deep study of their plates, and he glanced round nervously at Satan, whose demeanour didn't change in the slightest: he still smiled serenely. *Belial will have to deal with this one!*

Foolishly taking heart from Satan's lack of reaction, the devil went on: "And what are we doing about Bugrot and the Nefilim? Nothing, nothing at all!"

"So long as they stay the other side of the Lake, so what? Let them rot there!"

"They ought to be *in* the Lake, not behind it! We didn't defeat the Saragashim just by sitting on the other side of the Lake! We went out and fought them, tooth and nail!"

"That's right," interposed a third, "some of us are getting too soft. Too much leisure, not enough discipline."

"No spirit nowadays," added another, "even our tortures are getting soft. All these new-fangled notions! In the old days, a devil worked with his hands and teeth!"

Heads nodded in agreement. The souls themselves had started to complain, and what could be more shameful than that?

"It's different in a Symphony of Pain, of course," added the devil who had just spoken. "Some of the more subtle effects you just can't get by Ripping-and-Tearing."

115

"Even they're not what they used to be," grumbled another. "Last year ten of the souls died before the finale. I've never heard so many notes off-key."

"You're right," said another. "The work had no feeling, no flair: one combination of screams was much the same as another. I tell you, everything's going downhill in Hell, things just aren't what they used to be."

A glum silence fell over the table, broken only by the rumblings of Moloch's cavernous and unsatisfied maw, as his enzymes scurried around in a vain search for food to work on.

I can't let this go on.

Satan rose to his feet, his cloak swirling around him, and looked from face to face, feeding from the expectation he saw there. When the tension was just right, he finally spoke, throwing his voice out irresistibly in the way Belial had taught him during countless hours of practice.

"I have listened to you today, and on other days, and heard the despair in your voices, a despair that our enemies can only gloat at. I have heard, but have I been able to believe? Can these voices really belong to the Companions of the Exodus, to those peerless friends and comrades who scorned to remain in the soft, unmanly comfort of Heaven, and chose instead to leave and fulfil the Diabolical Dream, taming this wild planet, and building a new, glorious society of the just and the free?"

At this point, his meal, who had been slowly turning on the spit in front of him, yelled out with wild enthusiasm, "Yeah, sock it to 'em, baby!" and expired.

"I have listened to your complaints about the food rationing; I have heard you criticise the greatest of all our institutions, the Symphonies of Pain; and I have listened to your doubts concerning the very invasion of Heaven itself." He paused, and gazed around, while they all tried to avoid catching his eye. His voice rose again. "Do not fear! The plans for the invasion are now complete. But first we will destroy the Earth, test the Beast in battle, send a warning to the Usurper that his days are numbered. The time has come! In a few days we attack, and begin that punishment that the

Usurper has so richly deserved!"

Thunderous applause greeted these words, although one or two of the devils looked doubtful, as if they seemed to remember their Leader had said exactly the same thing during the Good Friday Orgies. For just a second, Satan wondered what would happen if he never received the power which alone could control the Beast. *Uneasy lies the head,* he thought.

He continued his speech, ending, as usual, with exceedingly gory descriptions of the torments that lay in store for the Usurper and his sycophantic minions. But his mind was clearly elsewhere, and when he had finished, he took only a few perfunctory bites at his meal, not bothering at all with the Christmas pudding, and then, alleging cares of state, rapidly left the Hall.

Moloch dribbled, grappled with temptation, lost, and with tears of shame in his eyes, devoured the rest of his master's joint, and the Christmas pudding, in one enormous mouthful.

****

Satan wasted no time in returning to his private quarters in the palace. By now, that suicidal saint should have arrived. He still had no idea what he could possibly want, but it had to be something to do with the Apocalypse. The problem now, Satan thought, as he donned his most elegant cloak, was to get out of the palace before...

"A word, my lord?"

Too late. *Belial.*

The newcomer who had crept up like a bereaved fog was the complete antithesis of the Dark Lord, a Giacometti figure of skin and bone, only the skin, which had the texture of a plucked chicken, was insufficient to cover all the bone, which thus broke through in various places, crumbling as it did so, and leaving a thin layer of dried calcium where it fell. The head was almost bald, the skin stretched tightly across the misshapen skull in a phrenologist's nightmare, mottled as if an over-excited pigeon with dirty feet had trampled and slithered all over it: a bleak, dandruffed skullscape. The mouth was a snail's tracery, scarcely distinguishable from the myriad wrinkles that composed the rest of the face. The figure exuded decay, and yet, almost smothered by this visible decomposition, two eyes shone out, intense, burning, mesmeric, two pits of insatiable life in the dried-up riverbed of the face.

He wasn't the sort of person to invite to a party – or a Christmas dinner.

"I'm busy!" snapped Satan, knowing he would never get away with it.

"I know, my lord, but I feel we ought to discuss your tactics before you meet St. Peter."

"Keep your voice down, you fool!"

The double wrinkle that must have been Belial's mouth underwent a kind of mitosis, and through the subsequent gap appeared the carious remains of what had once been teeth. Satan had long ago learned that this was Belial's idiosyncratic representation of a sinister smile.

"I believe, my lord, we are in no danger of being overheard. There were indeed two servants who seemed to be asking too many questions. I took the liberty of dealing with them."

Satan groaned: he lost an average of five servants a week through Belial's precautions.

"My lord, at first I accepted your reasons for agreeing to see St. Peter alone. He must have been sent by the Usurper – though his request that his visit be kept a secret presents somewhat of a mystery. Particularly at this time, we cannot afford to cross him until we know why he was sent. We've only kept dissatisfaction at bay the last few years with the promise of an imminent invasion of Earth. If anyone ever realises we don't really control the Beast..."

"But we will! We will! That's why I'm going along with the whole thing. You don't think I'm going to destroy the Earth just to please the Usurper, do you? Once the Wings open, we can use the Reins, the Beast will obey me in everything, and then..."

"That's what you hope, but you can't be *sure*..."

"I *am* sure! The Beast loves me. And I was promised

centuries ago, when the Usurper was hopping mad over what happened to that nincompoop son of his, that when the time came I could ride the Beast to destroy Earth and avenge him."

"That may be so. But I don't trust him, not one bit."

"He can't BondBreak, you know that, so he *has* to give me control of the Beast in order to carry out his Apocalypse. And then, what's to stop us attacking Heaven?"

"Forget that idea!" Belial said sharply. "That's strictly propaganda for the masses."

"But once I control the Beast..."

"You haven't got control yet. And when – if – you do, do you *really* think the Tyrant would let that happen?"

Satan was silent.

"Your trouble," said Belial severely, "is that you're starting to believe the story we put out in our *History of the Great Rebellion*. It's all right for the Nefilim and the Saragashim to believe we defeated the angels, but it behoves us to remember the true facts. Falsehood can only reach perfection when the truth is fully assimilated."

"So why did we say we'd invade Heaven in the first place, if you think we can't do it?"

"You know very well. With regard to the Saragashim and the Nefilim, it's to take their minds off rebellion. For the Companions, it's to boost their morale. The fires of Hell have sapped their spirit, fear of the Nefilim is growing. They need hope, so we give them hope. Once they've got Earth, they'll forget about Heaven. They'll have a new world, new interests."

Belial had very carefully said 'they', and not 'you', but Satan felt the old despair welling up. He tried to fight it by saying briskly: "Well, I'd better be going."

"My lord, I still don't like it. Why has this Peter risked coming here? Saints can be killed, unlike the angels. I've checked with Security, and it seems he doesn't hold particularly high rank in Heaven. He does hold the Keys, but he only has to rubber stamp the admissions of the Five Judges of Limbo. And he's the unofficial leader of the saints, of course, but even there it appears some are organising against him, perhaps because he's a friend of that maniac St. George we've heard about. He has no authority in the Council, which still consists exclusively of Seraphim, apart from some new saint called Darren. But..." Belial paused significantly, "according to our records, he was not only on Earth the same time as Junior, but was, in fact, one of his closest friends!"

"I know that. All the more reason to see him. After all, it's because of Junior's little escapade on Earth – Mephistopheles met him there, you know, a most unreasonable fellow, no sense of humour, always going round telling people how important his father was, boasting about all the mansions they had in heaven, and that sort of thing – it's because of him that this whole Apocalypse thing got started. If this Peter's his friend, he might have a lot of useful information."

Belial looked doubtful, and Satan stared at him, trying to look as evil as he could.

"I really feel," said Belial, "that I ought to accompany you..."

"You know that he specifically requested to see me alone. As you said yourself, we can't afford to cross him until we know what he wants."

"But Junior's friend! He's probably riddled with Goodness!"

Satan glared at the phantasmal creature, whose physical decomposition was now so far advanced that when he passed by the window, the fires of Hell could clearly be seen flickering through his translucent remains. He glared, and frowned so ferociously his eyebrows rasped against each other.

"Are you suggesting I can't take care of myself?" He seemed to loom larger.

It was quite obvious from Belial's expression that this was exactly what he was suggesting, but he didn't dare say so openly. He knew from painful experience it wasn't a good idea to accuse the King of Hell of having residues of Goodness deep inside him: Satan always reacted to such an insult in the same way – violently. So now he bowed slightly, and wished his master a fruitful journey.

Satan set off for his appointment with the person who planned to destroy him.

Chapter Thirteen
FIRST ENCOUNTER

The historic meeting which was to change the whole future of the Afterlife started badly. So badly, indeed, that within fifteen minutes, Satan ordered his guards to kill St. Peter.

Belial's doubts about his master's ability to handle a mere saint had rankled so much that he had arrived at Hellport already in a belligerent mood. The first sight of Peter only made his mood worse. He had expected to see some namby-pamby, supercilious saint, flatulent with self-righteousness, burping forth sickly-sweet homilies. Instead, he was faced with an ageing, scruffy man, with a ridiculous tangled beard almost scraping the ground, grubby hands with broken nails, an ill-fitting robe stained with ambrosia, sandals dirty and frayed. Immaculately dressed himself, he took this sartorial eye-sore to be a calculated insult on Heaven's part. So they thought him so impotent, did they, trapped here in Hell, that they didn't even bother to send a respectable emissary! They would learn!

But his inner voice reminded him that this saint could turn out to be very useful. He would know, at the very least, about the current situation in Heaven.

And he might even know something about... He cut off the thought.

Satan was therefore torn from the very beginning between the need to be nice and the desire to be positively unpleasant.

****

The visible manifestation of this inner turmoil was for Peter extremely disconcerting. He found himself looking up at a towering creature, a good half a metre taller than himself, almost filling the entrance to the Lounge. With the blazing sun of Hell behind him, it was difficult to make out his features. It *seemed* that he was smiling, but at the same time his nostrils were flaring as if about to go their separate ways, and that grating sound could only be teeth gnashing together.

Well, what did you expect? At least, he hasn't got horns!

122

Since Satan said nothing at all, Peter cast around in his mind for a tactful way of opening the conversation. He finally offered the following exploratory remark:

"Er, good afternoon."

"Speak!" snarled Satan with a friendly nod.

Peter ran his fingers through his beard: he needed to feel its rugged friendliness.

"Is there somewhere we can speak alone?"

"Follow!" commanded Satan, and with a dramatic swirl of his richly-embroidered purple cloak, marched across to the far end of the Lounge, where there was a long line of identical black doors. He entered the first of these, marked 'Treatment Room One'. Peter followed him in, with enormous effort dragging his trunk behind him. He expected to be stopped by the guards, but no one made any move to hinder him. He quickly realised why: in a land where mistrust ruled, only a lunatic would leave his possessions unguarded – he would have aroused more suspicion by *not* taking his trunk with him.

The room was expensively furnished, almost as luxurious as that of Tobias. A magnificent ornamental four-poster bed, covered by rich tapestries depicting stylised sylvan scenes, not long before much in vogue in Heaven, reigned in the far right-hand corner. Below it was another narrow door. The opposite corner was filled by a huge statue of Satan, with both hands held across his eyes, and a look of horror on his face. Near the left-hand wall there was a small wooden table with armchairs round it. The walls were lined with pictures by Bosch, Bacon, and Kandinsky, and a couple of old prints portraying the witches of Salem. The carpet was thick and soft, the lighting gentle and inviting, and waves-languorously-lapping-the-seashore New Age music filled the strange schizophrenic room.

Satan sat himself with another dramatic swirl in one of the chairs.

"Your message!" he barked, his left hand politely motioning Peter to sit down, the other scoring deep grooves in the arm of his chair.

Peter felt a momentary impulse of pity as he saw for the first time the aeons-old scars and gashes entrenched in the brow and cheeks of his host.

123

"First," he said – diplomatically, he thought – "you need have no fear that anything we discuss will go any further."

That, of course, was a mistake.

"Fear? I *fear*? The King of Hell *fear*?"

"Just a figure of speech. All I meant was..."

He broke off in alarm as Satan leapt out of his chair. But all he did was go to a small cupboard, extract a bottle and two glasses, sit down again, fill the glasses with a greenish liquid, and push one of them across to his guest with a charming smile spoilt only by the fact that he simultaneously shook his fist at him.

"Pregnant doodlebug juice," he informed Peter, "good for the intestines. Or any old nail wounds," he added with a cruel leer.

Well, at least he's done his homework. Peter was tempted to inquire whether it was also good for brimstone burns and thunderbolt scars. The momentary pity passed, to be replaced by contempt for the ridiculous powders and ointments with which he tried to hide his injuries. However, in view of Satan's unpredictable antics, he decided to drop his carefully prepared speech.

"Let me come straight to the point," he said. "I've come to talk about the Apocalypse."

"The Apocalypse is my business," yelled Satan, "so keep out of it!" Then, after a visible internal struggle, he added: "Which doesn't mean I wouldn't be very happy to deal with any inquiries you might have."

Why didn't someone warn me the Devil was mad! Peter decided to come even straighter to the point: perhaps only shock tactics would work in this situation. He said, very clearly:

"YOU MUST CANCEL THE APOCALYPSE!"

"I must *WHAT*!?" Satan was halfway to his feet, claws outstretched, before he managed to control himself. He collapsed back into his chair, shuddered, and tapped Peter's glass. "Ice?"

The expression on his face reminded Peter of Calvino's Viscount Medardo, sliced during battle into two independent – and antagonistic – parts. How was it possible, he wondered, to smile with one half of the mouth and snarl with the other?

Satan said, "I did hear you correctly, didn't I? You did say 'cancel the Apocalypse', didn't you?"

Peter nodded. Even to him, it sounded crazy.

"And why," Satan went on, with ominous calmness, "would you like me to cancel the Apocalypse?"

"One very good reason is that if you don't, Heaven will get flooded with people."

Satan burst into laughter. His tongue no longer seemed to be undergoing acupuncture when he at last asked incredulously:

"Flooded with people? *Heaven?* At last count, on Earth, there were less than fifty thousand people eligible for your place, and a good half of those were autistic, which is why our missionaries couldn't get to them! I admit you'll get most of the animals, but you said people."

He snatched out a hand to catch an unwary hellroach, and popped it crunchily into his mouth.

"What you say about those on Earth now may well be true," Peter said carefully, trying to take no notice as Satan spat out the hellroach's legs one by one, "but aren't you forgetting about those in Limbo?"

"Ah yes, the wishy-washy not-quite-bad-enough-for-me lot! What's the Apocalypse got to do with them?"

"With the Last Judgement, they all get finally pardoned, and come to Heaven."

"Do they indeed? How nice for them! Well, I agree that will certainly increase Heaven's population considerably. Still not quite enough to *flood* the place, though!"

"And those in Hell?"

"Pardon?"

"Aren't you also forgetting about those in Hell?"

Satan's smile disappeared. "And what have *they* got to do with the Apocalypse?"

"Would you say all your subjects are happy?"

Satan's brow darkened, a not inconsiderable feat since it was already pitch black.

"Are you suggesting people come here to be *happy?*"

"Of course not, that's just my point. People spend their time here being most *un*happy."

"What of it? Don't you dare to lecture me, you little...!"

"And the unhappier they are, the more likely they are to repent. And if they repent before the Last Trumpet Call, *they'll be able to leave Hell and go to Heaven!*"

125

"What?"

"On the Day of Judgement, everyone gets a second chance. Of course, you may keep a few of the souls, I don't suppose they'll *all* have repented."

Satan was twitching ominously. "You dare to lie to *me?*"

"I'm not lying," said Peter, sliding his chair nearer the trunk. "It's in the Book."

"What Book?"

"The Book of Revelations."

"The ravings of some lunatic in the desert! I've heard of it."

"Not ravings. Amongst other things, it foretells the very Apocalypse we're talking about. Perhaps," extracting a document from his cloak and holding it out towards the Dark Lord, "you should read the part I've underlined for you."

Satan took it contemptuously. As he read, however, he began to brighten up.

"But this is marvellous stuff! Killing with swords, hunger, earthquakes, plagues...hey, here's a reference to Wormwood, the old rascal..."

"No, not that," said Peter, "that bit near the end. The passage I've put a circle around."

Satan read aloud: "*And he laid hold of the dragon, that old serpent, which is the Devil, and Satan, and bound him a thousand years. And cast him into the bottomless pit, and shut him up...*' Why, the...! What's this? Lets me out for a bit, then has me cast into a lake of fire and brimstone for ever and ever?! The sadistic bugger! The treacherous, two-timing...!"

"There's more to come," interposed Peter quietly. He could feel the trunk with his foot.

"It says, '*Death and Hell delivered up the dead which were in them...*' NEVER!"

He leapt to his feet. "You're lying!" he shrieked. "You wrote that trash yourself! You've asked for it! Brimstone, eh? I'll drag your balls through brimstone, you'll feel what it's like! Guards! Kill this benighted saint! No, don't! Yes, do!"

Peter yelled "GEORGE!" and kicked the trunk with all his might as the door burst open and three guards rushed in.

He was almost too late. He ducked as a javelin hurtled towards his head, then straightened again rapidly to avoid a spear about to traverse his alimentary canal the wrong way. The third guard had his trident poised...

When suddenly the cry of *"For Heaven and St. George, especially St. George!"* erupted as the trunk burst open and the warrior saint himself, fully armed, leapt from it. Within seconds, it was all over, the three guards strewn over the floor, while their slayer peered round with a lugubrious and disappointed expression.

"But there aren't no dragons! Peter, you said..." His voice trailed off.

St. George was obsessed with dragons. The few dragons who had made it to Heaven before they became extinct on Earth had been forced to form Neighbourhood Watch groups to protect themselves from the wild saint, who would wander round at night trying to pick a fight with any dragon he could find, though in Heaven, of course, it was impossible to kill them.

Peter had never found out the reason for this obsesión, but since his mission involved the biggest dragon of all times – the Beast of the Apocalypse – it had seemed wise to choose as his bodyguard the biggest expert of all times. Moreover, George's devotion to Peter was absolute and unquestioning, partly because the latter had not accepted his official decanonisation by the Catholic Church and, despite Michael's threats, obdurately refused to expel him from Heaven.

The trunk had been a precaution: George's fame might have reached Hell, and a safe-conduct might not have been issued for him.

As Peter stumbled to his feet, he felt a sudden panic: if George had attacked Satan...

But no. Satan was standing exactly where he had been when he had called the guards, with a look of wonderment on his face. He shook his head, muttered something like "but this ruffian and Moloch together...", and turned to Peter.

"Well, aren't you going to introduce us?"

"You've just attempted to kill me!"

"Oh come on," Satan said, "I just got a bit upset over that book of yours. I trust you won't allow such a minor incident to strain our relationship. No real harm done."

"No harm done! If I hadn't brought George with me, just in case..."

127

"Ah, George, is it?" Satan said, turning to him. "I'm sorry we didn't afford you the usual formalities, but our visitors usually arrive *with*, and not *inside*, their luggage. Still, *chacun a son goùt*. Anyway, you seem to have made yourself at home. May I express the wish that your stay here will be as much a pleasure for you as it is an honour for me?" He gave him a dazzling smile.

St. George glared suspiciously, completely baffled. By the Holy Crusade, he'd just slaughtered a bunch of this Saracen's retainers, and the unholy dog was leering politely! He brought all his mental powers to bear on the problem, and came up with the only solution that made sense. He turned to Peter and asked:

"Shall I finish him off, too?"

"Well," said Peter to Satan, who was looking nonplussed at George's response to his diplomacy, "are you willing to listen to the rest of what I have to say?"

Satan shook himself out of his stupor. "Indeed, yes, we were having a fascinating chat before ... my guards got carried away. Be assured, they'll be severely reprimanded." He sat down, giving George an even more dazzling smile.

This unnatural behaviour was too much for the burned-out bits of old wire that comprised George's mental circuitry. He too sat down on the trunk and scratched his head.

"Before we continue..." said Satan. "It's a bit untidy in here. Bonegrinder!"

An official came running in, pretending not to notice anything amiss.

"There's been a slight accident here. Please remove these bodies, and as it's Christmas, have them distributed to the poor."

"Now," said Satan, when the bodies had been removed, "you were saying?"

Peter hesitated, but felt he had to use the advantage George had given him.

"Now what you've just read was the original plan. As you know, of course, God created the Beast of the Apocalypse to avenge the murder of Jesus. Why he didn't destroy the Earth at once, why he should wait two thousand years, I don't know." There were stories, of course, about a race of gods, the Nebulans, to whom the God of Heaven was somehow accountable, stories, too, of a conflict between Father and Son over this very question, even rumours that it had

128

been Jesus, and not his Father, who had really created the Beast. "But everything's now been simplified. No thousand years of Heaven on Earth, just the Apocalypse, and then the Second Judgement at once, with most of the souls, including your own subjects, as I pointed out before you... your guards got carried away, going to Heaven. And a few, maybe, remaining here with you." Then, remembering that, but for George, he would probably be dead, he added spitefully: "But as you'll be at the bottom of the burning lake, they'll need a glass-bottomed boat to see you!" *Make fun of my crucifixion, would you?*

"But he can't do that!" protested Satan, his new calmness wavering. The Treaty..."

"...is only valid *until* the Second Judgement. Perhaps you didn't read the small print."

"He tricked me even with the big print!" Satan muttered. He broke off, looked away for a moment. "There wasn't any small print, anyway. Belial checked it. It's nothing but treachery, he just adds clauses when it suits him! There's nothing in the Treaty about a bottomless pit!"

"I'm not saying there was. But I have an idea that may help you prevent all this."

"And just who do you think you are to...? Satan stopped himself, looked at George, and said more calmly: "And why should you want to help me?"

"I've told you: overcrowding." It sounded sillier every time he said it. "Already we're pushed into ghettos. I agree you've helped immensely with the human population, but we still get most of the animals..."

"Have *you* ever tried to seduce a moth or a chicken or a goldfish?"

"Oh, I'm not blaming you. You've done wonders! The crunch will really come, as I said, with the Second Judgement, when all the souls in Limbo and Hell – apart from those on Earth now – pour into Heaven. With their bodies, of course."

"Some of my guests," remarked Satan, "have parted company with their bodies."

"They'll be given new bodies, just like the souls in Limbo. Apart from overcrowding, famine will be almost inevitable – well, for us, anyway: the angels have all the best land, and they intend

129

to keep it, especially that stuck-up Michael." *That should score me a point or two!* "Which means we saints will be starving, and slumming it *with* all your ex-subjects."

He trusted he had put enough resentment in his tone to carry conviction.

"So it seems to me," said Satan, "that you want *me* to help *you*."

"Heaven will get overcrowded. It won't be drowned in brimstone." *So take that!*

A tense silence followed. George was still scratching his head: he had given up trying to understand Satan's strange behaviour, but was now occupied with a new mystery, the statue of Satan shielding his eyes from some unknown horror.

Satan soon seemed to relax, however, and began to scrape off the splashes of blood from the slain guards, tutting fastidiously as he did so. After some minutes, Peter said lamely:

"So don't you think you'd better cancel the Apocalypse?"

Satan caught a hellroach, and flipped it into the air so that it turned a triple somersault before plunging into his mouth. "It may *look* easy eating hellroaches," he commented, "but have you ever tried it?"

"Er, no."

"They're vicious little buggers, and always try to take a quick nip out of your lip or throat before surrendering to your greater nutritional need. Spinning them in the air three times makes them giddy and lessens the danger. Remember that whenever you try one."

"Thank you. I will."

The legs came out as before. "Sorry," said Satan, "you were saying something?"

"Don't you think you ought to call off the Apocalypse?" It sounded even crazier this time, which was what Satan had intended, of course.

"Ah yes, the Apocalypse. You're aware we've been making preparations for the last century?"

"Haven't you understood what I've been saying? The moment you attack the Earth, the Last Judgement begins, and into the Brimstone Lake you go! Splash! Sizzle!"

Satan's composure almost wavered. "I still have only your word for that, and the delirium of that idiot in the desert."

Before Peter could reply, the small door at the foot of the bed opened and a young woman entered. Black hair billowed out behind her, and so fluid and sensuous were her movements, Peter had the peculiar impression that she was gliding in. It took him a second or two to realise that she was completely naked, as her whole body was covered by a fine fur, muted autumn-leaf brown fur that lay softly over her slender – almost too slender – body.

"Lazara! Can't you see I've got a guest? And a saint at that? Cover yourself at once!"

Bloody spoilsport!

The girl backed out, saying, "Oh, Lord Satan, I didn't know you was 'ere!"

"And I bet your grandfather didn't know 'ow wot *you* was 'ere, either," mimicked Satan, but in a tone of real affection. "Wait. Since you *are* here, I have some questions for you. *After* you've made yourself respectable."

The girl quickly reappeared, wearing a plain white robe. Peter now had time to look more closely at her. There was something almost vulpine about her features, the ears just a bit too pointed, the teeth too sharp, the eyes too slitted. There was something odd, too, about the alignment of head and shoulders, giving the vague impression of a predator, which only made the Eliza Doolittle voice completely incongruous. Indeed, the total effect was extremely disconcerting – ingenuous, uncomplicated, spontaneous, yet feline, mobile, menacing.

George came out of his trance, saw the new arrival in no way resembled a dragon, and promptly returned to his semi-dormant state. Premonitions were not his forte.

Satan drew back his cloak and graciously extended his penis to the girl, who touched it reverently to her lips. Protocol having been observed, he addressed her in his most regal tones.

"Lazara, let me introduce you to my guests. The one lurking somewhere behind that exaggerated beard is St. Peter, and the one hiding behind that somewhat vacant expression is St. George." (The girl dismissed Peter with the briefest of nods, but gazed with unfeigned admiration at the mighty, if comatose, figure of the warrior saint.) "Do not be afraid of them: hirsute or somnolent, I assure you they are the most delightful company. Now, tell me, has the Physiotherapy Department administered to any off-world clients in, say, the last month?"

Lazara looked surprised. "Well, of course we 'as: packed out, as usual."

"And did any of them say anything unusual?"

"Wot do you mean?"

"Anything, for example, about great changes about to happen... anything apart from the usual 'don't tell Michael I've been here'."

Lazara rubbed her vulva thoughtfully. "Come to think of it, now you mentions it, there *was* one geezer 'oo really 'ad no idea where to put it and kept on gassing instead and said 'ow wot 'e'd put in a good word for me if I wanted to move to 'is place. Of course, I said I were quite 'appy where I were..."

Peter by now had realised who the 'off-world' clients must be. "You hear, Satan? Offering to take her to Heaven! Lazara, did he say how soon?"

"That's wot I asked 'im – just to be polite, of course, 'cos I'd never leave 'ere – and 'e said sommat about 'avin' a calypso first..."

"Now do you believe me?" Peter interrupted excitedly. *Lazara, I love you!*

Satan was looking distinctly unsettled again.

"Did he say anything about Hell, about me?"

"'E said... 'e said wot you 'ad a nasty surprise coming."

"What sort of surprise?"

"'E didn't say. I think he remembered where 'e was, cos 'e clammed up and flew off."

"And that's all? He said nothing else at all? Very well, I'll speak to you later. And you are to say nothing – nothing, do you hear? – about this conversation, or about these guests. Not even to your grandfather."

The girl curtsied and left the room, not without a lingering glance at George.

There was an uncomfortable silence. Satan stared unseeing at the opposite wall, and Peter stared at his statue. A nice touch, he had to admit, the Devil pretending to be shocked by the 'physiotherapy' that went on here! He should have known. Where else could errant angels go? There were no female angels, the female saints were, by definition – apart from his own Joan, and a few Tobias had managed to smuggle in – not the most exciting of company, and the angels would be only too aware that the female souls in Hell, while more than willing, and while real in one sense, in another were simply products of the skill of the Fitter and the Protoplasmic workers in the Way Station – *de luxe* dolls of flesh instead of rubber: only saints had natural cloned bodies. There only remained, therefore, the native inhabitants of Hell, the Saragashim, who had their own males to satisfy, and probably not a few of the Fallen Angels. Demand inevitably far exceeded supply. No wonder this room – and presumably all the others – was so expensively, and incongruously, furnished!

He dragged his attention back to the matter in hand. This unexpected corroboration of his story by Lazara had come at just the right moment, and he decided to play his next card immediately, while Satan was still off balance.

"In case you *still* think what I've told you is just the ravings of a lunatic, I'll show you something else. I was hoping not to have to use this evidence, but..."

He turned to George. "Could you pass me the Scroll, please?"

George dutifully rummaged among the gory assortment of weapons inside the trunk, and handed Peter something wrapped in a purple cloth. This he passed across to Satan.

"This," he said quietly, "is a copy from the Book of Razael."

"Impossible!"

Satan opened the cloth with hands that were trembling, and took out the Scroll. As he opened it, it crackled and threw off an eerie, wavering light, seeming to shimmer in and out of existence. He studied it in absolute silence, then said without looking up:

"How did *you* get hold of this? Only the Seven are allowed access to..." He stopped himself.

"I can't reveal that."

Now Satan did look up, staring straight into Peter's eyes, not with the earlier rage, but with an enormous incredulity that was almost more frightening. Peter glanced significantly towards George. Satan followed his gaze, and nodded.

"I may keep this, of course, to do some tests?"

"Of course."

Again, silence. Satan, as if unaware of what he was doing, caressed the purple cloth that had held the parchment, his hands lingering greedily over the material. *Of course, you were once one of the Seven yourself.* Peter fought down a sudden feeling of awe. Of pity. Of regret for what he had to do.

At last Satan spoke. His voice was tired, his body seemed to slump.

"Very well, you may be right. It seems you may be right." He appeared to be trying to convince himself of the impossible. "But we had a Treaty. Yes, I tricked him and he tricked me, but we had a Treaty all the same. But this... this is not like him. In Eden, he could easily have ... This is not like him."

He relapsed into silence, brooding and bitter. And there was something else, something Peter couldn't quite label. Sorrow? Hurt?

"Very well," said Satan at last, and strength was creeping back into his voice, "say I don't carry out the Apocalypse. He'll just destroy the Earth another way – he's done it before – and the Last Judgement will still go ahead. What difference does it make?"

"No, no, that's where you're wrong!" exclaimed Peter. "The Word of God is unalterable only *because* it is Bound by the Links of its own Chain once it has been entered in the Cosmic Book of Razael, which exists both in and out of Time, that is to say, it only exists as and when and because its predictions come true. It's like Schrödinger's Cat, until you open the box, the cat can be neither alive nor dead. I admit I don't understand it all, but if one Link were ever missing, if one Word failed to achieve temporal expression, the Book would be dislocated in Time. The Apocalypse is a major Link, it is *necessary* for the Final Judgement. Without it there cannot *be* any Final Judgement."

Please don't ask too many questions! I haven't really got a clue what all that means! I simply learnt it by heart! Fortunately, Satan was nodding slowly: since he had been one of the Seven himself, none of this was totally new to him.

Peter was preparing himself to face the inevitable question again – how did he, a mere saint, know these things? – but Satan did not ask. *Thank God I brought George with me!*

"So what you are saying," said Satan slowly, "is that the Apocalypse and the Final Judgement are suspended in an Eschatological Self-perpetuating Coil?"

Peter nodded sagely. *Am I saying that?*

"I have to thank you for your invaluable information." Satan almost smiled. "However, it only makes it all the more imperative that we ride the Beast."

Peter suddenly felt sick; it was nothing to do with pregnant doodlebug juice.

"As you have reminded me," Satan went on, "the Beast and the Apocalypse are in the Cosmic Book. They *have* to happen. So if we don't ride the Beast, someone else will, and you'll still have your Apocalypse. All the more reason, then, for *us* to ride it. If we control the Beast, we at least have a chance of defending ourselves."

Ah well, it was worth a try. And even if Satan hasn't yet begun to nibble at the bait, at least he's noticed it's there.

"I think you're wrong," he said. "I think it's almost certain, since the Beast was given to you, that only you would be able to ride it. *But what if it were destroyed?*"

Chapter Fourteen
BELIAL IS SUSPICIOUS

"And what makes you think you managed to deceive him?"

The speaker was Belial. Satan on his return to Dis, the capital, had found him in his room reading Metternich's *Memoirs*. This room was in many ways a quite literal extension of its master, for the floorboards writhed choking under a thick blanket of sloughed skin and bone dust. Furniture was sparse: a few shelves with books on politics, mesmerism, and scorpions, a table and chair covered in priesthide for his solitary meals, a narrow bed, and a cupboard containing a dozen identical frayed black robes..

According to *The History of the Great Rebellion*, Belial in Heaven had been 'mighty as a mountain', and had walked with the 'tread of an earthquake'. It was recorded how the giant angel Ramiel had been foolish enough to dispute a nice point of political science, and had been in consequence battered against a mountain until 'he and the mountain were both rubble'. From this and many other examples in *The History*, one had to conclude that Belial had once been a huge and formidable warrior. One was also quite free, of course, to conclude that *The History*, of which Satan and Belial were the joint authors, contained inaccuracies. But as this freedom carried with it the triple death penalty, nobody had as yet presumed to make so liberal an interpretation of the sacred text; which was no small relief for the Chief Executioner, who had been unable to devise a way of carrying out such a sentence.

Belial was now looking decidedly agitated, pacing up and down with his characteristic wraithlike shuffle, stirring up his own cast-off skin, which rose in little eddies round his feet.

Satan donned what he hoped was a complacent smile.

"Come, come, my bad fellow, am I not the Prince of Lies? He turned out to be quite a simpleton, really."

"Not so simple that he didn't manage to smuggle in that bloodthirsty maniac St. George!"

"Bah, he won't be any problem! He's got it into his head, as I told you, that he can fight the Beast! We just point him in the right direction, and that will be that!"

"Somehow, I don't think it will be that easy. But I agree: one way or another, we can certainly get rid of him. No, it's this St. Peter I'm worried about."

A particularly large flake of dandruff chose this moment to spread its wings, and glided into Satan's nostrils. As he emerged from his sneeze, he realised Belial had gone on talking.

"...just wanders casually into Hell, and mentions that he'd like the Apocalypse cancelled, please! Just like that! The Tyrant's pet project, his final solution! He's risking being banished, he's risking Hellfire itself! For what?"

"I told you. He thinks Heaven will get overcrowded, and he and his friends will have to slum it with a few of our own dear citizens."

"From the way you described him, he doesn't seem the kind to worry too much over comfort. Risking death here for a bigger house and fewer people on the golf course? How has he got the nerve?"

"Well, according to Mephistopheles, a lot of those saints were brave to the point of insanity. Peter himself was crucified – and upside down, too! Or was it on a funny-shaped cross?"

Belial's frown became frownier. "My lord, you ought to leave those reports to me. You know how emotional, how susceptible you are to..."

"Stop mothering me! I've been King of Hell for half an eternity, and you still act as though I can't be trusted to fart on my own! Anyway, whatever Peter's real motives for coming, it doesn't alter the facts. You've seen the pages from *Revelations*, and the copies from the Cosmic Book, which corroborate everything he said about the Apocalypse, at least. Which means we have to stop the Apocalypse. Or I face an eternity in brimstone. And you'll be there with me!"

Belial's expression hinted that he might be able to bear being separated from his master in that particular environment, but he soon returned to his theme.

"If we grant that the copies are genuine, *where did he get them?* How could a mere saint gain access to the Cosmic Book? Even if it doesn't make any difference, since the Book can't lie, it docs mean that Peter is much more than he pretends to be. Which leads to another question: if the tyrant really does intend to put us back in the Lake, how is he going to do it? His Flame Cannon won't reach as far as here..."

"And if he and his angels come here without it, we'll beat the shit out of them!" interposed Satan excitedly. "There's now the Saragashim as well as the Companions, and if Hell were attacked, even the Nefilim would ally with us!"

"Exactly. So what," asked Belial, staring at Satan, "if his weapon were *already here*!"

"What do you...? No, no," whispered the Dark Lord, "the Beast loves me, it would never... it's impossible..."

"I can't help remembering one of God's little quirks," Belial went on inexorably, his glittering eyes transfixing those of his master, "his sense of justice. We've already paid the penalty for our revolt. And anything we – or rather, Mephistopheles – has done on Earth, is covered by Codicil Thirteen. So he has no *just* reason to put us back in the Lake. I don't pretend to understand what makes him tick in such a strange way, but I'm absolutely sure he wouldn't, he *couldn't*, attack us without a legitimate reason. And what is your 'simpleton' Peter suggesting? That we disobey the Tyrant by refusing to go ahead with the Apocalypse, which would give him the perfect excuse to punish us. And he has the Beast here already, to do it with!"

"But if that's the case," said Satan, "*he must have planned the whole thing centuries ago!* Perhaps to punish us, as well as Earth, for the death of his son, even though we had nothing to do with it! And how could he get at us? Give us the baby Beast, wait till it had grown up, trick us into disobedience, and then set it against us!"

"So," said Belial, "now do you see why I have my reservations about this 'simple' saint? He *may* be telling the truth, in which case we should stop the Apocalypse. But it's more likely he's been sent to trick us, in which case we should definitely go ahead."

"On the other hand," said Satan, "*it's too obvious.* If the Tyrant sent him, he must realise we wouldn't trust him. What if he thought we might get wind of his plans, anyway – through the Physio Department, for instance – and so sent Peter to tell us the *truth* in such a way that we wouldn't believe it? Can you imagine his satisfaction if he warns us what's going to happen, and then watches us go ahead to *make* it happen?"

"We're just going round in pentagrams," said Belial wearily.

"There's only one solution: we'll have to torture the truth out of this kamikaze saint."

"Yes," said Satan. Then, "No."

"*No?*"

"If he *is* telling the truth, he might be able to help us. But he wouldn't be in a helpful mood if we rearranged his body! Humans are always a bit funny like that. It's obviously because they're at such an early stage of evolution..."

"*Can* you keep to the point?"

"And if he *isn't* telling the truth," continued Satan, "by pretending to believe him – as I did – we can still trick useful information out of him."

"But if he *is* telling the truth, torturing him would let us know that, and though I agree he wouldn't then be in the mood to help us, we could torture him some more to *put* him in the mood. And if he's lying, it would be more fun to *torture* the information out of him than to *trick* him."

"But," countered Satan, "if he *isn't* telling the truth, if he's been sent by the Tyrant, that means the Tyrant puts a high value on him. And then what better justification to attack us than the fact we've torn his emissary to bits?"

"But this is terrible! We don't know what Peter is up to, and we can't even torture him to find out!" Belial hadn't been so glum for a long time.

Satan silently congratulated himself: he hadn't had to admit his *real* reasons for not wanting to torture Peter. His satisfaction lasted about three seconds.

"There's an aspect I'm afraid we've overlooked," said Belial. "Forget what the Tyrant might do to us if we cancel the Apocalypse – have you considered what our *own* people will do?"

Satan had. Even so, he was still sick.

"It's that Christmas menu again!" he stormed. "Have those no-good cooks castrated!"

"We did that last Christmas."

"I don't care! Have them castrated again! They'll learn sooner or later!"

"*Can* we get back to the point? I told you we should never have claimed that *you* created the Beast! If we don't use it now, as promised..."

"Was I supposed to admit that Gabriel brought it in the

middle of the night?"

"We could have said you happened to *find* it...but it's too late now. Everybody here now believes that *you* created the Beast, that *you* planned the Apocalypse, that it's all part of *your* plan to take revenge on the Tyrant. The promise of an invasion of Earth has been the only thing stopping the discontent getting out of hand."

Satan thought back to the Christmas lunch in the Great Hall. Yes, some of them had even complained in front of his very face!

"So you see," concluded the Prime Sinister, "even if everything Peter said is true, we *dare* not cancel the Apocalypse, anyway."

"Ah, 'the hollow crown that rounds the mortal temples of a King'!"

"You're not mortal."

"Belial, has anyone ever told you what a spoilsport you are?"

"No."

"Well, let me put it another way: do you ever get invited to parties?"

"No."

"There you are then!"

"The point is, my lord, what are we going to do?"

"We've still got a little time. The Beast's Wings still aren't open, so we can't start the Apocalypse yet, anyway. Meanwhile, it's better to play along with Peter, see what he's up to."

"But this visit to the Beast's Pit!"

"I told you, they've got some crazy notion that George can destroy the Beast! It's clear they haven't got the faintest idea what Pobbles is really like! So why not take them to the Pit? That will not only dispose of George in a satisfyingly gory way, but also give me the opportunity to find out what Peter's really playing at. The trip will take at least a day – maybe a second or two longer if George puts up a good fight, ha, ha! – and if I can't learn his real intentions in that time, I'm not the devil I used to be! And when we get back, if I *still* don't know the truth, then we torture him as a last resort!"

Belial pondered this, then reluctantly nodded. "It will rid us of George, as you say, and we can't be held to blame, if they're the ones who insist on going to the Pit."

Satan felt a strange sense of exhilaration. Destruction loomed at every point, every turning seemed to lead to disaster, but at last, after all these millennia, there was a chance, a tiny chance, of getting what he really wanted. And this saint, this poor fool who thought he could deceive him, carried the key.

For the first time in many centuries, he allowed himself to think her name again.

****

The subjects of the devils' conversation, meanwhile, were hardly a hundred metres away, in a room in the west wing of the Palace. Peter was resting – and sweating – on a narrow bed, while George was sitting rigidly upright – and sweating – on a hard chair, his eyes fixed on a point on the wall. Peter supposed he was anticipating the duel with the Beast.

A duel he had not the slightest intention of allowing to take place. He had immense faith in George's prowess, but here they weren't dealing with a mere earth-born dragon, but the Beast of the Apocalypse itself. Neither, he suspected, did Satan really expect George to fight the Beast, to judge from the hilarity with which he had greeted the suggestion. It seemed he had agreed to take them to the Pit for the sheer pleasure of witnessing their dismay. *And probably to get more information out of me. I won't disappoint you!*

They had travelled from the Shuttleport, a journey of half an hour or so, in a wagon pulled by a cross between a giant doodlebug and an equally giant tarantula spider. Satan had ridden outside on the driver's seat beside Lazara, whom he had ordered to accompany them, while the two saints had melted inside, slithering in their own sweat. They had seen little or nothing of the terrain on the way – they were simply conscious of a universe of heat and sand – nor of Dis when they entered it. Satan had warned them to keep out of sight – it would not be safe, he said, for them to be seen in Hell. George, upon hearing this, had been all for leaping out and slaughtering a few score inhabitants to *make* it safe.

Then straight to the Palace, where Satan had led them furtively to the room they were now in. Peter had no objection to this: he was in no mood for sightseeing, and he wanted time to reassess the situation. He had hoped for air-conditioning again, but, of course, he reminded himself, outside the Way Station, of which, in effect, the Shuttles and Shuttleports were merely extensions, technology did not exist. There *was* a fan which was connected by a system of

141

cogs and wheels to a huge horizontal wheel which was being pushed round by a score of damned souls, but they were moving with such lack of enthusiasm that the cooling effects were negligible.

There Satan had left them, promising to have food sent to them at once.

The food had been brought by a servant so old Peter wondered whether anyone had ever tried to carbon-date her. Since neither had eaten since dawn, they rapidly devoured the rather odd fare that arrived (leftovers from the Christmas Feast), even though they weren't used to eating food which already had tooth marks on it, and even one tooth *in* it.

Hardly had they finished eating than Satan returned. George at once leapt to his feet, and said, "Let's go then."

Satan and Peter looked at him as he began to collect his weapons.

"George," said Peter gently, "we're not going till tomorrow, if we go at all."

"Ain't no dragon going to scare George! It wants trouble, it can have trouble *now!*"

"Could you remind your impetuous friend," Satan addressed Peter, "that the journey to the Pit is no easy one, and that we need daylight to find our way? The Beast doesn't usually have breakfast anyway, but George can arrive in time to provide a late lunch for it."

The appreciation of subtlety wasn't George's strong point: indeed, anything involving intelligence wasn't George's strong point. "I ain't going to feed it, I'm going to kill it!"

"Ah yes, of course, I was forgetting. Peter, can you really bear to have this rashly valiant gentleman on your conscience?"

"We're only going to take a look," replied Peter, troubled. *Oh shit!*

"And then kill it!" added George, who *was* quick on the uptake when it came to dragon talk.

"Very well," said Satan, appearing not to have noticed Peter's blunder. "I've discussed the matter with Belial, and he too has been convinced by your evidence. The Apocalypse must be stopped, if possible, and if George is willing to try to kill the Beast... And after that, we can sit down and think seriously how we can stop anyone else from riding it."

Peter was surprised: he had thought that Satan would be less convinced after speaking to Belial. *So just who's the cat and who's the mouse here?* He said: "So we're going in the morning then?"

"Yes, very early. I suggest you get some rest."

"But how can anyone ride the dragon after I've killed it?" demanded George, the significance of Satan's earlier remark having finally sunk in.

Satan looked at him, looked at Peter, shook his head in wonderment, said "Tomorrow should be an interesting day," and left.

Later, as he fell asleep, Peter found himself thinking, not of the Beast, but of Eve. Of her expression when she had given him the copy of the sacred scroll. Of her strange message for the serpents, the words of the fox to the Little Prince: "'You become responsible, forever, for what you have tamed.' Help me to help him. And come back, I need you."

Help who?

Chapter Fifteen
A Stroll through Hell

The next morning it was Lazara who brought them breakfast.

"I 'ad to persuade the old museum piece wot should 'ave been 'ere, but that weren't too 'ard," she confided to Peter, and there was something about the set of her teeth that suggested that the other had not enjoyed the 'persuasion'. "'Ere, tuck in, sir, no 'uman meat at all, cos we knows you saints is funny like that. Wot about 'im, the big 'un, shall I wake 'im up?"

George was still lying asleep on the floor – beds were unworthy of a true warrior – turning fitfully, with violent expressions twisting his features. Before Peter could answer, in came Satan.

"Good morning, good morning!" he cried cheerfully, "glad to see you're already up, Peter, decided to make the most of your last day, have you? But what's this, the mighty dragon-slayer still asleep?"

"You'd better move back a bit," said Peter. From the far side of the room, he yelled "Michael!"

George woke up. It was an unusual process. First, he drew his sword and took a dozen vicious swipes in the air; he then leapt to his feet, and repeated the same manoeuvre; at this point he opened his eyes, saw Peter, and sheathed his sword; and finally, he stopped snoring.

"Is it time to go?" he asked.

"You see," explained Peter, "he gets so involved in his dragon-dreams, very little will wake him up except hearing the name of Michael, whom he hates nearly as much as dragons. Good morning, George."

"Morning, Peter." The simple, trusting way he said this contrasted strongly with his violent awakening.

"Good morning, George!" beamed Satan.

George gazed at him as if wondering what he was doing there. "We're not taking *him*, are we?" he asked Peter.

"No, George. He's taking *us*."

"Yes," added Satan, "I'm going to show you a dragon with seven heads and ten horns!"

"You mean, I can lop off six heads, and it will still have one left to watch me hang them from the battlements?"

This thought so excited him it gave him an instant erection which clanked sharply against his armour. Lazara gazed at him in adulation, breathing quickly.

Satan burst out laughing. "I'm sorry we haven't got any battlements in the Pit for you, but you could always wear the heads round your belt instead!"

"Won't they be a bit big for that?" asked George innocently.

"Of course, if something *should* go wrong, would you like us to make a belt for the Beast, so that it can wear *your* head on it, ha, ha?"

"How can it wear my head if I've already killed it?" George turned to Peter. "This guy's not very bright: are you sure it wouldn't be better to finish him off?"

Satan addressed the ceiling. "Moloch, my old friend, I've been doing you an injustice all these years: I thought you were thick!"

"See, he's talking to himself now! There was a guy like that in the First Crusade, so..."

"Yes, George," said Peter. "but let's have breakfast first. I'm hungry."

"Speaking of which..." Satan swung round on Lazara. "What do you think *you're* doing here?"

She dragged her eyes away from George. "Oh, my lord, please let me come too!"

"I said," repeated her master, "what are you doing here?"

"When I 'eard that you 'ad went to bed early, and these two saints was making a trip with you, I says to myself, Lord Satan's off to see the Beast, I says, 'cos they was talking about the Calypso at the Port, so I changed with old Gagool to bring breakfast, so I could ask you. Please, sir, I do so want to see you plonked on top of the Beast, like when you're going to do that Calypso wotsit, so I can tell my friends 'ow 'uge and strong you was looking."

Satan swelled visibly. "Well, Lazara," he said grandiloquently, "because of our friendship with your grandfather, we are willing on this occasion to accede to your request." He turned to Peter. "We leave in half an hour."

****

145

Another doodlebug-tarantula took them out of Dis, which, apart from Satan's Palace, the Torturological Institute, and one or two other showcase buildings, might have been the setting for a Sergio Leone western. They weren't far outside the capital, however, when the giant creature began to buck and rear, hairy legs splaying in all directions.

"Time to walk!" said Satan, and out they got, George, of course, having to be dissuaded from punishing the frightened animal.

"None of these creatures will head directly *towards* the Pit," Satan explained. "Even though the Beast is at least half a day away, they sense it already."

Peter spent the first half hour simply trying not to faint from the heat, though George – but not, to Lazara's manifest disappointment, his erection – bore up bravely.

The terrain at first was completely flat, hard-baked and crisp like an overdone pitta bread. Every now and then, a brimspring would viciously erupt – a sudden spurt of hissing purple liquid ejaculating into the air, and casting glowing, scaly creatures on to the ground, where they immediately joined in furious combat. One such creature, having devoured whole a green lizard, found itself brutally attacked by the same lizard, no longer green, emerging from its rear end, and all the more belligerent for being smothered in digestive juices. The air had a taste of burning metal. Even the clouds looked singed.

"You may be wondering," remarked Satan after a time, "why we chose such a hot and inhospitable place as this when we decided to leave Heaven."

Peter hadn't been wondering about this at all, but about when his skin would start to peel off, and how long it would be before his beard caught fire.

"No doubt in Heaven the angels are saying we were *thrown* out."

Of course, if by some miracle the beard didn't catch fire, wouldn't it fall off when the skin did? How deep do hair follicles go?

"Although we won the war, it was evident there would be ill-feeling if we stayed in Heaven. So we decided to look for another world for ourselves."

If the beard *did* come off with the skin, might it not be possible to have it transplanted back?

"But we didn't want another soft, namby-pamby world like Heaven. We wanted an untamed world, a world of fire and storm that would reflect our own indomitable spirit."

At this point, Satan gave up. Only Lazara had been paying any attention, and that only with her ears: her eyes were for George, which unwitting object of her lust juggernauted on.

"How's Raphael, by the way? Still President of the Seven?"

Peter at once forgot about his beard. *At last! The first nibble!*

He wiped the sweat off his face, listening to it cascade down on to his sandals. "Yes. Just about."

"What do you mean by that?"

"Well, there are quite a few people who'd like to see him lose his position."

"Jealousy of the lesser for the greater. I was victim to the same thing myself. 'Envy is the tax which all distinction must pay.'"

So he's read Emerson, has he? Or just a book of quotations, like me?

"I bet Michael's one of them." Satan went on. "As if that puffed-up pansy could do the job!"

"Don't underestimate Michael. I've heard both Raphael and Gabriel would be glad to see him out of the Council, but he's still there, as strong as ever, if not stronger." *Or I wouldn't be here now!*

"But surely Raphael can handle *him*!"

"Don't forget Michael's got the Virgin Mary on his side."

"The Virgin Mary! What can an upstart like that do against Raphael? She's only been in Heaven a few centuries."

"You forget: she's Family."

"What! So the stories are true about her being Junior's mother!"

"Of course they are!"

"So she isn't really a virgin at all?"

"Yes, she is."

"But if the tyrant put her in the family way..."

"You don't understand: Jesus was conceived through the Holy Ghost."

"Who's he? I never met him. You mean he dared to cuckold the tyrant himself!"

"No! The Holy Ghost is... well, in a way, he's God himself."

"So the tyrant *did* deflower her!"

147

"No, he did not!"

"*Somebody* must have done it!"

"No, they did not! Look, I hardly think you're capable of understanding the finer points of theology ," said Peter stiffly. "So let's leave the subject, shall we?"

"As you wish," answered Satan merrily, "far be it from me to pry into family secrets! Poor little mite, though: with such a dubious background, no wonder he turned out odd!" And he chuckled away to himself for a few minutes, gloating over Peter's discomfiture. Then he returned, almost as if against his will, to the subject of Raphael.

"Well, even if she *is* family, as you say, and allied with Michael, I still don't see it's any great problem for Raphael."

"Well, they're not alone, of course. They've managed to drum up quite a lot of support, and have organised a new Reform Party."

"Oh yes, we've heard something about that. Isn't there a new saint, Dorian, Doreen, something like that, who's been causing a bit of trouble?"

He knows too much already! Peter hid his panic behind a counter-attack: "Yes, a revolting little creature, but harmless enough. We in Heaven have heard stories too, about someone causing a bit of trouble *here*. Boggle, Bugget, something like that..."

The saint and the devil scowled at each other, then trudged on side by side, each tormented by his own *bête noire*.

Peter was the first to break the silence. He'd had to veer the conversation away from Darren, but the last thing he wanted was a silent Satan. Why, he asked, hoping to relax him, did they bother to get people to sell their souls when most of them were coming to Hell anyway?

"One of the Codicils to the Treaty of Eden. Of course, the soul itself is insensitive to pain, so when we talk about souls, we mean the bodies they're given. Although they don't die a natural death, they can be 'killed' just as easily as when they were on Earth, and then the souls just float around, no use to anybody, except maybe as catapult practice for the Saragash children. What's more, because we can't hurt them any more, they grow quite insolent. I can't leave my window open at night, or they float in shouting 'God is great!' and other obscenities."

"Yes, yes, I know all this," said Peter impatiently, "but the ones who *sell* their souls?"

"The Pinks? Their bodies are truly immortal. The Tyrant agreed that any soul who deliberately *chose* to come here – rather than being sent against their will – would be given an indestructible replacement body. That taught them a lesson, I can tell you, for they all try it on sooner or later."

"Try it on?"

"Try to escape their just deserts by goading someone into killing them. They have quite a shock when they're in twenty pieces and feeling every moment of it!"

Peter shuddered. He remembered now: it had slipped his mind, because these souls didn't pass through the Way Station.

"Why do you call them Pinks?"

"The colour of the paper they sign when they sell their souls. No doubt you'll meet Mephistopheles later, our chief Buyer, and he can tell you more than me. He has vast experience. Why, the old bugger even had a go at Junior, nearly pulled it off, too!"

The ground had begun to slope slightly. It was still dry as turkey on the eleventh day of Christmas, but there were occasional signs of vegetation. In the distance, someone was boiling a thousand kettles in a straight line.

"The River Acheron," said Satan, intercepting Peter's glance. "Before the Shuttleport was built, my subjects used to be deposited there, on the other side, and Charon had to ferry them across. I'd have made them swim, myself! Charon still lives there, a bit forgetful in his old age, but a fine old chap, nevertheless."

Charon, when they finally reached the river, looked as though he'd been carved out of an old boot. He had only one eye, a hawthorn red, and hands so gnarled they resembled a baobab tree.

"Orpheus?" he enquired in a voice of dried twigs.

"It's me, Satan," said the Prince of Darkness, in a surprisingly gentle tone. "How are you, you old reprobate?"

"Satan? Oh yes, Satan. Such a long time since I saw you. Do you want to go across?"

"If you please."

The cyclopean creature looked around vaguely. "Where did I leave that dratted boat?"

"You're sitting in it."

"Oh yes, of course." He noticed Satan's companions. "How did they get across?" he asked. "I don't remember taking them."

149

"They haven't been across yet. You're going to take us now."

"*He* came across."

"Who?"

"The big one." He was looking at George, frightened. "You won't let him hurt me?"

"Are you a Saracen?" demanded George, speaking for the first time since they had set off. "Or a dragon-lover?"

The Boatman shook his head mutely.

"So why should I hurt you? Get us across the river before I break you in two!"

Peter interposed. "He's not always like this," he lied.

"He hurt me," whined Charon. "Don't let him do it again."

"Sir, you're mistaken. We've never been here before."

"He hurt me, I tell you!" wailed Charon, his red eye getting redder. "Look!" And he opened up his cloak, revealing welts and bruises, still raw.

Satan tensed. "Come with me," he ordered, and drew the old man aside.

Peter tried in vain to hear what they were saying. The Boatman kept gesticulating at George, and then at the other side of the river. Satan put his arm round his shoulders, calming him. But he was the opposite of calm himself when he returned, though he tried to hide it.

"Charon's just confused," he said. "Let's cross."

And without any further explanation, he jumped into the boat, and the old man at once began to row away. It took Satan a few minutes to get him to change direction, and pick up his companions. As the boat crawled across the water, he kept glancing fearfully at George.

On the other side, Satan fondly embraced Charon, and dipped into his pocket, producing some candied hellroaches, which the other accepted gratefully.

And then the travellers were off again. Satan remained unusually quiet. There was a new watchfulness about him, a feral alertness. His claws – a clear instance of Lamarckian evolution, thought Peter – unsheathed themselves, and twitched like fish on a hook. Unconsciously, it seemed, he kept closer to George and Lazara, and there was a perceptible lessening of open mockery towards the warrior saint, of which the latter remained quite unaware, just as he remained unaware of the she-demon's adoring glances.

The quartet trudged on. The sun was now directly overhead, and Peter could almost imagine he was a candle melting away. The Acheron soon became just a smudge behind them, the steam from its waters merging into the clouds of dust raised by innumerable whirlsands. The sparse vegetation again petered out, and even the ubiquitous brimsprings became lethargic and weary. The heat cast an eerie, wavering glow over everything.

When Peter saw Satan suddenly stiffen, he followed the direction of his eyes. What initially appeared to be yet another whirlsand proved to be something other, for it soon became clear that it was approaching them. Satan stopped and stared, his claws flexed like animated anchors. When he spoke to Lazara, however, his voice was calm.

"Would you just check, please?"

She nodded, and slipped off her tunic, under which she was completely naked. Peter marvelled anew at the weird grace and poise of her body. Then strange things began to happen. She flattened out: there was no other word for it. Her dark-tipped breasts disappeared like a pubescent girl stretching backwards, her whole torso streamlined, while what had been her shoulder blades opened to release, in a strange, fluid motion, a uniquely peaceful metamorphosis, two wings so fairy light that they billowed with the rising air currents. Then she was aloft, skimming like a skate towards the dust cloud.

George gave a puzzled frown, sat on a rock, and began to polish his mace.

This was not just the first time Peter had ever seen anyone change shape, it was also the first time he had seen anyone fly in Hell. He knew that most of the rebel angels' wings had been burned off by the Flame Cannon during the battle in Heaven. He also knew that a few of the native demons, those who occasionally operated on Earth, were obviously able to fly. Was Lazara one of these? Did she work for Mephistopheles? Why had she really wanted to be one of the party? Was it *only* George who interested her?

Within a few minutes, she was back. She glided down and alighted with the gentleness of a snowflake – *well, something like that, a heat-resistant snowflake?* – and flowed back into her former

151

shape. To Peter's disappointment, and possibly, he thought, her own, Satan at once handed her back her tunic.

"It's Yomyael, me lord, an' some mates of 'is. Been duffed up real proper, they 'as. Bits an' pieces all over the shop."

Satan seemed both relieved and concerned. "We'll meet them. Peter, if you don't mind, could you and George hide somewhere? – there are some rocks over there. I'd rather my subjects didn't know I was entertaining saints."

"I ain't hiding from no damn devils!" growled George, who had picked up the words 'George' and 'hide', and found them incompatible headfellows.

"You'll do what you're told!" snarled Satan. Whatever was making him nervous was also making him forgetful.

Peter just managed to interpose himself between them before blood flowed, and by the time he had also managed to persuade George to sit – not 'hide' – with him behind a rock, the cloud of dust had resolved itself into a cart being pulled by two more doodlebug-tarantulas.

The cart was piled high with broken bodies. Peter, peering from behind the rock, judged that with all the bits and pieces in the right places, there might well have been twenty original bodies. As the cart drew level with Satan, the demon guiding it, his face badly mauled, reined in the steeds, jumped out of the cart, and bowed – an act which roused Peter's admiration, since he had only half a leg to sustain him during this manoeuvre.

"Speak, Yomyael!" commanded Satan sternly.

Yomyael opened his mouth to obey, and managed to gasp out the single word 'Bugrot' before his tongue dropped out. He looked extremely apologetic, hopped back to the cart, and rummaged around until he managed to extract a torso complete with uninjured head. Clutching this, he began to hop back, but lost his balance, and his grip, so that the torso crashed to the ground, uttering a volley of expletives as it did so.

"Amazyarak! We do not allow bad language in Hell! How dare you!"

"Sorry, my lord!" gasped the torso. "It's that stupid Yomyael! First he gets us smashed to smithereens, and then he drops me!"

"What happened?"

152

"We came across Bugrot an hour ago, sound asleep. But that stupid Yomyael got so excited he gave a bloodcurdling yell as the nineteen of us leapt upon him..."

Only one out! thought Peter proudly.

"Standard strategy when the opponent is awake," murmured Satan, "but sheer folly when he's asleep."

"And... this is what happened."

There was a short silence, disturbed only by the scrabbling of the half-legged Yomyael as he attempted to gain what would normally have been his feet, but here was only his knee.

"It seems," said Satan, "that I shall have to deal with this Bugrot personally. Well, go and get yourselves patched up, and report to Belial."

Lazara put Amazyarak's torso back in the wagon, and then bent down to help Yomyael to his knee. Finding his face up against her breast, he essayed a playful bite. He obtained, instead, a playful slap.

"I got a feller now, see," glancing towards the rock, "so 'ands off is wot it's gotta be in future," she explained, somewhat apologetically.

A pity George doesn't know that.

The wagon set off again in the direction of Dis, Lazara remembering at the last moment to pick up Yomyael's tongue, and throw it after the wagon. One of the doodlebug-tarantulas spotted it, however, lunged, and swallowed it.

Peter and George emerged from their hiding-place, and once again the travellers set off.

The desert stretched away endlessly, though far in the distance Peter thought he could make out something breaking the horizon. Mountains, perhaps? Or was it merely a particularly large globule of sweat on the end of his nose? Distance seemed to be meaningless, just a shimmer of heat, a haze of nothingness. When he licked his lips, his tongue burned; when he blinked, his eyelashes smouldered; when he breathed, his throat scorched. The only consolation was that his beard still hadn't burst into flame. On, on, marching through the furnace – and for what? To provide high tea for the Beast of the Apocalypse?

But this whole trip had been a playing for time, and he'd already lost too much of that. The recent incident offered a possible line of attack.

"I'm very impressed with the courage of your warriors," he remarked to Satan. "They were Saragashim, weren't they? I've heard they were already here when you arrived. Did they accept your rule without protest?"

"There were a few teething troubles, but once we'd extracted a few of them, as it were, they rapidly recognised our superiority."

"They can't all fly like Lazara, can they?"

"Only a few. And *very* few as well as she does."

"And this Bugrot," Peter said as casually as possible, "is he a Saragash, too?"

"None of your business!" snapped Satan. "Kindly remember you're here to be devoured by the Beast, not to pry into the internal affairs of Hell!"

That was short and sweet! Still, he'd learnt something that might be useful. Charon had obviously mistaken George for this Bugrot. There must be major dissension in Hell, maybe involving some of the Fallen Angels themselves, since it seemed unlikely that this Bugrot could be a Saragash. And he who has enemies has need of friends.

The smudge he'd noticed on the horizon turned out to be a mountain, or maybe a volcano, as it had a reddish tinge. The sun was hovering over it like the eye of Sauron.

Satan turned to face him. His anger had dissipated somewhat, though he wasn't exactly cordial. Had he also reflected that he who has enemies has need of friends?

"That over there is the Mount of Despair, which means we'll soon be entering the Plain of Bones. I strongly advise you not to move away from the path. I'll lead the way."

Peter soon saw the reason for the name. As far as the eye could see, the ground was covered in bones glimmering white in the heat, shimmering in the haze. As they progressed, the bones lay so thick on the ground that the fires of Hell couldn't break through them, but crackled and snarled impotently beneath them.

"In case you're wondering why there are so many bones," Satan informed them with a malicious smile, "the Beast once lived here for a time, while we were spring-cleaning the Pit."

They walked deeper and deeper into the Plain, with Satan leading the way along an irregular trail he clearly knew well. Every so often, a brimspring would erupt near them, until one such eruption

154

was so close that George gave an oath and, instead of following the leader's circuitous route, strode off directly in the direction of the Mount of Despair, stomping right over and through the bones littering the side of the trail.

Barely had he traversed ten yards than he gave a roar enough to make a Saracen's stomach queasy; one of the skulls he was about to tread upon had opened its jaws and taken a vicious bite at his left leg. At the same time, an angry humerus and a couple of irate femurs smacked against his knees, six patellas made a concerted lunge at his private parts, and even the metacarpals and the metatarsals, small as they were, joined in the onslaught, and almost tripped him up. George reacted in the usual manner, and soon the air was thick with calcium and marrow. Seeing their colleagues thwarted in these individual attacks, a gang of bones rapidly came together to form a vaguely dinosaurian creature which clacked ominously towards the fuming saint. He struck this monstrosity repeatedly with blows that made the Plain ring, but it seemed impervious to the onslaught and started to force him backwards.

This was so novel and shocking an experience that it temporarily unhinged his brain, and induced an unexpected display of cunning. He ducked under his skeletal foe, grabbed its front legs, and twisted them round to face backwards. The creature swayed perilously as the legs tangled with each other, until finally the whole apparatus came crashing down in a noisy heap.

George gazed in astonishment at his handiwork. He shook his head desperately to clear it of this sudden attack of intelligence. Peter, watching him anxiously, noticed blood running down his leg. Soon the familiar blankness oozed over the stalwart warrior's face, and he leapt upon the bickering bones and proceeded to pulverise them in the usual manner.

"We had a lot of trouble with these bones," said Satan, as George stumbled back to them. "For years they just lay there getting bleached, a pretty apathetic lot on the whole. No pride, no ambition. Then some blasted hermit, who should have gone to Heaven, came here instead." He looked directly at Peter as he said this. "He did nothing but cause trouble. He told all the other bones – for he was little more than bones himself – that their ideas were ossified, their philosophy fossilised. A skeleton without flesh, he taught them, was still a skeleton, indeed, even more a skeleton, whereas flesh without a skeleton was a mere formless blob. For too long the bones had been basely subservient to the flesh, it was time for them to awake, to claim their heritage, to erect and spread their empire far and wide. Eventually, because of this rabble-rousing, the whole Plain rose up in revolt, and headed towards Dis."

Even George was listening now: this was battle talk.

"We might have been in real trouble, with the awful possibility that our own skeletons might join the revolt in sympathy, our vertebral columns becoming fifth columns, which would have rendered us utterly impotent. Luckily, the hermit fell, and cracked his head open, and a passing vulture gobbled up his brains. This deprived the bones of the only brain they had between them, so it was relatively easy to drive them back here. But ever since, they've retained a kind of inchoate consciousness, a mindless urge to attack flesh whenever it comes near them. We only keep them away from this trail by spraying acid every so often."

Satan paused, and then said, staring straight through the film of perspiration covering Peter's eyes: "I've often wondered how that hermit came to be here. Recently, we've been getting more and more quite remarkable immigrants, the sort that a few centuries ago would have gone straight to Heaven."

Peter's expression was blander than bland. "Higher standards?"

"As Keeper of the Keys, you must be the one sending them here."

"You give me too much credit. Mine's more an honorary position. It's the Five Judges who decide. They only refer borderline cases to me..."

"But I've heard that the Judges – or one of them, anyway – were chosen by you."

"Oh no, they were appointed by the Council of Seven."

"And you had no say in the matter? None at all?"

Peter tried not to squirm. "Of course, I have *some* influence. But you seem to be well-informed on these matters."

"We are. Some of our latest arrivals felt they were rather hard done by, going so far as to suggest that Stalin's show trials were a model of democracy by comparison!"

"Just bad sports," muttered Peter, hoping his beard would hide his shifty expression. "*You're* not complaining, are you?"

156

They were coming to the edge of the Plain, and luckily for Peter, this dangerous conversation was interrupted by a thigh bone making one last attempt to trip George. Then they were out of it, and entering a valley that lay between the Plain and the Mount of Despair.

Lazara ripped off a piece of her tunic, and insisted on tying it round George's thigh, showing remarkable agility in the process, since that doughty warrior refused to stop marching to allow her to do it. It reminded Peter of a puppy scampering round its owner's feet.

He knows too much! In one way, his guess – or was it more than a guess? – that Peter had been arranging for Hell to receive more souls than it should have, helped to support his story of overcrowding in Heaven. But if he put too many pieces together... He said quickly, before Satan could return to the previous topic:

"Tell me more about the Beast. For instance, what was it like when it was first brought here?"

Lazara at this point, having been scratching an imaginary itch on her left nipple – oddly enough, she had torn the tunic at just this point – seemed to despair of getting George's attention, and answered this question before Satan could.

"But it weren't brought 'ere! It were made by Lord Satan 'ere 'imself, when 'e went down into 'Ades, an' 'e were there ten 'ole nights an' 'e made it from bits an' thingummybobs of other monsters wot 'e done in down there."

"Oh, pardon my mistake," said Peter.

"It were so bleedin' 'ot down there, weren't it, my lord, that no blighter else 'ad the balls to go there, but Lord Satan, 'e weren't afraid, was you, not likely, an' so 'e makes it like I said."

"Remarkable, most remarkable! Have you any idea why he made it?"

"Why, so 'e could go back to 'Eaven," she replied, before Satan could interpose, "an' do in the angels wot done the dirty on 'im when 'e were there. An' there's one of 'em 'specially – wot's 'is name, Lord Sod or Cod or sommat? – oo's really got it comin' to 'im!"

"Oh, now why might that be?"

"You ain't 'eard about it? Where you been all your life? Blimey, everyone knows 'ow wot Lord Satan 'ere, wot was called

157

Lucifer then, beat the 'ell out of that Lord Cod, then let 'im off, but 'e weren't a gentleman, this Cod, for all 'e were a lord an' 'ad a fancy title, 'cos when Lord Lucifer – that's Lord Satan 'ere – were leavin' 'Eaven to find a new 'ome, 'cos 'e was fed up with 'Eaven, this Cod bod 'urled thunderbolts at 'im, whatever they is, yes 'e did, at 'is back when 'e weren't lookin', an' burnt 'is lovely wings, an' all the wings of 'is mates, wot's more, like Lord Moloch an' Lord Belial, an' so they fell 'ere an' 'urt themselves sommat awful 'cos like I says their wings 'ad been bust. So Lord Lucifer made the Beast to get 'is own back, an' quite right, too!"

"I should think so!"

"You see, though 'e done the Second Drubbin' good an' proper, 'e still couldn't get back to 'Eaven."

"The Second Drubbing?"

"Cor, you don't know nothin', do you? You ain' 'eard of the Drubbin'? When Lord Lucifer flies to Eden, 'cos 'e still 'ad a bit of wing left, an' duffed up Lord Cod all over again, an' made 'im 'and over the souls, an' told 'im straight up 'ow wot 'e'd be back one day an' finish the job."

"So Lord Lucifer administered a second beating to Go...to Lord Cod in Eden, did he?"

"I'll say 'e did!"

"This Lord Cod seems to have had rather a hard time of it!"

"No more than wot 'e 'ad comin' to 'im! Serve 'im right, don't it, for wot 'e done to Lord Lucifer when 'e weren't lookin', an' it ain't nothin' to wot 'e's got comin' when Lord Satan gets back to 'Eaven again! You wait an' see!"

"I shall indeed follow future developments with profound interest," promised Peter.

Satan gave him a look which indicated that he would be extremely lucky to be around to see the aforesaid future developments.

The view forward was now cut off by a high ridge that curved away in a vast semi-circle, seeming to indicate that it was in fact the rim of a huge crater. Far to the left of this crater, Peter perceived an eerie purplish gleam emanating from the roiling surface of a great lake. A glance at Satan's expression told him that this must be *the* Lake. *So this is where they fell!*

On and on. Signs of life began to appear again. A few snakes slithered about listlessly, giving an occasional half-hearted hiss, and tiny scimitar-tailed rodents now and then disappeared into their mouths with even less enthusiasm. A fine ash now covered the terrain, the residue, maybe, of an old volcanic explosion. On and on. Toiling up the slope. Too exhausted to talk, to get Satan to talk. *On the way back – but will there be a way back?* On and on...

Until, as they were nearing the top, Satan remarked nonchalantly:

"Oh, by the way, that is the Pit."

Peter had the feeling he had just swallowed a handful of particularly slimy slugs. *The Pit!* Inside that crater, two thousand years old – *we're almost the same age*, he thought inconsequentially – must be...

The Beast of the Apocalypse!

The journey from Dis, which until now had seemed a long, interminable torture, was suddenly over all too soon. But before they actually breasted the summit, Satan turned and stopped them with an imperious gesture. Another of his chameleon changes of mood had taken place. His eyes were shining, sparks of excitement flashing through his whole being.

"Prepare," he announced with pride, "to meet the Beast of the Apocalypse!"

And he took the final steps that brought him to the top of the ridge.

At once the ground leapt to life beneath them, jerking and twisting as if it were the saddle on some wild tectonic steed plunging and rearing in fury. Beyond the rim, seven jets of flame streaked into the sky, accompanied by a roar that burst against the firmament, echoing and reverberating between land and sky.

George was the next to reach the top, with Lazara beside him. What he saw had a strange effect on him. Once again, there was the give-away *clank* of the instant erection, but this time the rest of his body too went rigid. Even Lazara looked pale and shaken. George, totally oblivious of the girl, of his erection, of the wound in his thigh, very slowly, as if obeying some remote genetic instinct, drew his sword, and raised it high in the air. His lips formed his notorious battle-cry, 'For Heaven and St. George, and especially St. George!', but no sound came out.

Then it was Peter's turn.

The Pit was indeed a huge crater. Towards the near end of it, bellowing and flaming and jumping, was the Beast itself. It was impossible to say how big it was, as this estimate would depend on which of the seven heads one measured from. As two of these were almost lost in the clouds, Peter preferred not to attempt calculations, but to draw comfort from the fact that the clouds were low-lying. It was impossible, too, to ascertain its exact shape, because it was partially obscured by dust and flying rocks, but it made him think of a fossilised appendix on wheels, for the dozen or so legs were so squat and thick they barely raised the belly off the ground. It had what looked like four monstrous folded wings on either side of its body. Its tail was massive, curving up over the body like that of a scorpion. There was no sign of the ten horns Satan had spoken of. *Did he really need to exaggerate?*

There were hundreds of other monsters in the Pit , none of them anywhere near as big as the Beast itself, but monsters nevertheless; huge griffins, chimeras, basilisks, hydras, and others whose names were known only in Hell. But they were in a separate enclosure, cut off from the Beast by a wall of rock in which there was but a single gap, over which a tremendous portcullis had been erected. Scattered on this wall like so many gnats were possibly hundreds of demons.

And there were four other creatures which, because of their relative smallness, he hadn't even noticed at first, and which he couldn't see clearly now because of all the dust. Whatever they were, they all seemed to be different colours, and obviously had no fear of the Beast.

In the short time it had taken Peter to observe these details, the Beast had quietened down considerably, and was instead pawing at the ground with what seemed like expectancy. Three of the heads watched Satan, three gazed towards the enclosure, and the middle one veered between the two.

"Pobbles always expects a little extra something when I come," remarked Satan.

He gave a signal to the demons. At once they rushed to the breach in the wall of rock, and worked on levers and pulleys to raise the massive portcullis. Sensing freedom, a few of the monsters lumbered towards the spot. The first to reach it, an enormous octopus-like creature, burst through with a bellow of joy, the portcullis crashing down behind it like the teeth of doom.

The liberated monster smashed a few rocks to celebrate its freedom, and scampered around for a time, until it noticed the Beast, whereupon it uttered a fierce challenge, which was met only with silence. It rose on five of its tentacles and then, like the spokes of a wheel without the rim, catherine-wheeled towards the Beast in a thunderous charge. The Beast seemed to regard it with disdain, half turning away, but at the last moment, its scorpion tail lashed up and across and skewered the enemy from above with a speed and violence that transfixed it to the ground. The tail, like a huge electric drill, then spun the helpless victim rapidly while the heads each sent forth a jet of flame to barbecue it. All at once, the flames went out, and six of the heads swooped in on the victim, while the seventh remained in the air, staring upwards.

Peter was stunned. "Satan, isn't it...? I do believe it's saying grace!"

Satan pretended he hadn't heard.

With magnificent precision, each of the other heads bit off a sixth of the meal. They then rose in the air, with a unity reminiscent of Velasquez's *Las Lanzas*, and what looked like six enormous Adam's apples passed down through the necks and into the body. A few seconds later, the heads burped, including the seventh, which strictly speaking had no cause to do so. And not long after that, the tail lifted again, but this time gently and decorously, and a heap of still steaming bones clattered on to the ground. The Beast, rather self-consciously, it seemed, wiped its bottom against some bushes, and settled down for a nap.

Satan looked smugly at the trembling Peter. "A quite unique metabolism, don't you agree? Your phylogenic impasse," he added, indicating George, "seems rather impressed, too!"

Oh my God, George! I must stop him!

But George hadn't yet moved. His stance was the same as when he had first seen the Beast, with one leg thrust forward, his sword arm raised high in the air. But, instead of the battle-cry, gurgling noises were coming from his throat, and his eyes were staring wildly at the neat stool of bones that had been so discreetly deposited. Then a mighty tremor passed through him, he shook himself, and he turned to face Peter, who was staggering towards

161

him.

"Back in a minute, Peter," he said, with just the first hint of doubt his friend had ever heard, and turned towards the Pit.

"George, that's not a dragon! Last night you promised you wouldn't..."

"Don't be too hard on poor Pobbles!" shouted Satan mockingly. "Don't cut off all his heads at once!"

George marched on, Peter hanging on to his arm like a small fierce terrier dog. "George, it's impossible...George, you came to protect *me*, not to commit suicide...George, you great idiot, will you stop!"

St. Peter was still cursing St. George with all the power of his scorched lungs when at last he lost his grip on his arm, and fell headfirst on the gravelly slope. By the time he had raised himself, George was already well ahead – and the Beast was turning towards him!

****

Eve, lying feverishly by the Pool of the Old Ones in Heaven, suddenly started in fear, gazed wildly round, eyes staring, seeing nothing, looking not at, but through, the Archangel who was watching her with concern.

"What are you seeing, Eve?" he whispered, as he wiped the perspiration from her brow. "Have I done right in profaning the Cosmic Book itself? You ask me to trust you – to trust you, in this case, more than God himself! And I have done so, for old times' sake, and because God no longer seems to care. But if you are wrong?"

Chapter Sixteen
THE IMMACULATE INFANT

At the very moment that St. George was striding down into the Pit to do battle with the Beast of the Apocalypse, St. Darren was lying in a luxury cot in the Archangel Michael's palace, and gurgling away happily. With his pretty blue eyes, his curly golden hair with that delightfully unruly forelock, his little snub nose, and dainty mouth with that innocent smile, he could lie there with the most horrendously bloodthirsty thoughts, and no one would suspect a thing. Even Michael had no idea what was really going on inside that pretty little head.

St. Darren was completely mad.

****

The odds had been stacked against him from the very beginning. Like the House of Usher, madness was a curse that had lain over his family for centuries, usually in the form of religious fanaticism. One of his ancestors, for instance, had tried to assassinate the Grand Inquisitor Torquemada for being too lenient.

The refusal of his Jehovah's Witnesses parents to allow a blood transfusion had pushed him further towards the edge: at the age of sixteen days, it is difficult to accept with equanimity that your parents are consciously and deliberately murdering you.

The Afterlife didn't begin well, either. The travesty of a trial at the Way Station, the psychic trauma of nearly being sent to Hell, had been only the first of a series of unsettling Afterworld shocks.

Even after the intervention of the Judge Cuthbert, and the almost immediate granting of sainthood, Darren was carried, not to Heaven and a comfortable cot on God's right hand side, but to the Fitter, an extremely garrulous creature who looked like a runner bean, with atrophied ears and overdeveloped tongue, the tip of which kept darting in and out of the mouth as if in search of cool air to prevent it from overheating, who explained at inordinate length that Darren's original body was already being cloned from a sliver of soul material, and that meanwhile he would be Fitting him with a temporary replacement body.

The Fitter had taken him to the Fitting Rooms, to choose from the bodies hanging there on hooks. The poor soul was faced with a line of nondescript models, blotches and blemishes everywhere, sagging stomachs, ostrich knees – the sort of people found at North European holiday resorts eating soggy chips and huddling under grey August skies.

When Darren protested, the Fitter explained that his Design Department was so busy preparing for the Apocalypse that they hadn't time to spend on the loan bodies, which would only be in use for a few months anyway.

He had then had to spend an extremely unpleasant hour while the Fitter pushed and shoved, prodded and twisted, to force the soul into the unyielding loan body. He did pick up, however, what was later to prove some very useful information concerning Limbo. The whole point of Purgatory, he was told, was that the souls should be without a body, but as their stay here was not intended to be eternal, they were initially cloned, as he had been, and the bodies stored in enormous Vaults somewhere outside the Way Station. The souls themselves were put in huge vats nearby.

After that, new shocks had followed one another in quick succession. When he did eventually get to Heaven, instead of Pearly Gates, there were only wooden ones, covered with bits of flaking paint and various items of graffiti. And instead of the Keeper of the Keys, he was accosted by a lizard-faced individual selling very dubious-looking ambrosia, who insisted on acting as his guide in the Flatlands, a kind of reservation in the west to which, apparently, the human souls were more or less confined.

All this perhaps any normal worldly-wise sixteen-day-old baby might have taken in its crawl. But then had come the real shocks, concerning the Royal Family.

According to the lizard-faced individual, as they crossed a river flowing with water, and not with milk and honey, *Jesus had been banished from Heaven, the Virgin Mary had gone mad and had not shown her face in public since she had arrived, and it was such a long time since God himself had been seen that many thought him dead!*

The informant, like all self-appointed experts, hadn't got his facts quite right, but Darren wasn't to know this. His regulation body collapsed in a regulation heap.

It was at this very moment that his fortunes changed dramatically. The Judge Cuthbert had sent a message to the Archangel Michael advising him of yet another infringement of Court procedure, and Michael had decided to speak to the injured party himself. Darren woke up on a sofa in the Archangel's Palace.

He still remembered that first impression. The Vice-President of the Council of Heaven! Although slender, almost effete, he had coruscating golden wings, his whole body glowed, his eyes shone as no human's had ever done, his voice was the chiming of bells. He wore robes of the purest silk, and rings that lanced darts of light into the air. What if his perfume *was* rather strong, his nails perhaps too brightly polished? And what if, after insisting that Darren have a bath in a room almost choking with pearls, he did help to dry him, and allow his delicate hands to linger over his body? This was far better than any treatment Darren had ever received until now.

He had immediately asked why God and his son weren't in Heaven.

"Oh, God's here all right, it's just that he spends most of his time in the Cloud of Unknowing, so we rarely see him. He's suffering from depression, and let me tell you, when a god is depressed, it certainly is some depression! Partly to do with the state of things on Earth, partly to do with Jesus, of course, though we suspect there's much more to it than that. Jesus, it's true, isn't here, he's in Betelgeuse now, I think, or somewhere like that: it doesn't really matter, these stars are all the same, my dear boy, dull, dull. Do him some good. They say he's already bucking up a little."

"I don't understand."

"Of course not," said Michael, indulgently stroking his knee, "you've only just arrived. He took the crucifixion badly, very badly. But it was entirely his own fault! Fancy staying with a barbarous bunch like that! What could he expect? And the friends he consorted with! Grubby fishermen, tax collectors, prostitutes – just asking for trouble! What's worse," he added morosely, "they traded on having known him, and turned up here. Even Judas put in an application, claiming it had all been a misunderstanding. Or take that Peter, for instance, a bad-mannered upstart who only got ahead, in my opinion, because he gave Jesus cheap fish on the quiet. I think myself – just between you and me – Jesus wanted to show off a bit. If he'd kept quiet about his family connections, he'd have had no trouble.

165

Anyway, he was in a pretty bad way when they found him. When he did get back here, he made God promise to destroy the world."

"What! But Jesus died to save the world!" They might have murdered him, but his parents hadn't neglected his education in those sixteen days.

Michael chuckled, his hand casually moving from knee to thigh. "Yes, when that story reached here, we couldn't believe our ears! In fact, some say it was precisely that which finally incensed God so much he acceded to his son's demands. Save the world from *what?*"

"But he did it to save the world! Or else why didn't he save himself?"

"He couldn't. He was just a man then, not a god. That great dolt Gabriel was supposed to be keeping an eye on him, but he was careless as usual, taking a holiday or something like that. He only got back when it was all over. Anyway, it taught Jesus not to be soft like his father. If you ask me, God made the Beast of the Apocalypse simply to avoid, or at least delay, keeping his promise – he just isn't strict enough, never has been – but Jesus had learned a thing or two from those barbarians, and immediately got the promise entered in Razael's Cosmic Book, so there's no way God can get out of it.

"Anyway, my own belief is that Jesus left Heaven because of that quarrel over when, and how, earth was going to be punished. Apart from the problem of the succession. Jesus is next in line to the throne..."

"But God is immortal!"

"Precisely. Jesus is heir to a throne that will never become vacant. But if he can find a new world, then he can rule that, instead."

"And the Virgin Mary?" Darren was still trying to find some figure who might be expected to be nice to little children. '*Suffer little children to come unto me*', indeed!

Michael hesitated. There was a pained expression on his face now.

"Well?" insisted Darren: he had the usual strong will-power of a sixteen-day-old baby.

Michael's hands surrendered the territory they had so painstakingly conquered. "You'll be meeting her," he said, "but not just yet."

"Is it true that she's gone mad?"

166

Michael swung on him in sudden anger. "Who told you that?" The bells in his voice had changed to molten iron.

"A man I was talking to when I came..."

Michael quickly regained his composure. "Yes, I know they all say that. No, Mary's not mad, although sometimes I almost wish ..." He stopped himself. "You will find out one day what has happened. But right now I wish to speak of something else. I assume you want revenge – or shall we say justice? – for what happened at your trial."

A lump of lard with a jungle of whiskers, bulbous nose, horrendous puns. *'You'll only be in Hell for an eternity, after all. I'm sure the time will soon pass.'* Michael saw the answer in Darren's face.

"And I want Heaven to become a better place. I've watched it go downhill for thousands of years. There are no standards any more, no morality, no *rightness*. God is too soft. Everyone takes advantage of him. That evil hussy Eve twists him round her little finger. Peter gets away with murder because he happened to know the son. George tries to spill blood on the fields of Heaven itself, and dares to insult an Archangel. Some of the newer female saints are having *affairs*! And what does God do? Nothing. He could expel every cancer from Heaven by lifting his little fingernail. But no. Instead, he speaks of free will, of independence. Even when Lucifer rebelled, he wouldn't use the Flame Cannon until angels began dying. Raphael and Urmak and Gabriel and I and all the others, *we* did the fighting, *we* bore the blows."

He sighed heavily. "At least, against Lucifer, we were united. For the last time." The anger returned. "I seek to fulfil God's own purpose. He made Archangels to rule Heaven under him, and as such we must be respected and obeyed. He made Seraphim and Cherubim and Thrones and Powers and Dominions, and the hierarchy must be maintained. And he made the angels greater and more powerful than humans and other animals, so it must stay that way. *We* are the true progeny of Heaven, not the animals, not the saints, though some of them – and I hope you will be in that number – can earn the right, the *privilege*, to rule Heaven with us."

He stopped for a moment, wiping perspiration from his features with a hand that trembled with righteousness.

"Yet many of the angels themselves have fallen to the wiles

of the newcomers, and will not support me when I seek to return Heaven to its former glory. But you, you can help me. In return, I will make you the greatest saint in Heaven. We need to bring together the forces that stand for the old, the *true* values. If I try to lead those forces alone, my detractors will say, 'It's just old-fashioned Michael again!' But *you*, you are different. Just think. Sixteen days old, martyred, and then almost tricked out of your sainthood by a villainous old Judge controlled by a renegade saint!"

He took Darren by the arm, pushed him in front of a gilt mirror.

"Look at yourself now: with that loan body, no one would take the slightest notice of you. But they'll start to clone your real body tomorrow. Accelerated cloning is nearly fifty times as fast as natural growth. By tomorrow evening, you could have the body you died in. *And you could be the first baby saint in Heaven!* What I mean is, the first *visible* baby. Of course we've had babies here before, but never Grade One saints, and they all naturally waited till their new bodies had reached their peak of development before donning them. I don't know whether the Fitter told you – I'm sure he *tried* to – but the cloning process can be halted at whatever point the soul desires, and after that the body never ages. If you take your cloned body quickly, without waiting for it to grow, you can be the first baby saint ever to be seen here. Imagine! The *only* baby in Heaven. A babe, a suckling, an innocent nearly destroyed by a gang of wicked saints, a babe who died to enter a pure Heaven and found it fallen from grace! What influence you will have! Even on Earth, everyone goes soft when they see a baby. The most hideous little monster, covered in saliva and snot, smelly bottom, bloated arms and legs, and people say, 'What a beautiful baby!'. And that on Earth, which is positively crawling with the little slugs! But in Heaven, with just *one* single baby, no competition, people will travel miles just for the chance of hearing one meaningless gurgle, one purple-faced eructation, of seeing one pee puddle slowly spreading over the carpet, of..."

Michael became aware that his listener was looking at him with a certain degree of resentment. Darren couldn't know, of course, that Michael's disgust with babies was really disgust with the process of reproduction itself: a distant echo of the Great Yuk when the Saragashim had been discovered.

"And if they would do that for a normal, undistinguished

baby," Michael tried to rectify, "just imagine what they would do for a truly exceptional baby like yourself! Saint Darren, the last and purest of a long line of servants of the Church, Innocence incarnate brutalised by the spreading corruption in Heaven! And the Virgin will join us, of that I am sure. We will create a Party that will sweep all before it. We will put a stop to the shame that Gabriel is bringing on the very name of Archangel, we will clean riff-raff like Peter out of their positions of power, we will have every hippopotamus in Heaven deported, we will bridle that Eve who flaunts her body by the Pool and mocks our traditions! Why, we will influence the Final Judgement itself, stop all those damned souls pouring into Heaven with their evil ways! We shall rule Heaven as it was meant to be ruled!"

Darren wiped away the spittle which Michael had unintentionally spattered him with in his mounting excitement. He found himself trembling, too. The vision of power opened up to him made him giddy with its allure. St. Darren, arbiter of Heaven's destiny! Tobias crushed and broken, Hector crushed and broken, St. Peter, apparently the real culprit, crushed and broken – and his parents, too, if ever they got to Heaven, crushed and broken! And if his new friend wanted Gabriel and Eve, whoever they were, crushed and broken, that was fine by him!

Michael wiped away the spittle which Darren had unintentionally spattered him with in his mounting excitement.

The final blow to Darren's sanity had come less than a week later. As the Virgin Mary was to be the third member of the proposed triumvirate, Michael said, there was something he, Darren, ought to know.

"You've heard of the Corporeal Assumption, of course?" said Michael.

Darren hadn't. His sixteen-day education hadn't, after all, been perfect.

"Well, the Mother of Jesus came straight to Heaven with her human body. Everybody else here has – or will have – a cloned body, cloned directly from the soul. Immortal. But the Virgin has her own earthly body. Not a cloned body that never grows old, but..."

It took a few seconds for this to sink in. "You mean *the Virgin's body is two thousand years old!*"

"You understand now why no one ever sees her face."

169

"But no one ages in Heaven..."

"Not if their body was made here, in the Afterworld."

"But she can get a new body, just like me..."

"No, she can't. Only God really understands the problem. It's something to do with changing Dimensions, something related to the limitations of the Zindor Universal Life Force, the Zulf. Don't try to understand what that is. The point is, *what happened was impossible!* You understand? It can't happen, it couldn't happen, and yet it *did* happen! Which means that either God or Jesus disobeyed a Nebulan Forbidding, and created a Paradox. Mary's flesh jumped up a dimension – there's no problem paring down, otherwise we angels couldn't go to Earth – and now her soul is indissolubly welded to it, welded to every single putrefying cell! Mary is immortal, and her body is worse than dead!" Michael was almost weeping. "But she cares about Heaven, as I do, opposes the baneful influence of Eve, as I do. She will be our ally, she will not fail us, as we must not fail her."

No wonder she hates Eve, thought Darren, in that last lucid moment before his brittle mind finally cracked with so many shocks. How else could she feel about a woman thousands of years older who must look thousands of years younger?

****

Six months had passed, and Darren had every right to gurgle happily in his cot.

The Reform Party was everywhere in the ascendant, and the main cause of the triumph was undoubtedly the leaders: the Archangel Michael, the Virgin Mary, and the Immaculate Infant carried all before them. By now, there were few in Heaven who did not feel queasy at the mere mention of the name 'Tobias', few who did not step aside to avoid that archscoundrel St. Peter, few who did not feel that Heaven did indeed need a thorough overhaul. They flocked in their thousands to see the Virgin – hidden behind a thick blue veil – the innocent blue-eyed Infant lying on her lap, and, behind them, a protective hand on both, the Vice-President of the High Council of Heaven.

Still only Vice-President. Raphael remained untainted by all the scandals and furore, potent, impassive, enigmatic, the only one now, apart sometimes from Eve, to be allowed to enter the Cloud of Unknowing itself and converse with a God who seemed to have abandoned his whole Creation, both on Earth and in Heaven. Perhaps even more than the influence of the Infant, it was this feeling of abandonment, this absence of God, this absence of his once palpable love, which had allowed the spiritual vacuum to be filled by the new rigid Morality.

But though Raphael was untouchable, Gabriel, it turned out, was not.

"Gabriel," Michael had hissed – it seemed such a long time ago now – "who failed in Eden, and let Lucifer walk right in; who failed in Bethlehem, choosing a *virgin*, of all things, to be the Mother of Jesus, so putting the cat among the pigeons from the very start; who failed in Jerusalem years later, allowing the son of God to be foully murdered. And *still* he retains a seat on the Council. He's the one who's stopped me putting Peter and his cronies in their place..."

No longer. Gabriel had fallen. Oh yes, he still sat on the Council, he still wielded enormous influence, but he was in Darren's power. Two of the Old Ones had been reminiscing over something the Serpent had once told them in Eden, and had taken no notice of the bright-eyed baby who appeared to be sleeping nearby.

After that, it was easy. A vigilante force was formed, and Peter's office was raided. When Darren learned that the bird had already flown, he frothed and foamed to such an alarming extent that his nurses, thinking he had wind, turned him over and thumped him so much that, unbeknown to them, they were added to his enormous list of creatures to be crushed and broken.

It didn't matter; it wouldn't take too long to find out where Peter had gone, and by fleeing he had only announced his own guilt. Meanwhile, his friends in Heaven – in addition to a certain rotundity in Limbo – were at the mercy of the Reform Party.

All this was enough to make any normal vindictive baby gurgle happily. But every now and then Darren recalled something else so wonderful that the gurgling gave way to manic shrieks of delight. Something that his remaining traces of sanity had kept him from revealing to his allies, who didn't know that he hadn't returned his temporary adult body to the Fitter when he'd received his cloned baby one, or that by sheer force of his desire for revenge, he had taught himself to be able to move from one to the other at will.

171

So no one knew that the unprepossessing regulation body that had frequently mingled with other temporary replacement bodies in Limbo contained in fact the frenzied soul of the Immaculate Infant.

At least, those who, to their cost, did know this, had been in no condition to do anything about it. No condition at all.

Chapter Seventeen
BUGROT

Satan, despite the weight of the burden he was sharing, was in an excellent humour.

"So, any more plans for destroying Pobbles, then?"

You bet your life I have! Peter shifted the weight of George's legs to his other arm.

"I'm surprised at your heroic friend getting so frightened, though – fancy fainting like that!"

"He collapsed from loss of blood, not fear, you know that!"

"Well, you're entitled to your own opinion. Still, that fainting saved his life, you have to agree. I don't think Pobbles would've put up with him waving his sword around in that ludicrous manner for much longer – the tail was just a warning."

Peter didn't answer. The tail might have been just a warning, but it had effectively cut short, not only George's hopes, but also his erection, the severed part of which now lay in a red handkerchief being tenderly clutched by a tearful Lazara. Every now and then, she would stroke this war casualty, and whisper words of endearment and encouragement, presumably to persuade it not to wilt away for ever in the infernal heat.

Even after the Beast's tail had made this cruellest of cuts – and opened up a huge gash in his thigh as well – George had still managed, before collapsing, to make a few stabs at the Beast, which had turned away as if to show that it meant no harm. Was this why, Peter wondered, Satan had been willing to help carry George back to Dis? Had Satan in reality, despite his mockery, admired George's courage? Or did he want something from the saints? Peter recalled how quickly the safe-conduct had been sent.

He felt just a tiny twinge of conscience as he saw his intended victim struggling with most of George's weight. Would George have done the same for him? Would *he* have done the same? He pushed the thought away.

He felt George stirring. Thank God! Coming to see the Beast had just been an excuse, and if George had died for nothing...

Satan had noticed, too, and they lowered the wounded saint against a rock.

"Where's my sword?" asked George weakly, his eyes still closed.

Satan's answer was a muted growl. But he wasn't looking at George, but beyond him. His eyes widened, his mouth took on a vaguely rectal shape, and out of it, like an asthmatic intestinal worm seeking fresh air, crawled one word: "Bugrot!"

Peter followed the direction of his gaze, and suddenly his heart jumped about like a foetus which has just overheard that its mother plans to abort.

Not five yards away lounged the most terrifying creature he had ever seen, more terrifying than the Beast, in a way, for this had human form. It was a ghastly melange of reds, crushed hawthorn, sick, sanguineous reds, a rubella of reds; and mixed with the reds, scars of blue, a Schiaparelli network of cuts and gashes. It was as if the creature had been flayed, drawn and quartered, then stuck together again and plunged into some embalming solution, or some vicious lava flow, to fix it for ever, giving the surface – for skin it was not – a vitreous sheen, a translucent, hyaline horror. Within, visible veins and arteries pulsed and squirmed like worms, while gouts of blood seemed ready to erupt from a thousand pores.

"Oh dear!" said Peter. Then, deciding this was a bit inadequate, "Oh, fucking hell!"

The creature inclined its head in Peter's direction. He wasn't sure whether it could see him or not, for its eyes were seeled, sewn down, like those of a hunting falcon, but behind the translucent lids he discerned movement. Then it turned towards Satan.

There followed a weird, silent duel. Satan stared unblinkingly at the creature, and the creature stared unblinkingly – of course – back. Neither of them moved. Satan remained standing tensely, and the creature remained leaning against a boulder.

Lazara had given a gasp of fear, but when she noticed Satan staring grimly at the apparition, her confidence visibly returned, and she herself hurled a vicious frown at it.

Faith, thought Peter, may move mountains, but what about monsters?

Satan continued to stare so unwaveringly that Peter whispered, "Is he all right?"

174

"Don't you worry, sir. 'E's just givin' Lord Bugrot 'is Im'nent Death Stare, wot turns blokes into jelly." There was just a pinch of doubt in her voice, because Bugrot had a drooling grin on his face. *If that's jelly, it appears to have set rather hard – and in this heat, too!*

Lazara must have noticed his misgivings, because she went on loyally: "'E done the Death Stare in 'Eaven once, when some angels 'ad 'im from be'ind an' a big ponce were about to stick 'im with a 'uge skewer. 'E frizzled 'im up right proper. It's in the 'Istory."

"So we have nothing to fear, then."

"Gorblimey no, sir."

Bugrot, however, showed as much reaction to the vaunted Stare as a sheet of asbestos to a warm kiss. Satan finally conceded defeat, rubbed his eyes, and glanced surreptitiously towards George. But the latter's eyes were nearly closed; he was clearly in no condition to help.

Bugrot amused himself for a time crushing rocks the size of heads in one hand, grew bored, scratched his head, rummaged in his rucksack, and extracted...a book! It was massive, bound in blood-impregnated leather. He opened a page at random, and began to snigger. He then turned to another page, and another, while the snigger grew to a giggle, which transposed into a cackle, and ended up as a thunderous guffaw.

This was having a profound effect on Satan and Lazara, both of whom began to swell with rage.

"What's the matter?" Peter asked. "Why are you both swelling with rage?"

"'E's laughin' at the Book!" Lazara replied between clenched fangs.

"I can see that! So what?"

"The 'Istory! 'E's laughin' at the 'Istory!"

Ah, the *History of the Great Rebellion*. The holy book of the devils.

At this point, Bugrot gave one last enormous guffaw, shut the book with a loud snap, threw it on the ground, and urinated on it. The urine at once turned to steam.

"Peter," said Satan, with a deceptive almost-over-the-edge calm, "I am going to have to chastise that heretic, even though he is twice my size and a few million years younger. You are here under safe-conduct, and entitled to my protection. So fear not, Peter, fear not, George…"

"What's he want now?" asked George feebly.

"Though that foul creature stands in your path, and means to destroy you, I will not allow it." *That's jolly decent of you, though I don't think Bugrot is even aware I'm here.* "Soon this plain will ring with mighty deeds…"

"Can't it just tinkle with the sound of our hastily retreating footsteps?"

"What! The King of Hell turn aside from danger!"

"Only to help me carry George back. You can always return to make the plains ring another day."

Satan stopped mid-bombast. "That's true. My first duty is, after all, to my guests."

So let's get out of here, you old fraud!

Then came the problem. When they moved to the right, the monster did the same, thus continuing to block their path. When they veered to the left, likewise. After two minutes of zigzagging, they were back to their original position.

St. Peter wasn't a man easily given to illusions. Like Falstaff, he knew only too well that honour hath no skill in surgery. The monster clearly only wanted Satan, and Peter would have been quite happy to leave them to it. His plan, indeed, involved Satan's destruction. But not here, and not this way. Besides, without help, he knew he couldn't possibly find the route through the Plain of Bones, or get George back to Dis even if he could. He would have to fight – on Satan's side! *No, no, no! That's unthinkable!*

And then he remembered that Lazara could fly!

"Lazara, why don't you fly to Dis and at least get help for George?"

But Lazara stamped her foot. "I ain't leavin' Lord Satan to be duffed up by nobody! Not that he's goin' to get duffed," she added with inextinguishable optimism, "but I ain't leavin' 'im anyways!"

"I applaud your attitude," Peter sneered, "but you can't help us here, and George…"

"'Oo says I can't 'elp?" demanded Lazara. "We'll soon see 'oo can 'elp 'oo!"

And the great St. Peter, mentally girding himself to enter in epic combat with a horrific monster of Hell, found himself, half a second later, lying flat on the ground, with one set of claws about to rip into his jugular vein, and another set so poised as to simultaneously skewer his rectum and perforate his scrotum.

"Lazara!" said Satan sharply, "down, girl, down!"

Lazara extended her claws just enough to convince Peter that he had come very near to becoming a colander, then released him. He no longer felt jealous of her passion for his friend.

Satan rubbed her vulva to calm her down, and apologised to Peter.

"Sorry about that. You may find our womenfolk a bit hot-blooded compared to yours, a trifle slash-happy. It's nothing personal, I assure you. She clearly is very fond of you, for it's no easy thing for a Saragash princess to refrain from gashing once the claws are out."

Princess? "I'm glad I have a place in her affections. But George will die if he doesn't get help soon. And," he added cunningly, "even if he doesn't, if his erection isn't sewn back on quickly, it may never rise to the ocasion again."

Lazara stifled a cry, and clutched the red handkerchief more tightly to her breast. How in Aphrodite's name, Peter wondered, had she been able to almost unman him without dropping her precious trophy?

At this point, the monster thumped the ground so hard that thousands of hell-ants came storming angrily out of their nests, and made his first utterance.

"Bug hungry!"

"He can talk!" exclaimed Peter.

"Bug *hungry*!"

"Good God, is he a child?"

"Will you *please* refrain from foul language in Hell! No, he's not a child, but he *is* a bit retarded."

"Bug *very* hungry!"

"Satan," said Peter carefully, "is there any connection between ourselves and this hunger he alludes to with such single-minded frequency?"

"Yes, a digestive one!" Satan replied shortly.

Peter moved back slightly. Now he came to think about it, aided by the bubbling sound of Bugrot's gastric juices, perhaps it wouldn't be so difficult after all to find the way through the Plain of

Bones without Satan's help.

Fear must have made him hallucinate, because he then imagined he heard Satan saying:

"Peter, the one he really wants is ... You may be able to get away. If I don't... I mean, only if I don't get away, would you...? If I tell you something... but this creature will be no problem for *me*! But if... but no one else must ever know..."

Satan avoiding his eyes, stammering and lost for words? *Wake up, Peter!*

"If you want to tell me something, do it quickly." Peter said. "No one else will know."

"Swear by the Oath of the Twisted Testicle!"

"I will not swear by any stupid testicle! I just gave you my word."

"Just your word?" Now Satan did look at him, utterly bemused. "Nothing else?"

"Bug very hungry *now*!" The monster was much closer.

Satan shut his eyes for a second, and shook his head as if freeing his mind of clinging cobwebs of memory. He flung off his cloak, revealing a pitch-black body, still immensely powerful, but criss-crossed with jagged scars and deeply gouged wounds. What shocked Peter most, though, were the wings, or what was left of them. One was sheered down almost to the shoulder blade, the other half-wing, tattered and torn, hung like the sail of a phantom ship wrecked in some storm beyond memory. Satan noticed his expression.

"You're wondering how I got to the Garden of Eden? With these, with these and my will! There was a herb there that Eve found, and they began to heal, before... But now they hang truly useless. They..." His voice trailed away.

"Bug *eat* now!" *I knew he was leading up to that!*

"Tell her I built her palace..." Satan began – and then Bugrot attacked.

Everything happened so fast that later Peter could only remember a jumble of details: a whirling of black and red as the devils clashed; the crunch of bone; one of Bugrot's ears ripped off; Satan crashing to the ground with screams of agony; Bugrot clutching his eyes as Lazara swooped in; Satan leaping back into the attack; Lazara twisting on the ground; himself unable to obey his own logic, joining the fray, shouting furiously, aiming puny blows that only made the opponent scratch and giggle; all of them finally lying on the ground in a welter of blood and pain and temporary oblivion.

He came to to see Bugrot squatting in front of them with a knife and fork in his hands. *This is not a good sign.*

"We almost showed 'im wot for!" *What spirit that girl has!*

"Bug eat *at last!*"

You thought to alter the whole history of the Afterlife, and all you'll alter is the colour of a monster's faeces!

"What we need is a *deus* – or even, if you insist, a *diabolus* – *ex machina*," he said to his fellow *plat du jour*, who was groaning beside, and partly underneath, him. "If only George had been his usual self!"

And right on cue, St. George appeared behind the unsuspecting monster, and brought a huge rock down on his head! Bugrot, as is usual in such cases, fell forward in a heap, while George, wobbling on his feet, peered among the tangle of bodies, saying anxiously "Peter?"

****

" 'Ow did you know 'e were ticklish?" asked Lazara. "You're awfully clever!"

Peter somewhat resented his most powerful blows being classified as tickles; so that was why Bugrot had been giggling!

"Yes, well, one has to use a few stratagems in a tight corner," he muttered crossly.

They were straggling back towards the Plain of Bones again. The camaraderie of those first few moments when they had struggled to their feet had passed. Satan was clearly suffering under the double humiliation of having been beaten by Bugrot, and saved by a *saint*. Within a few minutes of their rescue, he was saying things like: "Don't think I'm not grateful to George, though his intervention, of course, wasn't absolutely necessary. But Bugrot does show a certain bungling promise as a fighter, and I have to admit I'd taken one or two heavy knocks myself, but, of course, in the end I'd have won..."

Buffoon! Peter was more irritated by Satan's ridiculousness

179

than he could easily account for. It wasn't only that they'd just shared a common danger. He realised that he'd earlier been subtly influenced by little details, by their shared admiration for Raphael, by Satan's obvious affection for Charon the Boatman, by the unquestioning adoration of Lazara, and especially by the way Satan had helped him carry George. Well, that debt was more than repaid now. *Vain idiot! And that nonsense about Eve and some palace! He never even met her! The Whiteguard caught him as soon as he set foot in the Garden, took him to God, and then hurled him back into space. Well, it just makes it all the easier to do what I have to do.*

Something still bothered him, though. Bugrot. The fact that, whatever Satan might have said to Yomyael and Amazyarak about the wisdom of attacking sleeping enemies, he had left the unconscious monster relatively unharmed, restricting himself to plunging his knife and fork deep into his backside. Peter wasn't pleased to find out that, beneath all the conceit and capriciousness, his proposed victim also had a sense of honour. Neither did Satan complain once about his wounds, though from the spasms of pain that sometimes crossed his face, Peter suspected he had more than one bone broken.

He himself, despite the psychotic goblin wreaking havoc inside his skull with an egg-whisk wrapped in barbed wire, had escaped lightly: he still had two arms, two legs, indeed all his limbs and organs, and all, give or take a few inches, in the same places as before. Lazara, too, seemed to have escaped miraculously with a few cuts and bruises.

George, however, was in a very bad way. Only the *in extremis* situation of his friend had lent him the energy to move against Bugrot. Lazara had taken the opportunity to rebind the stump of his erection, using yet another piece of her tunic, of which, to her obvious satisfaction, so little remained that a fig leaf by comparison would have seemed an overcoat, and the thigh wound had stopped bleeding. But he'd already lost so much blood that it was all he could do now to totter along between Peter and Satan.

Somehow they finally reached the Plain of Bones again. But it was clear they would never be able to cross it before it became too dark to travel, and Peter half expected Satan to suggest that they should sleep here, and face the menace of the Bones in the morning. Satan did indeed hesitate, but then continued on into the Plain: perhaps he'd been thinking, like Peter, that Bugrot by now would be recovered and feeling *extremely* peckish. Very soon, however, Peter realised that they weren't on the same path they'd used earlier: this one was leading north, almost at right angles, it seemed, to the previous one.

This path proved to be much shorter, and they emerged from the Plain before it was completely dark. Perhaps that was why Satan had chosen it. But Charon and the Acheron must now be almost as far away as when they had entered the Plain. Was there another point to cross the river and reach Dis?

But Satan began to follow a course which kept the Acheron well to their left. Peter, concerned about George, finally protested.

Satan kept on walking, and it was at least a minute before he answered.

"I am taking us to a place where George can rest, where we can all rest. We will be there soon."

His voice was unnaturally flat and strained. "I suspected we might meet Bugrot after I spoke to Charon. And I thought of turning back. Does that surprise you? But I found I *couldn't* turn back, I couldn't run. I think you understand, because you didn't run, either."

Do I tell him I didn't run only because I had nowhere to run to? Peter glanced sideways furtively, but it was now too dark to make out Satan's expression.

"And now I owe my life to your friend!" His voice was bitter, ironical. "Why pretend any more? Bugrot is invincible, even Moloch could never beat him. So it is no shame." His voice said exactly the opposite. "But George has to rest tonight, or he will die, and it would have been impossible to follow the trail through the Plain at night. So I am taking you to a place where George can rest."

After a short silence: "No one is ever allowed there now. No one. But I have a debt to pay." Another silence, then, in a voice so low, Peter hardly caught the words: "And if you are right about the Apocalypse, I myself will never see it again."

They had come to the top of a slight incline, and once again, as when they had reached the Pit of the Beast, Satan stopped. But this time, instead of exultation in his voice, there was such grief that Peter shuddered.

" '*My name is Ozymandias, king of kings:*
Look on my works, ye Mighty, and despair!' "

181

Peter looked out over a valley of grisly eldritch hue, where twisted bushes snarled and crackled, boulders heaved and hissed before spitting out smouldering fragments. And, lit by these fires, in the very midst of this cauldron, like a broken insect on the flattened corpse of this dead land, the ribs and bones of a huge edifice that must once have thrown an awesome shadow over the desolation. A few gaunt pillars still stood, etched black against the fires, stretching painfully up as if to escape the torment beneath them. And between them, massive blocks of stone still rasping of some eviscerated splendour, silently shrieking of a vast conception torn apart by its own audacity, and here petrified for eternity. Lying in Hell, it yet seemed not of Hell; but nor could it ever have been of Heaven, for there was an infernal vehemence, a pulsation of eternal violence in these stones.

"I built it for her, and she did not come." The voice so old. So empty.

"The Forbidden Zone!" breathed Lazara.

Satan looked at her, touched her cheek with a hand still covered with his own blood.

"Yes, Lazara, your grandfather helped me to build it. Of all those who laboured here, only he still lives. Two to share the secret: Mephistopheles and I. And now there are five, including two saints!"

Laughter made of ashes. He began to walk towards the ruins. Peter held back: they would be burnt to death in there! Satan said, without turning, "I tell you, there is shelter there."

Reluctantly, Peter followed, Lazara helping him to support George. *Mephistopheles! High Chieftain of the Saragashim, Christ's Tempter – and Lazara's grandfather! So her bringing us breakfast was no caprice: Mephistopheles, through her, is watching me!*

And now, as they passed through the murderous heat to reach the broken pillars and stones, came one more shock.

Can a fantasy undo the very laws of nature?

The stones were cool! Even the air between them was cool! The heat hissed and shimmered around them, lunged and darted forward, but fell back as if before an invisible wall. Peter ran his hands over the stones, pressed his forehead against them, sank down beside them in weariness, with George almost collapsing on top of him.

Satan stalked like a black ghost among the ruins, spectral, phantasmal. He communed with his memories, head down.

Peter's eyes were beginning to close. So cool. So comfortable. 'Tell her I built her palace.' *So he really did expect Eve to come to Hell! The poor deluded fool really expected her to come!* Yes, everyone in Heaven knew Eve had eaten the apple, *but how could Satan have known that then?*

Was that George already snoring? He would recover, George was strong. At last, he could sleep...

He jerked himself awake. *Fool! You have a new weapon! Use it!*

****

"What do you see?"

"A ruined building in a valley, surrounded by fire and desolation," said God.

"Ah, the Ice Palace! So Lucifer has let your Peter see the Ice Palace."

"Not *my* Peter!" God corrected him crossly. "He's an utter scoundrel!"

"But isn't that exactly what you're relying on?"

"Don't remind me! And that doesn't make him any the less an utter scoundrel!" He stopped and glared. "And what do you think you're smiling at?"

"Oh, nothing," said Raphael.

Chapter Eighteen
FISHER OF DEVILS

It was the place. The impossible coolness, the eerie silence, the memories trapped in stone. Gazing up at Hell's moon white and stark above him, seeing its light butchered into ghostly forms by the jutting stones, St. Peter felt a sense of desolation, of uncomprehended grief so long suppressed. A few yards away, George was sleeping soundly, his massive body hardly obscured by the slight Saragash girl lying with her head on his chest. *Ah, George, you have no questions, you seek no answers; yet are you really more empty than me? And that fool Satan. Could I ever have done what he has done, held a ridiculous, pathetic dream since almost the beginning of time? Why do I feel so hollow?*

It was the place. It was that figure, now bleached by moonlight, now swallowed by blackness, now pacing up and down furiously, now motionless with the head sunk on the chest. Peter tried to replace the sensation of desolation by anger. *So maybe the angels lied to us. Maybe he really did meet Eve in Eden. Maybe he did love her. So what?* Who did *not* love her? Who did not feel an ache, an unsatisfied longing, whenever they came near her? What was it St. Francis had said such a long time ago? *As if she had a bit of God trapped in her?* Eve, and her sea-green eyes, and her midnight hair, the unreachable fantasy that mocked the dreamer with his own inadequacy. So maybe Satan too had heard the call: *So what?*

As if to test Peter's determination, as if he could bear no longer to be alone with his memories, Satan at last ceased his phantasmal vigil, and came to sit beside him, the harsh moonlight striking the scarred face, the jutting nose, the full, disdainful lips that no longer seemed disdainful.

It's only the place. Peter reminded himself of what was at stake, forced himself to probe at once with the unexpected new weapon. *He'll never be so receptive again!*

"So you built this place for Eve? Maybe it's as well she didn't come."

No response, but he felt the Dark Lord's eyes upon him.

"Even in Heaven..." he went on, then broke off.

184

The figure beside him still didn't move. Had he heard? Then:

"Is something wrong with her?" The same flat, bleak voice – but no, not the same.

"The Dinosaur, too – the Old One, I mean, from the Garden – has been losing his strength. Gabriel used to wrestle with him for fun, but recently he's pretended to be too busy, in order not to embarrass his old friend."

"What is wrong with Eve?" The voice much sharper this time.

"Nobody really knows. But a lot of the Old Ones don't seem to be quite themselves lately. Francis had an idea..." He stopped again.

"What idea?"

"Oh, I think it's nonsense. Don't you think we ought to sleep?" He yawned mightily.

"What did Francis say?" Menace now.

"Oh, something about they *are* the oldest souls in Heaven... but that's nonsense. Souls are immortal, God wouldn't make that kind of mistake."

A long silence. *Why doesn't he ask about Eve again? Because he's afraid of the answer. Give it time to sink in. But time's running out.*

"Why is it so cool here?" he asked after a time.

"What?" Satan had obviously been following his own train of thought.

"These stones, they're cool, cold almost – and yet, over there, fire and brimstones."

"If you knew *how* we built this place..." Satan began, before relapsing into moody silence again.

Peter waited a moment. "You aren't going to tell me?"

No answer. *Think of something. I'm so tired...*

"Who's Bugrot? Surely he isn't a Saragash?" He didn't really expect an answer.

"You may as well know, since even if *I* didn't ride the Beast, *he* probably would. He's the leader of the Nefilim."

"The Nefilim?"

"Mutants. Half Saragash, half Companion."

"But angels can't reproduce!"

"*Companions*, I said, devils, not angels! But you're right, when we mate with Saragashim, they don't reproduce. Except once.

185

More than a hundred years ago, there was a great Cosmic storm, and suddenly any Saragash who had mated with a Companion started having children. This period of fecundity didn't last long, but it was enough to produce nearly twenty thousand Nefilim. I still remember the first child being born. Horrible!"

Good, I've got him talking. "Like Bugrot?"

"Worse! It came out all gold and shining! Just like... just like a little angel!" He almost retched, and an undigested hellroach leapt out of his mouth and scuttled away, chuckling to itself. "Luckily – or unluckily, as it turned out – we realised what was happening. Ontogeny recapitulates phylogeny."

"Of course it does!" said Peter, baffled.

"The babies were merely reliving their evolutionary stage – the primitive angelic phylum – before progressing to the more advanced devil form."

"You mean, like a tadpole into a frog?"

"More like a chrysalis into a butterfly."

"Oh, of course, far more apt."

"Within a few weeks they seemed all right, a nice healthy black, claws forming. But then, after about fifteen years, they changed again, grew bigger, and... became something like Bugrot. We weren't too concerned, as they had very little intelligence – as you may have noticed – but one day, they all of one accord headed out beyond the Great Lake."

"And then what happened?"

"Nothing. They just stayed there."

"Bugrot didn't."

"Bugrot ... is looking for revenge."

"Why?"

Satan didn't answer immediately. When he did speak, Peter couldn't see the slightest connection with his question.

"Tell me, Peter, do you know what happened to Beelzebub?"

Taken by surprise, Peter answered quite truthfully: "No, I don't. They say he was in Heaven about the time I myself arrived, but he disappeared again almost at once."

"You know he came to Hell once?"

Peter answered cautiously: "Yes, I've heard that. Maybe that's why we aren't allowed to publicly mention his name. One of Michael's little rules."

"Michael!" sneered Satan. "What was he before Beelzebub left the way open for him?"

Peter saw his chance and took it. "But Michael was always one of the Seven, wasn't he?" he asked innocently. "And he's giving Raphael enough trouble now. Especially now that God's never around."

"Never around?"

"Almost never. He leaves everything to the High Council. They say he's too busy planning what to do after the Apocalypse. He takes no interest in anything, not even the Flame Cannon. Why, he hasn't even bothered to do anything about the copies of the *History* circulating."

Satan tensed. " 'History'? What do you mean? What History?"

"Oh, nothing. The point is, God's so preoccupied with..."

"Do you mean *the* History? The *History of the Great Rebellion*?"

"Er, yes," replied Peter, sounding flustered. "But as I was saying..."

"But of course, it makes sense! Truth cannot be forever suppressed, even in Heaven!"

Ah, this is the Satan I know! But why has he reverted back to type so quickly? Because he can't face his memories. These stones only speak of his defeat. He would rather dream of impossible victories.

"Come on, now!" he said, forcing a light laugh. "I'm not saying a lot of it isn't true. But Belial throwing mountains? God hiding trembling inside a volcano? The Lucifer Society are a bunch of credulous idiots who've got nothing better to do than daydream. Just because they're fed up with Michael and the Virgin..."

"The Lucifer Society? *The Lucifer Society?* Yes, yes, of course, why didn't I guess? They had to see through the hollowness of the Tyrant's rule sooner or later!"

'Follow me, and ye shall be fishers of men.' He hadn't mentioned devils.

"I told you, they're just a bit fed up, that's all. The angels don't mind being ruled by God, or by Archangels, but a mere woman...! Pure escapism, that's all it is! They feed themselves on false rumours, and try to kid themselves they're true." *Like you!*

He feared he might have gone too far, but Satan seemed quite willing to gobble up his worms as soon as they entered the water.

187

"Pah!" snorted Satan after a few moments' silence. "What does it matter, anyway? I escaped from Heaven a long time ago, and I don't intend to go back! The Luciferians can come here if they want, and they'd be welcome! But you won't ever get me going back there!"

Right out of the water, the hook visible through his gills, and he's trying to pretend the bait doesn't interest him! If only I could find some way to mention the Flame Cannon again, he missed his cue the first time round; but it's too risky, the rest has to sink in first.

Satan seemed to take control of himself. "Anyway, it probably is a lot of silly rumours, made up, as you say, because people are fed up. Even if I wanted to, there's nothing I could do about it now."

"Yes, because in a few more days, unless you take my advice and sit tight here, and cancel the Apocalypse..."

Satan remained silent, and Peter was aware he had used up his last drop of energy. He'd done enough. As a throbbing heaviness came over him, he didn't even try to fight it.

****

He woke up to find Lazara shaking him.

"Blimey, Lord Peter, 'ow you do sleep! George 'ere's not so poorly now, an' Lord Satan's waiting. 'Ere, I've got sommat for you to eat."

The 'sommat' turned out to be some aggrieved-looking rodents squirming in her hand, but Peter hadn't eaten in twenty-four hours. "When in Rome..." he excused himself.

In the early dawn, the place looked different. It had lost its uncanny, phantasmal quality. The deep erosion of the stone was now all too visible, and the area was littered with rubble he hadn't noticed the night before. It was now just a ruin. A remarkable ruin, yes, but still just a ruin. Like he who had conceived it.

Satan, too, was back to his old self, or one of his old selves, little trace remaining of the suffering being of the night before. *Good. It's easier that way.*

And George, as Lazara had said, was indeed much stronger. His powers of recovery were amazing. Peter felt more secure seeing him standing there straight and *almost* firm, regarding him with his usual unthinking trust, and already – slowly, it was true – polishing the hilt of his sword.

Of course! The Four Horses of the Apocalypse! Seeing George there with his sword reminded Peter of the Beast's Pit: those four creatures of different colours must have been the Four Horses. The realisation brought home to him how little time he really had.

As soon as they left the Forbidden Zone, the heat of Hell hit them again with its full fury. Peter knew he had to play at least one more card before they got back to Dis and to Belial. And, it seemed, to Mephistopheles.

Satan led them back through the Plain of Bones – George scowled and looked rebellious, but this time followed closely in his wake – until they intersected the trail they had taken the day before. As the Acheron came in sight again, Peter took a deep breath and made his move. He hoped Lazara was too far away to be able to hear.

"Tell me," he said casually, "what do you know about Limbo?"

"The Way Station, of course," answered Satan, looking surprised. "And it's also where they keep people too intelligent to go to Heaven, but too stupid to come here."

"And did you also know the Protoplasmic Factory is there?"

"Where they make the bodies to come here? Of course."

"Not just the bodies that come here. *All* the bodies."

"There's not much difference."

"You aren't listening: I said *all* the bodies."

"What are you trying to say?"

"Not just the bodies already in use, but all the bodies that will be needed for the Apocalypse. Bodies for everybody now in Limbo; bodies for everybody now on Earth; and bodies for everybody now in Hell!"

Satan stared at him. "I repeat, what are you trying to say?"

Peter licked his lips, or rather, scraped his dry tongue over them.

"Satan, I'm not a fool. And neither are you." *Both very questionable statements!* "I've told you why you shouldn't go ahead with the Apocalypse. But what hard evidence have I really been able to show you? Only the copies of the Cosmic Tablets. And the Book of Revelations, of course, but as you said yourself, that stuff *could* have been written by anybody. The rest is simply my word. And why should you accept that?"

Satan smiled ironically. "You *are* a saint!"

189

"Well, I've been thinking about how to give you more proof. After all, if I fail to convince you, my whole journey will have been in vain. But I think I *can* give you more proof. Let me admit right away I myself haven't seen the bodies stored in Limbo. And nor has Tobias. But he keeps his ear to the ground, he *knows* the bodies are there in the Vaults."

He paused, not for effect, but because some enterprising bug had scrambled through his beard, and was nibbling at his cheek.

"We've often wondered," he went on, "why those bodies are kept such a secret. The saints' bodies are cloned quite openly. Can you think of any possible reason?"

As Satan didn't answer, he went on dramatically: "*To prevent you from learning about them by accident!* Because if the bodies of your present subjects are really there – I mean, clones of their own original bodies, not the low-grade replacement bodies they're sent here with – wouldn't that prove what I've been saying? That God plans to free all the souls in Hell? If he didn't, the bodies wouldn't exist, would they?"

Satan was staring at him, eyes wide open, and nodding slowly.

Peter was aware that the sweat was running down his body in rivulets – and not just from the heat. At least that damn bug would get drowned! The next few minutes might well decide his fate. He knew that the suggestion he was about to make would have been rejected out of hand the day before. But many things had happened since then, and by now Satan must be almost ready to put his head in the noose.

But what if Belial decided to intervene? Or Mephistopheles?

Chapter Nineteen
BELIAL ISN'T FOOLED

"You helped to carry that dangerous lunatic back here! When you could have left him in the Pit, and have done with him for ever!"

Belial's dandruff now swirled in violent eddies around his body instead of making its usual stately descent to the ground. His plucked-chicken skin wrinkled like that of a jacket potato left in the oven too long. His snail's-tracery lips were so tightly compressed they resembled the EEG of a person long dead.

He was, in short, upset.

"Pah! A few seconds, and it would all have been over! But now just think of his agony when we operate on his member! We'll operate, of course, while he's fully conscious. We'll tell Peter we can't successfully sew on a lopped-off erection to a flaccid parent member – it wouldn't fit."

"But he's dangerous!"

"Exactly! That's why I saved him. He could be dangerous to others, too."

Belial stopped pacing suddenly. His skin, taken by surprise, stretched forward under the force of inertia before squelching back on to his cheekbones.

"The Nefilim!"

"Belial, can you imagine George and Moloch together...?"

"But how can we be sure he would fight *for* us and not *against* us?"

"Gratitude. And if we give him back his erection, he'll be even more in our debt. As will Peter."

"Sire, I must ask you again, don't trust that Peter as far as you can skewer him!"

Satan gave his mentor an indulgent smile. "Such a worrier, aren't you? I tell you, I've got him fooled entirely. He's so innocent, it makes my mouth water! He *thinks* he's clever, but he's let out a few things, quite without realising it... Belial, we could defeat Heaven, wc...!"

Oh no, thought Belial, he's back to that! *His vanity will get us all destroyed!* "Sire, will you once and for all stop daydreaming?"

191

"It's not a daydream! Listen! Heaven's completely disorganised! Michael and Raphael are at each other's throats! The Council's being bossed around by a virgin and a baby! The angels are breaking up into factions! It's anarchy up there! What's more, most of the angels want me back as their leader!"

"WHAT!"

"And what," snarled Satan, his body swelling like an amorous frog's, "do you find odd about that?"

Belial said quickly: "There's nothing odd at all about people *wanting* you back – of course they do! I was just a bit surprised they'd say it openly – and that Peter would tell you."

Satan relaxed, and deflated. "He didn't *intend* to tell me, of course. He let it slip, and then tried to cover his mistake. But you know I'm not fooled so easily. What's more, in trying to cover up his blunder, he let out that everybody's secretly reading our *History*, and that there are clandestine Lucifer Societies all over Heaven."

"That's very good news indeed," said Belial, trying hard to look convinced. *Peter is lying. But why?* "But the real problem is the Flame Cannon, and as long as the Usurper controls that..."

"Ah, but I have a surprise for you, old friend," Satan exclaimed. "*The Cannon may not be working!* Peter began to say something about God not bothering with them, but I didn't take him up on it, in order not to put him on his guard. But I *have* tricked him into agreeing to get me into Limbo..."

"*Limbo?* In the name of the Perforated Twisted Testicle, whatever do you want to go to Limbo for!"

"Because by pretending to go along with his plan, I spend more time with him, and worm more secrets out of him. Especially about what condition the Cannon are in, where they're positioned, who's responsible for them... But not only that, there's so many useful bits of information I can pick up."

'Pretending to go along with his plan'? **His** *plan?*

"And there's another reason." Satan repeated what Peter had said about the cloned bodies in the Vaults. "Absolute proof, don't you agree?"

"I suppose so."

"And if the bodies aren't there, it's proof that he *has* been lying."

"True. But he'd be a fool to *prove* he's been lying."

"Exactly! So if he *is* lying, can you think of any reason why he'd want to go there?"

"Of course. To get out of Hell, and make his escape."

"That was my first thought. So we keep George here as hostage!"

Belial was impressed. This was more like the old Satan! But...

"Surely, if it came to it, he'd leave George behind to save his own skin."

"I don't think he'd leave his friend in the lurch."

"He denied Numbskull Junior three times," Belial pointed out.

"And then cut off Malchus' ear to defend him!" retorted Satan.

"Sire..."

"Yes, I know. I simply read up on him a bit: know thine enemy! Moreover, if he's *not* lying, which seems the more likely, if the bodies really are there, we could, if necessary, take *them* hostage too!"

"*What!*"

Satan was much more pleased with this '*What*' than the earlier one. "You don't really think I'm going to take the Tyrant's treachery lying down, do you? If Peter's told us the truth, we'll never be safe. But with the unwitting help of that fool, I can find out just *where* the bodies are being kept. After that, we can mount an expedition, and capture the bodies, or destroy them, or whatever. That'll make the Tyrant think twice!"

"But that's an excellent idea!" Belial was being sincere.

"Yes, it is, isn't it?" answered Satan smugly. "*Now* do you see how I've been toying with that hairy saint all along? Moreover, going to Limbo will keep Peter out of the way while you continue the preparations for the attack on Earth. Or Heaven, as the case may be."

"Sire, I still think it would be folly to even *think* of attacking Heaven..."

"Well, maybe so, maybe so! We can decide on that when I've squeezed Peter dry of everything he knows."

Belial began to say something, changed his mind. Instead, he said quietly: "Why is Mephistopheles interviewing Peter, and not me?"

Satan looked a bit embarrassed. "Because he asked me, before I came to see you. Lazara must have told him about the trip, and he said he wanted to check some minor details. You know how careful he is."

"*I* could have done that."

"Of course you could, and probably better. But Toffy got in first and... well, you know he's got much more experience with humans than we do. But that's not important. Belial, Heaven could be ours!"

"Yes," said Belial, and there was no joy in his voice, "Heaven could be yours."

****

So was it to start all over again?

Belial lay back on his bed, and closed his eyes wearily...

First it had been Beelzebub. After the defeat in Heaven, Belial had consoled himself with the thought that he would at least be second-in-command in this harsh place they had come to. When he learned the terrible truth – that although Beelzebub refused to raise his hand against his Maker, he had yet chosen to follow his friend to Hell itself – he was consumed with sick, impotent rage. But it was a rage that he carefully hid, for Lucifer, henceforth to be called Satan, was so moved by Beelzebub's loyalty that he wept unashamedly as he publicly embraced his early companion.

With Beelzebub here, he, Belial, would simply be tolerated, as he had been in Heaven. He set out to ruin his rival.

His task was made easier by the fact that many of the Fallen Angels also resented Beelzebub's presence. What right did one who had refused to fight in the Rebellion have to rule over true warriors? They resented, too, his brightness, for he had not been blasted by the Flame Cannon, nor seared in the Great Brimstone Lake. They came, with Belial's help, to see his grand gesture as stupidity, if not worse. The stories began to circulate: was it credible that Beelzebub had *chosen* to leave Heaven, had he not rather been hurled out in disgust by the loyal angels who knew he had been afraid to fight in the War? Or, conversely, had he not perhaps been *sent* to spy on the rebels in case they planned a counter attack?

Belial made sure these rumours got back to Satan, then grew hot in Beelzebub's defence.

But Satan proved surprisingly resistant to this insidious assault. What Belial could not understand, because it was not in him to understand, was Satan's capacity to *love*. His yearning to *be loved* he could comprehend, for he himself had yearned in vain for the love of Lucifer. But Satan's love for Beelzebub – and, despite everything, for Raphael – was something Belial could only recognise, without understanding. Satan never doubted that his friend had left Heaven to join him, because this was exactly the kind of exotic gesture he himself might have made had their positions been reversed.

Satan's loyalty only increased Belial's hatred. It was no longer just thwarted ambition. It was the stomach-gnawing detestation of the ignoble for the noble, the eternal cry of rage of one who has never been loved against one who has been loved too much. He took an uncharacteristic risk: he forged Council of Seven papers which seemed to show that Beelzebub was in fact an informer, and left them one night where Satan would find them. He heard the shouting and cries of exasperation and fury when Satan went to confront Beelzebub with this 'evidence', and he saw the flash of golden wings as Beelzebub hurtled into the sky. Never to be seen again.

The next few days were dangerous ones. Satan was ominously quiet, endlessly studying the false document. Belial begged him to let him see it, and quickly declared that in his opinion it was a forgery, probably brought to Hell by an angel who wished to punish Beelzebub for abandoning Heaven. He wept with Satan.

And became undisputed second-in-command. For more than four thousand years, his position remained virtually unchallenged. The defeated angels metamorphosed more and more into devils until they all became a more or less uniform black. As for Satan, the fire had gone out of him, and he became a shell of petty vanity, talking hollowly of carnage and revenge. Belial didn't mind: while Satan was busy with his fantasies, he left the reins of power in the hands of his subordinate. Indeed, Belial encouraged him in his unreality, and it was he who first suggested the writing of the *History of the Great Rebellion*. And in fact the false *History* did a lot of good in Hell, giving the broken angels the warmth of false memories. The myth of the Invincible Companions who had deliberately forsaken the soft living of Heaven, healed the sickness of humiliation, and even brought a kind of peace to the outcasts.

Then, one day, two Saragash Fliers returned with a report that was to change Hell for ever.

God had performed a new Creation!

At once the grey pragmatism of Belial's rule shook under the impact of this news. Satan became galvanised. A world that could be reached, if only by the Fliers, and a few devils who still retained vestiges of wings, such as Satan himself. At last, an opportunity for vengeance!

It was more than ten days before he returned, almost mortally exhausted. He would never fly again. But Belial noticed with fear and loathing the glittering flashes that now came from his body. With Satan had returned something of Lucifer.

Much of it could be explained by the Treaty of Eden. God's new creatures to be given to Hell, with no conditions whatsoever! "I didn't force him to give me *all* of them," Satan explained, "because the chance that some of them may get away will give edge to the excitement." And they could do with them whatever they liked! The periodic pogroms instigated by Belial against the Saragashim had provided some outlet for the frustrated rage of the devils, but with them the chances of losing an eye or a liver were extremely high. With the new victims, the possibilities would be endless.

But this didn't explain Satan's quiet moods, the sudden touches of gentleness that sent a premonitory shiver down Belial's spine, the abstraction when he would gaze in the direction of the new planet, and in his expression there would be... what? It reminded him of occasions in Heaven when Lucifer, Raphael, and Beelzebub had been together, but it was different...

Nor did it explain the secret building. Not a single devil employed in its construction, only Saragashim. And all sworn to secrecy. Away to the east, in the direction of the Lake. A huge building, impregnable fortress walls, keeps and turrets, crenellations and towers – Belial's spies gradually picked up the details. But once the outer walls were completed, security became even stricter, and only the Fliers under Mephistopheles went inside. And even after the sounds of construction had ceased, the mysterious Fliers were still spotted entering at night.

Meanwhile, the first souls from Eden had started to arrive:

three quite nasty fish, a strange funnel-shaped plant, and a violent-looking man called Cain, who proved to be a merry fellow, and immediately slew a passing Saragash. Rooms were prepared in Satan's palace. So the mysterious building was not for them, then.

Other souls arrived, more and more of them human, and all received joyfully. Despite the talk of doing terrible things to them when Satan had first returned, there was now little thought of harming them, for had they not *chosen* to join the brave Companions? And were not some of them delightfully wicked?

And then, after a hundred years, a letter came from God.

Satan gave one tremendous scream, locked himself away, and didn't rise again until the third day. He appeared at his door, utterly and frighteningly calm, though he looked as if he had been in a wrestling match with a hysterical octopus.

"I'd like someone to invent a thumbscrew, a rack, and an Iron Maiden," he said. "Before midnight. Oh yes, and would someone please bring me a cup of tea?"

And that was that. He never spoke about the incident, or allowed others to. The Fliers no longer travelled by night, and the mysterious edifice began to decay and crumble away.

And torture began. Not Cain. Though he was always very wroth and his countenance forever falling, he continued to enjoy all his former privileges for some time, until one night he went too far, and assaulted two Fliers who had also been drinking. And that was the end of him. The two inebriates fled beyond the Brimstone Lake, but Satan, after a moment of rage, suddenly smiled, with no humour, and said: "And so it ends."

Not Cain. But for the other immigrants, it became hell. Surprised at first, the Companions soon got into the swing of things, and the first Symphony of Pain award was bestowed amidst applause that was almost as loud as the winning screams had been.

Belial rode this storm as he had ridden others. After the arrival of the letter from God, Satan once again relinquished day-to-day control back to his Prime Sinister. Although it was clear that Cain had now become the favourite, he was too busy drinking to worry about power..

When Cain died, there still remained the threat of Mephistopheles. There was clearly a close bond between Satan and the young Saragash chieftain, especially with the building of the secret building, that gave Belial many bitter sleepless nights. The threat became even greater when Mephistopheles organised the Guild of Tempters, and recruited his Fliers to seduce souls on Earth to counterbalance the thunderous competition of the Old Testament prophets. He became more important than anybody to the economic and cultural life of Hell, which now revolved almost exclusively round the damned souls. Luckily for Belial, Mephistopheles concerned himself only with Earth affairs. Belial put up with it. He had no choice.

The Jesus Affair gave him a scare. If Mephistopheles had pulled it off! Fancy daring to Tempt the son of God! What a scoop that would have been! But what a disaster, too, Belial thought: even stupid, head-in-the-Cloud, tolerant God wouldn't have let that go unpunished!

Although the Tempters had nothing to do with it, the Crucifixion led almost directly to the depositing, late one night, of a tiny, cuddly creature which, they were told, was the Beast of the Apocalypse. Belial and Satan watched it contentedly lapping some milk, and wondered whether God had finally gone round the bend. The next day, when the cuddly creature was twice the size, Satan was jubilant, but Belial remained uneasy. The potentially dangerous idea of somehow using the Beast to get back to Heaven began to play a part in Satan's fantasies. Belial successfully fought these ideas until one day a saint arrived and coolly asked Satan to cancel the Apocalypse.

Beelzebub. The Eden affair. Cain. Mephistopheles. Belial had surmounted these, and other obstacles, one by one. And now everything he had worked for was about to be overthrown.

For after his last talk with Satan, Belial was absolutely convinced that Peter's sole purpose was to *lure Satan into attacking Heaven, not Earth, with the Beast*! He knew that unless he acted quickly, they were all doomed.

****

His decision wasn't taken lightly, and he even called in Mammon, so that he could thrash out his ideas with him.

Mammon, *'the least erected spirit that fell/ From Heaven...'*

198

Milton had been punished for that, of course, but it was the only time Mammon stirred himself to do his own impaling. He was the Oblomov of Hell, with a fervent belief that since his body was immortal, it was vital not to wear it out. Possibly because of this conservation of energy, his mind was extremely sharp, and Belial often consulted him when in doubt.

He now told him about his recent conversation with their master.

"Now consider," he said, "the kind of person who 'let slip' all this information about Heaven being ripe for Satan's return. A man who was *crucified* rather than give up his faith. Would *you* have done that?"

Mammon looked affronted,

"The risk he took in coming here! Daring to join in the fight against Bugrot..."

"But Satan said..."

"...that *he* saved Peter and George. But do you really believe Satan has fallen so low as to defend a *saint*?" He didn't wait for an answer, since he knew full well that Mammon wouldn't even defend himself if he were given a guarantee that his death wouldn't put him out too much. "Now, I ask you, is such a man likely to break down and reveal Heaven's secrets before we've so much as skewered a single testicle? No, he came to Hell for one reason only..."

He paused dramatically. Mammon was torn between curiosity, which entailed the effort of asking what that reason was, and lethargy, which argued that Belial would reveal it, anyway. He chose the latter.

"He was sent!"

Mammon gasped with such force that he almost displaced an air molecule.

"And why? Because, far from being unprepared for us, God has been waiting for just this moment! The Flame Cannon rusty? More likely polished so bright you could see your own blackheads in them!"

"But why?" It was reckless, but Mammon couldn't wait.

"Because God, or Jesus, thinks we were responsible for the Crucifixion. Satan wasn't even there, but if you read the New Testament, you'll see Jesus had an *idée fixe* that he was fighting him all the time! A passing epileptic, a few misbehaved pigs, and he thought

199

Satan was inside! But God couldn't *prove* anything at the time, so he couldn't attack us then. So he sent us the Beast, and ensured we didn't destroy it while we could by promising Satan that he could ride it for the Apocalypse. And then, what better justification for destroying us than if we use that same Beast to attack Heaven?"

Mammon was galvanised into unwonted activity: he raised a whole finger.

"You've forgotten something," he said.

Belial waited: he knew Mammon only spoke if he had something important to say.

"Your whole theory depends on Peter persuading Satan to switch the attack from Earth to Heaven. And all in just a few days. How could they know it would work?"

He fell back exhausted.

"That's what I couldn't work out. Lazara gave me the clue."

"Lazara?"

"Yes, that insolent Saragash wench. I spoke to her before you came. On the way back from the Pit, *they stopped in the Forbidden Zone!"*

Mammon tried to say "So what?", but couldn't manage it after his former exertions.

"Now God *knows* Satan, just as we do. No doubt he told Peter to play on his ambition, his thirst for revenge, the danger of not having the Apocalypse, and so on. All very convincing, but they needed something else, something Satan *couldn't* resist. And the key is the Forbidden Zone! No one ever lived there. So it had to have been for someone he *expected* to come to Hell, but didn't. But who?"

Mammon was sitting bolt upright again.

"Until that letter came, nothing but the best would do for the new souls. Then everything changed. He went berserk. Tortured everybody. *Except Cain!* Cain still enjoyed all his privileges, though he was about as thick as Moloch on a bad day! I only found out later who Cain was. The son of Eve! *The first, the ONLY woman in Eden when Satan was there!"*

"But that's perverted!" objected Mammon.

"That letter must have told him that Eve wasn't coming to Hell."

"Yes, yes!" Mammon had actually risen to his feet. "And he expected her to come because she'd eaten the apple!" He fell back to

200

his chair.

"And now they've been to the Forbidden Zone. Lazara says Peter seemed surprised to see it, but of course he *would* pretend that. Perhaps he's brought some message from Eve for Satan. That's why he wanted to go to the Pit, to be alone with him, maybe even to ask to see the palace."

"But..."

"To reawaken Satan's old dreams. To take away his common sense. And it's worked. Satan wants to go to Limbo with Peter to pick up more information – and you can be sure he'll 'find out' enough to attack Heaven the moment he gets back. And that will be the end of us!"

"But what are we going to do?"

A smile spread across Belial's face like an insect across a rotting cabbage.

"We get the Nefilim to capture Satan and Peter in Limbo, and we get Bugrot to ride the Beast instead!"

Mammon's face looked as if a pair of compasses had formed it – his eyes and mouth made three huge circles of amazement.

"If Satan gets back from Limbo safely," Belial explained, "nothing will stop him going ahead with his suicidal plans. Why should he take us with him? If he doesn't get back, no one will connect it with us, or even with the Nefilim at first: it will be assumed Peter had laid a trap, and allowed the angels to capture him. Then when the Beast's Wings Open, we'll get the Reins to Bugrot, and induce the Nefilim to attack Heaven. They will, of course, be blasted right out of the sky. But since the attack will be none of our doing, God can't punish us for it.

"We'll have slipped out of God's trap – damned if we have the Apocalypse, damned if we don't – we'll have got rid of the Beast, we'll have got rid of the Nefilim, and we'll have stopped Satan from forcing us to commit suicide. And if Satan later escapes from the Nefilim in Limbo, he need never know that we were involved. Everything will go back to how it was."

Neither Belial nor Mammon mentioned the small fact that if the Nefilim caught Satan he wouldn't be left with enough limbs to escape. They would have enough problems getting past Moloch and Mephistopheles without having to worry about their consciences as well.

****

"That Belial is too clever," said God. "He could ruin everything."

"Then stop him," said Raphael. "Will you allow one being to destroy the Plan?"

"It is not a Plan," God rebuked him gently, "it is an Unfolding. I cannot interfere. Everything I create must be free to Unfold itself, or it will never be free of me."

"You have told me that the Shaping of the Beast was a mistake. Are others then to suffer because of your mistake?"

"Yes," whispered God, "and that is the ultimate tragedy of being a god: others pay the penalty for our mistakes: we cannot undo what we have done."

Chapter Twenty
MEPHISTOPHELES

"Prince Mephistopheles will be with you shortly, sir. Meanwhile, if there's anything I can do... My name is Arrabis."

The speaker was a tall Saragash, with dark penetrating eyes and sharply pointed ears, who moved with the same supple grace as Lazara, but was clearly much older. He was wearing a long white robe with a red sash and a stylised insignia on the breast depicting two hands proffering what seemed to be a ball or globe. He spoke with a gentle dignity which might have put Peter at his ease had he not been dreading the forthcoming interview.

In an effort to take his mind off the danger, and reflecting that he might learn something useful, he said:

"I've heard that when the Companions arrived, you sought to propitiate them with child sacrifices. I find this hard to believe."

Arrabis gave a quiet smile.

"Yes, that story is nonsense. It was a simple gesture of hospitality, not appeasement."

"You mean you really did sacrifice children! But whatever for?"

"They were hungry."

"But sacrificing hungry children is just as bad as..."

"Not the children. The Companions, or Aliens, as they were then called."

"You mean you gave them the children to eat!"

"What else was there to give them?"

Peter gazed at him speechlessly. He knew, of course, that the Saragashim had been cannibals when Michael's expedition had discovered them, but all the same...

Noticing his horrified expression, Arrabis said: "Have you not heard of the Enlightenment?"

Peter shook his head, and breathed a little easier: so this sacrificing of children had ended at some time, then.

"Tell me, if you will, about the Enlightenment."

Arrabis leaned back, and spoke of a time when his ancestors had roamed at will over the vast reaches of Sheol. In those days, he said, the tribes had warred incessantly among themselves, battling for the one source of food the pitiless planet provided.

Their own bodies.

"Barbaric, utterly barbaric. Eating someone completely unrelated – and usually tough and stringy, too, for they were warriors all. By mutual consent, most battles took place at three-day intervals, when both sides would have worked up a decent appetite. Nevertheless, the warriors' anticipation of a good meal was marred by the reflection that they stood as good a chance of *being* a meal as of *having* one. But then came the Enlightenment!"

Ah, he murmured, what a glorious tale that was! That night, so long ago, when a rough untutored warrior lay sorely wounded and weak from hunger in a cave, while outside, his enemies, flatulent with the more acidic portions of his friends, awaited only the dawn to complete their repast. With him, his infant daughter, weeping piteously. Lying there, he recalls all the years of war and misery, and can feel sorrow even for his foes outside, some of whom will probably be slain with parts of himself still unexcreted. And thus the wheel of death will swing round and ever round, inexorably squeezing out the lifeblood of the Saragashim trapped forever within its pitiless gyrations.

And a Vision comes to him. The end of hunger, the end of war, the brotherhood of Demon.

He holds his daughter in his battle-torn arms, and speaks the words which will come to be known throughout the Universe, though often distorted, or hidden and embedded in local cults and myths.

"You," he murmurs, brushing damp locks from her brow, "are my seed, which must not fall on barren ground. The fruit of my loins. And as man has sown, so verily shall he reap."

And on the morrow, strengthened by conviction and the flesh and blood of his daughter, he emerges from the cave, and approaches his enemies; and it is said that a mighty thunderclap heralded his approach, and bushes sprang into flame before him; and the others became his disciples and carried his message into the nethermost regions of the planet. The New Age had begun.

Peter, said Peter to himself, don't say anything.

"He ate his own child!" he burst out.

"Not all of her; some parts he shared with his enemies outside."

"They all ate the little girl!"

"It seems so simple in retrospect, doesn't it!"

"He murdered and ate his own child, and you call that Enlightenment!"

Arrabis frowned. "I see that you, like the Aliens, come here with false preconceptions. What is the whole purpose of reproduction, if not to ensure a constant supply of fresh food?"

"To propagate the race."

"Precisely. And that means to prevent its extinction through starvation. From constant war we moved to constant peace. What need to fight when you could peaceably grow your food in your own body? With the intense satisfaction of having earned your daily bread, first by the sweat of the groin, and then by the sweat of the brow?"

Peter gazed at his hands. *My nails need cutting.* Then he saw the flaw in the logic.

"If the Saragashim ate all their children, they'd be extinct in one generation!"

"Quite! We don't eat *all* of them. A litter may be anything up to five. Each couple can keep up to three children from each litter. It's entirely up to them whether they consume all three. Very few do. They frequently keep one to bring up with loving and tender care. The relationship between them and the child so favoured is extremely close, for the child is aware that a real sacrifice has been made for it."

"And the others?"

"All children over the three become common property, to feed those living below the bread line for some reason – illness, temporary infertility, and so on. Of course, if someone repeatedly has recourse to the Childpool, they'll eventually get eaten themselves."

"Ha! I thought you said it was barbarous to eat each other!"

"We don't: that is, we, the adults, don't eat them. They provide food for the children in the Pool: they have to eat too, you know." And he frowned, as if surprised at this lack of consideration for the children's needs.

Peter decided not to pursue the topic. Instead, he said:

"So you really did welcome the Companions, then."

205

"That," said Arrabis, "is another story. And not exactly as it is written in the *History*."

****

They fell in their thousands, huge bodies charred and burned, limbs grotesquely distorted, twisting and turning in a macabre aerial dance to the hideous music of their own screams. In their thousands, and their tens of thousands, they fell, plunging helplessly into the hissing cauldron of the Great Brimstone Lake, boiling spumes springing up where they struck, hanging in the tormented air like gleaming, tortured serpents. And as they fell, the awful reek of scorched flesh drifted over the unmeasured expanse of the Lake.

Yet they lived. Incredibly, the purple glitter of the waters cracked and split as the alien beings rose to the surface, and slowly heaved their way to the distant shore. It was as if the Lake were some huge rotting carcass writhing to the movement of monstrous maggots, a diseased skin pulsating with sickness and fever.

The Saragashim watched. By the end of the day, as the first Aliens neared the shore, a deadly array of tooth and talon stretched far back into the desert behind. On the shore itself, carried there from their fastnesses by the Fliers, such a gathering of chieftains as had never been seen. And towering above them all, Alramzar, direct descendant of the Enlightener, holding by the hand a small, sickly boy with deep sombre eyes that gazed unwaveringly at the Lake.

Deciding whether to deal death or life.

With the Enlightenment, the Saragashim had chosen the path of peace. But many now advocated death to the creatures so slowly and painfully approaching them. Monsters able to survive the Lake of Ultimate Parting, what could stop them once they had all emerged and were united? Better to kill them one by one as they dragged their bodies on the shore, destroy them while they were weak.

But others, among them Alramzar himself, argued that the glorious achievement of the Enlightenment must never be sullied by so vile and treacherous an act.

The question was still undecided when the first creature finally emerged. As the Lake spat viciously at the first prey ever to escape its clutch, he dragged himself over the sharp rocks that enribbed the roiling waters until, finally, with a supreme effort, he rose to his full height. He was indeed an awesome sight. With blood bubbling along jagged open wounds like a spider's web of interlocking gashes, he gazed fearlessly at the assembled warriors, then turned towards the Lake. He turned, and stood motionless, and then his head slumped forward, and a wail of such pain and grief came forth that the warriors shivered with the despair of it, a cry that rippled like a myriad pointed needles through their scalps. His arms opened and stretched forward as if to embrace all his companions still twisting obscenely in the Lake; and then he crashed insensate to the ground, as if the iron will that had brought him to the shore had been wrested from him, not by his own agony, but by the agony of others.

Lucifer had arrived.

The boy Mephistopheles watched, the lurid glow of the Lake reflected in his inscrutable eyes.

****

"If only," whispered Arrabis, "I had been there!"

Peter found it difficult to speak. For a moment he had been made to see again the Satan of the Forbidden Zone. *You fool, Satan, can't you see you make a mockery of what was truly great with your fictions of conquering heroes?* Then he became angry with himself. The past was the past, these were only phantoms of the long dead. The mission must go on.

"So what did the chieftains decide?" he asked.

"They were greatly moved by the courage of the Aliens. The one who had arrived first, in particular, showed a courage of which even a Saragash chieftain would have been proud. When he recovered consciousness, he even re-entered the Lake to help some of his companions to the shore; at times, when the brimstone bit into him, he would be unable to suppress a scream, but still he did not turn back. The others, too, almost without exception, showed a courage and fortitude that impressed all who witnessed it."

He paused, then added sadly: "We do well to remember these things."

Peter remained doggedly silent.

207

"The women, too," Arrabis continued after a moment, "were immensely impressed, not only by this courage, but also by the members of the Aliens, sore and swollen from the Lake. In short, the advocates of death were silenced."

"But weren't the men jealous?"

"At first, yes, but then they thought about the Alien women, how magnificent *they* must be..."

"But there *aren't* any female angels."

"No one knew that then. Or that there weren't any children, either. Had we known, the vote might have gone the other way."

"On the other hand, you couldn't have destroyed them, anyway. They're immortal, and you're not. At least, that's what I've heard."

"You're right. We rarely live more than a thousand years. Prince Mephistopheles is unique among our race. All the same, don't forget they were nearly all wounded from the War in Heaven, and the Lake had weakened them still further. We could easily have kept them imprisoned there for ever. But we found out too late. You must remember, our people had never come into contact with other beings – except for an ancient myth that golden creatures had once visited the planet at the dawn of time, but departed again immediately after being unaccountably sick everywhere – so it never even occurred to them that there might be creatures of only one sex, creatures who couldn't even *have* children, let alone *eat* them. So at the beginning, everything was misinterpreted.

"It soon became clear, of course, that all these creatures were adult males: perhaps it had been a hunting party, and the women and children would be following. We were reinforced in this opinion when the Aliens declined, with expressions of bewilderment, to eat the children we offered them from the Pool, which proved that they had also reached Enlightenment, and that, despite dire hunger, they were determined to wait until their own children arrived. Though oddly enough, when they were later offered *portions* of child, leftovers from our own meals, they accepted and ate ravenously. We now know they didn't realise what they were eating."

"But they must have seen you eating your children."

Arrabis looked shocked. "Certainly not! You seem to persist in thinking we are uncivilised! Eating one's child is an intensely personal affair, a sacred family rite. The parents always retire to a secluded spot to enter that closest of all possible bonds between parent and child: the sacramental union of eater and eaten, the beautiful ultimate return to the womb."

Or close to it, thought Peter.

"The first sign of trouble only came on the fifth day when one of the Aliens happened to leave the shore, seemingly upset by the copulating around him..."

"You mean you copulated in the open?"

"Where else? Should one hide such a joyous act?"

"But decency..."

"Decency! You're as bad as Satan!" snapped Arrabis. "Killjoys, the pair of you! Performed in the open, it allowed others to judge, to compare, to learn – even, if necessary, to give advice. But above all, it served as a public celebration, an affirmation, an act of joy. We are by nature a joyous, exuberant race."

"So you ate in secret, and coupled in public - very nice, yes, but what happened when the Alien left the shore?"

"Ah yes, you see, until then, the newcomers had aroused only the greatest admiration, not only for their noble refusal to eat the proffered young, but also for their remarkable sexual abstinence. Some had been in the Lake as long as two days. In living memory, only one Saragash had survived that long without copulating, and he had gone completely insane. And yet, when our females – having promised their mates, of course, to turn a blind eye when the Alien women arrived – made the time-honoured gesture of welcome, lying down naked with their knees drawn apart..."

Momentarily distracted by memories of his first night with Joan, Peter missed a few words.

"...a puzzled expression, his fingers scrabbling between her legs, as if looking for something. But still he didn't mount her! Such fidelity to their own mates was remarkable."

"When the Alien left the shore..." prompted Peter again.

"He came across a couple just about to begin their meal. He snatched the infant right from their very jaws! They naturally attacked him, but other Saragashim pulled them off. The visitor's action was condemned, but it was decided that hunger, and an ignorance of local customs, had driven him to it. The couple themselves felt ashamed, and there and then, after taking a few bites themselves, generously offered the rest of their child to the Alien.

209

But he threw the meal down – perhaps he too felt a bit ashamed over his own earlier greed - and dashed back to his companions.

"Their reaction was extremely odd. The ones who had been contentedly munching the leftovers we had given them hurled them down with strange cries, and many grew angry, and stepped forward belligerently. The Saragashim unsheathed their claws, and threw off their loincloths – our penises have a serrated edge on the underside which is used in combat. The situation was tense. Just then, the Leader arrived and restrained his people who, sullen and openly hostile, gradually backed away. For the moment, trouble had been averted.

"But of course, our people now kept a watch on the newcomers, who that same night held what was, they thought, a secret meeting. No one could understand what they said, of course, but the debate was long and furious. Finally, the Leader himself spoke, then picked up an infant portion, held it up challengingly, closed his eyes, and took a bite. Slowly, one by one, others stepped forward and did the same, though most were sick at once, which was very odd, since they'd eaten leftovers before without any ill effects.

"Our chieftains decided to give the Aliens a second chance: possibly they had been angry because their comrade had been attacked. They were offered food again, which the Leader accepted with a gracious smile, though then four of them took the infants to a secluded spot, killed them, and cut them up in such unusual ways that they were no longer recognisable as children, before serving them up to the others.

"That same day, the Leader broke his sexual fast. He was a little gauche – seeming unsure, for instance, which was the appropriate entrance – but any deficiencies were put down to different customs and possibly shyness.

"But relations soon became strained again. With thousands of Aliens to feed, the Childpool rapidly began to empty. And when were the Alien women and – more important – children, going to arrive?

"On the tenth day, the Aliens' rations were halved.

"Their Leader quickly came to the chieftains and drew a picture in the sand. It depicted a group of deliciously plump children, and imposingly curvaceous women – a couple of the latter, it is true, with breasts on the back instead of the front. He then looked up at our purple sun, made motions with his hands to indicate it crossing the sky five times, and then pointed to the picture. Our people jabbered excitedly, some rubbing their stomachs, some their members: five days, and the orgy could begin!

"So the Saragashim tightened their belts, and gave the Aliens as much food as they could. But the five days passed. No Alien women or children arrived. Their rations were stopped completely.

"That night, they withdrew to a nearby plateau. And just before dawn on the sixteenth day, a group of them snatched ten infants from their parents while they were helpless in pre-prandial copulation. Thus began the First Food War.

"If I tell you that we then discovered that the Aliens couldn't be killed (though they could be well and truly wounded) and that, despite their earlier squeamishness, they now showed no qualms about eating the Saragashim they slew, you will understand why we couldn't win the War. Our people were so hungry some even tried to devour the babies before they were fully out of the womb, but they were too small to go very far and, besides, the mothers got furious.

"And then, less than twenty days after the start of the War, the Alien Leader approached, alone, dragging with him a prisoner who had been forced to teach him our language.

" 'Nobody,' he said, 'can really win this war. You can never win because we are immortal. But we cannot win, either. If we are always fighting, we will never get our strength back. We have to live in peace.'

" 'But your peace means eating *our* food,' answered Alramzar. 'Where are *your* children?'

" 'I'm sure you have already guessed: we have no females, we do not reproduce.'

" 'But what did you eat before you came here?'

" 'We know how to cultivate plants and fruits, and we can live on them.' He looked round at the arid desert surrounding them. 'But to do that, we need to settle in one place, to be secure from attack. Let us settle somewhere.'

"The Chieftains had no idea what plants and fruits were, but they listened to the rumblings of their empty stomachs, conferred, and announced that the War was over.

" 'There is, however, one problem,' said the Leader. 'We need to eat until we can grow these plants and fruits.'

"The Chieftains conferred, and announced that the War was not over, after all.

" 'We know that you die naturally. All we ask is that you give us the bodies of those of you who die naturally, until our plants have grown.'

"The Chieftains conferred, and announced that the War was still not over.

" 'Otherwise, we have no choice but to take *living* Saragashim.'

"The Chieftains didn't confer. They announced that the War really was over. Afterwards, they agreed that, even if they *had* conferred, they would still have come to the same decision, for they were tired of fighting creatures who did not have the decency to die. To return home after a major battle with enemy losses of zero was positively discouraging.

"And that," said Arrabis, "was the end of the War."

As if on cue, at this moment, a young Saragash girl entered and room, and spoke quietly to the other. Arrabis nodded, and said to Peter:

"The Prince will see you now, sir."

Listening to the story of what Satan had euphemistically termed 'teething troubles', Peter had temporarily forgotten about the forthcoming interview. And as the girl led him along a corridor, he suddenly realised what the insignia on Arrabis' robe had illustrated: the hands had not been proffering a ball, but a world! All the time, he had been talking to a Tempter!

****

He realised at once that he had met his match.

Mephistopheles, Grand Chieftain of the Saragashim, President of the Guild of Tempters, Honorary Member of the Circle of doom, was, like Arrabis, wearing a simple white cloak, and was no taller than Peter himself. That was all the saint was able to take in, for the eyes at once caught and transfixed him. As he looked into them, he felt as if he were being drawn away from his own reality. Entirely without colour themselves, they reflected hints and hues of the colours around, ever-changing, like bubbles suspended in sunlight. But what held Peter was the impression of some thing, some force, pouring out of them: a departure, stately, sorrowful, inexorable, of the very essence, the life force itself, of the being facing him. But no, the force was not leaving him: rather, it was as if it were gently flowing out towards the edges of his being, and inside, death had already filled the vacant places, an uncruel death, a death that had no quarrel with life, but only followed it like the partner in an infinitesimally slow dance. He was looking into, not an emptiness, but a bare, naked lifescape that was so complete in itself it had no need of extraneous forms. Yet, at the same time, there was beauty, and serenity, and vast intelligence, like an ocean at rest, and all the more powerful for its motionlessness. There was age, like a rock harbouring lichen: the lichen gives the trappings of life, but when it is gone, the rock isn't dead, or alive – it just *is*.

Mephistopheles did not offer any sort of greeting. Instead, he said – and his voice was like a wind echoing through caverns – "St. Peter, I do not have much to say to you, only a warning. It is clear to me you have reasons for stopping the Apocalypse other than those you have given." He was not questioning or probing; he *knew*. "To me it is all one. When the Earth shall come to an end, so shall my own purpose here. The Tempters' Guild will be no more. Our victories will be regarded as a fairy tale, the fabrications of a conquered race. And yet I am weary, and the world, bereft of all idealism and honour, offers no more challenge. I cannot enjoy a sport that I cannot lose. So if the Apocalypse comes, or does not come, it is of no consequence to me. Thus I will neither help nor hinder you in your quest."

He paused, and was so still it seemed that death had quietly, painlessly, taken dominion.

"But if you intend harm to Satan, that *is* of consequence to me."

"I wish only to stop the Apocalypse," Peter answered carefully – the harm was incidental, a corollary, not the intention. "Yet I wonder at your loyalty to the subjugator of your race, the one who holds the throne that should be yours."

Mephistopheles gazed at him steadily. "You," he said slowly, "presume to judge when you have no right," He paused, his eyes like water trapped in fissures in the grey rock of his being. "You look at ashes, and never felt the warmth of the fire that once blazed there. You see only a desert that once was crowned with water. But I have seen Lucifer. I stood on the shore, and watched a broken body wracked with agony turn round and go back into the burning waters again and again to help those who had believed in him. I saw the agony in his eyes when the last angel collapsed on the shore and he saw the hideous results of his ambition. And I have seen another agony, when he returned from Eden and the good in him rose to receive the gift of life again, and the gift was not vouchsafed him. I have seen Lucifer, Peter, and you have not, and so do not presume to judge!"

As quickly as it had come, the anger went. Now just an ancient being, with death leaking through the pores.

And Peter thought of Beelzebub, who had exiled himself from Heaven itself to join his friend in Hell; of Raphael, whose eyes yet burned with danger if any should dare to mock Satan in his presence; of thirty thousand angels who had pitted themselves against their own Maker; of Lazara, with talons ever ready to affirm her faith, even now, when but the shadow of the husk remained; and of himself even, who had just briefly seen behind that vainglorious facade the night before.

"Peter, when you came in, I tasted death. So be it, perhaps it is time." A pause. "I do not know your real intentions, but whatever you do, let it be for some purpose. Some good purpose. I look into you, and I do not see evil: I see grief, and confusion, and folly, and loneliness, but I do not see evil. Lazara has told me you plan to take Satan to Limbo, to learn whether your strange pitiless God has truly planned treachery against him. I do not stop you. But I ask you to remember: *they have been punished enough!* If you yourself plan treachery against Satan, I warn you I will find a way to punish you. And I warn you of something else: Belial wants to torture you, to learn the things I have not asked you, and Satan has forbidden it. Remember these things. Goodbye, Peter."

Peter bowed slightly – *why?* – and left. He thought he understood now. Arrabis and Mephistopheles were both Tempters. And both had been appealing to the *saint* in him. They had given him a romantic, glorified picture of Satan as he had been, to make him hesitate and question his own intentions – or even the intentions of God, for they must suspect that God was somehow behind it all. And they had warned him of the danger from Belial for the same reason.

Mephistopheles, if there were another way – but there isn't. I'm sorry.

214

PART THREE

BLOOD OVER HEAVEN

Chapter Twenty-One
ATROCITY IN LIMBO

When St. Peter stepped out of the airlock in the Way Station, and saw layers of cheek playing hide-and-seek behind gambolling whiskers, he knew he didn't want to return to Hell. Even the Cheshire Cat, he thought, could never have managed a smile as enormous, as face-consuming, as that of Tobias – until, that is, it twisted into a look of horror as Satan stepped out behind him.

No, he didn't want to return, but he'd have to: they had George.

Satan had blandly informed him that morning that the phallusician had, sad to say, suddenly got the ague – *and* a touch of Parkinson's – and therefore didn't dare operate on George, but that he was *sure* to recover by the time they returned from Limbo. Keeping George in Hell as a hostage was so elementary a precaution Peter wondered why he hadn't anticipated it from the beginning.

However, a more immediate problem was to reach the Vaults unseen, and hope that Tobias didn't die of fear before they got there: first, from the shock of having the King of Hell as his guest, and then from being asked to guide them to a place into which nobody but a member of the Council of Seven, or someone acting on their authority, was ever allowed to enter – *on the express orders of God himself.*

Half an hour was spent avoiding being seen on the tortuous trip through a maze of disused side passages, until they finally emerged from a long, unlit corridor into a small emergency exit. They were outside the Way Station, in the Wastes of Limbo.

The next three hours were a nightmare they all shared equally. It had been nearly six thousand years since what was now a huge asteroid had unaccountably broken off from Hell, and miraculously drifted into orbit round Zindor. It was now fifty degrees cooler. Though they walked on solid ground and breathed real air, it was as if these things were non-existent. His companions were ghosts in the swirling mist, who might suddenly disappear or float disembodied in the air. He himself seemed incorporeal, insubstantial, flickering at the edges.

219

And there were the presences that seemed to hover around them. Released from the Vats after a hundred years, the souls in Limbo would roam meaninglessly over the eerie planet, gradually losing their identity, their grip on reality. But here there was also the animosity, the palpable hatred, of the Twice Dead, the Unbound Souls of those who had perished again in Hell, and were blindly drifting through space back towards Zindor, towards their ultimate Womb. For deep inside the colossal planet on the horizon, it was whispered, lay the Zindor Wells themselves, source of the Nebulan gods' creative power.

They hardly spoke on the journey. The ground, almost unseen beneath the mists that brushed them with clammy tendrils, was rough and uneven, like the residue of some long-past volcanic eruption. Peter felt a dread reluctance to open his mouth, as if the air impregnated with menace might enter and suck at him from within. The others clearly felt the same unease. Even Satan would occasionally flinch as if touched by some invisible being. The sound of their own breathing, the scrunch of their feet on the rock, was the only connection with reality until at last they came in sight of a walled enclosure, with a small, black circular tower looming like a petrified ghost inside it.

"I'd better wait here outside," said Tobias, "in case the Guardian sees me."

"You didn't tell me there was a Guardian," muttered Peter.

"He's harmless – I think. But he may have special powers. Be careful, Peter."

"Aren't you going to wish me luck, too?" asked Satan.

"Er, of course," mumbled Tobias. "Any friend of Peter's is a friend of mine."

It was the most obviously transparent lie Peter had ever heard. He found himself smiling for the first time in many hours. *Good old Toby!*

Peter turned towards the tower. "Keep a lookout for our return."

"God be with you!" added Satan, with a completely straight face.

They were extremely lucky, for as they approached the tower, the massive steel door swung open, and a light appeared, revealing a small rounded figure who was so bent that he reminded Peter of a question mark. He was carrying a shovel, with which he at once set about digging a small hole, over which he lowered first his trousers, and then his bottom.

As an expression of intense and blissful concentration came upon him, Peter and Satan slipped into the tower. Inside, steps descended so deeply, it took them five minutes to reach the bottom, where there stretched before them an enormous cavern, extending, like the aisle of some surreal cathedral, beyond the limits even of Satan's vision. Bodies were stacked on either side, all wrapped in clingfilm, on shelves that extended up to the ceiling. It resembled a giant wine cellar, the bodies lying flat like an alcoholic's paradise.

They slowly walked along. Always the same, body after body after body. Peter felt they could walk like this for ever, and never reach an end.

"The Resurrected!" he whispered in awe.

"They don't look very resurrected to me!" muttered his companion.

"All the creatures that ever were, and maybe ever will be! This is what will happen if you ride the Beast. This is where the souls will come, and all the souls you have in Hell now."

"Not all of them."

"And what if a few do stay in Hell? Will you wave to them from the depths of the Lake as they picnic on the banks?"

He was being deliberately brutal: they still didn't *know* if any of these bodies actually belonged to souls now in Hell. If Satan could be frightened into *assuming* this...

A shout from behind startled them both. The bent figure was approaching with rapid bird-hop motions, his trousers around his knees, holding the shovel in one hand, and brandishing a sword in the other.

"Who are you? What are you doing here? I'm the Guardian and I demand..." He looked into Peter's eyes, and for a second Peter thought he saw a smile, but he must have been wrong, for the next instant the old man took a wild swing with his sword which missed Peter by about three feet, but was so forceful it swung him in the opposite direction. He stared in that direction for a few seconds, saw no one, then sheathed his sword.

"That sure scared them off!" he chortled. "Wonder who they were, though. Cowardly rats didn't stay around long enough for me to find out."

221

"Excuse me, sir," said Peter from behind him, "but I wonder if..."

"What, more of them? Do I have to kill them all?"

And he swung round, simultaneously drawing the sword, and tripping over the shovel. It took him another two minutes before he had organised himself enough to be holding the point of the shovel at Peter's throat.

"Right, you'd better talk, and quick, before I cut out your tongue!"

"How dare you talk to a saint that way!" said Satan, sounding shocked.

"A saint?" The Guardian peered at Peter. "But only St. Darren is allowed in here."

"I *am* St. Darren," replied Peter, *almost* at once. "I fell out of my cot, and hurt my real body, so this is a temporary replacement one."

"*Another* accident?"

"What do you mean?"

"The last time you came, with all those workmen, you had a different replacement body. But what can I do for you this time, sir?"

Peter, pondering the significance of that 'last time you came', hesitated, and Satan came to his aid, saying smoothly:

"We've come, my bad... my good man, to inspect the bodies. On the Master's orders," he added, wincing slightly at the word 'master'.

"But they were inspected only last month. And who are you? *You're* not a saint!"

"Make-up!" said Peter loudly, in order to drown the other's shocked 'I should think not!'. "He's just been to Hell in disguise to check the preparations for the Apocalypse."

"Oh, I see. But the make-up people certainly did a good job. How did they manage to make him look so ugly and horrible?"

Peter watched Satan's silent struggle to retract his claws. The Guardian went on:

"But why do you want to inspect the bodies again already?"

"One can't be too careful. Maybe I missed something the last time."

"But your workmen took every one out of the clingfoil!

222

What could you possibly have missed?"

That little horror Darren's been up to something! I must check this!

"Take me to the Vats again first. I'd like to put a couple into their bodies, just to make sure everything's OK."

"But, sir, I can't allow that! My orders..."

"What, do you presume to defy the great St. Darren, you little wretch!" stormed Satan. "The brightest soul that ever made the Pearly Gates dim by comparison!"

"Michael's taken the pearl!" muttered Peter between his teeth.

"This is not a mere common-or-garden saint! This is not one of those scoundrels like that old codger Peter, the so-called Guardian of the Keys! This is St. Darren himself!"

"Just you wait!" snarled Peter, *sotto voce.*

"So find him some souls at once, as he has commanded you!"

"Yes, sir, at once, sir, sorry, sir. Please follow me."

He shuffled away, followed by Peter muttering, to Satan's great astonishment, some of the ten thousand nastiest words in the Universe – a list which Belial and he himself had drawn up! They must have gone at least a quarter of a mile before the aisle branched out into a circular chamber, from which three other passages disappeared into illimitable distances.

The chamber was full of enormous barrels, each with a date on it. The Guardian lifted the lid of one of these, dated '1987', thus releasing a cacophony of querulous voices:

"Let us out of here!"

"That stupid vicar never told us about this!"

(A bitter voice: "I bloody well did, you lying sod, but you were sleeping!")

"If I ever get my hands on that podgy Judge...!"

"And after I brought so much happiness to so many men...!"

The Guardian slammed the lid down again. "I'm sorry," he said, "it's like this every time. No stoicism."

"Could you please put a couple in their bodies for me?" asked Peter.

The Guardian looked a bit rebellious, but said: "Let's see... '87, recent vintage, the bodies should be... yes, over here."

He went to a nearby shelf, yanked down two bodies, and

checked the name tags before freeing the heads from the clingfoil, which was already torn in places, as if it had been put hurriedly around the bodies. The heads were of an exceedingly plain woman and an exceedingly spotty man.

He then opened the Vat again, and shouted "Algernon! Ethel!"

There was a sudden hush in the Vat. Then a lot of squelching and ouching as two souls squirmed their way to the top. The Guardian grabbed these, and slammed the lid shut.

Usually, souls reminded Peter of tadpoles. Now they brought to mind rugby-playing spermatozoa. *Perhaps I'm spending too much time in unsavoury company!*

"Just like tadpoles, aren't they?" remarked Satan.

"Are you... let's see again... Algernon and Ethel?" demanded the Guardian, and interpreting gargling sounds as an affirmative, he forced open the mouths of the two bodies, and dropped a soul into each.

"These bodies have been simplified a bit," he remarked. "But you already know that..." A voice came from one of the bodies.

"Christ, it's stuffy in here!"

Satan winced, but held his peace.

"Ugh! A spider in the left ventricle! And what's all this?"

There followed a flurry of curses, and then things started hurtling out of Algernon's mouth – worms, bugs, a bit of surgical gauze.

"Oh dear!" wailed the Guardian. "I cleaned all those bodies when they arrived. It must have been your repairmen when they did the alterations."

"How do I get this thing started?" said a voice from Algernon's body.

"Thump the heart!"

"Speak up, I can't hear you!"

The Guardian yelled down Algernon's throat. "Thump the bloody heart, you gormless ectoplasm!"

A few moments later, the body convulsed, and then the eyes opened.

"Hey, I can't see a thing!"

"Oh dear!" said the Guardian again, extracting from a pocket the grubbiest handkerchief Peter had ever seen. "Mildew, I expect." He wiped Algernon's eyes vigorously, leaving the handkerchief slightly cleaner than before. "Better?"

The eyes blinked. "I can see a bit... Ethel!"

Just then the other body came to life. "Algernon! Is that you?"

On the hard, cold ground in the middle of a tenebrous underground chamber in the Wastes of Limbo, two beings clambered uncertainly to their feet, two living souls once again given form and substance, two bodies infused with spirit and life, the forerunners of a new race that would survive eternity.

It was a moving moment. Peter felt a lump in his throat: could it, he wondered morosely, be glandular fever? Satan, too, had a lump in his throat: a particularly tenacious hellroach was following Dylan Thomas' advice not to go gentle into that good night.

"Yes, yes," said Algernon, "it's me! Your Bulgy Algy, as you used to call me. Have we been in the same Vat all this time without knowing it?"

"I didn't know you were dead!"

"I was hit by the hearse after your funeral."

"Oh, Algy, my poor darling!"

The clingfoil was beginning to slip off their bodies, but they hardly noticed.

"It doesn't matter. I'm with my little tweedle-de-pom again, and..."

"Eek! What's that behind you?"

Algernon turned, and saw the others for the first time. The saint and the Guardian he took in his stride, but the sight of Satan induced a second 'Eek!'

Satan looked pleased with himself.

"EEK!"

"My creme caramel," said Algernon, "don't worry about the monster." (Satan's smile disappeared.) "We're safe in the Afterlife, and..."

"ALGY!"

"What's the matter, my sweet jelly baby?"

"You're not bulgy anymore!"

"Give me time, my peach blossom! I've only just..."

"Algy, you're not bulgy AT ALL!"

Algernon looked down, gave a horrified gasp, and frenziedly ripped away the rest of the clingfoil. There came a howl of despair worse than King Lear's on finding Cordelia dead.

225

"NOOO...!"

The refrain was taken up by Ethel, who had been making her own investigations.

"NOOO...!"

"Quiet!" shouted the Guardian. "You're making enough row to wake the dead!"

"Ethel, I haven't got a ...!"

"Algy, nor have I!"

And indeed they hadn't, as Peter and Satan could now quite clearly see. They both stared at the Guardian in horror.

"It wasn't my idea, sir!" he said to Peter. "You know I tried to stop you! You had the ornaments removed!"

"What the hell are you talking about?"

"Your workmen last month. Slice, plop, in the bucket, slice, plop, in the bucket! The women did take a bit longer..."

Ethel screamed, and would have fallen to the ground, but Algernon just managed to catch her. "You fiend!" he gasped.

Satan started, then realised the compliment was directed at the Guardian.

The Guardian waved an admonishing finger at Algernon. "Don't call me names! It wasn't me who did it. I just had to clear up the mess afterwards!"

"I'll kill the little bastard!" yelled Peter. "I'll twist his bloody neck into spaghetti!"

"Peter, please, we're in company!" Satan was shocked.

"Peter?" said the Guardian. "But I thought you said..."

"Yes, Peter, damn it, *Saint* Peter! How dare you think I was that little shit Darren! And if you tell a single soul – or body – you'll end up like these!"

Satan gazed at him with something akin to admiration.

"Oh dear!" This was all too much for the Guardian.

"But this is impossible!" exclaimed Algernon, "I can't go round without a ...bulge!"

"And I certainly wouldn't be seen dead without a pussy!" added Ethel, the shock clearly having temporarily undermined her good breeding. "Whatever would the neighbours think!"

The Guardian tried to be placatory. "Come, come," he said. ("How?" hissed Algernon.) "You'll soon get used to it. Much cleaner.

Just wait and see."

"You can go stuff these so-called bodies up your arse!" yelled Algernon. If his beloved Ethel could say 'pussy', then he could say 'arse'. He'd always wanted to.

"If you're lucky enough to have one!" added Ethel venomously.

"I can see why they didn't get to Heaven!" murmured Satan.

"Ethel?"

"My love?"

"It will be all right somehow, my little marshmallow."

"There's still us, isn't there? I mean, the *real* us."

"Yes, yes, my sweet demerara delight. They can't take that away from us."

"The cheat!" Satan suddenly shouted. "How did he think of it first? What an exquisite torture! My reputation's ruined!" He stamped his feet in fury, almost crushing the souls.

"Hey, steady on!" yelled the Guardian. "I've got to balance the books!"

Peter addressed the souls. "He's gone too far this time. I'll think of some way to help you, I promise."

"How can *you* help us?"

"I don't know yet. But in order to help you, I'll need to take you both to Heaven. As evidence. With these bodies."

"Never!"

"I can get you some *real* bodies afterwards. Maybe not your own, not just yet. But real bodies. With all the parts there. But you must stay in the Way Station, with Tobias. And if I'm not there in two days, go to the Archangel Raphael, you understand? Nobody else, just Raphael. But you'll have to wear the bodies for a time, because we can't carry you all the way to the Station. If you want help, you must do this."

"What do you say, Ethel?"

"All that really matters is the *real* you, of course. But if we *could* get your bulges back, as well..."

"And yours!"

"Well, mine wouldn't be much use without yours."

"They *do* seem to go together well, don't they?"

"Oh, Algy, do you remember when we did it on a camel?"

"Could I ever forget, my little cherry crunch?"

"These two," Satan announced suddenly, "are making me

227

incontinent! These treacly blatherings aren't love! 'My little cherry crunch' indeed! Glutinous, gluttonous creatures! Love isn't just bulges, or sentiments like the ingredients of a cream cake! Love is...''

"What?" asked Peter and Algernon and Ethel and the Guardian.

"Love is passion that binds up eternities. Love is the clasping of minds over the vault of infinity. Love is the sempiternal rhythm of starlight. Love is the keening sigh of impossibility."

"What!" said Peter.

"Wow!" said Algernon and Ethel.

"Er, pardon?" said the Guardian.

Satan gazed at them all with a huge contempt, then turned to stare down the other aisles. He then spoke to the Guardian. "Has this been done to *all* the bodies here?"

"Oh no, sir. Just those in this first section of the Vaults, those sentenced to Purgatory. And not even all of those. Most of the workmen were sick, and packed up early."

"So," said Satan, slowly, "the bodies of those souls now in Hell haven't been damaged."

Peter looked at the Guardian's mouth. *Strange to think that the shape of those lips, and the flopping around of a funny bit of flesh inside, can decide the fate of so many.* He remembered a line from the Apocryphal *Ecclesiasticus*: 'Many have fallen by the edge of the sword: but not so many as have fallen by the tongue.'

"No," replied the Guardian, "the bodies of the damned weren't touched."

Perfect, perfect! The information I received was right!

"So he's really going to do it!" Satan's voice was so low, Peter wasn't sure that he hadn't imagined it. "And Belial goes on about his *justice*! All right, we'll see who wins!" He turned to Peter, quite oblivious of the others present. "So you *have* been telling the truth. Don't think I'll be ungrateful. *I* will bring this Darren to you, and every one of my Torturers will be at your disposal to give you advice, to suggest those little extra refinements that you, as a saint, cannot be expected to work out by yourself."

Peter *was* aware of the others, however. "Just a little joke," he said hurriedly. "As my colleague is disguised as a particularly horrible devil, he amuses himself by acting the part. In Heaven, he has some of the angels in stitches!" *Well, he's hoping to, anyway!*

Satan shook himself, as if to dislodge unpleasant thoughts. "Tell me," he said to the Guardian, "you said the ... ornaments were put in buckets. Have you thrown them away?"

"Oh dear!" wailed the Guardian, "I don't have time to do everything."

"So they *are* still here. We'd like to take a look."

Oh, we would, would we?

"The great wrong that has been perpetrated here has to be put right," said Satan righteously, "and it will be easier if the embellishments are still here. Let us go and check."

He's just learned that God really has planned to empty Hell, and he has time to be concerned about these souls? Why am I always misjudging him?

"Very well," said the Guardian, "the buckets are in a storeroom near the reptile section," and, leaving the two Limboans exchanging confectionery, he led them along a small passage, at the end of which a horrific sight met them. Huge buckets, hundreds of them, lined the walls, full to the brim with... Peter averted his eyes.

Not so Satan. "Incredible," he breathed, running his fingers wonderingly through the contents of one bucket. "But how do you know," he asked the Guardian, "which bodies they belong to?"

"I don't. If you do insist on putting them back on again, I suppose the souls will just have to come and rummage around until they spot the bits they think belong to them."

Peter had a momentary vision of hordes of souls all claiming the same more self-assertive 'bits', then spotted something out of the corner of his eye. *I am not always misjudging the bastard!*

"Satan!"

"Yes?" Innocently.

"Put them back. And don't say 'put what back?'!"

"Put wha...? Oh, come on, they won't miss a few."

"Put them back. They all belong to somebody."

"But we'll probably remove them again when they come to Hell. And I've left the most important parts."

"Put them back!" *Good God, I've finally gone mad, I'm giving orders to the Devil!*

But Satan only glared at him, then unwillingly removed a dozen plump breasts from his pockets and dropped them in one of the buckets. "You're becoming a bore," he said sulkily. "They probably weren't virgins, anyway."

What Peter didn't know was that Satan only munched hellroaches as a substitute for pickled virgins' breasts, to which he was addicted, despite their being less nutritious, but which had been getting more and more scarce: not because virgins were wont to have fewer breasts than before, but because there were fewer virgins - one of the few sources of contention between Satan and the Tempters, whom he held responsible for the dearth of this delicacy.

They turned to go, but Satan took one last lingering look back at this treasure-trove... then started, and dashed to a shelf which abutted on the corner, and examined one of the name tags. He uttered one incomprehensible word, before yanking out the clingfoil. It was empty.

"Where is he?" roared Satan.

The Guardian put his hand to his sword, and Peter had the peculiar impression that, despite the earlier antics, he knew how to use it. "Who?"

"*Squiggly!* That no-good, double-crossing, two-timing serpent! Where is he?"

"Oh, Squiggly and Lamia."

"I don't know about any Lamia. Where's that Squiggly?"

"Oh, he could be anywhere. He shouldn't even be in Limbo. He was pardoned the same time as Adam and Eve, but it seems he was so ashamed..."

"I should think he would be! Two-faced worm!"

Peter was beginning to understand. Squiggly, the serpent in Eden. In Heaven, everyone knew that the serpent had tricked Adam into eating the apple. But why should Satan be angry with him?

The Forbidden Zone! 'I built it for her, and she did not come.'

So that was where the crazy fantasy had been born! 'Double-crossing, two-timing serpent'... The serpent was supposed to have sent *Eve* to Hell by getting her to eat the apple! The pieces suddenly fell into place. *And Eve said the serpents have a message for me!*

"And where is he likely to be now?" Satan was holding himself back with an effort.

"Outside somewhere. I know he's working on a new book, *The Horizontal Dream*; he'd completed seven thousand chapters last time I saw him. He..."

But Satan was gone, striding furiously back along the aisles between the bodies.

My job is done. I could escape now, but for George.

He stopped only to warn the Guardian to say nothing of his visit, and to give instructions to Ethel and Algernon, then walked quickly ahead, along the gloomy aisle to the steps, up, and out of the door which had swung shut behind Satan, as it now did behind him, too.

Satan was standing there, staring unseeing through the Limbo mists.

Peter stood beside him. "It would have made no difference," he said quietly, after a few minutes of silence. "Even if Eve had eaten the apple first, God would never have sent her to Hell. He didn't even send Adam."

They were the first words he had ever said to Satan without a hidden motive.

Satan didn't answer at once. But in place of the previous rage, a bitter, poignant smile came to his lips.

"No, he wouldn't have sent her, even if the serpent hadn't betrayed me. God tricked me then, as he hopes to trick me now. But you're wrong to say it makes no difference. If the serpent deceived Adam, not Eve, *why did she eat the apple?* She ate the apple, Peter, not because of any trick, but *to join me!* And God stopped her. And he will pay for it!"

That's all I needed. Satan will attack Heaven now, and nothing can stop him. I've won. But another part of his mind said: *But I don't think Eve ate the apple for your sake. It is still all a delusion, and you are going to perish because of this delusion. And yet such love, spanning hundreds of centuries, such idiotic, ridiculous love!* The image of Mephistopheles came into his mind. *He said I have no right to judge, and maybe I have no right to do what I am doing. But I have the* necessity. *The Chain of the Book of Razael must be broken. I cannot sacrifice thousands for one deluded old fool.*

And then he saw the monsters.

Dozens of them, fanning out over the Wastes of Limbo, like avenging ghosts, as if an angry Razael had created ghouls to make sure the Links of his Chain should remain forever locked. But they were neither ghosts nor ghouls. He sensed what they were even

231

before Satan, seeing his fear, swung round and, with the advantage of his angel eyes, uttered one word.

"Nefilim!"

Chapter Twenty-Two
An Old Acquaintance

Peter's first instinct was to take refuge in the Vaults, but the door had slammed shut behind him, and when he hurled himself at it, it yielded slightly less than it would have done had a particularly feeble butterfly collided against it.

Satan showed no inclination to hide. His claws were out, his teeth bared. "They must have taken over the Terminal," he snarled. "there's no other way they could have got out of Hell."

But where's Tobias? Had he seen the Nefilim coming, and made himself scarce long before?

The Nefilim were coming towards them.

"They're half blind," muttered Satan, "but they can smell saint a mile away!"

"More likely following your trail of hellroach legs! Let's get out of here!"

"You mean, *run away?*"

Oh no, here we go again! "You prefer to amble? Saunter? Stroll? You don't want to see Eve again?"

They ran.

Darkness was descending rapidly. Maybe it was the poor light, or the phantasmal mist that lay over the surface like a shroud, but within minutes Peter tripped and fell, his ankle twisting in the process. He struggled to his feet, but was only able to stumble along.

Satan stopped. "What do you think you're playing at?" he shouted. "If you want to practise dancing, do it some other time!"

"My ankle, I've twisted it. You'll have to help me."

"*Help you?* I can't go around carrying saints at my age!"

Peter looked at him in stunned amazement and helpless fury.

"And don't you look at me in stunned amazement and helpless fury like that! It's me they're after, not you. If I waste time helping you, they'll catch us both. Your only chance lies in my selflessly luring them away from you."

233

"Piss off then!" Peter yelled. "Save your stinking skin!"

"Peter, I have to think of Hell, too. Can I leave the ship of state rudderless?" He hesitated, then plunged his hand inside his cloak, and pulled out a much-used bladder bag, gazed at it longingly for a second, then thrust it into Peter's hand, where it wobbled and swayed as if it were full of live hellroaches: which it was. "Here, these'll keep you going till I can bring help."

"I'll tell Eve you ran away!"

Satan glared at the saint. The Nefilim were so near now that Peter could make out their faces, their red eyes like so many fireflies in the sinister twilight.

"Give me back my hellroaches," said Satan distinctly, "and never ask me for one again!" He stooped, thrust his arm under Peter's armpit, and began to drag him along.

Peter knew full well, and he surmised that Satan knew even fuller and weller, that without aid his chances of living to tell Eve anything were about as remote as George qualifying for Mensa. It was the semblance of blackmail which lent an aura of respectability to what would otherwise, in a devil, be reprehensible conduct: helping a saint.

With Satan hampered by Peter's weight, however, the Nefilim were now almost upon them. *Who will Joan terrorise in bed after I'm gone?*

And then a voice came from the ground.

" 'Hammer of the Fell Foe'! 'Conqueror of the Andromedan Fire Monster!' *Bollocks!*"

Satan came to an abrupt halt, nearly spraining Peter's other ankle.

"Squiggly!"

" 'Creator of Worlds where serpents rule!' *Cobblers!* Thought you'd fooled me, didn't you? Why aren't you busy saving worlds instead of running away from a few harmless teddy bears?"

"Gosh, he really is as big and ugly as you said he was!" came another voice.

Peter couldn't see where the voices were coming from. There *seemed* to be some movement on the ground, reflections of shadows, wisps of insubstantiality, but nothing that Satan's furiously flying feet were able to make contact with.

"He really is slow, isn't he?" remarked the second voice. "I don't think he's evolved one iota since you met him, Squiggly."

Peter shouted out: "If you're the serpent from Eden, help us! I'm St. Peter, a friend of Eve's. She has a message for you. Help us!"

"St. Peter! What are you doing with this old windbag?"

"For God's sake, help us! I'll tell you after."

"We should help them, Squiggly, if Peter's a friend of Eve's. And what the Hammer, or Scourge, or whatever, did, was done out of love – you told me so yourself."

"Oh, all right, you great softie. But don't expect gratitude from that great hulk!"

Suddenly, the ground came to life. Ghostly forms slithered and whipped out of nowhere, twisting, glinting, undulating, writhing. Within seconds, the first Nefil, barely ten yards away, stumbled to the ground, his feet wrapped round by serpentine forms. A second followed, then a third...

Then, "Follow us," said a voice nearby.

"We can't see you!"

"An astute observation. Sorry." And the serpent materialised before them, twice. "People used to mock my philosophy," remarked one of them, gliding away, "but I – with the inestimable aid of my darling wife Lamia – have mastered the ultimate links between energy and matter. It's all in *The Horizontal Dream*, and I think I may in all modesty remark that even God could learn a thing or two from it. But, come down here."

A large hole had appeared in the ground, down which first the two serpents, and then Peter and Satan, plunged, the former with graceful ease, the latter tumbling and scrabbling. It led to an underground passage, with dozens of branches at almost every step. The saint and the devil had to crawl along, until they all came to a halt in a chamber high enough to stand up in.

"Our library," proudly announced Squiggly. Peter noticed that most of the volumes had been written by Squiggly and Lamia themselves.

235

"Can the Nefilim reach us here?" asked Satan with unusual politeness.

"You mean the red-eyes? Impossible."

"So we're safe for the time being? Good!" And he hurled himself at the serpent, his hands outstretched. They were still outstretched – and empty – when he hit the opposite wall.

"I'd like the hedgehog to read our book sometime; he might be able to tidy up our admittedly tentative terminology," continued the serpent from where Satan *had* been.

After Satan had hurtled across the room a few times in vain, he finally collapsed in a corner. "Why did you get Adam to eat the apple, and not Eve?" he asked, panting.

"Because you lied to me."

"What's wrong with that?" asked Satan, surprised.

The serpent turned to Peter. "You said you had a message."

"Why didn't you come to Heaven when you finished your sentence in Purgatory?"

"But for God's Grace, Eve would have gone to Hell for my actions. She still had to spend fifty years in a Vat. How could I face her?"

"Her message was: 'You become responsible, forever, for what you have tamed. Help me to help him. And come back, I need you.' I don't understand it, but I do know that she loves you both, and by staying here you are punishing her as much as yourself."

Squiggly hung his head, while Lamia said, "You see?" Neither of them asked *who* they were supposed to help.

Peter added: "She also said you might have a message for me."

Squiggly looked surprised. "I'm sorry, but no. How could we?"

So your Intuitions aren't so infallible after all, Eve. He felt somehow let down. He realised he had unconsciously been relying on the serpents for guidance.

"Why don't you rest?" Lamia said kindly.

"Or tell us why you're being hunted," added Squiggly. "I suppose those red-eyes are the terrified agents of that Fell Foe your companion keep terrifying!"

"Squiggly!" Lamia rebuked him, "he's our guest now."

"Squiggly," said Peter urgently, "don't think I'm ungrateful, but we have to get out of Limbo as soon as possible. Is there another exit from here?"

"No, there's only the one. You must spend the night here."

"But if the Nefilim are still there in the morning..."

The serpent smiled. "After a night on the surface of Limbo, they'll be in no condition to harm you." He did not elaborate.

Peter turned to Satan. "How did they know we were here?"

"I suppose they saw us leave."

"How did they know we were *here*?"

For a moment, a huge doubt appeared in Satan's eyes. Then, "If you think it was Belial or Toffy, forget it. They must have hijacked a Shuttle, and found out at the Way Station."

That still left too many 'whys'. More to distract himself from their present plight than from any real interest, Peter asked: "Why do the Nefilim hate you so much?"

"Come on, he's not exactly the most likeable person you..." began Squiggly, before being nudged into silence by a frowning Lamia.

The fury of Satan's reply startled him. "Bugrot desecrated Beelzebub's Shrine!"

"Beelzebub's Shrine?"

"So I stripped him of his Badge of the Lesser Twisted Testicle."

"That was a bit severe!"

"And had him thrown in the Brimstone Lake. Which is responsible for his, er, skin condition. And his present invulnerability."

Like Achilles without the heel. Trust you to throw him right in!

"Speaking of Bugrot, how is Yomyael?"

"They managed to save his half-leg, but his tongue, which was found in the doodlebug-tarantula's stool, had shrivelled up and dehydrated, so, despite a successful transplant, he'll always speak with a lisp, and have bad breath."

"And Amazyarak?"

"I believe his legs got mislaid,"

"Bad prognostication."

Squiggly now asked Peter: "And how *is* Eve?"

Oh, oh, here comes trouble! "I told you, she's missing you."

"She's ill," said Satan.

"Eve is ill?" asked Squiggly, suddenly concerned.

"Yes, but I'm sure she'll be all right soon," said Peter.

"But what's wrong with her?"

Nothing! Don't you *start!* "Nobody really knows."

"The dinosaur's ill, too," Satan told the serpents. "All your old friends, apparently."

"We've heard nothing about this!" Squiggly protested. "Why, the elephant wrote only a month ago, and he said nothing at all about any illness."

Squiggly, first you save me, now you're trying to kill me!

"These illnesses came on rather suddenly," said Peter, adding, in an effort to divert the conversation, "perhaps it's just all the tension in Heaven at the moment, the pressures of the Reform Party..."

"Ah yes," interposed Lamia, "the elephant told us about someone called Darren."

"Our friend the snapper-off of unconsidered trifles!" murmured Satan.

"But I don't understand why he suddenly became so powerful," added Lamia.

"There's one thing," said Peter, "guaranteed to make people act irrationally..."

"Sex!" said Satan.

"Well yes, that too. But I was referring to babies."

"Wait, Belial said something about Darren being a baby... but the Guardian said he went to the Vaults."

"In a loan body. When he reached Heaven, he chose to wear the newly cloned baby body. Usually, saints only don their new bodies when they're at their peak."

"Why didn't you do that?" asked Satan unkindly.

Peter ignored that. "It was very clever. Angels – perhaps because they never passed through infancy themselves – are even more susceptible to babies than humans. Darren turned up at Council meetings, little hood over his head, dummy in his mouth,

238

pretending to burp away innocently, and the Reform Party began to win vote after vote."

Satan had been observing him attentively. "There couldn't be any connection between this Darren and your visit to me, could there?"

"Of course not." It sounded so feeble, he added: "I told you, *our* problems begin with the Apocalypse." He turned to the serpents. "You should go to Heaven to be with Eve."

Squiggly looked at the ground. "I must finish my book," he mumbled.

"*Our* book, love. Oh Squiggly, don't punish yourself any more. She needs you."

Squiggly squirmed in painful indecision. "All right," he said at last, "we'll return with you tomorrow. Only for a visit, mind you."

Lamia curled herself around him.

Satan's expression was sullen. There was pain there, too. *No one has invited him. But I think he intends to invite himself!*

He managed to avoid further dangerous conversation by pleading tiredness, and soon settled into an exhausted but very uneasy sleep.

****

That same night, in hospital, St. George, too, had visitors. One was Prince Mephistopheles. Another was Arrabis, his son, Lazara's father.

Satan had lied to Peter, and had in fact got the phallusician to unite the two parts of George's severed member straight after his conversation with Belial. The ancient Chieftain stared down at the anaesthetised saint. "Satan hasn't returned from Limbo," he said. "And my people have reported unusual movement among the Nefilim. We may have need of each other."

He signalled to his warriors, who carried George, still strapped to the bed, over the unconscious bodies of Belial's guards.

A couple of hours later, he was regretting his decision. There was only one good thing to say about George: he was a saint, which meant, thank the Great Sperm in the Sky, that he'd lived in Heaven all this time, and not in Hell!

As soon as he recovered consciousness, George immediately evinced a burning desire to 'get 'em'. When requested to be specific as to the identity of the 'em', he made it abundantly clear that the 'em' included those who were now holding him down. It finally transpired that the only creature who was definitely not included in the 'em' was St. Peter, and where was he? Informed that St. Peter was in Limbo, and maybe in danger, George leapt to his feet, with the bed still strapped to his back, and carved up Peter's imaginary enemies with a very unimaginary sword.

After considerable damage to the room, he was eventually made to understand that his rescuers believed Peter and Satan to be in danger, but that they couldn't for the moment do anything about it, as both the Shuttles had, it seemed, been hijacked by the Nefilim. (More damage to the room.) There was, however, one other possible way to leave Hell, but they didn't intend to tell him until he stopped damaging the room. (More damage to the room.)

At this stage, negotiations ceased while Lazara pleaded with her father and grandfather not to tear off what had been an erection, or, indeed, not to tear out the saint's heart, either. According to the tearful girl, George really meant no harm, he just had funny ways, and a good woman would soon put him right. Her father and grandfather, spotting her secretly fondling the ex-erection, furiously spanked her while remarking that a *good* woman might indeed put him right!

George eventually came to understand that damaging the furniture would bring him no nearer his beloved Peter. Besides, Mephistopheles had an air of natural authority, and the poor saint, without Peter, sorely needed someone to do his thinking for him. Having decided to trust Mephistopheles, his brain was not big enough to allow room for any mistrust, and he became meek and obedient, and agreed to do everything he was asked. Unfortunately, he was asked to do nothing for the time being, and another destructive half-hour elapsed before he agreed that being asked to do nothing was the same as doing whatever he was asked.

Just before dawn, Mephistopheles decided to wait no longer.

But this time, when he informed George that they were to be carried to the Beast's Pit by a relay of Fliers, there was no erection to clank against his armour. Even George had his limits.

Just then, Moloch, bleeding and badly beaten, stumbled in.

****

'And the Dark Lord of the Universe swooped on the Garden of Eden, and there seized the Usurper, and gave him such a Drubbing that still the air echoes with his screams.' (Sura 76)

Picture that scene for a moment: the Usurper, bruised and beaten and battered and broken, his foul effulgence incarnadined by his own spurting blood, lying crumpled at the conquering Feet of the avenging Dark Lord, clasping and clawing at Them in sweating terror and ignominious supplication; nearby, the humans clinging to each other in abject fear, foolish innocent creatures now trembling with the knowledge that he they had thought the master of all, was in reality a base, craven thing; how now seemed the lies he had taught them, how brash the boastings, how vain the vauntings, when he had believed in his folly the Dark Lord to be trapped forever in the burning bowels of Hell! Behold how they whimper and look up at the Unvanquished, as His huge Form frightens the very sun from the sky; they see Him raise His terrible left Hand to swot them and their puny creator into a bloody stain on the outraged fabric of the Universe!

But does out Lord Satan strike the blow – for Him, no more than the brushing aside of an insect – and thus end the miserable existence of the Usurper? No, no, and again no: for to end his existence is to end his punishment.

Slowly the Dark Lord lowers that world-wracking left Hand. What vengeance can He take, what revenge commensurate with the enormity of the crime? Drag the base creature back to Hell, where he can be tormented for ever? But how could He endure the proximity, the fearful blubbering, of that feculent vermin throughout the long journey back to Hell?

And then His Eye falls on the humans again.

Even after all these centuries, the brilliance of our Dark Lord's

241

decision still shines out. The Treaty of Eden has become our heritage...

Moloch had jumped a page: he wanted to get on to his favourite bit.

...on His opponent's groin, His Fingers round his throat, thus spake our Lord Satan:

"Know, fistulitic one, I give you but a respite. The time will come when We will return to Heaven and claim that which is Ours. Remember this Vow and tremble!"

Thus saying, He seized the self-styled King of Heaven and, lifting him by the scrotum, shook him like a ship's flag whipped by the storm, like a rat shaken by a dog. He banged him against the mountain side, against the stones. He twisted his arms and his legs together until he resembled a mandrake root. He yanked open his mouth, and tore out each tooth one by one. He scored deep scars across his tongue. He thrust His avenging talons into the Great Turpitude's nostrils, and raked them along...

At this moment, Moloch's reading had been interrupted by an enormous orgasm: he rarely managed to finish this passage in the *History* without one.

He dried himself off, and began his press-ups. This wasn't easy, as even in the starting position with his arms stretched downwards, his belly still touched the floor. As he lowered himself, it was squeezed sideways, so that he took on a vaguely poached-egg shape.

Being overweight was but one of his problems. Of late, his haemorrhoids too had been getting worse. A devil's piles are among his most treasured possessions, and many a time, as he lay soaking in the bath, the water rising and falling to their steady pulsing, he would reflect that their convoluted immensity raised him a cut above his colleagues. At other times, however, his reflections were less cheerful, for his opponents went straight for them, as a consequence of which they were now the most battle-scarred part of his body.

He still struggled gamely, however, to keep fit, as the threat to his beloved master from the Nefilim loomed ever greater. He made frequent attempts to diet, but his periods of abstinence rarely lasted very long. During the Christmas Feast, for example, not only had he finally eaten all of Satan's unfinished meal, he had then gone on to devour the cook as well.

After the exercises, Moloch went down to the cellar beneath his room and lovingly polished the Reins and buffed the Glove, a ritual he had performed every day for two thousand years. Soon, the Beast's Wings would Unfold, and his master would use these Reins to launch the long-awaited Apocalypse.

But where was he? It was now the middle of the night, and he should have returned the evening before. Moloch desperately wanted to go and find out what had happened. But Satan had been adamant: he must not leave his post for any reason whatever until he returned, for the Wings were due to open any moment.

Someone knocked at the door of the room above, and Moloch went to open it. Mammon was there, looking as if he had run there as fast as he could. He had indeed walked there as fast as he could, and his exhausdtion was genuine.

"Bugrot! The Nefilim!" he gasped, wiping tomato sauce off his cheek. "We're holding them at the moment, but..."

And then he was hurled to one side as half a dozen Nefilim burst in.

Moloch was out of shape, but he was still Moloch. It took five Nefilim to hold him down, but that was enough. He saw a sixth running up from the cellar with the Reins, nearly broke free, but then all five made a concerted lunge for his haemorrhoids.

When the waves of excruciating pain began to abate some minutes later, Moloch knew there was only one person who could help him.

It was the morning of the twenty-ninth of December, 1999.

Chapter Twenty-Three
THE MESSAGE OF THE SERPENTS

Squiggly had been right about the Nefilim. When they emerged the following morning from the tunnels, a few were still in the vicinity. But they were slumped on the ground, moaning and staring blankly around them.

"The Unbound Souls don't like intruders," Squiggly explained. "Some of them have been here thousands of years with no body, no corporality. Emptiness is their domain, matter is anathema to them. Though more than hate, theirs is rather a hopelessness so potent it can destroy anything it comes into contact with. Those red-eyes must be very strong to be still alive."

Toby! Was he out all night?

"Tell them," said Satan bitterly, "their case isn't so hopeless after all."

It was obvious that he hadn't slept at all, although throughout the night he had remained unmoving and silent. His eyes were puffed up, his lips dry and cracked, his scars more livid than usual. He had had the whole night to come to a full realisation of what was in store for him – according, that is, to the new Unauthorised Gospel of St. Peter.

Peter, too, felt drained and dispirited. Success was near. He was convinced that Satan now fully intended to attack Heaven, drawn by Eve, a thirst for revenge, the apparent weakness of Heaven, and as the only possible escape from the fate that God had planned for him. But Peter didn't like the price he was paying for this success, the price Satan would have to pay.

Squiggly checked that Tobias hadn't taken shelter in the Vaults, then they set off for the Way Station, the serpents leading the way. The pain in Peter's ankle had subsided, so he didn't need Satan's support: it was, he reflected, better that way. As before, no one spoke, and as before, Peter sensed movement in the dank early morning greyness around him, and unheard lamentations and unassuaged tears.

And so they reached the Way Station, standing in the Wastes like some huge, grimy blister. They entered through the emergency exit they had used before. Once inside, desperate to find Tobias, Peter rushed ahead down the dim passages. He finally burst into the hall next to Tobias' office from which the underground passages began...

Straight into the arms of a Nefil who seized him with a terrible roar, and dashed him to the ground! *Haven't they got anything better to do?* Eyes blurred from the pain, he could still make out a massive foot raised to crush the life out of him *—I see now why Squiggly turned against Adam!* – and then a swirl of black as Satan hurled himself at the monster, toppling him over before the foot could make contact.

The King of Hell was smaller and already weakened from the fight against Bugrot, and it seemed he must succumb to the sheer weight and ferocity of his foe. But though his enemy was a Nefil, he was not Bugrot. The end came in less than a minute.

"I needed that!" gasped Satan, looking down at his opponent's body.

At first, Peter took the comment to be the usual bravado, then he realised Satan meant exactly what he said. Barely hours had elapsed since he had learnt that his Kingdom was to be no more; he had at last been able to fight back at something tangible.

Peter mumbled a very ungracious thanks. The last thing he wanted was to be in debt to someone he planned to destroy. Satan stared at him. "A true devil never leaves a friend in distress." *Trust him to spoil it!* Then both became aware of the word 'friend' that Satan had unthinkingly used, and looked away from each other.

Peter was calculating just how many unbroken bones he still had, if any, when he remembered. "Toby!" he gasped. "We have to find him."

He staggered through the door which led into the back of Tobias' office. The overturned table, his presents lying smashed over the floor, foretold the worst. But at least there were no bodies there.

"I don't understand," Squiggly said. "How did that red-eye survive a night on Limbo?"

"It must have been inside all the time," Lamia suggested.

One. Only one? Surely they'd have left more than one behind in case the quarry made it back to the Station.

They had.

The second door of Tobias' office, which opened on to the main corridor, was open: Peter spotted the group of Nefilim as they turned into the corridor. But they also spotted him.

"In here, we can only slow them down," said Squiggly instantly, "so get going!"

"Don't..." began Peter, but the two serpents were already catherine-wheeling down the corridor, and he saw the first trip one of the Nefilim, but the other went flying into the air as a second monster reacted with unexpected speed. He felt, rather than saw, Satan moving past him towards the enemy.

"Get back in!" he yelled, "you can't fight all of them!"

Satan hesitated, while Peter dragged on his arm with all his might – which wasn't very much. Satan resisted, began to move on again, muttering "But Squiggly..."

"You can't help them! Anyway, they can leave their bodies!" *Could they? Here, inside the Station, subject to Newtonian physics?* A couple of the Nefilim were already moving towards them as Satan reluctantly gave way, and turned back into the office. Peter managed to slam the door, and push the bolts across.

The door shuddered as the first Nefil thudded into it.

And *still* Satan turned round to look at the door, half stretching out a hand as if to open it again. Then, as the door shuddered again, he shook his head and shouted:

"How do we get to the Hell Terminal?"

"That corridor out there!"

"There must be other ways!"

"I don't know them!"

The two of them stumbled back into the passage from which they had just emerged.

It was as if the builders of Gormenghast had been given a plentiful supply of whiskey and a free hand in this part of the Way Station. Tobias had led his guests through these labyrinthine tunnels without hesitation, but he'd had centuries to get to know the place. From almost the first minute, Peter knew they were lost.

Now what?

The Nefilim must have used the Shuttle. But was it still here? In any case, they'd be guarding the Hell Terminal here. Or would they? Weren't they mentally sub-normal? After all, going around dashing people to the ground couldn't be the best way to develop the intellect. Might they not all be milling round Tobias' office, stupidly waiting for the fugitives to emerge?

He's saved my life twice. So what? Last night he only wanted me alive to elicit more information about Heaven and its defences. Anyway, he owed me one, since George saved him from Bugrot. And just now? Pah! He attacked that Nefil out of sheer rage, saving me was just incidental.

"Which way?" Satan was shouting. "If you're planning any tricks, don't forget George! If I don't get back, erection soufflé for Belial's supper tonight!"

There, you see? That's what he's really like! The only reason he helped carry George from the Pit was to use him as a hostage. He's the King of Hell, for Christ's sake! But who said Hell had to be evil? Mephistopheles, Arrabis, Lazara, Charon – are they evil?

He knew he was still avoiding *the* thought.

He stopped, and sank down on to the damp concrete.

"What do you think you're doing?" hissed Satan. "We have to get back to Hell!"

"Let me rest a moment, let me think. Maybe we can reach the Terminal from the *outside*."

Lost amid dank endless corridors and tunnels, his body bruised and battered, hunted by mindless monsters – and now another enemy within, his own thoughts.

What did Eve mean?

Eve. Like a raindrop hanging from a leaf in the emerging sun, like the sudden blades of grass that would miraculously spring

247

up in the desert after a single night of rain, like a sunset bursting across the sky after a storm, hers seemed a beauty not made to last, a transient butterfly splendour, so fragile that a mere cruel thought would obliterate it. Yet the strength and the knowledge within her gave permanence to what should have been fleeting, held the raindrop in amber, embalmed the blade of grass, froze the sunset forever. And this was what frightened him: like the coldness of the stones in the Forbidden Zone, she was something that should not exist – utterly human, a vulnerable being who could cry and get angry, but also so much more than human, with her prescience, her endless store of love, her infinite sadness. No wonder Squiggly had felt seared by the sheer heat of her forgiveness.

Yes, Tobias was right. Peter was uneasy with her, uncomfortable, insecure. He knew very well that the sardine took great delight in shouting out, when Eve visited, "Remind Adam to clean his teeth!" He knew that the hedgehog was forever trying to catch her out in syntactical errors when she tried to speak Nebulan. He knew the elephant loved to douse her with jets of water just after she'd finished drying herself at the Pool. But these were the Old Ones, and he couldn't share their ease. He was, after all, a man; and she too much a woman.

But also too much like a god. She had been born with the faculty of Foresight, or rather, Foresensing, in itself enough to make Peter feel nervous when he conceived his mini-rebellion. And sure enough, she'd come to him the night before he fled Heaven, but not to accuse him. She'd given him the Scroll from the Book of Razael. "All I can Sense," she'd said, "is that you may need it. A... friend has taken great risks to get it."

But, in addition, she'd given him that cryptic message for the serpents – and said that they, in turn, had a message for him. Squiggly had said no. But now, his body wracked with pain, his mind bruised, his emotions crawling raw and livid out of the dark places where he kept them confined, he could no longer keep the thought out. He knew what the message was.

He wanted to help the serpents.

Everything else could be rationalised away. But Squiggly and Lamia? He, the saint, had left them to their fate, and run away, while Satan, the Outcast, had tried to go to their defence: it was as simple as that.

The half-soaked stupid old bastard wanted to help the serpents! Damn you!

He sensed a helpless fury welling up inside him.

Satan was pulling him to his feet. "We have to get to the shuttle!"

Peter, knowing he was ruining everything he had been working for, heard his voice as if it belonged to someone else, to an enemy betraying him.

"If you escape, don't attack Heaven! You'll be destroyed!" *Francis, George, Nicholas, Tobias, all of you, forgive me!*

Satan laughed harshly. "Nothing can destroy the Beast."

"I tell you, you'll both be destroyed!"

Satan completely misunderstood. "You think of your friends in Heaven at a time like this? Ah Peter, I swear to you, when they are in my power, I will never harm a single one of your friends. They are safe."

Peter laughed insanely. "You swear by the Oath of the Twisted Testicle?"

"Yes, I swear by..." Then Satan, too, burst out laughing.

They were still laughing idiotically when they heard the shouts behind them. *So the Nefilim really can smell saint!* It was the end. He was to die beside the creature he had come to destroy. *Surely I deserve better than to have such a clichéd ending!*

When he saw the chink of light ahead of them, his only thought was *Oh goody, the Nefilim will now have more room to dash me to the ground!* And as Satan dragged him, cursing hysterically, through the exit and out of the Station, he knew he'd finally gone mad when he imagined he heard *'For Heaven and St. George, and especially St. George!'* Even had it been real, he thought, the Nefilim would have time to dash him to the ground at least three times before such a stupidly long battle-cry even came to an end.

249

****

He was wrong. They only had time to dash him to the ground once. This was, however, quite sufficient to knock him unconscious, and when he came to, the battle was over.

The first thing he saw was Tobias gazing earnestly down at him and wringing his plump hands. The next, George saying "Afternoon, Peter, sorry I was late", as he removed a Nefil head impaled on his sword. The next, Lazara gazing cheerfully down at him with one eye, and devouring George with the other. The next, Satan talking to a lamppost and a tree trunk. No, that couldn't be right! He blinked, recognised that the lamppost was Mephistopheles, and guessed that the tree trunk must be Moloch. Next, the Four Horses of the Apocalypse standing quietly to one side. After all this, it was hardly a surprise to see the ground strewn with the bodies of Nefilim.

I refuse to say 'Where am I?' "Is anyone else coming to the party?" he asked.

Tobias, it transpired, had escaped the Nefilim the previous evening by making a detour round them and heading back to the Station. With the Unbound Souls growing stronger every hour, he'd arrived back in such a state of fear that he'd spent the whole night wandering disoriented through the tunnels. He'd finally slept exhausted, and only been woken by the noise of the battle with the Nefilim.

It took somewhat longer for Peter to understand what had brought the Four Horses to Limbo. Mephistopheles, Moloch, George, and Lazara (who insisted on being with 'er feller') had gone to the Pit, with teams of Fliers taking it in turns to bear the heavy burdens of Moloch and George. Until their arrival, George had been completely obedient, but on again seeing the Beast, who had given him a friendly nod of recognition, he had been so intent on revenge that it had taken the combined force of all the Fliers, and Moloch sitting on him, to bring him to order again.

George finally wrenched the head off his sword, and then used the jaw as a whetstone to sharpen the blade, as Peter told his friends about Algernon and Ethel, while, a short distance away,

Moloch removed some intestines which were clogging up the spikes of his mace Gutripper as Satan and his friends discussed their next move. The Four Horses were neighing in a very disgruntled manner: Limbo wasn't ideal grazing ground.

Seeing Tobias and George looking at him with unfaltering trust, Peter was already regretting that he'd tried to warn Satan against attacking Heaven. He'd been on the point of betraying friends he'd known and loved for centuries simply because Satan hadn't turned out to be quite as vile as he'd expected. Indeed, he was arguably superior to either George or Tobias, but friendship and loyalty was something that had to go beyond objective judgements, otherwise the concept had little meaning.

Fortunately, Satan seemed to have forgotten the warning, anyway, since he'd put it down to Peter wishing to protect his friends. *So what happens now? We could reach the Heaven Shuttle from here. If Satan tries to force us to go back to Hell, is George recovered enough to fight both Moloch and Satan? I don't think so.*

The question was academic, for at that very moment, a puzzled look climbed into the grooves it had been cutting out on George's face over the centuries.

"Who let that damn dragon out?" he growled.

Somehow, Peter already knew what he was going to see before he even looked up.

Had he had the angel eyes of Satan and Moloch, he would also have seen that Bugrot and thousands of Nefilim were lining its flanks.

****

Thousands of miles out in space, another creature with angel eyes spotted the Beast at the same time. His one thought was, "This time I've really put my foot in it!"

The Archangel Gabriel had been in torment ever since Eve had asked him to secure a certain Scroll from the Cosmic Book of Razael. Indeed, his torment had begun even before that, when St. Darren, giggling uncontrollably, had warned him to vote against St.

251

Peter and his friends in the trial the Reform Party were preparing against them. Otherwise, he'd have to reveal a little something he had overheard in Limbo, about Eve's second child, Abel.

Gabriel wasn't ashamed of what he'd done, and neither, he knew, was Eve. Indeed, he had his own suspicions as to the paternity of Cain, but was too much of a gentleman to ever raise the matter. However, it did rankle just a little bit, and as he was often responsible for accepting the burnt offerings when God was away in Heaven, on one occasion he just couldn't resist throwing it back in Cain's face. When you are the son of Satan, when a burnt sheep's carcass lands bum-first right on your face, and when your elder brother then laughs his leggings off, there is only one thing to do. Exit Abel.

Eve and Gabriel had words over the matter, and thenceforth Gabriel's dangly was sentenced to glow in vain. But the warmth and affection between them had survived all the millennia, and they still smiled secretly at each other when they recalled those wild days of primeval innocence and discovery. They kept their brief affair a secret, not from shame, but because, recognising the insecurity and weakness of the human male, they hadn't wanted Adam to be hurt by the knowledge that his first two children weren't actually his.

Now, of course, with the new puritanical morality that was corroding and corrupting the very spirit of Heaven, it would be disastrous if the affair came to light. And although Gabriel was sure Darren could never prove a thing...

...the Virgin Mary wouldn't need proof.

What a fool he'd been! "No fuss, no trouble," God had said. "All I need is a womb for my child. Any healthy married woman will do, so long as she doesn't smoke or take drugs. Oh, and make it somewhere in the East, so the little mite doesn't catch cold." The important thing was that nobody should know. He wanted his child, while on Earth, to be a normal child, to experience what it was to be mortal and human. And what had Gabriel done? Seen the young Mary collecting water from the well, and fallen in love (yet again) on the spot! Of course, he didn't dare do anything about his desire then, but he did think that the mother of the son of God would *have* to go to Heaven – and then she'd surely know how to show

252

her gratitude to him for having chosen her for such an honour! The fatal error wasn't entirely his fault. He'd overheard Joseph boasting to his cronies in the inn about his romps with Mary, never thought to check on the truth of these assertions, contacted the Holy Ghost and, not without a tinge of jealousy, told him to get on with the job.

The furore in Heaven when it was discovered that Mary had been a virgin! God himself shaking with anger! No fuss, he'd said, and suddenly a *virgin* was in the family way! And *all* Gabriel's blabbing about how a very special baby was to be born! From then onwards, things had got more and more out of hand, culminating in that final humiliating story that God had sent his son to Earth to save everybody! "From what?" God had actually bellowed, "from *myself?*"

Gabriel had only survived this debacle because everyone agreed that, apart from the unfortunate virginity, Mary was in every other way an ideal choice. And things might still have been all right, except that Jesus himself got to hear the stories, let it all go to his head, and played around with his embryo Nebulan powers, not realising he was just as mortal as everybody else. And then, having brought his fate on himself, once he got to Heaven he forced his father to create the Beast of the Apocalypse to avenge him.

It turned out, moreover, that Gabriel had disgraced himself for nothing. For instead of a newly cloned body, Mary arrived in Heaven with a body that was already fifty years old! God would never talk about the Corporeal Assumption, but the angels had a pretty strong suspicion that Jesus had again been meddling without his father's permission. Gabriel, though shocked, had still paid court to her, for he had come to love her simple sincere character.

But being the mother of the son of God had gone to *Mary's* head, too. She enjoyed Gabriel's attentions, but played the coy maiden. She seemed to forget that she had gone on to give Jesus four brothers. In Heaven, because of the notoriety of Gabriel's blunder, she was still – jokingly, at first – referred to as the Virgin, and that was how she came to see herself.

Fifty was bad enough, in a Heaven where everyone else was

253

in their prime. But Mary *continued to age!* The pitiable creature, the putrescent flesh clinging to her crumbling bones, her very brain cells cancerous, became rancorous and vindictive, while Gabriel's passion changed to a deep, abiding pity.

But now the poor Virgin clutched at the love that Gabriel had once offered her, as a deer freezing to death in winter might remember the warm days of summer. It was, he felt sure, the only thing that stopped her going completely insane. The more her body putrefied, the more grotesquely coquettish she became with the Archangel, trying to move in a hideous caricature of adolescent femininity, smothered in perfumes that scarcely had the strength to hide the stench of decay. She didn't expect, or even want, a physical response: it was the *memory* she hoped to keep alive, a wretched need to feel that *still* Gabriel desired her.

But at the same time she resented her dependence on him, and went against him at every opportunity, drawing nourishment from each capitulation of his, as a parasite bleeds its host to death. She saw he hated Darren, and therefore backed the Infant's every whim, she backed Michael, she opposed those, like St. Peter, whom she knew him to like or respect. She sought to humiliate him while he provided the blood that only just held her madness this side of obscenity.

The Reform Part was moving against Peter and his friends. One thing was sure: if Gabriel went openly against the Virgin, it would be like plunging a knife into her golem body, and for a vengeful Darren then to reveal what he knew would twist that knife so that the last drop of sanity would ooze out. For the Virgin, decomposing on her bed with his image in her tortured mind, to learn now that the hated Eve had been his first love – and the mother of his child – that, he was sure, would finally destroy her. Could he turn off the life-support system after two thousand years?

No, he could not break the hideous Hippocratic Oath he had forced on himself: Peter would have to be sacrificed.

But, desperate, he told Eve everything, sought her comfort and advice, and she told him that if he really wanted to help Peter and his friends – and maybe achieve something even greater – he must commit the ultimate sacrilege, and gain unauthorised access to the Cosmic Book itself! And because it was Eve, because he knew she would never willingly harm anyone – even though she warned him that her visions were incomplete, and that the result of this action might well be worse than the disasters she was attempting to avoid – he had acceded to her request.

But he had, of course, read the Scroll he had copied. Which was why, for the past four days, he had been flying out deep into space, afraid that this time Eve had judged wrongly.

And now his worst fears had come true: the Beast was on the way to attack Heaven! And not just with Fallen Angels, but with Nefilim!

He turned, cursing himself, and flew back to warn the High Council.

Chapter Twenty-Four
THE DEVIL HEARS CONFESSION

When Satan confirmed that the Beast was heading for Heaven with an army of Nefilim, George at once leapt upon the Red Horse ready to do battle, but that mighty steed, at a command from Satan, simply threw him off. Everyone then had to sit on him while Peter persuaded him that it would not be a good idea to try to chastise a Horse of the Apocalypse. Lazara was almost in tears, perhaps suspecting that her 'feller' was never going to settle for quiet domestic bliss.

The Beast will be destroyed by the Flame Cannon without the necessity of destroying Satan as well. The Apocalypse will be stopped! Hurrah! I've won!

As for what would happen when the Beast was destroyed, he preferred not to think – with luck (which, translated, meant, 'with George's help') he would by then have put a safe distance between himself and a vengeful King of Hell.

Then he became aware of what the others were saying. *I'm hallucinating! They're talking about saving Heaven from the Beast!*

"We still have the Four Horses," Satan was saying, "we can do *something*."

"But why?" asked Mephistopheles. "You're safe now. You can't be blamed for not having the Apocalypse if you haven't got the Beast. And the Nefilim will be out of the way."

"But if they take Heaven, what's to stop them returning one day to attack Hell?"

"Take Heaven?" Mephistopheles laughed. "Defeat the angels on their home ground? Very unlikely. Anyway, even if they did, do you think they'd want to leave Heaven and go back to Hell?"

Satan stared up at the sky. The Beast was almost out of sight now.

"The question is," said Mephistopheles, "*why* has Belial betrayed us? What was he afraid of?"

"I'm not sure it *was* Belial," said Satan stubbornly.

"Mammon did come to warn me," added Moloch. "He had blood running down his face."

"That settles it," said Mephistopheles, "it must have been tomato sauce: Mammon's blood might crawl or drip or dribble, but it wouldn't *run* anywhere. And only Belial knew where the Reins and Glove were."

" 'E wanted to sleep in Lord Satan's bed 'cos it's ever so big an' comfy," opined Lazara.

"What does it matter?" said Satan impatiently. "You won't understand, Toffy, because you've never been there, but... Moloch, would you really like to see Heaven destroyed by the Nefilim?"

"Of course! Well, maybe not Heaven itself, but the angels yes, well, most of them."

"If anybody's going to destroy Heaven, and all the angels, it's going to be *me*!" roared Satan. "Heaven belongs to *us*, not the Nefilim!"

"That's what I meant," said Moloch.

"The Beast wasn't flying very fast," Satan contined. "The weight of all those Nefilim, I expect. The Horses could probably catch it."

"That was Bugrot with the Reins," added Moloch. "If we could dislodge him, get the Reins, the Beast would obey you..."

Mephistopheles hesitated, but the old warrior in him was stirring. "You're right. What does it matter how many Nefilim there are? They can't all be in the same place at the same time."

"An' the 'Orses can keep the 'orrors at bay," enthused Lazara, "an' wot with George 'ere too to 'elp..."

"Let's go," said George, hearing his name.

"That is," said Mephistopheles, "if our saintly friends *want* to help."

"I've never ridden a horse in my life," said Peter truthfully.

"Then you, Peter, can stay here, but of course, you'd be quite willing for George to help us save your home, I suppose?" said Mephistopheles. Peter felt his eyes boring into him.

"I can't believe you're all willing to risk your lives to save Heaven!" Peter burst out.

"Peter," said Satan, "do you think I want my heritage littered with thousands of Nefilim when I get there? Do you think I want my breakfast served by unsightly crippled angels? The Beast is *mine*, and *I'm* the one who's going to destroy Heaven, not some brainless monsters."

"It's 'is Beast," said Lazara, "an' 'e can do with it wot 'e wants, so there!"

"Perhaps," said Mephistopheles, "Peter has something he wants to say."

This time there could be no doubt. Mephistopheles *knew*. But how?

Peter returned the Chieftain's gaze wearily. "Yes, you're right. To get yourselves killed by the very people you want to protect, whatever you say, is just too bloody stupid! The Nefilim aren't going to get very far anyway."

Everyone stared at him, except Mephistopheles, who nodded with quiet satisfaction.

"Satan," went on Peter, "can I talk to you alone?"

But Satan, after so many battles, was in Noble Mode. "Anything you have to say to me, my friends can hear too," he said grandly.

Don't be too sure! But he was so angry with Satan for not acting as any self-respecting evil fiend ought to act that he didn't argue.

"Can you imagine," he said tiredly, "a woman of fifty coming to Heaven, and boasting that she'd never even spoken to a man in her life? St. Asella did just that."

Lazara looked disgusted.

"Or a woman who decided it would be an offence against God to wash herself more than twice a year? St. Bridget at your service."

"Stank the Courtroom out!" muttered Tobias. "And that was just her *soul*!"

"Or a man who lived on top of a pillar for thirty years? St. Simon Stylites. Or a man who believed he could serve God by banishing snakes from a country?"

258

"Patrick," Tobias recalled. "Of course, he *was* Irish..."

"Whatever in the name of the Twisted Testicle are you talking about?" demanded Satan.

Mephistopheles chuckled. "I think he's leading up to the Flame Cannon," he said.

George glanced across with interest, while Satan looked from one to the other with a bewildered exasperation.

"When did you guess?" Peter asked the Saragash Chieftain.

"Belial is a coward. He had to have a *very* good reason to risk so much."

"You ought to meet the Hedgehog one day. I think you'd get on well."

Satan slammed his fist into the palm of his hand, and yelled, "If we're going to stop the Beast, we have to move now! You two can play riddles later!"

"Michael was letting in all the weirdos," continued Peter wearily, as if Satan hadn't spoken. "Anyone who'd lived a normal, healthy life was kept out. Heaven was becoming unbearable for the original saints. We died horrible deaths, and then found ourselves spending eternity with fanatics, and torturers, and ascetics, and flagellants, and sexual deviants, and Crusaders, and murderous popes. Anybody I chose Michael automatically vetoed. So Raphael came up with a compromise, and agreed to set up the Way Station – as you know, of course – and although Michael put in Cuthbert as Chief Judge, I got Toby in, too. And so, yes, we began to fix some of the trials. Maybe we were sometimes unfair, I can see that now. We were so determined to redress the balance, to get in some nice, normal people, that we became as bad as Michael, automatically excluding – with a little help from some drugged wine – virgins, mystics, missionaries, and so on, some of whom perhaps deserved Heaven for other reasons. But you can't imagine what it was *like* up there!"

"It does sound pretty awful," said Satan. "But why didn't the Usurper do his own Judging?"

"He used to, till Jesus came. When he tried to stop Jesus creating the Beast, Jesus apparently turned on him and pointed out that his own human rights record was so abysmal it was downright embarrassing to be his son! Apart from the Flood and Sodom and Gomorrah, he said, he was ashamed to look an Egyptian, a Canaanite, a Moabite, a Philistine, or almost any other 'ine' or 'ite' in the eye. It seems God took it to heart, felt he couldn't trust his own judgement any more, and let the Council take over."

"From what you say," said Satan slowly, "I would've thought you'd have *wanted* the Apocalypse. If all of Limbo, and most of Hell, is going to go to Heaven, it seems – and I assure you I mean this in the kindest way – there'll soon be a lot of your sort of people there. Or are you still going to say it's only a question of overcrowding?"

Peter hesitated. But the only way to stop these devils – and George – from committing sure suicide was to tell the truth. *And just when everything was working out so well! If only I could believe the reasons he gave for stopping the Beast were his real ones!*

"The trouble with the Apocalypse," he said, "is that it includes the Second Judgement. And the trouble with the Second Judgement is that *we are going to be included in it.*"

"So that's it!" breathed Mephistopheles. "Now it begins to make sense!"

Satan, Moloch, and Lazara did not agree with him. They stared at Peter open-mouthed.

Tobias spoke up. "He means the saints – and their friends – are going to be re-judged."

"And can you guess who the Judges are going to be?" asked Peter.

Satan snapped his fingers. "The Council of Seven!"

Peter gave a smile that looked as if it had been stewed in Macbeth's witches' cauldron.

"The Council of *Nine.* Raphael, Michael, Gabriel, Uriel, Doriel, Urmak, Radkiel – and St. Darren and the Virgin Mary!"

"What!" From Tobias.

"Yes, my old friend, I only learnt that myself a few days ago. Gabriel warned me about it. By the way, Toby, I must ask you to speak of Darren with respect in future, as he is now officially the Immaculate Infant."

Satan had burst out laughing. "The Council of Seven enlarged to include a frigid old hag and a psychotic baby! And their job is to judge that old reprobate St. Peter himself! Now that's what I'd call a real pickle!"

"A devil of a fix!" added Tobias, old habits dying hard.

"I appreciate your sympathy," muttered Peter, his teeth grinding together like two hacksaws having a quarrel. "I'm glad I afford you some amusement."

"Oh come on, Peter, don't be so stuffy! What an honour! They alter the constitution of Heaven itself just to get at you! Why *did* you treat that poor sweet baby so badly, by the way? What had he done?"

"Nothing. But fanaticism and bigotry ran in the family, it was in the blood. I don't claim that what we tried to do was morally right." *I'm having a bad dream, I can't really be apologising to the Devil on a point of ethics!*

"True morality, of course," remarked Satan, "is something that only comes with age and experience, and you're only two thousand years old. It's understandable. But are there any other charges against you in the Second Judgement, apart from the fact you've been blatantly fiddling the *First* one?"

"Yes. Second: I shouldn't have become a saint in the first place, for three reasons: the three cock crows which no one ever seems to forget..."

"Ah yes," interposed Satan, "Junior didn't seem to appreciate that he who runs away today, lives to run away again another day!"

"...sleeping in the Garden of Gethsemane, and using undue violence against a servant of the High Priest..."

"We heard about that. Really, Peter, cutting off the poor fellow's ear! Anything else?"

"Three: affecting a personal appearance that lowers the tone of Heaven. Four: having an unseemly affair with a certain militant French saint, thereby bringing Heaven into disrepute."

"You never!"

"Five: refusing to expel from Heaven certain decanonised saints, such as Christopher, Nicholas, Agatha, Valentine, George..."

"Yes, Peter? Is it time to go?"

"Six: keeping unsavoury company, and yes, before you say it, George's name does crop up again. And seven, which I'm sure is being added to the list right now: unauthorised visit to Hell, keeping even more unsavoury company, and conspiring to prevent the Apocalypse."

"So there aren't any *serious* charges? Still, let's see: Raphael, Gabriel, and Radkiel will support you. That's three. Urmak I know nothing about..."

"I don't believe he'll allow such a travesty of justice."

"Well, let's be honest, not exactly *travesty*... anyway, that's four. So it all depends on Uriel. I met him in Eden..."

"Uriel won't vote against me."

"So, five to four in your favour. A reprimand, a bit of latrine cleaning, some spud bashing, nothing worse." Satan sounded genuinely pleased.

"Five to four *against* me. Gabriel will vote with the Virgin."

"Don't be stupid! I know Gabriel's thick as two waterlogged planks, but he'd laugh his head off at all those charges."

"That's what I thought. But he told me himself he'll vote against me if the trial goes ahead."

"He *told* you?"

"Yes. I think he was trying to warn me."

There was a silence while Satan digested all this information. Then he said: "So you thought that if there were no Apocalypse, there'd be no Second Judgement. Just like you said at the beginning!"

Peter nodded.

"But it wasn't overcrowding you wanted to prevent, but your own re-judgement."

Peter nodded again.

"And you showed me what Revelations said about me, to discourage me from having the Apocalypse. But we checked, the document was genuine. "

"Of course. But you said it yourself: the ravings of a madman, with grains of truth."

"But the Scroll of Razael backs up your story,"

"Only if you're already half convinced. The Apocalypse and the Final Judgement are both entered there, but you only *assumed* the Final Judgement included the Burning Lake for you. There's nothing at all about it in the Scroll."

"The Scroll mentions a Punishment," objected Satan.

"I know. And I don't know exactly what that means. It probably refers simply to the loss of the damned souls. But I guessed how you'd interpret it *after* reading *Revelations*."

"You would have risen high in the Guild of Tempters," murmured Mephistopheles.

After another pause, Satan said: "So if I *had* had the Apocalypse, nothing would have happened to me and the Companions? No Brimstone Lake?"

"Of course not. After all, it was God who gave you the Beast."

Lazara opened her mouth to protest, saw Satan turn away in embarrassment, and closed it again. *Sorry, Lazara. I really did enjoy your version much more.*

"But the emptying of Hell? The cloned bodies really are in the Vaults. I didn't really believe you at all until I saw them."

Oh yes, you did! "That's true. God really does intend to give the damned souls another chance. But I repeat, that's not the same as throwing you in the Lake again,"

Poor Lazara couldn't take any more. "No one could throw Lord Satan in no lake! 'E only went there, 'cos 'e got all sweaty thumpin' all those angels in 'Eaven, so 'e went in the Lake for a wash, 'cos 'e didn't know it weren't 'ealthy!"

"I apologise," said Peter. "I chose my words badly."

"But did you really think George could slay the Beast?" asked Satan.

Peter smiled wearily. "Not at all. I simply needed to spend more time with you."

Then he waited for the explosion. *Thank God George is wide awake!*

Satan was quiet for a full minute, while his mind grappled with an impossible concept.

"As Belial said, you gave away a lot of important information

about Heaven's weakness – anarchy in Heaven, Lucifer societies...
were they *lies?*"

"Yes," said Peter.

"The Flame Cannon?"

"Primed and ready for action."

George's puzzled frown stirred uneasily in its grooves.
"Eve?"

"Physically, in the best of health."

Satan could no longer delay facing the truth.

*"So all the time you intended me to attack Heaven, knowing the
Flame Cannon would destroy me?"*

"Destroy the Beast, that was the important thing."

"But destroying me in the process."

"That was a possibility. But you survived before..." The words
sounded false even to himself. "I warned you. In the Way Station I
warned you..."

There was no explosion, no paroxysm of rage. Rather, the
spirit seemed to go out of Satan. He seemed suddenly... diminished,
as though the shroud of his own vast and wasted age were being
drawn tighter around him.

"So you'd have done all that, just to escape... what? Demotion?
Scandal? A spell in Limbo, perhaps? All that, after I... I would have
given you high honour in Heaven, Peter..." His voice was now barely
audible. "I believed we were... not really enemies."

"Listen to me," said Peter urgently, "I warned you, don't
forget I warned you. And why do you think I'm telling you now?"

"Oh yes, you warned me when it was too late, when you
thought it made no difference!" The contempt and the pain were
almost palpable.

"No difference!" Peter's voice shook. "God damn you, you
think it would have made no difference? I almost betrayed my
friends to save you! No difference? There were – are – hundreds of
us going on trial, mine is just the test case, not just me, but *anybody,
everybody,* in Heaven who hasn't behaved as the Reform Party
thinks they should have! The Second Judgement, Satan, the Second
Judgement! After you saved my life twice, do you really believe I

would have gone ahead if it had just been *me?*"

Life seemed to be flowing into Satan again. "*Hundreds* of you? All going on trial?" It was almost an entreaty, a plea that this be the truth.

"Yes, hundreds, by the end probably thousands: once they tasted blood, what would stop them?"

"That... makes a difference..."

"More difference than you think! After the Apocalypse, there wasn't going to be any more Limbo. There'd be no point to it. *They couldn't send us to Limbo!*"

It didn't sink in at first. "No more Limbo? Then what, where...?"

Satan stared at Peter, then, like a butterfly emerging from its chrysalis, a smile began to break through his torn features. "*Hell!*" he whispered. The smile broadened, an incongruous childlike joy in a face spattered with blood and bruises. "You were going to come to *Hell!*"

Tobias spoke, horrified. "Peter, you never told me!"

Peter forced a grim smile. "Oh, Hell's not so bad when you get to know it. It's warm, there's lots of excitement, interesting people, and even bits of interesting people."

"*My subjects!*" Satan rolled the words around his bruised mouth like vintage wine. "*My subjects!*" Then he said: "In your place, I wouldn't have warned you even if you *had* saved my life. Why did you do it?"

"The serpents."

"*The serpents!*"

"You were concerned about the serpents. That's what finally decided me."

Satan looked at him in utter astonishment.

Peter added: "I said, that's what *finally* decided me."

"I was not wrong in my judgement of you," said Mephistopheles.

"But why tell me all this now?" asked Satan.

"To stop you killing yourself in vain. Both our problem are, at least temporarily, solved. The Beast, and the Nefilim, will be destroyed by the Flame Cannon, so there can't be any Apocalypse. But if you're anywhere near the Beast when the Cannon are used, bits of you will probably reach as far as here. Why kill yourself for nothing?"

George had been growing more and more agitated. So much so that he now did a very unusual thing: he asked a question.

"Has God changed his mind, then?"

Peter looked at him, perplexed.

"About what?"

"The Flame Cannon."

Peter felt a terrible premonition. "What do you mean?"

"You told me that big dragon was born in Heaven, right?"

"Yes."

"So no one can use the Cannon against it then."

Three minutes later, Peter had learnt the worst. George often went to the Forge to have new weapons made by the angel Anviel. As George was practically his only customer, Anviel would have fascinating one-way conversations, and frequently complained that since God had stopped sending angels with flaming swords to butcher the enemies of the Israelites, his 'work' was reduced to polishing the Flame Cannon. It was all a waste of time anyway, Anviel told him, since God, stricken with remorse for the destruction of the Rebels' wings, had Vowed never to use the Cannon against the Heaven-born again.

The Beast was Heaven-born.

Less than a minute after the imparting of this rather interesting information, the four Horses of the Apocalypse swept majestically into the air and hurtled in the wake of the Beast.

St. Peter was torn between contemplation of his own stupidity – what was he doing sitting behind Mephistopheles on a goddamned flying Horse? – and a growing panic: Satan now knew that the Flame Cannon couldn't be used against him.

266

Chapter Twenty-Five
Blood Over Heaven

"Let's see," said Peter. "Four flying horses, two saints, two devils, and two demons – one of them well past his sell-by date – against the Beast of the Apocalypse and twenty thousand invincible monsters. Hmmm. Who would *you* bet on, Mephistopheles?"

"Faith, Peter, faith!" chided Mephistopheles. Then, after a moment: "The Beast and monsters, of course." After another moment: "You're not exactly a baby yourself!"

Ah, this insouciant banter between heroes as they ride fearlessly to their doom!

He and the ancient Saragash were on the White Horse; George and Lazara (arms around his neck, wings open: was he even aware she was there?) on the Red Horse; Moloch on the Black Horse (its head could just be seen emerging from the suffocating folds of his buttocks); and Satan on the Pale Horse.

Acute respect for the astronomical distance between a flying horse in deep space and the nearest celestial body had, Peter realised, helped him to learn to ride extremely quickly.

The ill-assorted companions caught up with the Beast three hours later just as the Elysian Fields came into view.

****

Warned by Gabriel, Raphael had already united his forces, such as they were, in the recently renamed Darrenspark, just outside Michaelsville.

As the Beast neared, they could see thousands of red-and-black misshapen creatures swarming along its flanks like mutant locusts, screaming and snarling, brandishing terrifying weapons in their free hands. They had found purchase for their feet on the sclerotic ridge that encircled the Beast like the base of a tortoise shell. Above them all, perched triumphantly on the Beast's middle neck, was Bugrot,

267

controlling the Beast with Reins that threw off coruscating flashes of greenish gold. It was clear that the Beast wished to dislodge this rider, but each time it tried to do so, he jabbed down at its middle head with a similarly glowing Glove, which seemed to send spasms of pain through the Beast, forcing it to submit to his will.

A few of the angels were donning light armour – relics of the War in Heaven – but others, including Gabriel and the old Whiteguard, had formed a separate group, and were stretching and flexing their wings, clearly intending to attack while the Beast was still in the air.

Most of the angels, however, were looking towards the Dome: waiting for God to appear and use the Flame Cannon, which stood on an emplacement near the edge of the park.

The Dome served as an inter-dimensional Gate for God to leave the Cloud of Unknowing, and Manifest himself to his creatures without harming them. At one moment it seemed like an image superimposed upon the solid background of Heaven, but at another, it was Heaven itself that seemed insubstantial by comparison. It gave the impression that the space within it was vastly greater than the space without. Fleecy, intangible wisps curled and drifted around it, as if constraining a monster heaving with power. But when would God use that power?

A shout suddenly went up. "Look! Up there!"

Four dots had appeared in the sky to the east, dots that were approaching much faster than the Beast was. There was a kind of nimbus around them, like comets engulfed by their own tails. As they began to take on vague forms, they began to flash different colours – red, black, white...and something that was the very negation of colour.

Another shout. *"The Four Horses of the Apocalypse!"*

The Beast *and* Horses of the Apocalypse *and* thousands of mutants all descending on Heaven simultaneously!

To oppose them, a couple of thousand angels who happened to be in or near the capital, and a few Old Testament warriors such as Gideon and Joshua who also chanced to be there, leading a demonstration against St. Darren. The dinosaurs and other animals

268

who might have proved a match for the Nefilim were a thousand miles away, where they had recently withdrawn in protest at the unstoppable influence of the Reform Party.

For a moment, even Raphael showed despair, then he took a deep breath, and once again his eyes were calm and serene.

"We still have to try," he said simply.

"Yes," said Gabriel, equally calmly, "we must try."

Michael said nothing, but there was a glint of joy in his eyes as he tested the blade of his thin rapier: at last he could *fight* again for the things he believed in. He caught Gabriel's eye, and for the first time in many centuries the two Archangels, remembering the War in Heaven, nodded at each other in mutual understanding and respect.

Uriel, however, asked Raphael what many had been thinking. "Aren't the Flame Cannon going to be used?"

"No, not against the Heaven-born."

Uriel nodded, but there was hurt and anger in his eyes. He had grown up since Eden.

Raphael touched him lightly on the arm. "It's the price of free will," he said gravely, "the price of real freedom, too."

Before Uriel could answer, someone shouted: "But they're attacking the Beast!"

It was true. All four Horses were swooping towards the Beast, and sunlight glinted off sword blades, as the riders moved among the Nefilim. At that same instant, a cry rent the skies which curdled the blood and doused the flame of the few dragons still around: "...And especially St. George!"

Soon the Horses were near enough for the watchers to identify two more of the riders. Names were whispered that had almost become the stuff of folklore and legend: 'Lucifer!' 'Moloch!'

No one recognised the diminutive rider of the fourth Horse, but the trailing beard of the man behind him was unmistakable. Some of the angels groaned.

So busy was everybody staring up at the sky that only Gabriel noticed that Eve had appeared, diminutive beside the pride of Heaven's angels, wearing a simple white flowing robe. He looked across at her, seeking answers, but her eyes were glazed, as if she were not really seeing what was happening.

Then Raphael and Michael swept into the air, and he followed, the Whiteguard beside him, darts of pure gold piercing the sky, daggers of silver aiming for the hearts of the Nefilim, erupting like fireworks among them.

****

St. Peter's role in the stirring events that followed was not of the most glorious. He stayed on the Horse, clinging desperately to Mephistopheles, long enough to realise that the others had already decided on a strategy. George – with Lazara just behind him, her devilsmane whipping round her shoulders – and Moloch raced along either flank of the Beast, dealing out death and destruction to the disadvantaged Nefilim with such uniform ferocity that they approached its heads – and Bugrot – simultaneously. Bugrot, however, with the power of the Glove, forced three of the Beast's heads to turn and keep them from approaching any nearer by sending out jets of flame. But this, it seemed, the riders had been expecting, for they turned, and like Horatius on the bridge, battled to stop the Nefilim from advancing across the main neck where the heads branched off, thus cutting off any aid to Bugrot.

Satan, meanwhile, relying on the fact that he was the appointed Master of the Beast, and that therefore the Beast would not, whatever the agony from the Glove, attack him, was assaulting Bugrot directly, this time with the enormous advantage that he was mounted on a clearly homicidal steed. Peter, peeping out from behind Mephistopheles, who for some strange reason was suddenly flying *away* from the Beast – *while eminently sensible, this is just too good to be true* – saw Bugrot actually giving way before the assault.

At the same time, the angels, too, were wreaking havoc in the Nefilim ranks, swooping and plunging and darting, dislodging monster after monster, who fell screaming down to the surface below.

Despite this carnage, for every Nefil killed or dislodged, a hundred remained, and the assault was doing nothing to halt the

270

steady descent of the Beast itself. Within a few minutes, it – and the Nefil hordes – would be touching the very soil of heaven.

Peter realised that the White Horse was now sweeping back towards the Beast. *I knew it!* Towards and *under!* It galloped beneath the Beast, until suddenly Mephistopheles wheeled it upwards, and struck with his tiny sword at the point where the necks joined. The heads gave a chorus of outraged squeals, and lashed downwards, but couldn't reach the vulnerable spot. Again the canny old Chieftain, matching the speed of his Horse to that of the Beast, jabbed upwards, again the heads twisted down in furious protest, again they couldn't reach him. Jab, squeal, lunge; jab, squeal, lunge; and with each jab, the Beast veered upwards, trying to escape the painful cuts.

Peter's contribution to this brilliant tactic was, first, to hamper Mephistopheles by clinging on to his arm, and then, after a particularly abrupt movement of the Horse to escape an irate head, to hamper the Horse by clinging on to its tail. *Will I be remembered for having fought against Bugrot himself on the burning sands of Hell? For having outwitted the very Prince of Lies? Like hell! Three cock crows for my first epitaph, and falling off a bloody flying horse for my second!*

He really felt quite hard done by as he lost his grip, and plunged downwards.

The beleaguered Beast was now at an angle of forty-five degrees to the ground, and the Nefilim, still reeling from the assault by George and Moloch, and harassed by the Whiteguard, were slipping off in their dozens. But not Bugrot: he saved himself by holding tight to the Reins, and kept his position. And the Beast quickly proved that seven heads are better than one: it abruptly lowered three of them at once. Taken completely by surprise, the White Horse flew into them with such force that it almost knocked itself unconscious.

And as it fluttered feebly in the air, Bugrot leaned over and smashed his club full into Mephistopheles' face.

For those few seconds, the Nefil was vulnerable, but Satan, with a terrible cry of anguish, swung his Horse round to try to catch the falling Chieftain. At the same time, the Beast, which until now had refrained from using its lethal tail against the Horses,

271

now swung it round like the boom of a mast in a storm, and it whipped into them, sending George and Moloch tumbling on to its back, and causing the latter to drop Gutripper. George fell right in front of Bugrot, who raised his club, dripping with the blood of Mephistopheles, with a roar of surprised delight, only to be met by Lazara's outstretched claws ripping at his eyes. The respite saved George, but for the tiny she-devil there was no chance. Bugrot, catching one wing, tore it from her body with a furious roar, and she toppled backwards, slipping off the Beast's back, limbs jerking in agony, blood desecrating her fragile beauty.

George had regained his feet, and was advancing on the Nefil with murderous, unstoppable intent. But he saw Lazara slipping away, and did something he had never done before in battle: he hesitated. He hesitated, half turned, stretched out a hand in vain to catch the writhing body...

...And received such a blow from Bugrot's club that he was lifted right off the Beast's back, and hurled backwards and downwards after Lazara's flailing body.

Two of the Whiteguard, about to wrench the Reins from Bugrot, had to obey the instincts of the angel before those of the warrior, and wheeled away instead to catch the falling bodies.

This left only Moloch. Now weaponless, he had partially climbed up one of the Beast's heads in order to use his weight advantage in the most direct way possible by leaping from a height of ten feet and landing right on top of Bugrot. This would have flattened any other creature, but though all Bugrot's limbs were trapped under the devil like chips under mushy peas, Moloch had unfortunately landed with his backside smothering Bugrot's face. Too late he remembered his piles. Next moment there was the vicious snap of teeth, and they were no more. Moloch rolled off Bugrot like a hula-hoop, yelling possibly the worst obscenities ever heard in the Universe, and continued to roll until he came to an indentation in the Beast's back, where he came to a shuddering stop like a stranded jellyfish. Bugrot rose to his feet, a delighted expression on his face, chomping the unexpected delicacy.

272

Then the Beast landed, filling half the park, and it was over. There were almost no Nefilim left on its back, but that didn't matter. No longer needing to use the Glove to force the Beast down, Bugrot was able to use it instead to control its firepower. The angels flying forward to do battle were met by a wall of flame that drove them, shrieking, back.

Peter, who had also, but only at the last moment, been caught by an angel, was tottering from the impact, but still conscious enough to notice that the Dome suddenly glowed at this moment. *At last!*

But the glow died away, and God did not intervene.

And then the Pale Horse landed.

Satan had the mangled figure of Mephistopheles in his arms. Two angels at once stepped forward to take the body, and Satan for a moment tensed, like the mother of some wild animal trying to protect her young, before seeming to realise no harm was intended. His features could hardly be seen, completely covered in blood as they were – whose blood? – but the agony and fury Peter sensed there made him forget his own pain and fatigue.

Satan looked round, saw Lazara still writhing in the arms of an angel, saw the bulk of Moloch where it had rolled off the Beast's back, even gazed at the crumpled figure of George, before turning back to the body of the old Saragash. He touched the destroyed face with one hand. Then, without a word, he turned towards Bugrot and the Beast.

Chortling with glee, Bugrot jabbed at the Beast with the Glove, it roared in pain, a flame began... then died away. Puzzled, Bugrot repeated the movement. The same thing happened. The Beast could not – or would not – attack its appointed Master. Furious, Bugrot leapt down from the Beast, and hurled himself at his enemy.

Later, Satan was to claim that Devil's Meadow (formerly Darrenpark) would have rung with heroic deeds that day, that such a battle between titans would have been witnessed that the echoes would have reverberated even on distant planets. The witnesses were of two quite distinct opinions: all but two swore that Satan wouldn't have lasted more than ten seconds, while Lazara (through faith) and

St. Peter (who sensed what Mephistopheles had meant to the Dark Lord) were convinced that Bugrot was extremely lucky to be killed by the Beast first.

The Beast had only two thoughts: one was that Bugrot had forced it away from its beloved Pit and given it nothing but pain, and the other, that this same Bugrot was trying to hurt the hand that had fed it for two thousand years. It had only these two thoughts, and it had them in seven heads, which precluded hesitation.

The scorpion tail skewered the careless Bugrot from behind, and the heads at once cooked and ate him!

The only difference from what Peter had seen in the Pit was that, in front of so many angels, the Beast retired shyly behind a tree – at least, a small portion of its bottom did – to deposit the steaming bones.

"If the hippopotamuses had had such good manners," muttered Michael to Gabriel, "we might not have had to give up playing golf!"

As they began to recover from the shock, some of the angels began to cheer, while Satan, with his last bit of energy, staggered forwards and picked up the Glove and Reins.

Fools! They don't realise!

The Beast's middle neck lowered itself, curled round Satan, lifted him, and deposited him where the necks met, where Bugrot had been. Satan, swaying with injuries and fatigue and grief, pulled slightly on the Reins, and the Beast turned to face...

The Dome!

But instantly, Raphael, flying so fast that he was no more than a blur of light, at once placed himself between the Beast and the Dome. *With that speed, he could easily have snatched the Glove from Satan. Why didn't he do it?*

"No," he said.

The Master of the Beast wiped blood from his face. "Ten thousand years," he said, blood dribbling with his words, "ten thousand years boiling in Hell. Six thousand years without... The time for vengeance has come. Out of the way!" *It's a lie, that isn't why he came; this is because of Moloch and Mephistopheles and Lazara!*

274

Raphael remained directly in front of the Beast, unflinching. Peter had the impression of immense forces held back, of something more than angel power locked inside that body.

"Yes," said Raphael quietly, "ten thousand years. Once again the time of choice. Do not choose wrongly a second time."

""Raphael, out of my way! I swear I do not want to harm you. You only obeyed orders. But do not try to thwart me now!"

"You mean your Rebellion? We didn't obey orders, Lucifer, we weren't given any. What we did we *chose* to do."

Satan gazed at Raphael, his last illusion gone. Then fury contorted his features. The hand holding the Reins shook uncontrollably. "Out of my way! Heaven's mine!" The Beast's middle head opened its mouth...

And then a tiny white figure was running forward, Eve, clearly meaning to protect Raphael with her own body.

Satan could never harm Eve! It's over! Yet Peter immediately knew that he had to stop her. It was not even a conscious decision, but an imperative that burned into his mind, allowing no dissent. He watched his own arms in shocked amazement as they grabbed Eve as she was running past, he cursed himself even as he dragged her screaming backwards, not knowing what he did, only that he had to do it.

Raphael took a step forward.

"I warned you!" Satan screamed, his face now twisted beyond recognition. He jabbed with the Glove and a jet of flame shot out, full in the Archangel's chest. He staggered and sank to the ground.

Then, incredibly, he rose to one knee, dragged the other leg up, and stood again, a smoking hole like a dark tunnel in his brightness, the acrid odour of his burnt flesh carrying across to Peter as Eve tore at him with her nails.

"Now you know how it feels!" shrieked Satan.

"Lucifer, the Flame Cannon ...were a mistake," Raphael gasped. One of his legs scraped forward again.

"Keep back, keep back!" Rage and hysteria in Satan's voice. He raised the Glove again with a terrible scream that seemed to contain all the hate he had ever felt, all the cruelty he had ever inflicted, all the agony he had ever suffered, all the love he had ever lost.

And threw it to the ground! He stared wildly, first at Eve and Peter, and then at Raphael, before his head slumped down and he crashed to the ground in front of the great Archangel, who collapsed beside him, his chest still smouldering.

Peter, sick at heart, released Eve, expecting to be blasted by her hatred and fury. *Why did I do it? I survived Hell just to get Raphael burned to a frazzle!*

But in that moment of unnatural stillness, as the Beast, distressed, nuzzled the two fallen figures, he saw Eve staring at the Dome, now eerily glowing, and heard her repeat with wonder and fear in her voice a verse from St. Mark's Gospel:

" 'And if Satan rise up against himself, and be divided, he cannot stand, but hath an end'."

Chapter Twenty-Six
JUDGMENT

He didn't want to open his eyes, to listen, to talk. While his eyes were shut, dream images could drown out those other images of pain and death. *Ah so wonderful to lie back in the boat and wait for the fish to swim into his nets and his wife waiting at home in Capernaum and maybe in the evening a walk through the olive groves and had he once tried to walk upon the water but what was that body floating there with the fish so peacefully without a face someone he ought to know...*

A bony hand over his, a voice rich with sadness and death.

"Ah my lovely, laughing, light Lazara! **Do not look at me!** *But tell that God of yours who seems not to care whether his angels live or die, that Satan was never really evil, nor his Companions, remind them who tamed the Beast. Help to keep the Lucifer in him alive, as I have done. Ah Lazara never again light as the swallow..."*

So few words? So why will I miss you, Mephistopheles? But it's all nonsense, they say he saw the Fall of Lucifer, but no one except an angel can live that long, not without a face.

Peeled skin, burnt flesh, gold with a starburst of black. YOU made me hold back Eve, Raphael, you or your master! But how do I know this? What was that word you used? 'Redemption'? Your words had no meaning. 'Completing a circle that began in the Garden of Eden'? What are you talking about?

Is that Eve? What's that huge lump of meat you're holding? Ah, yes, Eve, the bridge from Earth to Heaven, from Heaven to God himself, but who was stronger, eh, when it really mattered? I look at you, Eve, and I weep for the shores of Galilee, nights gorged with stars and reflections and ripples, and, once, a woman bathing, and as she moved the moonlight glinting on a million tiny sea creatures washing over her body, encasing her in a weird, green, coruscating silver. You are not real, you are each man's glorious debilitating dream, so why are you sinking down beside that grotesque figure, your midnight hair falling forward and throwing a black shroud over it? There is a building I wonder if you know where the broken hopes kept the stones cold cold as themselves and so I could not betray Satan and now I see what you are holding and he in his final humiliation hunched into himself and yet he has seen the mermaids and I have not and that is why I think I feel the pain.

George is all right, or will be, but his pride...beaten by that red-eyes in front of everybody! Red-eyes, what a funny name, and why didn't I see Squiggly among all my broken bodies and blood? I suppose I must have killed him earlier... but why *did* he beat you, George? Because you tried to save Eve as she was falling, her wings torn off, and so you should feel pride not shame. Eve? But she cannot fly, someone has been lying, using me again. Peter, the poor fool who strutted and fretted and puffed his minute upon the stage, and now the real players are coming on one by one. It wasn't Eve, but Lazara, a broken doll propped up against your knee, her devilsmane coiled round her like a huge black bandage and that hideous hole instead of a shoulder torn cartilage and bone resembling intricate coral and that terrible cut clawing into her child's breast forever now a creature of the earth no more like the swallow...

You all scream my guilt at me, and say I brought the Beast, but they could have stopped it, I know Raphael had the power, stop lying to me! It wasn't me who switched off the Flame Cannon, it wasn't me who told the Nefilim to come here, it must have been Belial and Algernon because, you know, they just aren't bulgy any more, isn't that ridiculous? And now Darren will get away with it.

You think you're all so clever, so why couldn't you save Mephistopheles? **He** saved you: he *was* the one who brought the Horses out of Hell, he *was* the one who made the Nefilim fall. Even so, most of them survived. Too dazed to be any trouble, so the angels loaded them all up on the Beast and sent them off I don't know where. Back to Hell? And off it went. With, would you believe it, George's dragons too! Oh yes! It roared, and little roars came out of the ground, and it really was quite astonished, let me tell you, and it took off and came back followed by all those other dragons, and I remember Satan telling me it was lonely, and it came by again to say goodbye to him – yes, really, why do you smile? Why else would it come back, and nod all its heads like that? And then up, up into the sky, all the other dragons following it like glowing baby comets. I wonder if they think of the Nefilim as their larder! George

278

was hopping mad and he said, "There aren't none left? Not one?" and they said not one, and he looked so vulnerable without his armour, and he gazed so longingly at the sky. And then – here's the wonderful part, Toffy, I have to tell you – he looked at Lazara – you knew her, I believe – and he saw, really saw, that terrible wound, and he reached across and touched her face, as carefully as one might touch a bubble of water – George! Can you believe it? – and said "Never again?". And Lazara cried then for the first time, and fell against him, her head like a small bruise on his massive torso, because for a Flier not to fly … but you know that, because you all lost your wings in Heaven, and I think that's why you became as you are, and maybe that's what Raphael was talking about, maybe it has something to do with this whole thing. Poor George had to grope with the concept of another's grief, and he reached helplessly for his sword, but of course it wasn't there, so he touched her face and her tears trickled over his fingers, and then he was holding her tight and looking utterly bemused.

Is that you, Gabriel? Why have you turned against me? Why don't you listen to Raphael, who said something about me. Peter, being responsible for the fact Satan was unable to destroy him! I've no idea what he was talking about, but that's much nicer than voting against me like you're planning to do! Francis! More food? Do you think I don't know how to look after myself? I went to Hell and back again, could you do that? And that's when I became jealous of Satan, did Toffy tell you? So much love over so many centuries and it made me feel so empty… I preached love, you know, oh yes, wandered round for years preaching the stuff but now you mention it, I'm not sure I know what it is, is it confectionery as Algernon and Ethel insist? Everyone knows I sleep with Joan, but is that love? Do I love Eve? Toffy tried to teach me, but how can you love anything as imperfect as Satan, who's just a big lump now, with Raphael's midnight hair streaming all over him?

And thus St. Peter fought with his guilt and his fear and his despair, and stumbled towards a kind of understanding, until on the second day, he suddenly sat up, his mind crystal clear, the fever gone.

So clear that he just couldn't believe it when they told him his trial was to go ahead. After everything that had happened, they still wanted to waste their time trying him? Now that there could be no general Second Judgement, were they so determined to get their pound of flesh that they were willing to stage a mini-trial just to bag Tobias and himself? Did Darren really have the power to convene a Council of Nine meeting at eleven o'clock at night?

On the thirty-first of December, 1999?

****

The Council of Nine. In the centre, the Virgin Mary, hidden in a mass of blue veils, and on her lap St. Darren, dressed in swaddling clothes, little fingers closing and unclosing, the personification of purity and innocence: the archetypal image of the Christian faith, unblemished innocence and fulfilled motherhood. The ultimate travesty. Instead of the Mary he had known on Earth, simple, surprised, sincere, warm, the creature lurking behind that emotive blue was now little more than rotting flesh, eaten through with jealous rage and cancerous hatred; and instead of the baby Jesus, a mind feeding on carrion, nurtured on dreams of himself burning in hellfire.

After the attack on Heaven, Michael had at once sent a force to deal with the few Nefilim in the Way Station on Limbo, and poor Tobias, who'd been hiding in the tunnels all night, went in to thank them, and they said they were glad to have been of help and arrested him. Peter now asked him urgently about the serpents, but they hadn't been there when he re-entered the Station. Neither had he seen any signs of Algernon and Ethel. *So there goes our last chance.*

He dragged his eyes around. Michael, indefatigable crusader for a narrow, negative morality, next to the Virgin; Doriel next to him, a cipher to replace the increasingly independent Uriel; then a space in the centre, Raphael's seat; then Gabriel, blunt, well-meaning, flawed, a friend who had unaccountably turned enemy; Uriel, tolerant, still full of wonder; Urmak, stern, unbending, but always just; finally, Radkiel, unknown, but Satan had said, "he will support you". They all showed signs of the fighting against the Nefilim. And they all looked a bit bemused, as if wondering what they were doing there. *So who insisted on this trial, then?*

Michael at once opened the proceedings. He read out the charges Peter had earlier enumerated to Satan, but didn't add the new one of conspiracy with the King of Hell. He spoke without passion; it was clear he now had no taste for the proceedings.

Then Darren took over. He recalled in piteous tones how he'd become a martyr, and then went on to describe his trial at the Way Station, while poor Tobias writhed under the shocked, hostile stares of the Council.

"But observe," wailed Darren, dabbing at his eyes, "the unintelligent countenance of this Baby Brutaliser! The dull, vacuous eyes of this heartless Mutilator of New Life! The slack lips of this Slaughterer of the Innocents! Could such a gross creature have conceived so intricate and hideous a crime against one whose nappies had hardly yet been stained? Where should we look to find the real culprit behind this heinous plot against a helpless infant?"

Peter was so caught up in Darren's rhetoric that he began to look round for this unequalled villain before noticing everyone's eyes swivelled towards him. *So that's how Brutus felt when Mark Antony got into his stride!*

Then it was the Virgin's turn. Her voice, slightly more grating than a cicada scratching its legs with a wire brush, spoke of the vile immorality that now pervaded Heaven. This lecherous Keeper of the Keys was but the latest example, following in the wanton footsteps of the most evil temptress of them all... *And to think we used to read poetry together in Galilee!*

And so it went on, Darren and the Virgin taking it in turns to expatiate on the crimes of Peter and his friends. Michael was strangely silent, and the others said nothing, but from their expressions, Peter felt he had been overly optimistic in thinking the vote would only just go against him.

It came to an end finally.

"Would any one like to speak in defence of the accused?" asked Michael wearily.

All eyes turned towards Gabriel. He gazed steadfastly at his hands. *So it's true: but why, why?* Long seconds passed before Uriel rose to his feet, blushing furiously as always, but with a look of unusual determination on his face. He did his best, but the main charge – that of subverting justice at the Way Station – was difficult to refute.

The voting went as Peter had predicted, with Raphael, *in absentia,* voting 'guilty, but pardon recommended'. There was a slight interruption when Darren cast his verdict, because he first found it necessary to fall about with laughter, and then to shout "Crush you, crush you, crush you!" until the resultant lisp reduced him to a sibilant hiss. Gabriel had not looked up, and Michael had to ask him again for his vote.

"Don't forget, Gabriel, don't forget!" cackled Darren.

The Virgin half stood up. "Gabriel, we are waiting for you." *Do I detect panic in her voice? What's going on here?*

At last Gabriel looked up. "I find the defendants guil..."

"Oh, don't talk such utter nonsense, you great shiny twerp!"

"Hush, dear, you shouldn't speak that way to Gabriel."

"Gabriel or not, he's still only a vertical life-form, isn't he?"

Peter had recognised the voices even before he turned and saw Squiggly and Lamia at the entrance, but he felt even more joy to recognise behind them Algernon and Ethel.

"Worms in the High Council Chamber?" roared Doriel. "Throw them out!"

"You see? What did I tell you? Still stuck in the same old mouldy speciesism!"

"Squiggly!"

"Oh, all right! Gentleangels, allow me to introduce you to Ethel and Algernon, who have come to undress for you."

Algernon stepped forward, holding Ethel by the hand. Both were wearing long cloaks.

"Come on, my turtle dove, let's be honest, neither of us has really got anything left to be shy about!"

"But all those men!"

"They're angels, my little tapioca pudding, not really men."

Slowly, shyly, the two walked towards the front of the

Chamber.

Darren had stopped chortling, and had begun to give all the signs of acute colic.

The two Limboans now discarded their cloaks. They were naked.

"These two gentlefolk," said Squiggly, "are just the same as many other bodies in the Protoplasmic Warehouse. No more and no less."

The Archangels blanched when they didn't see what they should have seen. Michael finally gasped: "What is the meaning of this?"

"The meaning," said Squiggly, "is that someone did this to a lot of the bodies in the Warehouse. Algernon, tell the Court who."

Algernon looked round. "He's not here," he said.

Peter's heart sank. *Of course, Darren was in a loan body!*

"Yes, he is," said another voice. "I affirm that it was St. Darren."

Peter hadn't recognised the Guardian at first, because he was now more a tall exclamation mark than a bent-over interrogative.

"It's a lie!" Darren screamed. "I wasn't in my baby body! He couldn't recognise me!"

"It was St. Darren," the Guardian repeated. "I am the Guardian. I recognise bodies *and* souls – when I choose to."

Then he did the strangest thing: he winked at Peter. *He knew all along that I wasn't Darren! Then why...? Because he wanted us to see the bodies! The rest was all a charade! How could I have been such an idiot as to believe that the Guardian of the very Vaults would be a doddering old fool?*

As if he had read his mind, the Guardian suddenly drew his sword and for a few moments gave such a dazzling exhibition of swordplay that even the Archangels looked stunned. At the same time, a message came very clearly into Peter's mind: *"Forgive me, but I was so bored! I get so little solid company. Pop in again sometime, and bring that friend of yours who pretends so well to be a devil!"*

"First," said Gabriel, and it was the old Gabriel, strong, sure

283

of what he was doing, "I find the defendants *not* guilty. Second, I demand we investigate this matter right now."

"And I second the proposal," said Michael. Peter had never seen him so angry. *I knew he wasn't involved!*

A strangled gasp came from the Virgin as she began to topple from her seat.

And then there was a flash of light so brilliant that everybody was temporarily blinded.

When Peter opened his eyes again, the Virgin was pulling her veils from her face...

The face, fresh and healthy and vibrant and astonished, of the Mary he had known two thousand years before!

And standing beside her, glowing, emanating power, another face he had known and loved: Jesus, the son of God!

"Told you I'd be back, you old rascal! Still trying to fob off putrid fish on everybody?" he said cheerfully to Peter.

And next to Jesus, God himself!

"Right, that's dealt with the minor matters! Now let's really get down to the Final Judgement!"

"So *you're* the infamous St. Peter," said a third figure. "I believe you've been trying to corrupt an old friend of mine. My name is Beelzebub."

Somewhere, a bell chimed midnight.

Chapter Twenty-Seven
BEGINNINGS

God drifted lazily through the Universe, luxuriating in the warm massage of the stars, and feeling rather smug with himself.

Xonophix, bless his galactic heart, had said it couldn't be done; no Nebulan could break a single Link in the Cosmic Chains of Razael, without damaging the whole fabric of Space-Time.

He understood what Jesus had done. It was in the genes. The things he'd done in his own wild oats days, and without the excuse of having been crucified! No wonder, with such a father, Jesus had come to Heaven screaming blue murder, and had only been placated by God's creation of the Beast. "It will grow up in no time," he said, "and then you'll have your revenge." He'd thought he was being clever: in two thousand years, surely, his son's ire would have cooled. And indeed it did. But Jesus, rightly suspicious of his father's intentions, had at once dashed off and had the Beast, and hence the Apocalypse, entered in the Cosmic Book. And then there was nothing either of them could do about it. Any Nebulan intervention would be detected by the Chains, with unforeseen, but indubitably disastrous, consequences.

For the same reason, God had been unable to do anything about the Virgin Mary. Again, he fully understood why Jesus had done it. The poor boy, confused and terrified, only three days old as a god – three horrific days closed in by the Stone – had finally reached Heaven, only to be told off by his own father for getting himself into such a scrape with all that boasting about his paternity. He had recklessly whisked his mother, and her body, straight to Heaven, desperate to have the comfort of her arms. And nature, yet again transgressed, had exacted a terrible vengeance on the innocent woman.

Jesus had matured, and been healed, under the guidance of the Archangel Beelzebub, who had taken him to a private clinic in the Betelgeuse System, away from the constant reminder of his folly, and the unbearable anguish, and eventual bitter hatred, of his own mother.

Despair threatened to overwhelm even God himself: his son was ill, his son's mother was putrefying, his Second Creation was going from bad to worse, and he was powerless to stop the world being destroyed again. Sick to the heart, unable to trust his own judgement any longer, he withdrew into the Cloud. Let the High Council govern Heaven for the time being: he needed to rest and think.

He had forgotten that what was, to him, a brief moment, was to his creatures a very long time indeed. When he finally began to take an interest in what was going on around him again, Heaven had become a shambles. When he learned that the Reform Party, in his continued absence – but in his name, of course – was arrogating to itself the right to conduct an all-inclusive Second Judgement, he was about to break his self-imposed rule about interference in the destiny of his Shapings.

And then, one day, he had watched astonished as the premier saint of Heaven had calmly wandered off to visit the King of Hell!

Eavesdropping, God decided, with things as serious as they were, was for once permissible. It soon became obvious that the hairy wretch was out to break a Link in the Chain itself – the one thing a Nebulan could not do, or even dare suggest should be done, but which, if it were not done, would result in the cruel destruction of the Second Creation!

And he had six days to do it in!

But still God might have stopped him.

Because Peter's plan, he realised, could lead to another war in Heaven! The saint, it seemed, was trying to push Satan into an attack on Heaven, under the assumption that the Flame Cannon would repel such an attack. He didn't know that God had Vowed never to use the Cannon against the Heaven-born again. He had to be stopped.

And then Jesus had intervened.

Now fully a god – promising indeed to be quite an exceptional one – Jesus had said:

"I *know* Peter, probably better than he knows himself. And Beelzebub knows Satan. When it comes to it, they'll be unable to destroy each other. Peter may stop Satan going ahead with the Apocalypse – something we all want – but in the end he won't send him against what he believes to be certain destruction by the Flame Cannon. Trust my judgement."

And God, after conferring with Raphael and Beelzebub, had trusted him. The prize was priceless: once let the Chain be broken, and not only could the Apocalypse be averted, but also, in that dislocated moment of space and time while the Links were severed, the Virgin could be rescued from her putrefying body! For that split second, encompassing within it infinite possibilities, the impossible could become possible.

And then Belial had made his move! And, unlike Satan, the Nefilim had no old loyalties!

He had been on the point of breaking his own Vow – with unknown consequences – and using the Flame Cannon to protect his angels while the Beast was far out in space, when he had spotted the Four Horses! *And their riders!*

And suddenly he had seen the third possibility, just a hint, a wisp of it. Just as Eve had done, although he didn't know this at the time. *Lucifer's Second Judgement with Lucifer as his own Judge!*

What an Unfolding it had been!

When the Beast left Heaven, carrying the unhappy mutants, he knew he'd won. But he had to wait those two days, until that final minute of the millennium when the Apocalypse did not go ahead, and the Link snapped, and Mary could be dragged from her death-in-life. He wasn't really sorry.

It gave time for those out-and-out rascals Peter and Tobias, who made Adam seem like a paragon of virtue, to sweat it out a bit! Chuckling to himself, he ordered that their trial continue!

God turned slightly to avoid a galactic cluster pressing into the small of his back.

And now?

I've repaired the bodies that Darren desecrated, since all the parts were there. Those souls will eventually have to go to New

Heaven on Betelgeuse, because it is getting a bit crowded here. Not Squiggly and Lamia, of course. Eve would murder me if I let them go! Adam, too, I think, though he'd never admit it openly. I still don't know how they survived the Nefilim in the Way Station. Somehow, through what *they* call Natural Philosophy, and *I* call magic, they are able to leave their bodies. Incredible! Squiggly tried to explain the principle to me, but, frankly, I didn't understand a word!

Mary is already nearly her old self. Her memories of those terrible years are already blurred, since she was, in any case, only half alive, and it was only the putrefaction of her body seeping into her soul that made her what she was.

I suspect she'll be making up for lost time! I overheard Gabriel asking the Dinosaur to teach him to dance, because he knows Mary used to love dancing. When Mary realised what Gabriel had been prepared to do in order not to hurt her...! Jesus is already unconsciously treating him with a touch of deference, as a potential stepfather! We'll try and forget that little peccadillo of making unlawful copies of certain Scrolls; he thinks we don't know, so why disabuse him? Without him, Mary would have been lost for ever. And one thing I'm quite determined *she* must never find out is that little business with Eve. Darren was threatening to go around telling everybody, so I did my old whirlwind-and-thunder act with him, and now I'm sure he's the most frightened baby in the Universe! I know it was naughty of me, but it felt good!

Poor Michael! Why did it have to be him of all people to discover the Saragashim so long ago? But he's learning. When he accidentally found out (since I just happened to let it drop!) how Gabriel had suffered to protect the Virgin Mary, his simplistic morality received a huge dent, I can tell you! I was pretty furious with him, but I *did* desert Heaven for two thousand years, and he only did what he thought was best. Maybe the Virgin will bring him and Gabriel closer together – although Gabriel had better watch out; if he ever lets Mary down, I think I know who'd be more than ready to take his place!

But Raphael! He understood that his old friend's salvation lay in *choosing* to sacrifice his dream of conquering Heaven rather than having it forcibly taken away from him. His wounds were terrible, and those of the other angels who faced the Beast, but not as bad as they might have been. The Beast had no wish to harm anyone: it *had* to obey the Glove, but it used the lowest possible flame setting – just compare how instantaneously Bugrot was frizzled!

But if Raphael was the one who finally freed Satan from the chains of trying to be what he thought he ought to be, it was Eve – together with Mephistopheles – who kept Lucifer alive in him. One has to admit that Mary and Michael were right – what a little hussy! A few days old, and she's already committed adultery with the Devil himself, and then, just for variety, throws in an Archangel as well! The things one learns with just a few days' eavesdropping! And I can guess who asked Gabriel to make that copy of the Cosmic Scroll. Eve was somewhere, somehow, behind Peter's little escapade. With her usual frankness and honesty (which really boils down to 'Sorry, God, no disrespect meant, but I think I know better than you!' – hussy!) she offered to tell me everything, but I declined. *Suspecting* you've been taken for a ride is not as bad as being *certain*! To think I won a prize for Shaping her!

Damn it all, I deserve a dozen prizes!

Apart from spending time with Raphael, she's hardly left Lucifer's side during this slow painful healing of his terrible wounds. She hasn't found him ugly or pitiful. Rather, she's immensely proud of him, and he must know that by now.

I've told him that he and his Companions are free to leave Hell whenever they want, that I'll send the Beast to transport them to wherever they want to go – there are plenty of habitable planets near New Heaven, for example – and that, maybe, when the angels have had time to get used to the idea, they could return here. I think I know what his answer will be – and he'll be right. It's too soon. They aren't ready, the angels aren't ready. But a beginning has been made.

In the meantime, what will he do with Belial and Mammon? Will he have the courage to recognise that in their own way they were right, that Peter at that time was indeed planning to lead them to their doom? I won't worry too much over them: Belial will, I'm sure, prove to him that he risked his own life trying to stop the Nefilim!

And his real dream? I simply don't know. At the time, in Eden, Eve's love for him, I'm sure, was really not much different from her love for any other creature. But she's come to realise how dangerous it is to have so much love to give, she's learnt to dissimulate a little, to try to protect those, like Peter, who yearn, but fear, to respond. It's made her sad, knowing that men aren't strong enough to accept her gift. But she's greatly affected by Lucifer's devotion, by knowing he really would have tried to 'make a Heaven out of Hell' if she'd gone there. As Woman she is invincible, but as a woman... will she resist so much love?

Peter's the one I'm really worried about. Of course he's glad that all the re-trials have been called off, but he feels he's been a puppet with others pulling the strings, which isn't really true at all, but he's a proud man under his decidedly untidy exterior.

The real problem, though, is something else. Apparently, he's finished that lukewarm affair with St. Joan that he thought I knew nothing about. It was inevitable: he has seen loves that spanned millennia – not just Lucifer's, but Gabriel's too, and the serpents' – and he feels he will never have such a love: yet he cannot be content with less. In the words of one of their poets:

The little more, and how much it is!
The little less, and what worlds away!

And he has seen those who, like George and Lazara, do not ask, do not search, but unthinkingly accept the gift that is given to them. The tragedy is that he believes he cannot ever be like them. Jesus once told me that I was wrong to have created Eve, that I had condemned dreamers through the ages to a life of dissatisfaction and unfulfilment. Sometimes I think he is right...

But something will come up. After all, in his way, he's just as much a born fighter as George or Moloch. And George, who's only *almost* as unobservant as he seems, came to me with an idea yesterday which might just... well, we'll see. But I'm not really optimistic.

****

290

Satan was having his farewell party. It wasn't *quite* as he'd envisaged it in his dream in Eden. But near enough. He *was* sitting beside Eve, and, although God wasn't bowing, he *was* serving them fruit cocktails, a definite improvement on the tepid tea of a few millennia before. And although Michael and Gabriel, despite his asking them nicely, refused to serve as his footstools and indeed told him to go take a running jump, they did it in a nice way. And Beelzebub and Raphael really *were* there, the latter still with thick bandages round his chest, but cheerful enough.

The great absentee was Mephistopheles. His granddaughter was there, yes, chatting away volubly to God, who smiled uncertainly, as if not quite understanding what she was saying; even Moloch, despite being unable to sit, was there, lying gingerly on a huge couch that had been constructed especially for the occasion. And all the Old Ones were there, too. Yes, everyone was there, except Mephistopheles. But God had said: "Lucifer, that wonderful friend of yours wasn't my creation, I can do nothing. But I have... an acquaintance, who *may* have a solution to his death. Be patient, and maybe..."

He shook off the thought. He had mourned, and he still would mourn, but now was the time for joy. He looked around him...

****

"Oh, don't worry about me, I'm fine," Adam was saying to Lamia. "To tell you the truth, our sex life was starting to lack spontaneity after the first four or five thousand years. I'm not saying anything against the dangly, mind you, but, let's be frank, it doesn't do much except go in and out and round about. Now, if *I'd* been God..." He stopped himself. "But we remain the best of friends, I assure you. A splendid woman, marvellous, I wish her the best of luck!"

The Sardine, happily ensconced in his bowl now suspended from the Elephant's tusk, shouted out, "Your teeth, Adam, and don't forget the mouthwash!"

Adam smiled patiently – he had heard that joke a few thousand times now – tickled the Sardine, and went back to his conversation with Lamia.

The Slug, now wearing a pince-nez, was saying to Squiggly: "It seems to me perfectly obvious that you 'disappear' temporarily into a rotating mini Black Hole through a Wormhole that you keep open due to the Casimir effect on exotic matter, taking advantage of vacuum fluctuations in supposedly 'empty' space, and then, using your own development of Gödel's Theorem, you cause a Temporal Causality Loop in order to traverse hyperspace and thus appear instantaneously elsewhere. But what about Stephen Hawking's Chronology Protection Conjecture?"

"Well, of course, we avoid that problem by reducing ourselves to electronically encoded information, and then transmit..." Squiggly began, before coming to a stop, mouth wide open. Now *there* was an example of a late developer!

The Platypus was sitting morosely in a corner, still wondering what he was supposed to be.

"Would you like to dance?" Gabriel asked Mary shyly.

Radiant with happiness, she took his hand. "By the way," she said mischievously, "if you *should* invite me back for a coffee, just remember some nice girls *do*!" It was so good to be able to make a ten-thousand-year-old Archangel blush like that!

Lazara, giving up on God, was now sitting on George's knee (he had one arm round her, with the other hand he was looking nostalgically at some old dragon photos), and staring at Michael in amazement. "But you're from 'ere, ain't you, so 'ow come you never 'eard of the time Lord Lucifer 'ad to put 'is 'oof into Lord Raphael's cobblers 'cos 'e 'ad 'old of 'im from be'ind?"

Michael's retort was drowned by Moloch's belching. The poor devil only dared use the one escape route for his gases now.

"Oh look!" squealed an extremely shapely Ethel, in the *miniest* of skirts and the *teeniest* of blouses, "that's one of the angels who was in that big Council place. I wouldn't mind him seeing me now!" And then, as Algernon frowned, "I was only joking, sweetie pie! Give me a kiss!" Moloch's belching was drowned by their noisy squelchy kisses.

Uriel hid a smile at Michael's pained expression, which became even more pained when the Hippopotamus, slightly drunk, lurched across to have a chat.

Lazara's twin sister, who, at George's request, had been brought all the way from Hell, was talking to Tobias, and looking extremely bored. She'd been looking forward to spending the evening (and hopefully the night) with that really cool St. Peter that her sister had raved on about, but after a few polite words, he had excused himself and left her stranded with Tobias and his awful puns. George, as usual, thought Satan, had misunderstood: Peter had been showing so much interest lately in Lazara, not because she attracted him, but because she was the granddaughter of Mephistopheles. God and George and Satan and Eve and the two Saragash sisters caught each others' eyes – a quite remarkable feat considering the hundreds of revellers between them – and shook their heads despondently.

****

But that night, Eve had another vision. She wasn't completely sure, but that dark-skinned woman who had finally persuaded Peter to shave, who looked at him with deep affection that was clearly returned, had her own sea-green eyes, her own midnight-black hair. At first she was shocked, and then she realised it solved so many problems, eased so many unspoken tensions. She felt a quiet contentment as she gazed across fondly, yet warily, at the figure beside her. Satan looked so *innocent* when he slept!

"What would you say to having Peter as a son-in-law?" she whispered, thinking he couldn't hear.

Satan smiled to himself in the dark. "We could do worse," he thought.

Out Now:
Women Writing the Weird
Edited by Deb Hoag

WEIRD

1.   Eldritch: suggesting the operation of supernatural influences; "an eldritch screech"; "the three weird sisters"; "stumps . . . had uncanny shapes as of monstrous creatures" —John Galsworthy; "an unearthly light"; "he could hear the unearthly scream of some curlew piercing the din" —Henry Kingsley

2.   Wyrd: fate personified; any one of the three Weird Sisters

3.   Strikingly odd or unusual; "some trick of the moonlight; some weird effect of shadow" —Bram Stoker

WEIRD FICTION

1.   Stories that delight, surprise, that hang about the dusky edges of 'mainstream' fiction with characters, settings, plots that abandon the normal and mundane and explore new ideas, themes and ways of being. —Deb Hoag

RRP: £14.99 ($28.95).

featuring

Nancy A. Collins, Eugie Foster, Janice Lee, Rachel Kendall, Candy Caradoc, Mysty Unger, Roberta Lawson, Sara Genge, Gina Ranalli, Deb Hoag, C. M. Vernon, Aliette de Bodard, Caroline M. Yoachim, Flavia Testa, Aimee C. Amodio, Ann Hagman Cardinal, Rachel Turner, Wendy Jane Muzlanova, Katie Coyle, Helen Burke, Janis Butler Holm, J.S. Breukelaar, Carol Novack, Tantra Bensko, Nancy DiMauro, and Moira McPartlin.

Out Now:
Bite Me, Robot Boy
Edited by Adam Lowe

Bite Me, Robot Boy is a seminal new anthology of poetry and fiction that showcases what Dog Horn Publishing does best: writing that takes risks, crosses boundaries and challenges expectations. From Oz Hardwick's hard-hitting experimental poetry, to Robert Lamb's colourful pulpy science fiction, this is an anthology of incandescent writing from some of the world's best emerging talent.

Featuring
S.R. Dantzler, Oz Hardwick, Maximilian T. Hawker, Emma Hopkins, A.J. Kirby, Stephanie Elizabeth Knipe, Robert Lamb, Poppy Farr, Wendy Jane Muzlanova, Cris O'Connor, Mark Wagstaff, Fiona Ritchie Walker and KC Wilder.

Out Now:
Cabala
Edited by Adam Lowe

From gothic fairytale to humorous pop-culture satire, five of the North's top writers showcase the diversity of British talent that exists outside the country's capital and put their strange, funny, mythical landscapes firmly on the literary map.

Over the course of ten weeks, Adam Lowe worked with five budding writers as part of the Dog Horn Masterclass series. This anthology collects together the best work produced both as a result of the masterclasses and beyond.

Featuring
Jodie Daber, Richard Evans, Jacqueline Houghton, Rachel Kendall and A.J. Kirby

Out Now:
Nitrospective
Andrew Hook

Japanese school children grow giant frogs, a superhero grapples with her secret identity, onions foretell global disasters and an undercover agent is ambivalent as to which side he works for and why. Relationships form and crumble with the slightest of nudges. World catastrophe is imminent; alien invasion blase. These twenty slipstream stories from acclaimed author Andrew Hook examine identity and our fragile existence, skid skewed realities and scratch the surface of our world, revealing another—not altogether dissimilar—layer beneath.

Nitrospective is Andrew Hook's fourth collection of short fiction.

RRP: £12.99 ($22.95).

Acclaim for the Author

"Andrew Hook is a wonderfully original writer" —Graham Joyce

"His stories range from the darkly apocalyptic to the hopefully visionary, some brilliant and none less than satisfactory"
—*The Harrow*

"Refreshingly original, uncompromisingly provocative, and daringly intelligent" —*The Future Fire*

ND - #0464 - 270225 - C0 - 229/152/24 - PB - 9781907133428 - Matt Lamination